"*A Long Way From the Creek* is a thriller in every sense. It grabs your attention from page 1 and keeps you hanging on until the very end. Howard Blank has constructed a colorful, intricate plot filled with suspense and surprises."

—Kay I. Gilman, Co-author
The Savvy Woman's Success Bible

A
Long
Way
From
the Creek

A Thriller

by

Howard E. Blank

Pikesville Press
Baltimore, MD 21208

First printing 1998

ISBN 0-9661751-1-5

LCCN 97-76068

Editing, design, typesetting and printing services provided by About Books, Inc., 425 Cedar Street, POB 1500, Buena Vista, CO 81211, (800) 548-1876.

ATTENTION: Quantity discounts are available on bulk purchases of this book. Special books or book excerpts can also be created to fit specific needs. For information, please contact Pikesville Press, 3404 Deep Willow Avenue, Baltimore, MD 21208, (410) 484-8644.

DEDICATION

To Amy, who got me started; to Judy, who kept me going; and to Ray, who helped me finish.

Part I

CHAPTER 1

They passed through the toll booth and the Bentley accelerated smoothly onto the Maine turnpike. Tall forests of pines, rich and full, stretched on either side, and to the right occasional glints of morning sunshine could be seen cutting through the overcast gray of the September sky.

In the rear of the car, his mother and Penny, his fourteen-year-old sister, were sharing their views on the latest fall fashions. Beside him, his father was playing with the radio to bring in a clearer reception of the classical station that kept fading in and out. Mike looked over at the man clad in khakis, blue plaid shirt, and Docksiders. He studied his father with more scrutiny than he ever remembered having done in all his seventeen years. The profile seemed no different, thin face jarred by its broken nose, high forehead crowned with straight black hair, dark eyes patient and quiet. He turned briefly to Mike, wide lips splitting in a brief smile when he noted the boy watching him.

Mike turned quickly away, staring out the window at the highway as a blast of Beethoven suddenly came in so loudly his father adjusted the volume sharply down.

Who is this man?

Mike had asked himself that question ten times during the two-hour drive up from Weston—a hundred times since the previous afternoon. Before yesterday, the question had never even occurred to him. Before yesterday, if there was anything in his life of which Mike was certain, it was who—and what—his father was. So what in hell did it all mean? Mike pondered as he let his thoughts return to the events of the day before.

———

Turning left through the ivy-laden iron gates, Mike negotiated his vintage Chevy up the curving drive that swept the hill. Mike always enjoyed the view of the imposing edifice as it came clear of the trees at the last turn. At this time of year only the peaked roof and stone chimneys of the house could be seen from the road below because of the lush foliage. The rounded white balconies seemed to beckon, softening the exterior and making it appear less massive.

Home.

He was always glad to arrive there, a feeling he'd had ever since they'd moved in nearly twelve years earlier. He'd been only five then, but he still remembered the thrill he felt as, holding his father's hand, he'd walked up the broad front steps and entered the marble foyer.

"Gosh," he'd said, turning wide-eyed to his father and feeling as if he had stepped into a movie. "Is it really ours?"

"It is, Mike," his father had answered, ruffling his hair and looking down at him with that oddly sad expression in his eyes Mike never quite understood. Beyond them, Mike saw his mother's flushed and excited face as she stood in the open doorway holding Penny in her arms. His two-year-old sister had seemed intent only on restraining herself from sucking the thumb that edged tantalizingly closer to her pouting lips.

Parking below the open garage, he'd noted his mother's white Mercedes coupe beside his father's Bentley and felt a quick stab of remorse when he recalled the recent argument he'd had with the man. Two of Mike's best friends were driving new Porsches, and Mike, stuck with his eighty-two Chevy, had pressed for better. Not a Porsche, maybe—certainly not a new one—but something better. His father had been uncompromising, however, and Mike, despite recognizing the man's determination to draw a line, had not really understood. After all, everyone knew the Frosts were as rich—if not richer—than anybody else around.

"Your old man's got more money than God," one of the kids at school had thrown at him once in a taunt that was half jest and half envy.

Mike had not known how to respond because he suspected it was true. Everybody said so—at least, everyone around here. But outside of Boston, Mike had no idea what the family's reputation might be because his father was careful not to be exposed to the media any more than was absolutely necessary.

"That's just my style, Mike. Low key," he'd said once, in response to Mike's question as to why he'd turned down an invitation to appear on the *Today Show* to discuss the phenomenal success of his investment firm. Mike had been disappointed, thinking it would have been cool to see his father on national television.

He entered the house and went into the large country kitchen of which his mother was so proud. He opened the refrigerator, took out a piece of cold fried chicken, and after a brief hesitation, reached in to take a beer from the bottom shelf. His mother would be reading in the lower garden, he justified to himself, and besides, it was Friday afternoon.

Grabbing a plate, he headed toward the den in hopes of catching the end of the Red Sox game. Instead of turning on the set, however, some impulse led him to the bay window.

He stood there and took a sip of beer, watching the late September sun setting behind the trees. The day-long drizzle had stopped only an hour before, and shortly after, the sun had broken through with a suddenness that was almost breathtaking. He could see the moisture on the trees as the rays cut through obliquely. He shivered involuntary as he sensed the dampness and inhaled deeply as he imagined the rich dankness that would pervade if he went outside.

Dad's trees, he thought, as he always thought of them.

And Dad's room, he added, looking about the comfortable den with its dark-paneled walls and bookshelves bracketing the massive stone fireplace, blackened from use. He took in the wet bar from which Mike occasionally was offered a weak drink on some special occasion, the Picasso above it Mike was still uncertain he appreciated, and the antique roll-top desk in the corner where his father often worked at night.

Mike remembered his father was due home that evening and the next morning the family would leave for Maine. Suddenly, he was anxious for Charley Frost's presence, something that had less and less importance to him lately. Once, when he was younger, he'd missed Charley terribly when the man was not around. But this past year or so—

Mike realized for the first time he had begun to think of his father as "Charley," wondered what that implied.

He walked to the desk, picked up a photo of the family standing below their jet, four arms waving wildly, grins so genuine the excitement seemed to pulse from the paper through his fingers. His father's expression was especially electric, and Mike smiled himself as he studied the long, broken-nosed face that seemed almost split in the photo by the wide lips. Beneath heavy brows, the dark eyes sparkled even as they squinted into the sun and the straight black hair above Charley's high forehead seemed to glisten.

March 17, 1982, he noted, reading the inscription inked to the side in his father's hand. Five happy years and a lot of fun miles ago, he acknowledged, forcing from his mind the image of the gleaming Porsche he coveted.

He studied the picture, remembering the thrill of that day. Charley had been mysterious, acting comically like a spy as he helped them pack a large picnic basket, whispering and looking about as if their mission was of the utmost secrecy. He kept quieting them as they giggled, rolling his eyes and looking sideways and showing great relief as he ascertained they were still undiscovered by whomever it was he pretended was searching for them.

Kate had seemed as perplexed as he and Penny, but they were all infected by Charley's mood, especially when he'd gone to the refrigerator at the last moment, removed a bottle of champagne, and thrust it surreptitiously under his leather jacket. With a final "shh" he'd hurried them out the door, which he closed with elaborate care.

Wherever they were going, Mike had known it was no ordinary picnic.

They'd driven through Weston but instead of heading north as Mike anticipated, Charley had turned south onto the Mass Pike toward Boston.

Penny's "Hey, Dad—" was interrupted by a sharp "shh," and from then on they'd all sat in quiet anticipation. Pulling into the parking lot at Logan, Charley had taken the picnic basket and had led them to a side gate, avoiding the main terminal.

A guard let them through when Charley showed a pass. Then they were on a runway, walking toward the hangers, when Charley suddenly stopped, bowed low, and with great flourish indicated with open palm a gleaming plane that stood alone.

They looked at each other uncertainly, Mike finally breaking the silence as he slowly began to understand. "Geez, Dad—but that's a jet!" he whispered.

Charley had laughed, breaking the mood, and they'd all run together to inspect the silver beauty.

"Charley!" Kate exclaimed. "Is it really...?"

He looked at her fondly. "Yes, it is. Really."

She came into his arms with an excited "Oh-my-God!"

"Hey, Dad! Look!" Penny was pointing to the plane's side. "Look what it says!"

Mike looked, too, saw "Pretty Penny" inscribed on the fuselage.

"Pretty Penny!" his sister exclaimed. "Is that me?"

His father had swooped her high in his arms, brought her down and hugged her tight as he said, "It sure is, sweetheart."

"Pretty Penny," she repeated softly.

"I'll bet that's what it cost, too," said Kate.

"That, too," Charley acknowledged wryly. "But she is a 'Pretty Penny'. What do you think, Mike? Excited?"

Mike had been thrilled beyond belief when he first registered the surprise but felt odd emotions as he lingered on the name.

"Yeah," he managed.

Now, five years later, he looked up from the photo and across to the bookcase where the trophies were kept. Most prominent were the two that read, "Wood Valley Country Club, Father and Son Doubles. Charles and Michael Frost. First place." There was one for 1986, another for this year, 1987.

On the paneled wall to the left was another memento, this a hammerhead shark with a plaque below inscribed, "December 28, 1984. St. Thomas, V.I. Michael M. Frost."

He turned his eyes to the fireplace, looked for a moment at the quiet portrait of his mother hanging solitary above the mantle, and as he replaced the photo on the desk, he thought of the "Pretty Penny" and felt good about his father.

7

He didn't know why it was that something seemed to nag.

It wasn't that his father wasn't good to him. He was—that and more. In fact, Charley Frost was probably the kindest and most considerate man Mike had ever known. And, busy as he was, he always had time for his family, keeping his business trips to a minimum and rarely being gone for more than four or five days at a time. Even his father's denying of things such as the Porsche Mike reluctantly conceded to be in his own best interest, despite the fact they could well afford it.

No, Mike reflected, it wasn't that, for he was very secure in his father's love. It was something else, something he couldn't quite touch but was unquestionably there.

The thought suddenly surfaced, and he wondered at it.

There was something he feared about his father, he realized, something in the soft-spoken man that made Mike uneasy.

And he remembered then when that feeling had first begun.

It had been about three years ago. Just over three, because it was the spring before the Democratic Convention, and that would have been the summer of 1984.

He'd been sitting with Charley in this very room, watching the early evening news and waiting impatiently for the Red Sox–Yankees game to start.

"Who do you think he'll pick?" Charley had asked.

"Huh?"

"Mondale—who do you think he'll pick as his running mate?"

"Oh." Mike was embarrassed at not having been paying attention, but the truth was politics bored him even though he tried to take an interest because his father stressed it as important.

He'd focused on the screen, quickly trying to catch up on what the commentator was saying.

"…and seem to be the probable choices."

Four faces were boxed on the screen, faces with names under them Mike vaguely remembered having seen from time to time.

As the commentator outlined what each would add to the Mondale campaign, Charley had asked again, "Who do you think, Mike?"

"None of them," he'd responded, surprising himself at the definite tone of his statement.

"No?" Charley looked at him quizzically. "Who, then?'

This was adult talk, and Mike determined to sound informed.

"Ferraro," he'd replied, not knowing why. He didn't even know the person; in fact, he had only recognized the name vaguely when he'd said it.

"Ferraro? She's been mentioned, but she's certainly a long shot."

Charley was interested in Mike's opinion now, trying to draw from him its basis. But Mike had none and suddenly felt cornered. "You'll see," he'd rejoined, sounding as certain as he could. "It'll be Ferraro. I'll betcha."

Then, not wanting to have his position further examined, he'd said, "Hey—I'm going to get a Coke before the game starts. Want one?"

"No, thanks," Charley had replied, turning again to the set, but not before having fixed Mike with that kind, understanding look of his that made Mike feel it was okay even if he wasn't as up on things as he should be.

But that look had been quite different when, some months later, the Democratic nominee for the presidency, Walter Mondale, had dramatically announced his selection of running mate.

" . . . Stateswoman from New York—Geraldine Ferraro!"

And, as the exultant figure on the screen had extended his arm to the wings, as the floor of the Convention Center had risen in hat-waving pandemonium, Mike had turned to his father with a grin on his face.

And for the first time he'd seen the look.

Instead of smiling at him, as he'd expected Charley to do, even coming over to shake his hand perhaps in some acknowledgment of Mike's cleverness, his father had sat quietly. The look on Charley's face had been so somber, so—*searching,* that was the word—and continued for so long Mike had become uncomfortable and averted his eyes. It was as if his father had disapproved of him, had thought he'd been a smart ass. And it hadn't been that way at all. He'd just had a hunch, that's all, and he was sure his father knew it.

But it was the same every time he talked to his father about what he thought would happen. Even little things, like ball games.

"Hey, Dad—I *know* the Brewers'll win today," he'd say in excitement as the close pennant race continued.

And when he did, his father's own excitement seemed to fade and the look came. Especially if Mike turned out to be right, as he almost

9

always did when his hunch was *really* strong. Just like his father, he had often thought with pride.

Charley would bet on the Patriots, sometimes heavily Mike suspected, although he never knew for sure. But he was incredibly lucky, and Mike marveled at his almost unerring ability to sniff out a Patriot upset in advance.

"How do you do it, Dad?"

Charley had shrugged. "They're that kind of team," he'd answered finally, leaving Mike unsatisfied.

Mike had noticed Charley rarely if ever bet on the games the Patriots ended up losing, surmised that his father had guessed right again and was grudgingly proud of him for not betting against his own team even when he was reasonably sure they would lose.

"Can't do that, Mike," his father had said when Mike questioned him.

But Mike could.

And did, sometimes, although he felt disloyal to his father's ethic by doing so. But Mike couldn't help it. Lately, he'd become a good prognosticator himself, better than good, and his hunches paid off week after week as he bet with his friends and his amazing streak held.

Three straight weeks he'd won the pool.

And he'd hit virtually every side bet he made.

Why not take advantage of your hunches, if you trust them? he thought. Even if it meant betting against your favorite team once in a while.

But his father would never have agreed with that, Mike knew. Always do the right thing—that was Charley. To a fault, Mike sometimes felt, although he admired him for that.

But a guy had to be selfish sometimes, take advantage of things, as Mike was beginning to see it. However, when he had tried to discuss that attitude with his father, Charley had looked at him with that odd, probing stare. It was as if his father didn't want to hear his opinion, but Mike knew that wasn't true either. That was one thing about Charley— he always tried to draw Mike out, discuss things with him on an adult level.

Whatever it was, Mike knew, despite their closeness, something had come between them, something embodied in that searching look he never understood and that always chilled him.

So he'd begun to keep his thoughts to himself, especially his hunches, and he regretted not being able to share that part of himself with his father because he was growing particularly proud of the way he was so often able to figure things out.

Charley's safe combination, for example, he thought, looking to the wall of bookshelves. Behind the third, he knew, protected by some leather-bound volumes of Shakespeare, the small safe was set into the wall. He'd come upon Charley once as he'd been opening it. His father had seemed startled, and Mike's curiosity was aroused.

"Just some valuables, Mike," Charley had said, putting something into the aperture and then closing its face. "Your mom knows the safe is here—but nobody else," he added by way of explanation as he spun the dial before replacing the books.

"Sure, Dad," Mike had responded, understanding his father to mean the secret should rest with him. It made Mike feel good to have something up on his sister Penny anyway, and that it was his father's suggestion he do so seemed to put a stamp of approval on that sense of power.

Although they never discussed it again, the thought of the safe behind the books held an odd fascination for Mike. And so one day, no longer able to resist and knowing the house was empty, he'd gone to the shelf, removed the Shakespeare volumes, and looked at the exposed square steel face.

What lay inside? Mike wondered. His hand moved to the dial, and he began to spin it aimlessly, feeling the heavy metal turn solidly as he did so.

If I were Dad, what combination would I use? he wondered. The thought came softly at first, but quickly it grabbed Mike's imagination and he found himself almost frantically turning the dial in a various combination of numbers that came to him.

His father's birthday. His mother's. Penny's. His own.

But as he made the final spin, the lock always failed to click.

Mike knew the odds of his discovering the correct series were so small as to not even be calculable, but something in him drove him to try.

It was a good half hour before he replaced the books, defeated.

As he started to leave the room, his eye caught the picture of the *Pretty Penny,* and he stopped, transfixed.

The numbers on the side of the plane drew his eyes like a magnet: XE2647830.

And in a flash, he saw it: 26-47-8-30.

Why he broke it out that way he couldn't have said, but somehow he knew it was right.

And a moment later, as he spun the dial back again and the last number stopped the turn, he'd felt a great excitement as he pulled gently and the small door swung out.

Tentatively, Mike put his hand on the bottom of the black hole that held his father's secrets. Then, his heart pounding, he cautiously moved his fingers forward. They found nothing.

Quickly, Mike went to the cabinet where the flashlight was kept. Coming back to the wall, he turned on the beam and looked in.

The safe was empty.

Mike stared at it a long moment before slowly closing its door, spinning the dial, and replacing the Shakespeare.

He felt an odd emotion as he stood there, part of him sorry the safe had revealed nothing and part of him glad it hadn't. But he also felt elated at having been clever enough to figure out the combination.

Mike remembered that feeling now as he stood in the den, the plate of cold fried chicken still on the coffee table, untouched.

The house was quiet. His mother was outdoors reading on the terrace; and Penny would be playing tennis now that the weather had cleared. The day maid was gone by this hour, and the live-in servants— Clarissa and Ben—would be off for a long weekend, since the family was leaving the next day for Maine.

Raising his eyes to the bookshelf, Mike stood still a moment, and then walked slowly to the wall.

He'd feared his father might have changed the combination for some reason, but the lock clicked home solidly as he spun back to thirty.

Before him, his father's safe swung open again.

Was it still empty? he wondered.

Reaching inside, Mike felt a small packet. His fingers grasped it and he took it slowly from the safe.

In his hand he held three passports bound by a rubber band. He hesitated briefly, then slid off the band and opened the top one.

His father's face stared up at him, appearing very stilted in the small photo. Under Charley's picture was the name "William Stuart Jennings."

Mike felt a chill come over him as he lingered on the strange name typed with such permanence beneath the familiar face. It seemed a violation of his father and upset Mike greatly.

He opened the second passport and again Charley's face appeared. The line beneath it carried the name "Brian J. Cunningham." The third was "Walter Benton."

Slowly, Mike closed the blue cover over Charley's last picture. He bound the three passports together again and stood thoughtfully, holding them in his hand. Then, almost against his will, he went to the cabinet, got the flashlight, and went back to the bookshelves where the dark hole waited.

Mike snapped on the beam and looked in.

Money. Set well back in the long, narrow safe, were stacks and stacks of money.

Mike reached in and removed one of the stacks.

The crisp one-hundred-dollar bills looked mint new.

Mike counted them quickly. Fifty. He was holding five thousand dollars in his hand.

He took out a second packet: one-hundred-dollar bills again, as were the next two.

There were three rows of ten stacks each and when he took a closer look he saw another three rows behind those. Except those bills were something he had never seen before: five hundreds. Twenty-five-thousand dollars in each packet.

Mike calculated and realized before him lay nine hundred thousand dollars in cold hard cash.

Slowly, he replaced the money, looked at the passports reflectively, and put those back into the safe. The click of the lock when he closed the safe door sounded sharply in the quiet room.

Mike walked again to the window, unaware now of the trees as he stared out. Fake passports. Cash—an incredible amount of it. What did it mean? A vague fear began to rise in Mike that was quickly overridden by a flash of anger.

Charley Frost, he thought to himself, and his lips tightened.

Charley Frost, the All-American boy, that generous, upright model of citizenry, that staunch and patient mentor of all that was just and good—that low-key man with the easy air whom Mike had so long aspired to one day emulate.

Charley Frost. An open book of a man with three fake passports and a fortune in cash hidden in his safe.

Knowing the man, who would have guessed he could hold such secrets, whatever their import?

No one, Mike reflected. No one would suspect Charley Frost of anything untoward. At the thought, the line of his lips softened into an almost smile.

"That sly son-of-a-bitch," Mike muttered to himself, but there was a grudging admiration in his tone. He'd always loved and admired his father but had viewed him as essentially a simple man, despite the trappings. But now he understood that there was some deeper side to his father, some dark side, perhaps, and that realization, while threatening, was at the same time surprisingly exciting to Mike. What did—Mike's thoughts were broken abruptly as he heard the front door slam.

"Kate! Mike! Penny—*anybody*," he heard his father's voice call cheerfully. "I'm home."

———

"I'm home."

Yesterday's words echoed again in Mike's mind as he shifted his eyes furtively to his left where his father effortlessly steered the Bentley north.

I'm home.

The words were innocent enough, but for the first time in Mike's life they raised a question he'd never have thought to ask—yeah, Charley Frost, you're home, but where in the hell have you *been*?

CHAPTER 2

The day was blustery, the Saturday morning sky slate gray as the van moved slowly up through the trees. Gusts of a sharpening breeze skittered across the boughs hanging heavy above them and the rustle of leaves could be heard through the open windows.

"How much longer you think the rain'll hold off, Harry?" the driver asked.

His companion ignored the question as he had every time it had been posed since they'd hit the Maine turnpike a half hour earlier. Although he wouldn't have admitted it, Harry was concerned himself as he looked at the darkening clouds that promised more than the scattered showers that had been predicted.

He hoped they'd have the hour they needed but doubted it. Not that the rain, even a heavy rain, would necessarily spoil things. It might even make them easier. But he didn't like having to worry about it.

The narrow road turned left, and suddenly the trees were less dense and the house was visible on the top of the rise to their right. A black and silver Bentley stood in the drive. An eighty-seven, Harry guessed by the look of it.

Glancing at the mileage indicator, he noted it was 3.6 miles since they'd turned off the main road. Exactly as he'd been told. He was comforted by that fact.

"Keep going," he told the driver, annoyed with himself because he knew the order was unnecessary. They'd worked together before and had been over this part of the drill a dozen times.

15

About two hundred yards past the house he pointed to his right and the van pulled over to park in a stand of pines. The young man with the heavy-lidded eyes who waited there in the gray Volkswagen nodded in recognition.

* * *

On the court below their weekend house, Charley returned the ball as hard as he could with his backhand but knew it was no use anyway, visualizing the ball coming again in a white blur to the far side of the court even before that happened. He reversed his body in a futile attempt that left his racket far short and stumbled to keep his balance.

Looking across the net, he warmed to his son's grin as the boy said, "Gotcha that time, old man."

It was the first time Mike had referred to him as "old man" and Charley appreciated his son's tentative step in taking their relationship to a different level. There was something more in the statement, too, something almost aggressive which Charley quickly attributed to the boy's glee in having beaten him.

"Your first set ever—don't be so smug," he rejoined, walking to the net and extending his hand.

Mike reached over and, still exuberant from the victory, ruffled his father's black hair. They laughed at Mike's use of the gesture that had so long been exclusively Charley's.

He's growing up fast, Charley thought, and he couldn't help but feel the slightest touch of both loss and envy as he noted the youthful vitality emanating from his son. Mike was tall, almost as tall as Charley himself, and his body, although muscular, had the supple grace of the swimmer he was. His face was square, nose straight, and chin strong and slightly cleft; the brown-flecked eyes twinkled at the world with interest and humor. When he'd been younger, the freckles he'd inherited from his mother had been pronounced, but they had almost disappeared now although there was still a distinct trace of red in the sweat-damp hair that now ringed his forehead.

I envy him, Charley admitted to himself. The looks as well as the youth. Charley had always thought of himself as plain-looking, his long face angular, nose thicker than it should have been from a long-ago break, mouth a bit too wide, forehead too high. He felt his eyes were his best feature, large and dark with a little boy's sadness, and he credited them with whatever success he'd had with women. As he looked across the net at his son, Charley wished the boy well.

He was proud of Mike but resented the spoiled streak, the why-not attitude that seemed to flourish in the boy despite Charley's efforts to maintain a reasonable perspective within the family. And there was also an arrogance in Mike that rankled Charley, a sense of superiority that revealed itself from time to time in a cockiness Charley found offensive.

But Charley realized he tended to overreact to those characteristics because of his own background, and therefore tried to keep his displeasure in check, keep his own perspective. For, above all, Mike was basically a nice, bright kid.

Still, he worried about the boy. More than he should, probably. But, he reflected, he had reason to.

How much did Mike know? Charley wondered. Was there anything *for* him to know?

The boy got moody on occasion in a way that might have been just adolescence but was nevertheless out of character with his normal buoyancy. He'd certainly been in a funk when Charley had returned home the evening before, his eyes downcast during dinner. He had retired to his room immediately thereafter. And today, on the trip up, the boy had hardly said a word.

Mike seemed his usual self now, though, Charley thought as he observed his son across the net.

"Think you can take one more?" Mike challenged, looking up at the sky as he did so. "Maybe we can get it in."

"Six-two, six-one—shouldn't take me more than half an hour."

Mike winked, tossed him a ball. "Loser's serve."

Charley walked back to the fence that screened the court from the trees and thick underbrush beyond, picked up the second ball, and came to the service line.

"Ready?"

Mike nodded.

Charley threw the ball high in the air, racket poised to smash as it descended.

But it never came down.

The "thup" he heard was almost like the sound of his racket hitting hard, except he never got to swing it. Instead, the ball disappeared at the top of its arc, and he looked at the empty space above his head, glanced quickly at his son and had only a split second to note the boy's confusion before he heard the guttural, "Just to let you know we're not fuckin' around."

He turned quickly and saw the ski-masked figure emerge from the woods to the side of the court.

The gun in the man's hand was leveled squarely at Mike.

"No heroics." The mask muffled the words.

Charley nodded understanding. He looked up toward the house.

"Don't worry." He could sense the sneer on the hidden mouth. "They're being looked after." The man motioned with the gun. "Move," he said, and Charley walked to the sandy path, Mike behind him as they were herded to the house.

They crossed the patio, strewn with the wooden deck furniture that should be stored this weekend, and entered the kitchen. The breakfast alcove brightened as the sun momentarily broke through to flood the surrounding windows, and Charley noted the breakfast dishes had already been washed and put away. Good old reliable Kate, he thought fondly.

"Charley?" she cried as they entered the living room. She stood framed in the light from the sun porch beyond but came quickly to his arms, head pressed to his chest as he stroked the soft brown hair. She was still in her housecoat, the lavender one they'd picked out together so many years ago in Rome, which she wore with surprising habit.

So small, he thought, so tiny and vulnerable. But strong—stronger than she looked, for he had always recognized it was her resolve, her dedication, more so than his own, that had welded the family into the tight bond so important to him. He loved her, but less deeply than she believed, and depended on her as his anchor more than she had ever understood. He tilted up her face now and looked into the frightened and questioning blue eyes. He squeezed her arm in reassurance, then looked over her shoulder at his daughter.

Penny, in plaid slacks and blue crewneck sweater, sat frozen on the hearth of the stone fireplace that dominated the room, tears running quietly down her cheeks. A carbon copy of her mother, he thought, wondering now if he'd ever see that fourteen-year-old promise blossom.

"Hey, baby," he said softly, and she met his eyes bravely.

Another ski-masked man stood off to her side, foot on the hearth, gun dangling insolently as he rested his arm on his knee. He seemed to appraise the silver trays and goblets displayed in the breakfront on the opposite wall, behind the sofa and armchairs that faced him. It crossed Charley's mind the man would be surprised to learn the breakfront itself was far more valuable than the silver it contained.

The man behind Charley broke the brief silence. "Okay. Let's get this show on the road."

The other man nodded, stood straight, and produced a length of rope from his belt.

"What—" Charley began, but the man raised the gun quickly.

"No questions now. We'll tell you all you need to know soon enough. You first," he said, indicating Mike.

Mike looked at his father, and Charley nodded. Mike's body was tense, and Charley hoped the boy wouldn't do something foolish.

"Just a necessary precaution. Keep you out of trouble," the man behind said, almost as if reading Charley's thoughts.

Mike stepped forward and put his hands behind his back as he was directed to do, and the other man quickly tied them.

"Sit," he said, and Mike sank down onto the sofa, uncomfortably upright as the ropes were pulled tight about his ankles.

"Now you."

Penny rose as ordered. She was silent during the ritual.

The man motioned to Kate, and Charley released her gently. Her eyes locked with his as the man knelt behind her.

"Okay," the man from the tennis court said, addressing the three stiffly seated figures on the sofa. "Listen. And listen good.

"We're taking your old man with us. Now I know Charley here won't give us any trouble, 'cause he's smart. Everybody knows that. And if you're half as smart as him, you'll do just like I'm telling you.

"One." The man raised his forefinger. "No calls to anybody, especially the police. We don't figure you'd do that, not after we told you not to, but just in case—" he looked toward the other man who walked to the phone, picked up the wire, and pulled it viciously from the wall.

"Where are the other phones?"

"Kitchen and upstairs bedroom," Charley replied quickly.

The first man nodded, and the other left the room.

"Two," the man went on, raising another finger. "You wait one hour, then you go to work on those ropes. Shouldn't take long, and make sure it doesn't because you've got to be back in Boston by six-thirty—to get our phone call."

He let that sink in.

"And three," he said as the other man reentered the room, an array of Charley's clothes clutched under his arm. "Just remember the stakes," he moved his gun toward Charley, "and do everything we tell you—exactly like we tell you. Understood?"

The three on the couch, who seemed almost hypnotized as they stared at the mask, nodded in concert after the briefest hesitation.

"Good." The man walked to the mantle, turned the clock toward them.

"Remember. One hour," he said, prodding Charley toward the door. "Be smart and nobody gets hurt."

Charley stopped and put all the confidence he could into his expression as he faced them. "Do just what they tell you. We'll pull together, and we'll get through this before you know it."

"Good advice," the other man said, but the one behind Charley stopped him short by raising his gunned hand and motioning toward the door. The second man left quickly.

Charley moved again, but looked back one last time. "I love you," he said.

"Dad—" Mike's statement hung.

Penny gave her brave smile.

Kate's eyes held his deeply.

Then he was outside, the gun hard in his back, wondering how and when he would ever see them again. He looked through the pines toward the ocean, which showed as gray now as the sky. He heard the dull roar of the surf and turned away finally as the van pulled up and the voice behind said, "Let's go."

CHAPTER 3

The men removed their masks as soon as they entered the van, surprising Charley.

"Don't worry," the man to his right said, reading his thoughts when Charley looked at his face. "We're gonna spend a lot of time together, and masks aren't exactly practical, especially in public. But this is a clean deal, understand? Pay up and that's it. No revenge either way. Got it?"

"Got it."

The man faced forward again as the van moved down toward the main road. "I'm Harry—that's Eddie," he said after a moment.

"Pleased to meet you," Charley said dryly and Harry gave him a wide grin.

"I like a man with style," he said.

Harry's face was beefy and pock-marked, his eyes somewhat beady in their heavy sockets, but his grin was infectious and Charley almost smiled back despite himself. Dressed in a conservative business suit, complete with tie, it was hard to think of the stocky man in his true role now that his mask was removed.

The one called Eddie was hatchet-faced, nose sharp in profile, as he drove. He exuded an animal nervousness that transmitted itself to Charley. In the black turtleneck sweater that was tight against his wiry frame, he seemed perfectly cast for his part in the drama.

"Don't worry," Harry said, anticipating again.

When they reached the turnpike Eddie pulled over at the first phone booth and Harry explained about the plane.

21

"How did you know it would be here instead of Boston? I didn't even decide to have it flown up until yesterday."

"Just make the call," was Harry's answer.

* * *

The Lear jet was waiting off to the side of the runway when they reached the Portland airport, fueled and ready for take-off as Charley had instructed.

Bob Dyer came out to meet the van when they pulled up to the hangar. He was wearing the habitual plaid flannel shirt despite the changing weather, and tufts of his shaggy mane of gray hair blew in the wind.

"All set, Mister Frost. Where you off to?"

Charley hesitated, glanced at his watch. Twelve-thirty—just forty-five minutes since they'd left the house. Harry and Eddie were at the rear of the van for the moment, unloading several large suitcases. And, Charley realized, managing to stay well removed from the scrutiny of the maintenance man. Charley looked at Bob and thought about his momentary freedom, but remembered, as he was obviously intended to, the gray Volkswagen that sat guard on the road just down from the house in which he had been forced to leave his family.

"Just a precaution. No heroics, remember?" the man called Harry had said as they exited the driveway, raising his hand in a signal as they passed the Volks. He had picked up the two-way radio that rested on the dashboard, turned it on and said, "All clean."

"Check," came the reply from the Volks, and Harry had shut off the radio.

"Understand?" he had asked Charley.

Charley understood all too well and now responded to Dyer, "Chicago," although he hadn't been told.

"Well—have a safe trip."

The man's voice held a slight admonition. A native "Mainiac" as he called himself, Bob Dyer took a deep pride in the beauty of his state and appreciated the frequency with which Charley and his family made use of their weekend hideaway. They visited as often in winter as in summer, and he thought of them more as locals with a vacation home in Boston rather than the other way around. So, at times, did they.

"All set," Harry called. The suitcases stood at the foot of the stairs leading into the body of the jet.

"See you," Bob waved, walking off.

"Put the van on the parking lot," Harry directed Eddie. "And make it quick."

The van moved off, and Harry motioned Charley toward the jet. "Let's go," he said, picking up one of the suitcases as he mounted the stairs, indicating Charley to do likewise. The suitcase was moderately heavy but told Charley nothing about what it contained.

Just as they entered the plane, a clap of thunder broke and a light rain began that increased rapidly as Eddie ran up and grabbed the last two suitcases.

"Good timing. Must be our lucky day," Harry said to the smaller man.

"Close her up," he ordered, and Charley swung up the aluminum ladder, folded it to the side and secured the door while Eddie placed the suitcases in the luggage compartment to the rear.

"Nice layout," Eddie commented as he returned, indicating the wide, comfortable-looking seats that could accommodate twelve, and just behind the cockpit the black leather couch complete with side tables, lamps, and large coffee table that doubled as a work space. Noting the wet bar set in the wall, his face took on a more intensified look.

"That thing stocked?" he asked, moving forward.

Charley started to respond but Harry stopped him with a hand on Charley's arm.

"That ain't your worry," he said to Eddie. "You just sit back here and do your job. I'll call you later when I need you."

Turning to Charley he continued, "Let's get moving," and ushered him to the cockpit. Charley shed his leather jacket, pushed up the sleeves of his sweater as he always did when flying, and took the pilot's seat.

Harry settled into the co-pilot's seat, took his gun almost casually from his jacket, and held it on his lap as Charley checked the controls. He looked inquiringly at Harry. "I'll have to call in a flight plan."

"Tell 'em Chicago."

* * *

They'd been in the air for an hour, were heading southwest with Portland nearly four hundred miles behind, when the unbroken greenery below ended abruptly at the edge of a large body of water that extended ahead as far as they could see. A few islands were visible

23

through the continuing rain, almost exclusively green themselves, but other than that the gray water dominated, punctuated by tiny whitecaps.

"Lake Ontario," Charley said, breaking the silence.

"Smart boy. That should be Oswego," Harry said, indicating a town visible through a break in the trees at the shoreline to their right and behind them. "About twenty miles, I'd guess.

"Okay." Harry looked at his watch, checked the plane's speedometer, which stood at three hundred fifty miles per hour, and said, "Give it two minutes thirty seconds and change your heading to zero-one-zero."

Charley glanced at the man.

"Was a pilot once myself," Harry said proudly, responding to the unasked question. "Korea."

Charley was surprised at receiving such relevant information.

Despite himself, he looked over at Harry and was less than reassured as the man said, "Remember, we got a clean deal here. No revenge either way, like I said. And besides, it's only money." But there was an edge behind the words and a hard light in the eyes that belied the easy words.

"What are you asking, anyway?" Charley threw out finally.

"Two million." Harry dropped the figure. "Shouldn't be a problem, should it?"

"Two million is always a problem."

"True. But I'm sure they'll work it out."

Charley looked back to the watered expanse below. He knew the man was right, but was also certain in the end it would make no difference.

* * *

"All clean," Eddie had said into the transmitter as the jet lifted off. "Check. All clean, here."

The call had come over the power receiver at exactly twelve-forty, and the gray Volkswagen left its hidden post immediately. It was twelve-fifty-five when the driver reached the pay phone, the same one Charley had used an hour earlier.

Taking some change from his pocket, he dialed a number in Boston.

"All clean," he said, hanging up after he'd heard "check" from the other end.

The man in Boston replaced the receiver, rose, and walked to the window. South Boston was dreary on the best of days, at least in this section, and even more so under the present steady downpour. Looking out at the mean street that made the hotel room seem more seedy than it actually was, Masters was glad he'd be there for only two days.

His reflection showed almost as a figment against the rain-washed windows with their gray backdrop, and Masters thought again he had surely not been intended for rooms such as this. He prided himself that his chiseled features—the aquiline nose and piercing blue eyes—were out of place here. He felt he radiated a sensitivity that rightfully required far more gracious surroundings.

He decided then if all went well, he'd never return to Boston.

But he was uneasy. Saturday was a bad time to start a job like this, he thought again. What with the banks closed. On the other hand, the setup in Maine was a lot simpler than pulling it off in Boston, the seclusion a great advantage. And besides, they'd need at least two days to get that much cash together anyway, he reflected, knowing the family could work with the banks if they were open or not.

He rubbed his eyes wearily. He'd been over the choices a hundred times, was tired of thinking about it. It was done. They were irrevocably committed, and he felt a sudden exhilaration in the actuality of danger.

Still at the window, he reached into his shirt pocket and took out a cigarette. He had time only for one deep drag before the phone rang again from its resting place on the scarred Formica night table.

It was exactly one o'clock.

He picked up the receiver. "Yes?"

"Well?" came the familiar voice, a trace impatient.

"All clean," Masters responded.

"Check." The line went dead.

The man on the other end left the phone booth, walked out into the warm sunny day. He looked across the mall to the Lincoln Monument, registered the heavy turnout of visitors congregated on the marble steps, and felt good about all of it.

Smiling to himself, he thought about how nervous Masters and the others must be despite their cool demeanors, how nervous he himself should be but how calm he actually was. Because he had one distinct advantage. He was totally confident of the outcome.

Glancing at his watch, he saw he had less than a half hour to get to the club for his tennis game.

He stepped into the street, raised his arm, and called, "Taxi."

CHAPTER 4

"Bring her down to five hundred feet and get ready for an approach when I tell you."

Charley estimated they were perhaps two hundred miles northeast of Ottawa. He couldn't tell exactly because during the past half hour he'd seen no discernable landmarks in the striking array of color that undulated endlessly over the contours of the earth below.

Fall came early here, he reflected, thinking those same colors would appear, equally rich, in his own New England within two weeks.

Fall had always been his favorite time. The family took long walks through the deep woods bordering their home in Boston, kicking the leaves as they went while often holding whatever hand was nearest. He recalled the previous year when he and Mike had an impromptu foot race that ended with the boy barely winning. He himself had stumbled just after the finish, rolling on the soft ground and propping himself gratefully against a tree as he caught his breath. The other three were quickly around him, the predictable concern on Kate's face mirrored in the children's as well. When they ascertained he was fine, they'd showered him with the crisp leaves as he feigned protest.

Maine's fall was different, at least on the coast where they were. Different, but equally stirring in its no-nonsense simplicity. Those weekend days generally began with catch football on the lawn, progressed to a stroll through the green and brown pine scent of the surrounding woods, colors subdued here but blending in a stark perfection with the ocean below as they came through the sand and pine-needled path to the edge of the rocky precipice and looked down.

"Gosh," Penny had said that first year. She'd been eight then, and he lifted her into his arms and held her tight as he'd looked over her shoulder into his wife's gentle blue eyes.

Those days—the best days—always ended with long hours before the fireplace, reading, working at an occasional jigsaw puzzle. Or doing nothing, as often as not. Just watching together as the flames died and soft music played in the background.

That picture changed to the last one he had of them in the same room, barely three hours before. They should be free by now, he thought, had to be if—

The thought was interrupted by Harry's hand hard on his shoulder.

"Over there," Harry said. Charley followed the pointing finger to his left and saw the runway break through the trees.

* * *

"Come on, Mom, take it easy—we'll be there in plenty of time."

Kate looked over at Mike, tension evident in her eyes.

He reached over and touched her hand, and her expression seemed to soften. She'd raised Mike from infancy, marrying Charley not long after Mike's real mother had died when he was only three months old. My mother, Mike now thought. It never occurred to him not to think of her as his mother. To Mike, Kate was as real as any mother could be, and his eyes misted slightly as he looked back to the road.

I've got to take charge, he said to himself again, exactly as he had when they'd heard the van drive away from the house and he'd immediately insisted, despite the ski mask's warning, that Penny lie on the floor so he could begin working on the knots that bound her. In the end, though, it was his mother who had to come on to the floor so her smaller fingers could pull free the last of the knots his own bleeding nails had only loosened. She'd broken two fingernails herself in the process.

"Mom—" he'd said, feeling a new outrage as he helped her to her feet and looked at the blemished hand in his own.

"Let's get out of here," she'd responded, taking her hand from his almost abruptly and turning to the door.

27

The three of them had run to the Bentley, and Mike, still in his tennis clothes and feeling the rain cold against his skin, had negotiated the winding back road as rapidly as he'd dared. Once on the turnpike, however, he'd driven with deliberate moderation.

"Go a little faster, Mike. Please," Kate urged again.

He shook his head and despite himself grinned at their role reversal. "No, Ma. We don't want the police stopping us." Looking at the dashboard clock, he said, "Three-thirty. We'll be home in an hour."

* * *

It was raining harder now.

The force of the drops against the thin windows of the phone booth sounded in a deep staccato that lulled Masters as he waited, and the sudden noise of the phone when it finally rang was jarring.

He looked at his watch. Three-thirty.

"Yes," he said.

"All clean." Eddie's voice sounded thin on the long-distance connection.

"Check."

He hung up and lit another cigarette.

* * *

"Good game, Owen."

His younger opponent wiped his hand on his shorts before offering it across the net.

"Buy you a drink?" the man asked, indicating the glass enclosed lounge above the courts.

Owen glanced at the wall clock.

"Order me a bourbon and water," he said. "I'll be two minutes."

He walked from the court, took some change from his pocket, and entered the phone booth in the men's locker room.

* * *

"Check," Masters said. Eddie's message was delivered to the man from Washington. Leaving the booth, he ducked through the rain back toward the hotel.

Three hours to wait, he thought.

* * *

Charley watched as Eddie went to the small hangar, unlocked the door, and drove out in a small fuel truck moments later. In ten minutes, they had refueled the plane.

As Eddie returned the truck to the hangar, Charley looked around again. Nothing more than the long runway lined to one side by power poles and the large paved area that fronted the hangar. Other than that there was only a small building Charley guessed housed sleeping quarters. And miles of deep forest in every direction, as Charley had seen from above.

"World War Two special," Harry said behind him. "For emergencies. We're the first."

Charley looked down the runway, then up past the trees to the sky.

"Relax," Harry smiled. "This place hasn't made a map in forty years. Come on, let's get back in the plane."

Charley folded the ladder and secured the door.

"How long do we stay?" he asked.

"Two days. If we're lucky."

Harry opened one of the suitcases.

"Here," he said, tossing Charley a sleeping bag.

Eddie had been busy unpacking groceries. He paused and looked up at Harry.

"How about it?" he asked. Harry glanced to the front of the plane, considered, said finally, "Why not?" as Eddie headed quickly toward the bar.

"How about you, *amigo?*"

Charley nodded.

"Hey, Eddie! Absolut on the rocks for our host. And remember, no olives—just a twist of lemon."

It was exactly what he would have ordered himself, and Charley eyed the man narrowly.

* * *

"Why haven't they called!"

Kate's voice was imploring and, despite himself, Mike was getting annoyed.

"For Christ's sake, Ma!"

Kate looked sharply at him and Mike lowered his eyes.

"I'm sorry," he mumbled , "but it's not even six, and he said six-thirty."

She sighed. "I know." She was still wearing her lavender housecoat although she'd draped a pink cardigan over her shoulders. He himself had changed long since from his tennis clothes into khakis and a navy pullover, but the chill from the afternoon rain had not left him.

"Hey," he said, touching her hair, noting the reddened eyes and haggard expression.

Inadvertently, his eyes were drawn to the bookshelf on the far wall where they lingered on the leather-bound volumes of Shakespeare. Had it only been yesterday he'd removed them from the shelf, opened his father's safe, and reached inside?

Mike considered sharing with his mother the details of his discovery but quickly discarded the idea. She had enough on her mind at the moment without having to ponder, as he did, the import of false passports and a fortune in cash hidden away not twenty feet from where they stood.

The secrets of his father's safe troubled Mike now more than ever, but he buried all thought of what they might imply as he brought his eyes back to his mother.

"Dad'll be fine." Mike forced the words, feeling it was his job now to take charge. "I'll bet he's calmer than any one of us," he went on, confidence in his tone.

Kate smiled, finally. "Oh, Mike." She held him with moist eyes. "You've done fine. And you'll do fine."

Behind him he heard Penny suddenly begin to cry.

"Hey," he said, going to the couch and taking her in his arms. "Hey. It'll be okay." He held her tight against his chest as the sobbing rose and finally broke with a cry that left her breathlessly gulping for air.

30

It felt good to have his sister in his arms now, gave Mike a warm big-brother feeling. He felt protective suddenly of this girl who was his sister and whom he often disliked with an intensity he was careful to conceal from his parents. He knew he was jealous of Penny, who was so much like Kate, but that knowledge had not changed things for him.

How insignificant and petty those emotions seemed to him now as he stroked his sister's hair and said, "Shh, Penny. It'll be over soon. You'll see."

Beyond her shoulder he looked out at the trees—his father's trees. They were framed now in the gray, cloud-brushed backdrop of an early evening sky.

He squeezed Penny's shoulders, released her, and walked to the bay window that had become his home base as they waited. Past the garden he could see the pool in the last of the dim twilight, remembered covering it with Charley only two weeks before. And it's getting cold already, he thought, feeling the chill reach in from beyond the glass.

He looked out to his left to the tennis court, turned after a moment, and moved to the fireplace. Kneeling, he rapidly started a fire, using the trick his father had taught him years ago, rolling up a page of newspaper, lighting it, and holding it torchlike up into the chimney for a moment before placing it under the logs.

"Makes the air above warm and helps draw the fire up quickly," Charley had explained.

As the flames grew now and the crackling of the dry wood began, the room seemed almost cheerful, even more so as the deep, rich tone of the grandfather clock in the hall suddenly sounded.

"Six o'clock," Kate said as the last reverberation died.

"He said six-thirty." Penny's statement was matter of fact. He looked at his sister, knew she had grown as well that day; he wondered how much they'd all have to grow before this was over.

They sat silently watching the fire, he at the window resisting the urge to pace, his mother on the couch, Penny arms-about-knees on the floor, waiting. Mike, who had never smoked, wished suddenly he did.

The clock and the phone sounded together.

"Hello?" Mike was at the phone in the middle of the ring as Kate rose quickly, too, hurrying toward the kitchen. He heard a click when she picked up just as the soft voice began.

31

"Mike? You on, too, Kate? Good," Masters went on after they'd responded affirmatively. "Now listen carefully. First of all, Charley's okay. He's comfortable—not tied up, no rough stuff, don't worry about that sort of thing—he's just being watched in an out-of-the-way place. You know we took the plane?"

"No!" Mike and Kate said in unison, their surprise so obvious the man on the other end chuckled briefly. Mike realized it had been a trick question.

"Yes. Charley's with the plane and they're both in good shape, so don't worry about that."

Masters continued speaking, affecting an easy manner and making deliberate use of their first names. He wanted to put them at ease, to relegate the situation as closely to a business transaction as he could manage, and his next words were intended to strengthen that impression.

"Now let's get down to business," he said. "Kate. We want two million dollars for Charley's safe return." The statement hung.

Kate broke the brief silence. "Where? When?" It never occurred to her to negotiate.

"Monday. We'll call you at two. That should give you enough time. Then we'll tell you what to do next."

"Let me speak to Charley! Please!" Kate's voice had a touch of hysteria the man soothed quickly in his calm and reassuring voice.

"We can't do that, Kate. Not now. Charley's with the plane a long way from here. But he's fine, believe me. We only want the money, and once that's settled he'll be back home. Monday night, if you do exactly as we say."

"Two million," Mike injected. "It might take more time to raise that much."

"Not with Bill Chambers helping you. You'll work it out. Twenties only. And remember, no police. You'll have to be sure to make that very clear to Chambers when you speak to him.

"Until Monday, then," the voice ended reassuringly.

Kate was back in the room by the time Mike replaced the receiver.

They had certainly done their homework, Mike realized, because Bill Chambers was the one they'd have to call.

Mike thought of his father's friend, who was also president of the largest local bank. Their bank. Charley was on the bank's Board of Directors, but he and Bill were far more than business associates, having teamed as doubles partners for a good ten years.

"What did he say?" Penny interrupted his thoughts, and he turned to his sister.

"Dad's okay. They want—" he began, but was quieted by a harsh "shh" from Kate, who was on the telephone.

"Bill," Kate spoke into the phone. "Bill, something's come up, something we desperately need your help with..."

* * *

Masters returned to the car, pleased with himself.

So far, so good, he thought. The family seemed under control, and he was fairly certain of the outcome of that part of it.

He would have liked to spend the evening in some different kind of action, unwinding from the tension of the day. But that would have to wait. Right now he had to figure out the other part, and he didn't have much time.

Turning east, he headed past the Quincy Market, crowded as usual with Saturday shoppers despite the continuing rain, and was relieved to see there was no backup as he approached the Callahan Tunnel. He glanced at his watch and slowed his speed. He'd make the last plane for Washington in plenty of time.

* * *

Owen stood before the mirror and pulled his black bow tie up just a notch to the right. Perfect, he thought, looking at the finished product.

He regarded his reflection critically but with satisfaction. At forty-two, his rangy frame was still trim and youthful, the dark eyes clear, deep-set, and penetrating. The mouth was a bit thin, perhaps, but the quick smile was a winner, and he had learned to smile often. Only a slight thickening of the jowls and neck gave evidence of aging, he thought. That and the sag beneath his eyes he'd begun to notice recently. But, all in all, he felt the changes made him appear more substantial, and the touch of gray at his temples accented his full dark hair and added a distinction he liked.

"Ready, darling."

He turned to his wife, noting with approval her radiance in the lush emerald-green formal gown she was wearing. It matched her eyes perfectly. He had given her a rose earlier and was glad he'd thought of it. Those things were important to remember, and he thought with a twinge of sadness how far he had come from spontaneity.

Extending his arm he took her hand, bowed deeply, and kissed it.

"You are beautiful, Missus Reid," he said as if in awe, making certain to infuse an adequate amount of affection into his tone. He neglected that sometimes, although the emotion was not counterfeit. But it was hard not to treat those things as inconsequential especially now that the rest was accelerating.

She smiled a tribute to his gallantry and he kissed her lightly.

"Bert's waiting," he said, opening the door and ushering her to the limousine waiting at the curb.

* * *

"Get some sleep," Harry said.

Charley shrugged.

Eddie had been asleep for some time, his light but steady snoring the only sound in the passenger's cabin. Only a few reading lamps were on, and the plane's interior had an almost cozy look.

Outside, all was black.

CHAPTER 5

Monday morning broke bright and sunny.

Masters looked down onto Boylston Street feeling very good about everything. The trip to Washington had led him far beyond his expectations. Any conceivable expectations, he thought with excitement.

He hadn't put the whole puzzle together yet, but knew now that he would. Because now he had the answer. He just didn't know what it meant.

He glanced at his watch. Nine-thirty. By this time tonight it will all be over, he thought.

The man in Washington had bothered him for a long time now. Two months, he reflected—ever since he'd received that first phone call.

Not the man himself, Masters amended. He didn't bother him. It was the identity that was irking him, or rather the lack of it.

As far as the man who gave the orders was concerned, he'd been fine. Perfect, in fact. Masters had never been involved in anything that had run more smoothly.

"John Masters?" the voice had asked over the phone the first time. Masters had thought he recognized it vaguely, couldn't place it.

"Yes," he'd answered. "Who is this?"

"Never mind that for now, Mister Masters. You were referred to me by a friend. I'd like to meet you and discuss a possible business transaction."

"Which friend?" Masters asked cautiously. "And what kind of business?" He asked the question although he already knew the answer.

"Just a friend. That's all I can say now. I'll tell you more when we meet today."

"Today?"

"The sooner the better. This is a very pressing deal."

He had agreed to the appointment, considering the possibility of entrapment but knowing he wouldn't commit himself until he was sure of the unknown party.

But it hadn't worked out that way.

When he'd reached the picnic grove off the small country road, a tan Chevrolet had been waiting. The door opened and a large ski-masked figure had gotten out. Masters could tell nothing, either, from the other's casual but nondescript clothing.

"Don't be alarmed, Mister Masters." The voice held a soft but unquestionable command. "It's just that I must be cautious."

"What friend?"

"Easy now. I understand your concern, and I assure you that before we conclude this meeting I'll give something that will convince you of my good intentions."

They stood facing each other beside the picnic table.

Masters had been wary, but something in the man's attitude convinced him to listen.

"Okay. Shoot. But it had better be good."

"It will be. Ever hear of Charley Frost?"

"Sure. Everybody around here has. At least, everybody who ever reads the financial pages."

Then the man laid out the simple plot, as they sat opposite one another at the picnic table on that warm summer afternoon. He concluded with three words: "Two million dollars."

Masters' eyes narrowed. "Two million dollars," he repeated.

"Certainly. Of course only one million will be yours. The other is mine."

"Sounds too easy," Masters said skeptically.

"I assure you it will be easy. Just as easy as I've said."

"What makes you think I'd be interested in something like this?"

The man had remained silent. Ski masks were not unknown to Masters; he'd even used them himself. But he always knew the face on the other side, and as the silence continued Masters found himself more and more bothered by his disadvantage.

"What friend?" he asked again.

The man shook his head. "But I did promise to show you something that would convince you. Here," he said, reaching into the pocket of his light sport jacket. Removing a large envelope, he handed it to Masters. "Open it."

Masters did. "Jesus Christ!" he said, pulling out the bound packets of one-hundred-dollar bills. "There must be fifty thousand dollars here!"

"Forty thousand. A token of my good intentions."

Masters realized the police would not risk this kind of money on a bluff, especially for someone as low on their priority list as he would be even if they'd fingered him, which he doubted they had. His business had always been relatively small, clean, and unspectacular. And above all discreet, which was the trait he imagined had brought this man to him.

The tall figure extended a hand. Masters looked into the masked face and considered for a long moment before taking the other's hand in a firm hold. He noted the grip was exceptionally strong.

"That's it, then. You'll hear from me. One more thing."

"What's that?"

"I need your car keys. You'll find them in an envelope a half mile down the road."

Masters hesitated.

"That's how it has to be."

He handed the keys over.

"Take care." The man had driven off. Masters had followed on foot, finding the keys exactly where he'd been told.

That had been their only meeting. The telephone calls came on schedule and with similar brevity and precision. And more important, the information was flawless.

The only thing Masters knew was the man lived in Washington. Or at least received his calls there.

Pay phones to be sure, but still—Masters felt there was some way to track it and began to have an idea as he noticed a pattern to the various exchanges he dialed. By checking the exchanges in the Washington directory, he discovered weekday calls would go to anywhere in the city. But weekends were always to Georgetown.

The numbers, of course, had never been the same.

Masters hadn't worried about it too much at first; mostly he had just been curious. But two weeks ago that had changed when the man from Washington had been giving him the final details. "Take your share, divide it up with your people in whatever way you've decided, and send my half to a post office box I'll give you."

"What if the money doesn't get there?"

"I'll take that chance. I have great faith in the postal system."

Masters hesitated.

"How do you know I'll send it?" he asked finally.

"I have great faith in your intelligence. After all, I know who you are."

Masters had realized then the threat would hang not just through the successful delivery of the money, but beyond—for his entire lifetime. He had to even the stakes or he'd never be comfortable.

Watching the post office box would be no good. The man was too smart to be trapped that way. And besides, it could be days, even weeks before he showed. Another idea had taken hold then, and he'd flown to Washington, spending two full days searching out every phone booth he could find in Georgetown. He wrote down each number and its location, finding all five he'd called before. They didn't matter, of course, because the calls would not be made from any of those. Still, finding them made him feel better.

He knew it was a long shot, but maybe—so he took it.

"You'd better give me a number where I can call you over the weekend. Just in case there's a problem."

This had been Friday when the man from Washington called to tell him it was "go" for the Saturday morning rendezvous with Charley Frost.

There was a hesitation on the line and Masters held his breath.

"I'll call you."

"You may not be able to get me if there's a problem."

Another pause. Then, incredibly, "Okay. I'll give you a number when we talk tomorrow."

And he had! "I'll be there at exactly eight-forty five Sunday morning if you need me."

Masters had replaced the receiver, eager with anticipation. He wondered briefly why the man hadn't thought to reverse their method of communication from the beginning. Instead of having Masters call a variety of phone booths in Washington, he could have phoned Masters at prearranged numbers in Boston, as he now did. That one slip had given Masters his opening.

The man from Washington had made a mistake, and Masters was glad he had. He hoped it was his only miscalculation, however.

He hardly slept after arriving in Washington late on the evening of the kidnaping, and he'd been seated on a bench by the river by eight o'clock Sunday morning. From there, he had a perfect view of the phone booth by the walking path, the booth with the number the man from Washington had given him. As he turned the pages of his newspaper, he knew the chance of his being recognized at this distance was slight. And even so, so what? He planned a confrontation later, anyway.

But his immediate goal was the man's identity.

He intended to follow when the man left the booth, hoping to find his residence, but at least expecting to be led somewhere that would allow him to track the man later. Because once he'd seen the face he could always find the man.

The wait had been intolerable, Masters forcing himself to maintain an easy, natural air. Finally—right on schedule—he'd seen the man approaching the booth. He recognized the tall, athletic build and imposing carriage.

He'd watched as the man stood in the booth for a few minutes before opening the door and retracing his steps. Masters kept his face to the paper but raised his eyes over its edge, prepared to fold it leisurely and move once the man was far enough ahead for him to follow.

But that hadn't been necessary.

Instead, Masters almost dropped the paper as the man passed some fifty yards away from him. Because even at that distance, he was recognizable.

Jesus Christ! Masters thought, and he almost spoke the words out loud—was afraid for a moment he had. Jesus Christ! he repeated to himself as he fought to keep his hands from shaking.

Owen Reid!

It was Owen Reid. Beyond question, the next president of the United States.

CHAPTER 6

The sun rose slowly in the cold Canadian woods, its copper rays slanting through the surrounding trees like searching fingers. Charley felt warmed by the sight of it as he looked out the oval window of his plane. A hawk suddenly broke from some high, secluded limb, and Charley watched as the graceful bird glided effortlessly against the peaceful morning sky. It was hard to imagine disaster on such a beautiful day.

Although, he reflected, he'd been given no cause for immediate concern.

His captors had been polite, even friendly, and although their mere presence was threatening, they in fact exuded a quiet confidence that was almost reassuring.

They were right to be confident, too, because he knew their premises were correct. No one other than his family would know he was missing until it no longer mattered, and the men were on target in assuming the family would come through.

Charley was proud of his family, loved them deeply, singly and as a whole. He hoped they would never have reason to learn his loyalty and commitment had not totally been to them, as they now believed without question. As he, with better reason, believed in them.

They would handle things, despite their anguish, do what had to be done, support each other, a strongly welded unit at whose center was Kate. He'd chosen well for himself, Charley reflected, his resentment of that practical decision now a memory so dim he could hardly reach it. That long-ago wrestling of conscience lay buried as in some still, silent pond, resting with the romantic boy-girl dreams of his youth, dreams that had once seemed so important to him but that he had nonetheless forced himself to drown when his other dreams had been threatened. He had long since come to terms with that sacrifice, but some part of him still mourned the lost, bright promises that had never been allowed their chance.

But he'd crossed that line when he married Ellen, he reminded himself. It was only later he had chosen Kate. He'd needed a mother for his infant son, and Kate had fitted the role to perfection. Then and now. It wasn't that he didn't love her. He did, in his way. But not in the other way, the way he had once known, the way when every day had broken flush with the pulse of excitement.

There had never been excitement with Kate. Affection, certainly, respect, and above all confidence in the woman who was his wife. Those, after all, had been the reasons for his choice.

But no excitement together. Never that.

Just quiet and gentle companionship. That had been there at first, and now, seventeen years later, it was still so. Only now, as they entered middle age, that texture of the relationship seemed to him more easily acceptable.

A good deal of what he felt to be lacking in their marriage he realized to be of his own doing. The choice had been his own, and he had well understood his motivation to have been essentially pragmatic. He had needed a wife and a mother for his son—someone in whom he could have confidence—and Kate had been there. But beyond that compromised beginning, through all the years of their marriage, Charley recognized he had never really shared himself with her. There were things—the most important things—he could never share. Who and what he really was could never be shared, no matter how close he and Kate might have been.

But there was more, those private feelings within which he always seemed to hold back because of the distinct sense of separateness that had lurked in him for as long as he could remember. No, he admitted, he never gave himself completely, not to anyone. He always kept something in reserve.

Those faults were his.

Kate's, he felt, were that she had never noticed, never seemed aware that the excitement and the real Charley were missing. During their courtship she hadn't questioned his lack of ardor; she had only looked forward eagerly to their marriage and to her assumption of the role of wife and mother.

And later, through the building years when he'd amassed that portion of the wealth and trappings of which she was aware, she had taken all of it in stride, no wonderment it was so, no fear it might be lost, merely simple acceptance that good fortune had come the way of her family.

No questions, no *deep* questions, as to how that had come about.

And that, Charley conceded, had been important to him, too.

Yes, Kate was a good woman, and had been good for him. But it was ironic the very facets of his wife that had served him best—her simplistic outlook on life, her need to fulfill her roles, her ability to rationalize, her essential practicality—were the very things with which he was so often privately annoyed.

But those were the things that would carry them through this, Charley reflected as he gazed through the window at the sun which had now risen clear of the thick forest that fringed the narrow runway on which the plane rested. Kate would hold them together and the family would come through. The men who held him hostage had every right to be confident in that.

And the money—as they had said, the money was no problem. Charley knew that better than anyone. At least, he told himself, they'll have absolute security, no matter what. The thought gave him comfort, as it always did. That had always been important to him, for himself as well as for his family. He rarely dwelled on it but understood that his deep need for security stemmed from fears he had never outgrown, fears that even today were a prime motivation in all he did. That his own security had been an important by-product of the whole, lofty enterprise brought a curl to his lips, and he reflected on how inconsequential that really was when viewed in the total context of what he had really been about these many years.

"Nice day," Harry said, interrupting his train of thought. The man had come to stand by Charley's seat. He looked as rumpled as Charley felt after two days on the plane. "How about stretching outside a little?"

Charley responded affirmatively, eager to be outside—if only for a little while. He was just as eager to leave his thoughts as well—if only for a little while.

* * *

Bill Chambers brought the money late that morning. Kate had signed the necessary papers, and now Mike waited for what he hoped would be the final call from whomever had taken his father. It seemed that two o'clock would never come. When it did, the phone rang.

"All set?" the now familiar, smooth voice asked.

"Yes," Kate answered breathlessly as Mike listened in on the extension. "Tell us—"

"That's why I called. You've got it all?"

"All of it," Kate affirmed.

"Good. Now listen carefully. Mike, you on?"

"Yes." Mike's nervousness intensified.

"Okay. Mike, you take the cases into the Bentley and drive to Highway 90. That should take about six or seven minutes, right?"

Mike agreed.

"Okay. Give it ten. Let's say you enter on the northbound ramp at exactly two-fifteen. Got it?"

"Got it. But what then?"

"Turn your CB to thirty-six, and we'll pick you up."

"How about me?" Kate broke in.

"You stay home, Kate, like a smart little lady. Charley'll be home for dinner." There was a minute's pause before the voice continued, "See you in ten minutes, Mike."

* * *

Masters watched from the woods as the Bentley stood by the side of the road. It was exactly two miles east of the Mass Pike. He gave it one more minute, saw no cars pass in either direction, and then walked back to his own car, parked on the far side of the road out of Mike's vision.

Picking up the CB microphone, he said into the speaker, "Breaker three-six for Mike."

"You've got him," Mike's voice came back hoarsely.

"Head back up the Pike and get off at the next exit. Wait at the same spot—two miles east."

Masters drove off then and came around the turn not far behind the Bentley, which had made a rapid U-turn. He slowed down a bit but the precaution was unnecessary as the other car outdistanced him quickly.

He went east a mile at the next exit, pulled over to the shoulder, and said, "Breaker three-six for Mike."

"You've got him," the breathless response came immediately.

"See the trash barrel to your right? Just put them in there."

"But—"

Masters cut him off, wanting to maintain complete control over the wound-up teenager. "In the trash barrel, Mike. Then go straight home." He broke off, turned, and drove on the overpass above the Pike, stopping at a point where he had a view of the westbound traffic on this secondary road. A moment later he saw the Bentley come to the southbound ramp of the Pike and enter.

Good boy, Masters thought, observing the traffic for a moment to ascertain no cars appeared to be positioning themselves near any of the exits. He was sure it was a clean drop, but it paid to be careful.

When he was satisfied, he drove east again, stopped, left the car, and reached into the trash barrel.

The suitcases were there.

He placed them quickly into the trunk of the car, surprised at their weight. A sharp nervousness overtook him and he wanted to slam the trunk shut and be gone, but he squelched his anxiety. Taking a deep breath, he placed his thumbs on the locks and sprung the top case open.

* * *

Eddie had been in the hangar waiting for the phone call for a half hour, and Harry was getting edgy.

"Where the fuck is he?" It was the only profanity Harry seemed to use, but he repeated it often as he strode up and down the aisle of the plane.

"It's almost three o'clock," he said again.

He was making Charley nervous.

"What if they can't—" Charley began, but Harry turned on him with an uncharacteristically harsh "Shut up!" as he paced again.

Suddenly there was a clamoring on the ladder and Eddie's face appeared, almost gamin-like, in the doorway.

"Let's go!" he shouted, giving a thumbs-up to Harry.

Harry broke into a grin, clapped Charley on the back, and said, "You heard the man! Let's go!"

They rushed to the cockpit, strapped themselves in, and with what he could only think of as a festive air, Charley started the engines.

* * *

Kate and Penny were at the door when a perspiring Mike returned; four blue eyes stared at him, wide and questioning.

He nodded and they both embraced him, tears of relief coming as if it were all over.

* * *

They were still over the forests, but Charley estimated they'd crossed the border already as they headed southeast at 130 degrees on a direct line for Portland.

The clear sky had held. What few clouds there were appeared almost make-believe, small puffs that looked like piles of shaving cream hung suspended. To his right, the midafternoon sun made the wing shine like a silver mirror.

Charley was glad it was almost over.

"He got it!" Eddie had exclaimed over and over again as they'd taken off. "The son of a bitch really got the money!"

Only then did Charley realize how doubtful the men must really have been. They'd seemed so patient, so sure, and now their excitement and relief were so infectious he almost felt as if he too had pulled something off.

The good feeling persisted as the plane headed south.

"We're leaving you now, kiddo."

Charley looked back sharply, saw Harry standing in the cockpit door adjusting a final strap across his chest. He noted the parachute on the man's back, looked into his eyes as the other nodded.

"She's all yours from here."

Harry withdrew a hunting knife from his belt and Charley stiffened.

"Relax," the man laughed, placing a hand on his shoulder. "It's all over. Almost, anyway," he went on, reaching to the control panel and grabbing the wires that led from the radio. With a quick motion he sliced them through.

"No more calls. Just a precaution—so we'll have time to get out in case you have thoughts of sending our position. Not that I think you would, but—" he shrugged, worldly wise.

Charley nodded, trying to ignore a sudden unexpected fear at being left alone in the plane.

Harry noted the quick widening of the eyes, misread it.

"Don't worry," he assured. "The radio being out won't hurt you, not on a clear day like this. Just keep your eyes open, wag your wings if you have to—but what the hell am I telling you this for? You're a better pilot than me, anyway."

"Hey, Harry. Cut the chatter. We gotta go right now."

Looking back into the cabin, Charley saw Eddie struggling with the emergency exit. The man was braced to the side, and as the door came open the quick rush of air slammed him to the wall and rocked the plane sharply.

Harry lurched forward and Charley felt his own chest push into the wheel but was able to sit back after only seconds as the cabin pressure leveled and the plane righted itself.

The noise of the air was so loud he couldn't hear Eddie's words. His eyes registered Eddie's wave as he positioned himself at the door, looked back a last time, and leaped outward.

Harry's eyes met his briefly. Then the man turned, quickly following his companion.

* * *

They hit the ground within fifty yards of each other, pulling their chutes in immediately and holding them to their chests as they ran across the large meadow still deep in late summer grass.

"That kid better be here," Eddie panted as they neared the woods.

"Don't worry," Harry came back just as they both saw the familiar figure step from the trees and wave.

Almost as one, the men stopped.

Harry looked at his watch, then at Eddie.

The other nodded almost imperceptibly, raised his eyes and looked south.

Harry followed his gaze.

The plane was almost thirty miles away by then, but both men thought they could still see the barest touch of light burst in the clear sky.

* * *

The *Boston Herald* carried the story in a special edition that evening. As he boarded the Delta flight for Washington, Masters looked again at the headline.

"Charles Frost Killed in Plane Crash."

CHAPTER 7

"Air Explosion Claims Frost, Investor."

The headline in the *Washington Post* wasn't nearly as big as that of the *Boston Herald*. And it was on page 3. But then, Reid reflected, Charley wasn't nearly as well known in Washington as he was in New England. But he was known.

That probably couldn't have been helped, he reminded himself, under any circumstances. But he wouldn't have to worry about that anymore.

He returned his eyes to the paper, reread the brief article.

> **September 29 [AP]** A mysterious mid-air explosion has apparently claimed the life of one of New England's most prominent investment counselors.
>
> Investigators from the CAB have confirmed the wreckage of the Lear jet that exploded this afternoon over Northern Vermont was that of the plane registered to Charles Frost of Weston, Mass.
>
> Although no bodies have as yet been recovered, a spokesman for the investigative team said, "We have every reason to believe he [Frost] was on board. As far as bodies are concerned, I don't think there's much hope for that. This explosion was as devastating as any I've ever seen." The cause of the explosion is as yet undetermined, the spokesman said.
>
> Frost was apparently returning to the Portland, Maine, airport, to which he'd radioed approximately fifteen minutes before the 3:40 P.M. occurrence.

Portland airport manager William Wylie stated Frost's plane had been missing since early Saturday afternoon when he'd taken off for Chicago with two unidentified men. When asked why he hadn't reported the plane overdue when informed by the Chicago airport it had not arrived as scheduled, Wylie stated, "That wasn't unusual for Charley Frost. He'd file a flight plan for one place, end up at another. I would have reported it, but it happened often before and he always showed up in a day or two."

Wylie also confirmed he had himself spoken to Frost in the last radio communication, confirming Frost had mentioned he was flying alone.

For the past ten years, Frost, forty-two, had headed the highly successful Frost, Associates. Founded in 1977, the firm rapidly became one of New England's premier investment advisory concerns. Frost was noted for an exceptional ability to forecast trends in various industries, and the firm has been identified with a highly speculative approach and frequent spectacular results.

In Weston, Frost's wife and two children were unavailable for comment.

Reid put down the paper, leaned his head back against the soft leather of the armchair and reached into the brushed silver box on the table at his side to retrieve a cigar. Lighting it, he blew the smoke upward toward the sloping beamed ceiling, thought of how much he enjoyed the rich taste, and regretted he could only indulge the pleasure in private.

Image, he thought. Always image. It would be nice if life could be simple, but that luxury had been denied him ever since he'd first understood how it could be. And that had been a long time ago.

1963. He'd been just eighteen then, he thought, shaking his head in wonder.

He got up, went to the built-in bar in the far corner of the dimly lit study, and poured a small bourbon into the cut crystal glass. Not a few of his peers would have rung for a butler to do the chore, but Reid did for himself whenever possible, seeing anything else as affectation. But at some barely conscious level he recognized that the deeper truth, for him, was no matter what their value, he considered others to be underlings in the total sense of that word, and he always struggled against that arrogance in himself for he well knew it to be an impeding and dangerous attitude.

In any event, both the servants were off tonight, at his suggestion. And Nancy, too, was out, although she'd been a little difficult.

"Darling, I'd rather stay home with you. You seem upset," she'd said, putting her hands on his forearms and looking with concern into his eyes. "The symphony isn't that important to me, anyway. You know that."

He'd nodded, stroked her cheek. Her green eyes had glistened as he did so, and her strong, well-featured face had softened in expectation. She was so easy, he thought.

"I'll fix a nice dinner for the two of us, okay? I'd like to do that, for a change," she said.

He shook his head, containing the touch of irritation he felt at her persistence. "You go on, honey," he said kindly. "Really. I am distracted, as you say, and I've got a lot of thinking to do—and I do that best alone."

His voice had carried a finality that left no room for discussion.

Charley Frost, he thought now, looking over at the unlit brick fireplace on the wall opposite the bar. Large French windows stretched between, hidden now by the tweed textured drapes that shielded the garden beyond. Charley would have had a fire going by now, even this early in the year, especially in this dark-paneled room that almost demanded one. Charley had always loved a fire as he had loved most of life's simplest pleasures.

It had always amazed him how Charley had managed to cling to that perspective. And frustrated him as well, because the trait had ultimately presented problems.

He reflected on the brief newspaper notation of Charley's meteoritic rise, then pondered his own as well.

They'd left the orphanage only twenty-four years ago, two raw-boned kids out to take the world and turn it on its heels. Now Charley was gone. Finally.

And here *he* was, alone in the elegant town house in Georgetown, the junior senator from Colorado. Waiting.

* * *

It was almost nine-thirty when the taxi dropped Masters at M Street. He walked leisurely north on Wisconsin, past the understated red brick of the Georgetown Inn from which a handsome young couple was just emerging, and decided he'd stop in for a drink there afterwards.

He moved along the crowded streets, stepping off the pavement at one point to pass a group of long-haired kids who commanded the sidewalk as they ambled laughing and chattering. Beyond them, he adroitly avoided conversation with a plump, acne-faced girl who thrust a pamphlet at him.

A block later, the pedestrian traffic diminished, and shortly thereafter he turned to his right.

The tree-lined street looked quiet and ordinary, but Masters knew it was not. Both incredible wealth and power nestled well entrenched and carefully tended beyond those small, neat gardens, and he rankled at the world's inequities.

"Money goes to money," his mother had often told him, explaining away the near poverty in which the family had seemed always to exist. He had realized early the statement was an excuse, but he recognized its truth nonetheless.

He had money, now. A lot of it. But it was still unfair, based on who had taken what risks in the enterprise.

Although he'd taken advantage of the same system himself, he thought. Six hundred thousand dollars for himself, and four hundred thousand for Harry and his crew who had really been on the line. But it had been his deal, and Harry had been delighted.

On the other hand, the man from Washington had cleared one million. Or thought he had. It had been his idea and his information, but still—

Masters was not yet certain how he'd handle it. He wasn't even sure where he wanted things to go. He had the man's money stashed with his own in a locker at Logan. He would confront the man and play it by ear.

He came to the house, noted the downstairs lights were on, and opened the gate. Mounting the steps, he rang the bell. The chimes that reverberated within sounded serene through the thick oak door.

When it opened a moment later, he was surprised to find Owen Reid himself facing him. The man was dressed casually in an open-

51

necked sport shirt, looking elegant as ever with that touch of gray at the temples of his square, rugged face. Masters had to admire the man's composure. Masters knew Reid had to be terribly shaken at seeing him, but there was no way to tell that from either his face or his voice which, after only the briefest hesitation, said, "Can I help you?"

"Hello, senator," Masters said.

"I'm sorry, but—should I know you?"

The voice was innocent and Masters marveled again at the cool of the man.

"Come on, senator. Let's not waste time. I think we need to have a talk."

Pushing forward, he entered the foyer. Noting the large double doors that stood open to his right, he moved toward them.

"Anyone else home?" he turned to ask, and the other man shook his head.

"Let's go in here, then," Masters asserted himself, walking through the doors.

His quick impression of the dark-paneled room which was enriched by a glowing fire had barely formed before the other voice came softly from behind him.

"Masters."

Turning quickly he looked into the face of Charley Frost. He had only an instant to register the dark, sad eyes before he felt the strong arm come across his windpipe from behind and quickly close in a powerful, suffocating grip from which he knew, despite his struggle, there would be no escape.

Part II

CHAPTER 8

"One more set, Mike. Come on."

Shelly's voice was plaintive. She was beginning to annoy him.

Looking at the broad freckled-face ringed with perspiration-soaked blonde hair, his annoyance changed to guilt at how their relationship was subtly eroding. He was at fault, drawing away, and she was becoming more assertive as he did so. His eyes dropped to the breasts thrusting beneath the tennis shift, and he felt a quick stirring that became even sharper as his eyes caught the wet stains that encroached on the white cotton beneath her arms. He remembered a clear, spring day just like today, and the shower, that long ago baptism of their youth when they'd come together, fresh with soaped innocence. He thought of the vows he'd made, both spoken and silent, vows he thought he'd meant, as they joined feverishly on the bed in the guest house.

That had only been a year ago, he thought regretfully. He wanted desperately to bridge the brief passage of time and recapture what he'd felt, but he knew their relationship was irreparably beyond that somehow. Was that what growing up was about, he wondered? Losing relationships you believed were forever?

"Okay," he said in a way that told her it was with reluctance. "One more set."

He tossed her the ball and walked to the far side of the court.

* * *

"I'm leaving, Mom," he said.

The statement was as deliberate as he could make it, delivered as he'd practiced it.

Kate looked up quickly, sat straight as she replaced her cup carefully in its saucer. She looked very young today, he thought, in the pink and green plaid shirt whose sleeves she had rolled past her elbows. She'd let her rich brown hair grow longer, shoulder length, and the lightly curled ends had a softening effect on her oval face.

"What exactly does 'I'm leaving' mean? Of course you're leaving for Europe. I know that. But that's two weeks away."

He pushed away from the table, stood, and shrugged. Can I really carry this off, he wondered. Do I really want to?

"I'm not going to Europe. I've already told Rick and Ben."

There was an almost smart-assed tone in his voice he immediately regretted. That was the last impression he wished to convey. It was his graduation gift from her, after all. He wanted to go to his mother, make it right, but somehow they seemed always at cross purposes now.

"I'm going to look for him, Ma," he said more softly, breaking the silence.

Kate rose and came to him, took his face in her hands and looked up into his eyes. He must have grown two inches these past months, she thought. He was even taller than Charley had thought he'd be.

"Mike," she said finally, "your father's dead. You know that."

He pulled away and went to the open French doors. He stood on the small balcony and looked down at the pool where Penny and a few of her friends were enjoying the warm June afternoon.

Taking a deep breath, he expelled it in a heavy sigh, said, "I know. I mean I guess I should know. But deep down I just don't believe it."

"It's hard for me, too, Mike. Charley was always so full of life. It's hard to think—"

"No, Ma. It's not just that," he cut in, turning back to her. "I *feel* somehow he really isn't dead, that he's out there somewhere."

"Mike, if your father were alive he'd have contacted us. You know that."

"I guess. But suppose he couldn't, suppose—"

"Mike," she chided gently. "Come on. You're a big boy. You know better."

"I suppose so. But I can't get it out of my head, Ma. I felt that way all along, and at first I thought it was dumb just like you're saying. But lately the feeling's gotten even stronger, especially since that guy came around last month."

"You're reading too much into that, Mike. It was simply follow-up."

"Maybe. But still—"

He thought back now on that brief meeting in early May, only a week before his surprise party.

———

The doorbell had rung about nine-thirty that Saturday morning. They were still having breakfast in the alcove. Clarissa had put down the coffee tray and gone to answer the door. She returned after a moment, her eyes wary in her round cinnamon face.

"Gentleman to see you, Miz Frost."

"Who is it, Clarissa?"

"Don't know him, ma'am. But he said he's from the government—something about the—" she broke off, finished lamely, "you know."

Kate had risen and they'd followed her into the foyer.

The man stood waiting, briefcase under his arm. He was young and well-dressed in a three-piece tan suit. Every feature about him, from the short blonde hair down to the polished cordovans, could have been described as regular.

"Missus Frost? I'm sorry if I've disturbed you. I can come back if it's not a convenient time."

"No, not at all," Kate responded, extending her hand. "Mister—"

"Barnard. Jonathan Barnard."

"Mister Barnard," she finished. "This is my son Mike and my daughter Penny. What can we do for you?"

"Well, ma'am," he seemed the slightest bit uncomfortable as he said it, "I'm from the FBI. Kidnaping." He reached into his pocket, removed his wallet, and briefly flashed an identification. "We just wanted a follow-up on your husband."

Although visits such as this one had been commonplace during the first weeks following the accident, it had now been over six months since anyone had come to question them.

"Certainly, Mister Barnard," Kate said, ushering him into the living room. "But I don't know what we can tell you we haven't already."

He shrugged, seated himself on the wing-backed chair as she indicated. Kate sat opposite on the sofa, Penny next to her. Mike stood behind them, hands placed stiffly on the back of the couch at either side of his mother's shoulders.

"You're probably right," Barnard said, looking across at the family grouping. "But then..." His voice trailed off.

"I understand. What is it you would like to ask?"

"Well, suppose you just tell me again what happened those couple of days. Whatever details any of you remember, even the smallest."

He took a tape recorder from his briefcase, placed it on the coffee table and looked at her inquiringly. "You don't mind?" he asked.

"No," she replied, and he turned it on, testing the mike and placing it before her.

"Why don't you start, Missus Frost?"

Kate had done so, reviewing in her throaty voice those three days with as much detail as possible. Mike and Penny broke in occasionally to help fill in the picture.

As his mother spoke Mike's mind drifted back to that Monday when the call had come informing them of Charley's death. It had been late afternoon, and Bill Chambers had been waiting with them in the den.

Kate had taken the call at Charley's desk. She had not said a word beyond "Hello. Yes, this is Missus Frost," but stood silent, framed in the bay window for some moments with the phone to her ear before slowly replacing the receiver and turning to them dry-eyed.

"He's dead," she managed after a moment in which she'd examined their expectant faces one by one. "Charley's dead," she whispered, breaking down only when Mike rushed to her.

She collapsed in his arms, sobbing wildly. After a moment, she repeated, "Charley's dead," but it was a scream this time as she suddenly pounded her fists in frustration against Mike's back.

It had taken a few moments for them to extract from her what little information she had. By the time she was done, the phone had already rung again twice.

"The reporters will be here in a minute," Bill said as he hung up the second time. "Better get her upstairs, Penny." The girl had nodded but looked dazed as she went to her mother. Mike knew she was in shock. He expected the full impact of their father's death to hit her later but was grateful she could function now. It never occurred to him to question his own icy calm.

"I can handle this, Mike," Bill said as the women ascended the staircase.

Mike nodded, relieved.

"I think we'd better call the FBI before we do anything else."

The statement had confused Mike briefly before he connected the fact of his father's death with the kidnaping—a fact he seemed almost to have forgotten.

Bill had made the call and handled the reporters as well, but in less than a half hour the FBI men had been there, and the CAB men, and the state police, and he could never remember how many times they'd gone over the story then and in the weeks to come.

And after eight months they still had no clue to the kidnappers' identities. No trace of the money had been found, although it had been marked. They did not even know where Charley had been those two days. Canada, they suspected, but it was only a guess.

All they knew for sure was that the *Pretty Penny* had been destroyed at exactly three-forty P.M. by two massive charges of plastique. Mike had heard one FBI agent call it "overkill," referring to the amount of explosives used. They also knew, of course, Charley Frost was dead.

As he'd listened to his mother finishing her latest re-cap of the story, he thought of the overwhelming evidence supporting that conclusion and wondered why he alone had nagging doubts.

When the interview was over, Barnard had risen. Mike noticed that he pulled at the creases of his pants after he stood.

"Thank you for your time Missus Frost." He nodded to Mike and Penny as well, including them in the effort. "I know it must be painful, but…." he trailed off.

"We understand," Kate murmured.

Barnard's gaze was a study of understanding that somehow remained impersonal. "One more thing, if it's not too much trouble. I'd like to look at your husband's den."

"Why?" Mike had asked quickly—too quickly maybe, he thought to himself as Barnard's eyes swung to rest on him.

"Well, you never know," the man said easily. "Might be something. I'll only take a minute, if that's all right."

"Certainly," Kate replied. "This way."

Barnard had only stayed in the den momentarily as promised, but Mike felt he took in every object of the room with his sweeping gaze. He thought the man's eyes had settled briefly on the bookshelves but wasn't sure.

"Nothing's been changed," Kate said quietly.

Barnard nodded and idly picked up the picture of the *Pretty Penny* from the desk. He looked at it briefly, then replaced it.

"Well," he said. "Thank you."

After he'd gone, Mike had sat quietly.

"What's troubling you, Mike?" Kate had asked when he still didn't speak.

"I don't know, Ma. Something, but—"

"Going over the story again? That bothered me too."

He shook his head. "No, Ma. It wasn't that. It was that guy, Barnard."

"He was polite enough. And it's his job, remember."

"I know. But it was the way he looked at us. More like he was checking our reactions than listening to the details. I had the feeling he wasn't even listening to what we said. He was just was watching us and looking around the house for something."

"You're imagining things, Mike. What would he have been looking for?"

He looked up at his mother, then shrugged and said uncertainly, "I had the feeling maybe he was looking for Charley."

Kate shook her head slowly.

But he hadn't imagined it two days later when he called the FBI and could get no trace of an agent named Jonathan Barnard.

"Maybe we didn't get his name right," Kate offered by way of explanation.

"We got it right," Mike insisted.

"Well, maybe you called the wrong office. There are so many of those people running around."

"They'd know him. They'd be able to look him up."

"I don't know why you're making such a big thing of it. You must be mistaken. And anyway, what harm was there?"

And he hadn't imagined it two weeks later, when on a hunch, he examined all the phones in the house. He'd unscrewed the speakers as he'd seen done on television and had found the small black obscenity in the den receiver.

"Well, of course they'd have tapped our phones, Mike," Kate had said when he silently placed the round disc before her. "I'd expect them to. After all, we could have gotten a call from those men or someone else, maybe. And they were looking for any possible lead, remember."

"Mom, that was nearly eight months ago."

"They probably just forgot to remove that when they were done. I bet there was one in every other phone in the house, too."

Mike was exasperated at times with Kate's need for simple answers, pat conclusions. It seemed to him she could take anything and rationalize it into some comfortable niche. Especially now, when he most needed her support, and she relegated every suspicion to his imagination. He knew she believed he was suffering from a deep paranoia. But she was wrong.

Barnard—and that had been his name, Mike was sure of it—had been looking for signs of Charley's presence. Why he was certain of that, Mike didn't know. But he was. And the phone tap. They hadn't simply forgotten it. And whoever had kept it wasn't looking to find the kidnappers. Not after this long. His conclusions gave him hope. Because it looked as though somebody else thought his father might be alive, too.

Once the initial shock of the accident had worn off, Mike had gone into a deep depression. He had spent a great deal of time in his room staring at the ceiling or taking long, aimless walks. He had no appetite and he picked at his meals. His schoolwork had suffered and all attempts to draw him out socially had been futile.

61

Kate and Penny had suffered likewise, but they seemed to be getting over it. Although Kate's expression was often tinged with a soft sadness and quiet tears still sometimes came, she was getting better every day.

And Penny was completely back to normal, he thought now, looking back again through the window to the pool where he saw his sister arch from the board as three of her friends stood chatting at the low rail of the redwood deck.

Only he himself was going nowhere. But it was as much confusion as grief he felt, because for him, and for him alone, there was the other element, the knowledge he'd shared with no one: Charley's safe and the secrets it contained. The strong implication his father was something other than the straightforward man he had seemed. Mike felt a deep need to set that question to rest, to somehow understand and to know his father in whatever ways there were to know the man.

Only then could he be free to put the finishing touches on his own healing process and on his emerging self-image as well.

The contents of the safe, which he checked from time to time, remained untouched. Why that had meaning for him, he didn't know. He'd even been tempted, on occasion, to take some of the money and use it for some extravagance his mother would not have allowed. But something had held him back. He wondered if his mother really was aware of the safe's existence, as Charley had told him.

Upon reflection, he thought not.

But overriding all else was the simple fact he had a growing certainty that his father was still alive.

When the feeling had started, he'd discounted it as wishful thinking. But it had hung on and grown, a nagging pull that had solidified into decision with the events of the past few weeks. Barnard, the phone tap—Kate might see them as nothing, but to Mike they were some kind of proof.

Turning back from the balcony to face her now, he took a deep breath and plunged. "I'm leaving, Ma," he repeated, voice firmer than he felt.

"Mike," she started, but he cut her off.

"I'm going. I mean it. Tomorrow."

The expression on her face was terrible for him, and he softened despite his resolve. "I've got to, Ma. I just know he's out there somewhere. I don't know how, but I know it."

Kate remained silent but her disapproval radiated.

"You can't stop me, Ma," he went on gently, but his voice remained firm. "I'm eighteen. I've graduated high school. And I've got money of my own now. Besides, I'll be back way before college starts. That's over two months away. And Rick and Ben will get along in Europe fine without me."

She held his gaze as long as she could and said nothing as he turned and left the room. He took the wide curving stairway quickly up to his room. If I don't do this now, I never will, he told himself once more.

Placing his suitcase on the bed, he opened the closet and considered what to pack. He was going to do a lot of driving, and it would already be hot where he was headed. He tossed jeans, shorts, and T-shirts into the suitcase. He contemplated another moment and grabbed his barely worn sports jacket, a nice pair of slacks, and a few dress shirts.

He had almost finished packing when he sensed his mother behind him.

"Where will you start?" he heard her ask after a moment.

He turned and met her eyes, surprised at her capitulation and greatly relieved by the inference of support, no matter how slight.

"I thought maybe at the beginning," he said. "At the orphanage."

CHAPTER 9

Charley watched as Owen threw the line. The splash of the lure as it hit the still water suddenly reminded him of St. Mary's. The creek.

They'd come a long way from that creek to this cold, secluded lake in West Virginia, he thought. They had been two lonely orphans who'd once only been hungry to steal what precious moments of privacy they could. Who would have ever thought them capable of cold-blooded murder? No one, least of all themselves.

But they'd done it, and Charley wondered again if there hadn't been another way. He and Owen had been over it so many times, and the conclusion had always been inescapable. Masters had to be eliminated.

The reasons were sound, even noble, he mused wryly, if such a word could be used to describe the act of murder. But that hadn't made it easy. In the end, though, there hadn't really been a choice. Charley was convinced Owen had agonized over the decision as much as he himself had. Although more and more, especially of late, he seemed almost to detect a single-minded intensity beneath his friend's controlled surface. That was of great concern to Charley.

But no, he told himself again. In the end, Owen would honor their plan. It was just that Owen was more pragmatic. And, he conceded, that was a quality that had often served them well.

Like the time Owen had deliberately broken Charley's nose, as Charley had told him to do.

But would *he* have been able to do the same, had the situation been reversed?

He would, he thought, but he was glad the situation hadn't been reversed, for the action was abhorrent to him. But yes, he'd have done it. He'd have had no choice.

How many times had they both, individually and collectively, capitulated to that premise? No choice. Even murder, now. Their gains were high, but their sacrifices seemed higher still.

And they had no choice.

Owen, in his navy windbreaker, played his line as they sat on a flat ledge on the shore of the quiet lake. Charley looked on with faraway eyes. St. Mary's, he thought again with rare nostalgia.

Take Route 230 south about ten miles out of Asheville, North Carolina, and suddenly the green woods begin to thin until all that's left are some scrub pines that look skinny and naked against the brown rocky hills. A little further down the scraggly, ugly bushes start. A mile or so on the right is a dirt road where there's a small sign that reads "St. Mary's Orphanage."

Follow that up about a half a mile, watch the dirt kicking up all around, especially in summer, and you dead end in front of a large dirty-white building with a big porch where there's always a kid or two around. If you look to your left across the scarred, sparse lawn, you can see the rusty sliding board and the three swings, the middle one hanging from one chain. The sandbox is broken like it always was.

Once you're in the house, it's dark and quiet. And cold most nights, when you can hear the wind pushing through the cracks of the grimy windows.

That's how Charley always remembered it whenever he thought about it, which wasn't often anymore.

But as Owen pulled in his line and tossed it again, Charley let his mind drift back.

* * *

The creek didn't have a name, or if it did they never knew it. It was only "the creek," but the words were magic when one of them whispered to the others, "Let's sneak off to the creek." Stifling giggles, they'd make their way furtively to the pines in a cautious Indian file, running with abandon as they came to the safety of the trees, coming up breathless finally when they reached the muddy bank at the bottom of the hill.

They knew they'd be punished later but that never mattered. Only the few golden hours of freedom counted.

There had been three of them then.

Charley Frost.

Owen Reid.

And Richie Peters.

They had been inseparable from the start and had remained so despite repeated attempts by Mr. Summers to break up their "gang." Mr. Summers ran the orphanage and was chronically irritated by their noisy laughter and backyard wrestling, not to mention their occasional brief disappearances. They'd all come under the belt more than once in the man's frantic attempt to find out where they'd gone off to, but none of them had ever told.

Mr. Summers would remove his wire-framed glasses, pinch the bridge of his thin nose, and call them "undisciplined." Maybe they were, but they stuck together and somehow got through the years maintaining a spirit they found sadly lacking in their companions.

If that's what "undisciplined" meant, they preferred it greatly to the quiet voices and downcast eyes of the other kids around them.

All three were gangly even in the earlier years, although Owen's build had been less arms and legs than the others. They were pretty evenly matched athletically, but he seemed to have the slight advantage.

If they had a leader, it would have been Charley. There was something in his spirit that brought them up even on the worst of days. He pushed them to a sense of adventure none of them could have achieved alone.

Richie was more quiet, thoughtful even. But he turned out to be the one with the power. That had been slow in developing, and none of them recognized it as it grew. It had just crept up on them like the blossoms in an apple tree: you knew the buds were there but you never really noticed them, and suddenly they sprung full-blown and you wondered how you missed that along the way.

The first time they had witnessed Richie's power had been in a basketball game, but they never realized it until a long time later.

The three thirteen-year-olds were all first stringers on the Mills River junior varsity: Charley and Owen were the forwards and Richie, the tallest, played center. They were psyched for the game because it was the first of the season.

And, more important, it represented their own private victory, their first at St. Mary's.

For months they'd been practicing in the school gym whenever they had spare time, rushing to phys ed for the extra few minutes before class and taking advantage of the half hour when they generally had to wait for the orphanage bus at the end of the day.

Mr. Anderson had watched them for a few days, then had started working with them. The broad-shouldered young gym teacher was patient, and with his private coaching the boys had rapidly improved.

"You guys are getting pretty good," he'd said one day as they were leaving for the bus. "How about coming out for the team next week? You can make JV easy—probably varsity next year if you keep up."

They'd grinned at each other, run to the bus, and whispered excitedly during the twenty-minute ride. But the budding dream was shattered in their meeting with Mr. Summers, which had taken place just before dinner,

Mr. Summers, or "Old Man Winter" as they called him behind his back, had been adamant about not letting them even try out in the first place.

"No boy from Saint Mary's has ever done such a thing. It would completely disrupt our schedules."

He took off his glasses, placed them on the desk and blinked his small eyes rapidly as he looked up at the three boys who stood before him.

"Please, Mister Summers. Please let us try out." Owen was their spokesman, because of the three, Old Man Winter seemed to dislike the shy boy the least. "I really think we can do it, sir," Owen finished lamely.

Summers didn't respond for a moment, but they suspected he wasn't thinking it over. It was just his way of tantalizing them, and the man affirmed their hunch when he finally shook his head with an emphatic "no."

They hadn't really thought it would work, anyway, but they'd had to give it a try. As they closed the superintendent's door and shuffled to the dining hall to start their dinner chores, Owen turned suddenly away and walked to the corridor wall. He stood there with his arms folded across his chest.

"I really wanted to try out," he said softly, looking at the other two boys.

Charley's face suddenly took on a grim determination. "We're going to do it, Owen. We-are-going-to-do-it!" he said, slamming his fist against his palm with an intensity that gave Owen a hope.

Mr. Anderson had been sympathetic when they talked to him the next day. Sympathetic but hardly encouraging.

"I'm really disappointed, fellows. I know Saint Mary's has never had any kids in extra-curricular activities because of the practice time involved, with the bus and all. But most of them never wanted to go out for anything, anyway.

"But with you three, I thought maybe—heck," he said, looking at their faces. "I'm really sorry I made the suggestion."

"You could help us, Mister Anderson," Charley spoke up.

"Well, sure," the teacher said uncertainly, brushing back his thinning black hair. "I'll do anything I can. Would it help if I wrote a letter?"

Charley shook his head.

"What then?"

"You've got to go see him. Mister Summers."

"Go see him?" the gym teacher repeated dubiously. "And tell him what?"

"Don't you see, Mister Anderson?" It was Richie, now. The rangy boy who was just shy of being gawky stepped before the teacher's desk. His dark eyes burned with intensity. "You said it yourself. The other kids from Saint Mary's never tried to do anything before. Doesn't that tell you something?"

Richie paused before continuing with intense emotion in his voice. "Think about all those kids, Mister Anderson. Kids with no hopes, no dreams—no spirit! Kids going nowhere.

"But maybe if we do something, break out a little, then they'll start thinking maybe it's not so hopeless after all." There was no doubting Richie's plea was really for all of the orphans, not just the three who stood anxiously before their teacher.

Anderson was deeply touched. He stood suddenly, deeply angry, and said, "Son of a bitch!" His eyes were moist, and it was only through his greatest effort his voice hadn't broken. Unable to speak further he waved the boys from his office.

They never knew what he said to Summers, but as the bus pulled up to the orphanage that afternoon, they'd seen the teacher's car pulling away. He had turned his face toward them and they knew he'd seen them, but he didn't nod or wave and his face had appeared grim.

"Shit," Owen muttered uncharacteristically, thinking that was it.

But they'd been summoned to Old Man Winter's office a short time later. Entering with a fear of retaliation tinged with just the barest hope, they lined up before the man's desk. He kept his glasses on and stared up at them in silence. They could tell nothing from his face.

Finally he cleared his throat, gave a thin rendition of a smile. "Well," he said heartily, "I've just had a visit from your physical education teacher. Seems you all have made quite an impression on him."

He paused as if unsure of what to say. "He told me you boys were good in basketball, 'real good' I believe he said. Thinks with you playing he feels Mills River has a good chance to develop a winning team, maybe even state champs. They've never had one, and he's right, it would be good for the area.

"Anyway," he went on, authority now clear in his voice, "now that I understand the facts I'm happy to encourage you to try out for the team. Mister Anderson said he'd either arrange a ride back after practice with some parent or he'd bring you himself."

Summers stood, extended his hand. "Good luck," he said, shaking a moist palm with each in turn.

"I'll bet Anderson threatened to kick the shit out of him," Charley said as they ran excitedly across the yard. They all agreed—hoped— that's how it went.

When they stopped to catch their breath, Owen looked reflectively at Richie. "You'll be a great salesman someday," he said seriously.

Richie blushed even deeper below the flush of his cheeks before he turned away.

All three boys made the team and by late fall were involved in daily practices that sometimes kept them away from the orphanage almost into the dinner hour. Initially they'd been fearful this additional infraction of their schedule might jeopardize their opportunity, since they had not been excused from their normal duties at St. Mary's. The first time they'd been late, they'd half-expected a "what-else-can-I-do" shrug from Mr. Summers, indicating he had no choice but to revoke his permission. They didn't know how they'd handle that if it happened, and Charley had worked himself up to high frustration as he imagined that scene.

"It won't happen! It can't!" he muttered over and over again as Mr. Anderson's car drove through the early darkness, headlights picking up the pines as he negotiated the narrow dirt road.

The boys rushed into the house as quickly as they could, anxious to make amends by being as helpful as possible, but it wasn't necessary. All their work had been done.

As they seated themselves at the table, Mrs. Kurtz, the matronly lady who supervised the large unadorned dining room, had merely said, "Good evening, boys." The rest of the kids had held them with large eyes.

Owen nodded, solemn-faced, and Richie's eyes were moist. Only Charley could manage a hoarse "Thanks."

They were thankful it didn't happen often, but whenever they were inordinately late it seemed their work was always done.

The support from the kids and staff continued to grow, and they could sense a change in the whole place that made them feel good.

"We really are making a difference, guys," Richie shook his head in wonder. His concern for the other kids had transmitted itself to Owen and Charley as well, and all three began to see their effort as more than just individual achievement.

"We're going to do it for Saint Mary's," Charley thought sometimes, although he never would have said it.

They worked hard, improved, and as the season approached it was evident all three would be starters as Coach Anderson had predicted.

"Congratulations," Mr. Summers offered when he heard the news. He even seemed to mean it but they weren't really sure.

Other things were happening, too.

Charley had a girl, or sort of.

She was one of the cheerleaders, small, blonde, and bubbly, and after practice sometimes they'd stand by the bench and talk until he had to run and catch his ride. Her name was Bobbie, and it was obvious she watched Charley during the entire practice.

The three of them had even been invited to a party one Friday night by one of the other players. They had declined, of course, feared testing yet another rule, but still—

But most important of all was the team, and on the afternoon of their opening game they were high, almost giddy with anticipation. The team was good and they knew it. They could be winners.

"Let's go and get 'em!" they cheered in unison as they left the locker room, certain they'd beat Jeff Davis, a school from nearby that consistently humiliated the Mills River teams. There was a long-term debt to settle, and they intended to do it.

Charley particularly relished the fact the victory would be at home.

But as they sat in the locker room at half-time, all their expectation had drained. They were down 32–17, and felt they were lucky to be that close.

Even Mr. Anderson's pep talk seemed to lack a ring of conviction, and although the players slapped each other's backs and said, "We'll get 'em!", they knew they were kidding themselves.

Only Richie seemed removed from it. Sitting away from the group with his back against the locker, long legs sprawled on the concrete floor, he seemed to pay no attention to the coach's words. He merely stared ahead totally relaxed.

Charley was annoyed at his friend's seeming indifference. He challenged him as they were leaving the locker room. "Come on, Richie. For Christ's sake! We still got a chance."

The other players stopped and gave them a little room.

Richie turned to Charley. His eyes were clear as he said, "I'm sorry. I wasn't listening. What did you say?"

Charley was angry now. "What's with you, man? You act like you don't care. Sure, we're losing, but we got a chance. We can't throw in the towel. We're not quitters."

Richie seemed confused, looked at all the surrounding faces. He shook his head finally, and said, "Charley—what the hell!" He stood and grinned at all of them. "Hey," he shouted, suddenly exuberant. "Hey, what a game, huh!? That shot, Wally—"

71

Charley's voice cut him cold as he roughly grabbed the other's shoulder. "Richie," he said, obviously controlling his patience as if dealing with a child, "Richie—we're down by fifteen. Remember? And Wally only has one lousy lay-up. Now for Christ's sake," he added after a lingering look at his friend he expanded to include the rest of the team, "let's go out and play some basketball."

He turned and walked toward the door. The others followed quietly. Only Owen and Richie were left.

"Hey, Richie," Owen said quietly. "You okay?"

He was perturbed by the perplexed look on his friend's face, and only less so when something vague shifted in Richie's eyes and he managed a weak, "Oh—sure."

The second half started badly, and they were quickly down 36–17. The gymnasium was crowded, primarily with Mills High students who sat on the tiers of benches beneath the steel rafters of the high-ceilinged room. Some boos came from the crowd, along with a lot of foot stamping and clapping. But gradually it started to change and by the end of the third quarter they had closed the gap in the score. It was now 42–31.

They were still behind, but they felt as they touched hands before the fourth quarter tip-off that maybe, just maybe, they were going to pull it out.

Taking their time and playing with discipline, the team showed amazing poise and maturity. Slowly they continued to cut into the Jeff Davis lead, and suddenly, unbelievably, they were ahead 49–48. With less than thirty seconds left, victory was almost theirs.

Jeff Davis brought the ball up but Mills River's defense was tight, and the other team tried in vain to get a clear shot off. With ten seconds left, their right forward took a desperation shot that hit the rim and bounced off, but the ball was rebounded by the Jeff Davis center who hooked the ball high over Richie's outstretched arms. The "swish" could be heard clear above the shouting, and the Mills River players stood still.

Coach Anderson called a quick timeout, and as they huddled around the bench Charley glanced at the time clock. Four seconds to play. He looked over at the scoreboard although he didn't have to: Jeff Davis was ahead by one point.

Richie had shown little emotion during their dramatic comeback. After the scene in the locker room, Charley had expected his friend to play like a man possessed, leading them to victory. But it hadn't gone that way, Richie only doing a workmanlike job as they'd crept back into the game.

That had seemed to work out okay, until the last seconds. Now the passive look on his friend's face annoyed Charley. It's almost like he doesn't give a damn, thought Charley.

They went back on to the court. With only four seconds left, they'd be lucky to get one shot off, and that would have to be from half-court. Charley expected the ball to come to either himself or Owen, which was the play they'd called, was prepared to turn and shoot if it was him, but instead Richie passed in to Wally Curtis, the small guard, who dribbled once, leaped high in the air, and threw a long one-hander whose "swish" coincided with the buzzer.

The whole team rushed around Wally and raised him on their shoulders, almost breaking his ribs in their enthusiasm. Except Richie, Charley noted. He was still standing on the sideline from where he'd thrown the ball in bounds. His black hair was disheveled and sweat soaked, and he had a faraway but distinctly frightened look on his face.

CHAPTER 10

Mike was tired. The drive down from Boston had taken two full days, and as he passed Asheville he thought of getting off the interstate, checking into a motel, and having a swim before dinner. It was four o'clock already, and by the time he reached St. Mary's the superintendent might be gone. He hesitated for a moment, said the hell with it, picked up 280, and continued south.

He saw the sign that read, "Mills River 12 Miles," knew his turnoff came about five miles short of that and checked his mileage indicator so he'd know when to anticipate it. 2072. That's where it would be. He winced, thinking of how much mileage he'd already put on the car, over half of it in just the last two days.

He thought back to the night of his birthday party, a month earlier, when the dancing had begun to die down and it became apparent people would shortly begin to leave.

Phil Downs had come up to him, taking him aside.

"Come on outside with me for a minute," Phil had said conspiratorially, level blue eyes revealing nothing.

Mike looked back at Phil and seemed to hesitate but his best friend pressed it. "Come on, Mike. Just something I want to talk to you about."

They walked together onto the flagstone area that led off the lower driveway, stopped and faced each other under the basketball hoop Charley had erected so many years before.

"Mike," Phil began seriously. Mike drew back a bit, anticipating yet another lecture probably inspired by his mother about his out-of-touch attitude, but the outside flood lights had suddenly gone on and everyone was yelling behind him again, "Surprise! Surprise!" And there in the driveway, alone in the lights, stood a silver Porsche.

He was reminded instantly of the Porsche he'd seen in a showroom window and secretly coveted that past September, just before everything had happened, thought how incredible it was the exact car he'd imagined himself owning was now his. He'd never discussed that wish with anyone. Putting that thought away, he turned to look at the crowd of well-wishers before running to the car.

He traced his hand over the hood, touched the soft black leather of the bucket seats. His mother came to stand quietly at his side. He hugged her tight and whispered, "I love you, Ma."

"Happy birthday, Mike."

Over his mother's shoulder he'd seen Shelly watching, radiant in her low-cut green dress, freckled face expectant. He grinned at her broadly.

"How about a ride?" he asked with a grin and she came running.

"See you later," he called as he spun the Porsche down the driveway.

Shelly leaned across the console, put her arms through his, and snuggled against him. The stars were bright and the wind rushing through the open car whipped her blonde hair against his cheek.

"Happy birthday," she said into his ear. "It was a nice birthday, wasn't it?"

Things between them had been almost normal that night, and he traced her face gently with his finger later as she buttoned up her blouse. But the old feelings just weren't there.

The day before he headed south, he told her he was leaving.

"Where, Mike?"

"I don't know. Just away for awhile."

"When will you be back?"

He shrugged. "Soon, maybe. Certainly before college. I just don't know, Shelly."

He felt a finality to their relationship that saddened him. But he recognized his feeling of loss wasn't just about Shelly.

Checking the mileage indicator now, he began to look for the inter-section and saw the blacktop road with the sign "St. Mary's" coming up on his right.

As he drove through the thin pines, he remembered the clouds of dust his father had told him about. He regretted the road was paved now. Things must have been simpler then, he thought, remembering "the creek" of Charley's childhood. He wondered if perhaps he could find it later and decided to try after he talked with Mr. Winston.

The orphanage looked bright as he parked the car. He could see it had been freshly painted. To his left he saw a bunch of younger children on the swings and see-saws. Mike watched for a moment as an older child helped a tentative three-year-old onto the top of the sliding board while another kid stood waiting at the bottom, motioning encourage-ment.

Further over he saw a basketball court. The excited shouts of the game in progress came across the well kept lawn.

He couldn't see the tennis courts or the pool from where he stood. But he knew they were there.

"Mister Frost," Winston's voice had been warm when Mike had phoned. "Of course I'd be delighted to see you. Visitors are always welcome at Saint Mary's, but I can think of no one we would rather host than you."

Mike was ushered now into the superintendent's well-appointed of-fice, and the slightly paunchy man rose and walked quickly around a massive antique desk . With his round, cherubic face and ring of wispy gray hair he could have passed for a parish priest in blue seersucker. "Mister Frost, it's a pleasure to meet you," he said taking Mike's hand in both his own. He seemed to be searching Mike's face for something.

"Is something wrong, Mister Winston?" Mike asked.

"Nothing. Just looking for your father, I guess." He kept staring at Mike. "It's been many years," Winston added almost hastily.

Mike wished now he had stopped off and changed into a sportcoat and slacks. He wondered if the khakis and blue denim shirt he wore, though neat and pressed, were perhaps a little casual for this visit.

Winston motioned Mike to one of the tufted corduroy armchairs and sat opposite him on the matching couch.

"Charley Frost's son," he said after a moment, still looking deeply at Mike's face. "I'm sorry about your father, Mister Frost."

"Thank you, sir. And please call me Mike."

"Mike, then. Your father was a great man. A kind man and a good friend. We all miss him."

Winston rose and walked to the fireplace. "Did you know your father had this built?" he asked. "It was right after the fire, a long time ago. There was a fireplace in the living room, but Charley insisted on another in here. I'll never forget what he said to me over the phone: 'I spent a lot of time being frightened in that room,' he said. 'I always thought of it as being so cold. I'd like to picture a warm man there and a cozy fire in the winter so kids won't be scared like I was.'"

The superintendent paused, his voice almost faltering as he said the last words. Blinking his watery blue eyes rapidly, he looked down at Mike.

"That's the kind of man he was," he went on after a moment. "He was only twenty-three then, perhaps twenty-four. I know he hadn't been out of college long. And he wired me twelve hundred dollars to have it built. You couldn't do it today for ten times that, of course," Winston ran his hand lovingly over the heavy stones, "but twelve hundred dollars was a lot of money then—especially for a young man just starting out.

"I remember being almost jealous he could do it. Here I was thirty-two years of age, already having worked for ten years, and twelve hundred dollars was about what I had in savings. If that." Winston walked to the window and opened it. The sounds of shouting children filled the room. Leaning out, he was quiet for a moment, then turned back to Mike.

"Look at that," he motioned, and Mike came to the window and stared out at the crowded, noisy pool. Beyond it, he saw the tennis courts where three heated games were in progress.

"All this," the man said indicating what Mike could see and more. "He certainly changed a lot of lives."

Mike was deeply touched by the superintendent's words. The man he'd described, the thoughtful, giving man—that was the father he had known. He was surprised at the relief the thought gave him. Had he really come to doubt even that part of his father, he wondered?

77

"How well did you know my father?" he asked after a moment. "When he was a kid, I mean."

"Not well at all, really. I only came during his last year, not much more than a kid myself. I had my degree in sociology, and this was going to be my first stop." The twinkle in Winston's eyes telegraphed the punch line. "That was twenty-six years ago."

Mike regarded the kindly man.

"This must be pretty rewarding," Mike offered, wondering if he himself could make that kind of commitment, knowing he couldn't—at least, not to such an unglamourous post as he perceived the superintendent's to be.

"It is rewarding, Mike. Very." Winston faced him. "Thanks to your father. If not for him this would only be another rundown orphanage with a bunch of sad kids going nowhere."

Winston closed the window and returned to the arm chair. "You know, Mike, they started to change things even while they were still here. As kids, I mean, even before your father began to support us financially."

"They?" Mike asked.

"It's funny," Winston said, "I still put them together in my mind even after all these years. Your father and Richie Peters of course— they were the leaders here. And their friend, Owen Reid. It's funny to think now he was the more quiet one, the shy one—seeing where he is today."

"Owen Reid?" Mike broke in.

Winston nodded. "Your father must have told you. They were close as could be."

Mike tried not to appear puzzled. His parents had often discussed Senator Reid. The were as convinced as most other Americans the charismatic Coloradan would win the Republican nomination that summer. Mike planned to exercise his own initial voting privilege by casting his ballot for Reid in November. Charley had mentioned Reid had been at St. Mary's with him, but he had dropped the information casually, implying they'd barely known each other. Now Mike found it odd in light of what Winston was saying.

"It was more, though," the man continued. "The three of them seemed so alike. They even looked alike—all tall, with those deep dark eyes. Almost like brothers. Not really, of course, but that's the way you thought of them because of how close they were. Funny, I always thought they'd end up doing something together. That's what they always talked about. But of course, Richie was gone so early, and then your father wound up in Boston and the senator out West."

"Do you have any pictures of them, Mister Winston?" Mike asked on impulse. "My dad told me so much about those days, but he didn't have any pictures."

Winston shook his head. "We used to have some, especially of the championship basketball team. But there was the fire, and they were destroyed along with all the other records."

"When was the last time you saw my father?" Mike asked after a brief silence.

"I never did see him again. Not after he left here, and he was about your age then. We spoke often, of course, and I asked him time after time to come down and see what he'd helped create. He always planned to, but he never did. He was a busy man, but—I know he'd have been very proud," the superintendent finished. "Very proud."

"He was never back?"

"Never," Winston shook his head firmly. "Neither was Owen Reid. I remember the first time I saw him on television, maybe seven or eight years ago. It had been so long, I hardly recognized him," the man said, raising his eyes to Mike's and shaking his head slowly. "A lot of years. They go so fast, Mike. That's hard to understand at your age. But they do."

At that moment the grandfather's clock struck six, and Mike rose. "I'm sorry. I didn't know it was so late," he said, extending his hand to Winston. "Thank you for your time."

"Please," the man said, rising himself. "Stay for dinner. There's plenty. And stay the night, too. We have a guest room—the Charles Frost Room—," he added with a smile, "that's as comfortable as any you'd find in Asheville. I'm sure your father would have liked that."

Mike hesitated for an instant. Why not stay the night? he said to himself. After all, his father had spent years here, in far less comfortable accommodations than Mike would be given. "Sure," he said with an enthusiasm he hoped carried. "I'd like that. Thank you."

"You're more than welcome. Besides, you should get over to see Frank Anderson while you're here."

"Frank Anderson? My dad's old basketball coach?"

"Not so old," Mr. Winston said with a slight smile. "Perhaps five years my senior. He's head of the physical ed department at Mills River High—has been for ten years now. I'm sure he'd like to meet you."

* * *

Driving to Mills River the next morning, Mike suddenly remembered he had never tried to find the creek.

Oh well, he thought. The bright faces and excited conversation of the kids had given him more of his father than he'd hoped to find. Charley's spirit was alive and well there, and the ghosts at the creek could rest for now.

He was feeling very good about his father that morning, and his eyes misted briefly as he determined to emulate Charley's example. Maybe I can make a difference too, he thought. He already had his own money. Not much, but there was more to come. Lots of it. Mike didn't know how much, really, but he knew the initial trust, which he received when he'd turned eighteen, was only the beginning of the funds that would come into his hands as the years went by.

And, of course, there was the money in the safe. That and the fake passports. The thought dampened his reverie. Its existence, which represented some unknown dimension of his father that impinged the man's otherwise flawless image, nagged him continually. Mike was still frustrated at never having been able to confront Charley with his knowledge.

He wondered now how he'd handle that if and when he ever found his father.

He'd talk to him outright about it, like a man, he decided, feeling more comfortable again as he turned off Main Street onto Willow Glen Road. Going down three blocks he saw 1707 on the mail box and pulled to the curb.

The man who was sitting on the porch reading the paper rose and came down the steps.

"Mike Frost?" he asked, extending his hand.

"Mister Anderson?" Mike responded as he took the firm grasp.

"Good to meet you," the man said warmly, putting his arm about Mike's shoulder and leading him toward the steps. He was almost as tall as Mike, and the arm on Mike's back felt very strong.

"Sit down," the coach said, indicating a comfortable looking rocker. "Coffee?"

"No thanks."

"Iced tea, then? Or lemonade? It's gonna be a hot one today."

"Lemonade sounds good. Thanks."

Mike noted the sweat stains on the denim shirt that seemed tight across the broad back as the man entered the house. There were beads of perspiration on the bald head as Anderson returned a moment later, letting the screen door slam behind him.

"Never did like hot weather," he said, placing a glass on the table in front of Mike and reaching into his pocket for a handkerchief with which he wiped his brow. "That's a silly thing to say, I guess, for a man who's lived his whole life in the South. But winters get awful cold up here, which northerners don't realize."

He seated himself, hunched forward with hands on knees, looked long at Mike. "Charley Frost's kid," he said finally.

"Yes, sir," Mike forced, politely. Was he always to be referred to in that context?

"Damn," the man said softly, shaking his head as if the motion were involuntary, almost a shudder. "I'm sorry about your father. Still can't believe it." Although the man looked directly at him, the pale blue eyes seemed to go through Mike, looking beyond him to some other place.

"Charley Frost's kid," he repeated. "I never would have thought it. Your old man was some hell-raiser." His eyes brightened and he seemed younger in the remembrance. "More spirit than any kid I ever coached. I always worried a little it might get him into trouble but look how it turned out. Just shows you."

"What was he like as a kid?"

"A little feisty, like I said. But a great kid. A tough kid. I was sure proud of him. Lead us to our only state championship, Charley did. He pushed that whole thing at St. Mary's, too, gettin' the kids to reach out finally. Him and Richie Peters, of course."

"He was my dad's best friend, wasn't he?"

"Well, yes—him and Owen Reid. The senator, you know. The three of them were so tight you almost thought of them as one person. At least, I did. I even got 'em confused sometimes. Coached 'em all the way through high school, but once in a while I'd turn on the bench and say, 'Get in there, Richie,' but it was Charley or Owen I was calling for, or vice-versa.

"Not that they were all *that* alike, you understand. They just seemed so. They had spirit all right, those three kids, but your dad was the hell-raiser, like I said. A real competitor, Charley was, and could he get fired up! I'm sure you saw that often enough yourself, though," Anderson chuckled. Mike nodded.

"He had a temper, your dad did. Really got on the other players when he didn't think they were putting out like they should. Especially Richie, when he got funny—spacey, I guess you kids would call it to-day. I guess you know about that."

It hung like a question and Mike shook his head. A bee buzzed lazily at some nearby bush, and he registered the faint bark of a dog as he ceased the gentle motion of his rocker.

"Your dad never talked about it, huh?" Anderson went on. "Only a couple of us knew about Richie, and we never really understood it."

"I don't know what you're talking about."

The man hesitated, but continued reluctantly. "Well, maybe it wasn't so, but some of us thought Richie had some kind of—," he paused, seeming to look for the right word. "Well, power."

Anderson looked at Mike as if waiting for the boy to offer something.

"You dad never talked to you about it, huh?" he asked when Mike didn't respond. Mike shook his head. "About the basketball games or the time your dad got hurt? Not even the raffle? Or the thing with those people from Duke?"

"He never said a word, Mister Anderson. I just knew Richie Peters had been my father's friend here, they played basketball together, and he died in that accident when the two of them left here to go out West."

"The two of them?" Anderson repeated. "All three of them went. Owen Reid was there, too."

"My father never said." From behind him he heard the sound of a car passing on the quiet street.

Anderson mused. "That's funny. They all went off together, just after graduation. Never even stopped by to say 'so long.' Just took off. Kind of pissed me off, too," he grimaced an easy apology for his vulgarity, "especially after all we'd done together. But...."

The man was obviously still upset at the slight. Mike was uncomfortable with this knowledge of his father's behavior toward the man who had been so close to him, but he could think of nothing to say. He was silent for a moment. Then he asked, "What about when my dad got hurt, Mister Anderson? You were talking about that."

"Well, it didn't seem like much at the time, but I remembered it later. We were playing Southern Cross. A grudge game. They'd beaten us bad year after year, you see, but we really had a team now. We were psyched to finally take 'em."

Anderson's broad face lit as he recounted the story. "We did, too," he added with pride, "by fourteen points. But anyway, during halftime I saw Richie kinda slumped in the corner, and I went over and said, 'Hey, Richie—whatcha down about? We're looking good.'

"He looked back at me as if he didn't know who I was, and then he kind of shook his head, like he was clearing it, and said, 'I'm not worried about the game, Coach. It's something—a feeling I have. I dunno,' he said, like he was real confused. I asked if I could help, but he just shook his head again.

"Anyway," Anderson went on, "after the game, some kids from Southern Cross were waiting for our players when they left, and there was a fight. That's when your dad got his nose broken. Got hit over the head, too, with a bottle. Took eighteen stitches—I'm sure you've seen the scar."

Anderson paused but Mike said nothing. "When I got there," the man continued, hunching forward, muscular forearms resting on his thighs, "Richie was holding your dad in his arms, and he kept repeating, 'I knew it. I knew it.' Then he said something real odd. He said, 'I've got to learn to change it.' All the time he was just talking to himself. Didn't even seem to notice I was there."

Anderson's eyes narrowed a bit as they held Mike's. "Like I said, I didn't think a lot about what Richie said then, what with your dad hurt bad and all. But when the raffle thing came up, I started thinking. You see, they decided one year to have a raffle at the high school to raise money for a new gym, and they were selling tickets as hard as they could. The prize was a '63 Mercury convertible, and I remember your dad and Richie and Owen could only buy one ticket between them because they cost three bucks each.

"Well, Richie really made a pain of himself. He insisted on looking at all the tickets, went through them until he picked the one he wanted. Wouldn't take anything else, and some people got mad at the trouble he put them to, although that wasn't usually his way.

"Anyway, the sum of it was, they won the car."

Anderson stopped for a moment, then said quietly, "Most folks thought he was just lucky, but I knew it was something else."

"You mean he had a sixth sense or something?" Mike asked when the man went silent, and for some reason he felt an odd chill as he said the words.

"Yes, he did. At least, I believe he did. I think it was something growing in him, getting stronger all the time, and I think he was just beginning to understand it. Like knowing how the basketball games would come out. I think he believed those were just hunches, but the raffle ticket was different.

"That's why I called the people at Duke. They've got this parapsychology department there, you know, where they work with ESP and that sort of thing. Give people tests and all.

"Anyway, I knew there was something strong like that in Richie, something real different from other people, and I called to arrange for him to go down to Durham for the tests. He didn't want to go but changed his mind all of a sudden."

"What happened there?" Mike could barely contain his curiosity.

"Funny thing. He flunked the tests cold. The fellow called me after and said it was one of the worst scores they ever had—way below the average of probabilities. They thought that might mean something, too, but couldn't figure anything. When they finally did get it worked out, the fellow from Duke came up here the same day to see Richie.

"But it was too late, then. We'd already heard he was dead."

"What was it they found out?"

"I never did know. But the fellow was all excited. Couldn't believe Richie was gone. I never saw a man so disappointed."

Anderson sat quiet now, lost in the memory.

After a moment, Mike stood, uncomfortable for some reason. He put his hand on the porch railing. "Thanks for talking to me, Mister Anderson. You helped a lot."

Anderson looked up at him. "You look like a basketball player yourself. Are you?"

Mike nodded. "Forward," he said.

Anderson shook his head as if in wonder. "It's amazing how big you kids get today. Forward. That's what your dad played. But in his day, you'd have been tall enough for center."

"Do you have any pictures of my dad from those days?" Mike asked almost as an afterthought.

"Used to. Plenty of 'em, pictures of the state championship team all over my office."

"Where are they now?"

Anderson shook his head. "All gone," he said. "Vandals broke in fifteen, maybe twenty years ago. Stole all kinds of things, but I regretted those pictures most."

He rose and took Mike's hand. "Good of you to stop by. Where you off to now?"

"I don't know."

"Well, stop in again if you're ever out this way."

Anderson watched the Porsche move off down the street and waited for a long time before entering the house. Walking to the living room, he picked up the phone and dialed.

"He just left," he said.

"Where to?"

"I don't know, but I think maybe Durham."

"How much did you tell him about that?"

"Just enough to get him there, maybe."

"How do you read it? Does he know anything?"

"I don't think so. I'm pretty sure he's just got a hunch his dad might still be alive. Or hopes so, anyway, like you said."

"You tape it?"

"Yes," Anderson said, involuntarily touching his pocket. "Like I promised. But that's it," he added, not attempting to disguise the distaste in his voice.

Anderson hung up the phone and walked into the den. Opening a drawer in the desk, he removed a faded news photo captioned, "Mills River High State Champs. 1963." He looked at it reflectively, wondered again that he'd allowed the man Barnard to get him involved in this. He'd loved Charley Frost.

But America was his country and Barnard's card established him as government.

* * *

Mike took out a road map and checked it quickly. About three hundred miles, he estimated. He got back on 280, then headed north to pick up the interstate highway. With luck, he'd be in Durham by evening.

CHAPTER 11

Charley walked from the shell-strewn beach and climbed a small way up the rocky precipice that rose abruptly beyond. Looking to the east, he noted the Ensign floating softly in the sheltered cove, about forty yards offshore where he'd anchored so as to protect the hull from the thick stands of white stag coral showing beneath the surface of the clear blue waters. The boat's sails were down, and she would be out of sight to even the rare ship that passed close to Thatch Key. The small green-capped island with its white stretch of beach looked inviting from afar, but other than an occasional diving boat that would anchor well offshore, the plethora of surrounding coral in the shallow waters kept any knowledgeable sailor at bay.

Great boat, he thought, eyes still on the lazing Ensign. The best island boat ever built, with that eight-hundred-pound keel keeping her steady in even the most unpredictable of the violent, sudden squalls in which he'd been caught. He turned away and sat against the rocks, locking his hands about his knees and gazing across the water back toward St. Thomas.

Home, he thought, and his wide, thin lips tightened across his bearded face. He'd been there for eight months now, ever since early October, and he had tried to force himself to think of the island paradise as home. He'd have to keep at it. There really was no other choice, now that he was dead again. Poor Charley Frost, he indulged himself briefly. You should have had better.

He squinted his deep-set eyes—almost azure blue in the tanned, angular face—and looked toward the green hills that rose up behind Sapphire Beach, three or four miles across the water. He'd left the small marina there at nine that morning and could have made Thatch within a half hour under the strong offshore wind had he not gone to the far side of the small, uninhabited rocky stretch of land that punctuated the Caribbean midway between St. Thomas and St. John. The precaution of having the Ensign out of sight had taken an extra half hour but had been necessary.

Not that Charley felt he need worry. He was certain no one was following him. But he'd believed that before. And besides, he wasn't concerned about himself today.

A sudden noise behind him broke his reverie.

Looking back to the beach, he saw the head and shoulders of a man break through the water just off shore. The figure moved slowly onto land, hampered by the tank on his back. Once ashore, the man quickly slipped out of the straps and leaned the tank against a rock. Unzipping his black wetsuit, he flipped his diving mask to the top of his head and looked around.

Charley rose, and when the man saw him he waved. Charley scrambled down the rocks, accepting the outstretched hand.

"Good to see you, Owen," he said, unable to hide the emotion in his voice.

"You, too, Charley," his friend responded, reaching out and tousling his friend's hair. Owen grinned as he noted Charley's faded denim shorts. "You really look the beachcomber." He touched Charley's gray-flecked beard lightly and stepped away. "It goes well with the long hair. And the blue eyes suit you. You look good, Charley. Relaxed. I'm glad to see it."

"No problems getting here?" Charley asked.

Owen shrugged. "The usual. Bert, my security man, threw a fit when I insisted on going off alone. I know damn well he's on the dock at St. John right now with his binoculars fixed at my boat. I made sure to anchor in close to the north shore so he wouldn't be too concerned. But I don't have too long."

Charley nodded. "Let's get to it, then."

They sat side by side on a rock overlooking a small pool that encroached the beach. Owen opened a waterproof sack tied about his waist, extracted a cigar, and lit it.

"You really look like a politician when you do that, even in your wetsuit. No beachcomber in you, senator."

Owen blew above the smoke and watched it slowly dissipate against the backdrop of blue sky. "My loss," he said, turning to Charley, a momentary wistfulness in his eyes that hardened into purpose even as his friend watched. "Well, about the convention," he said. "It's only six weeks away. I'd like to go over it again, see if you have any more thoughts or any changes to suggest."

Damn, Owen thought to himself. Happy as he was to see the other man, even under these circumstances, he was beyond this part of things now. He resented the necessity of charade and wished he could be honest with Charley, but he knew that could never be again.

Charley considered a moment. "I don't see any problems, Owen," he said. "The primaries went exactly as we'd anticipated. You won't believe the coverage you got down here, by the way. You're almost as well known now as the president is and you're a helluva lot more popular. And as far as the convention is concerned, and the election itself—we always knew how those would go."

Owen nodded. "I'd like to nail down the strong points of the platform we'll go with, though," he pressed on, managing to keep interest bright in his eyes. "After all, we've got another four years to think about."

"Well," Charley said, feeling vitalized now, as he always did in these conversations, wishing things could be as they once were. "There's no question energy conservation should be your cornerstone. You'll look especially good when the Saudi thing blows—you'll have it both ways."

"I agree. That's about where I started myself. But what about the business with Jason Coleridge?" Owen was referring to a young black militant who was only then beginning to make his mark on the national scene. "How do you think we should prepare for that one?"

They discussed Coleridge and several other issues briefly, reaching rapid agreement as they moved from topic to topic. Owen took pains to have Charley feel his special input was still important. Why not? After all, that's why he'd taken the trouble to come down. And besides, it was nice to see Charley, if only for those few moments.

But finally Owen looked at his watch and lifted his eyes to Charley who nodded.

"I wish," Charley began hesitantly, then continued, "I wish we could just have gone diving today. Or taken a sail. Something simple for once."

"It could all have been a lot simpler," Owen agreed, face softening as he regarded his friend. "If only we hadn't bought that damn raffle ticket. And bet on those horses. But," he said as he rose, "we were kids then."

He donned his gear and stepped into the water. Mouthpiece in hand, he turned to face Charley.

"You have a girl, don't you?"

"Yes. Janine. Two months now. Does it show that easily?"

"Easily enough. And that's good for you. But, Charley," Owen hesitated, "keep it low key, right? I don't want to lose you again."

Without waiting for an answer, Owen flipped down his mask, positioned the mouthpiece inside his lips, and moved deeper into the water until he finally dove and kicked forward, keeping just above the sharp coral that lined the cove.

Charley watched the trail of bubbles move slowly off. He looked at his diving watch and saw it was nearly one. He decided to wait a bit before starting back. Climbing again to his perch on the rocks, he sat, leaned his head back, and looked toward Sapphire Beach, which gleamed white against the hills that rose on the eastern shore of St. Thomas.

His small house was beyond those hills, just a five-minute drive down the narrow winding road which brought him to the beach. He would have preferred a Jeep to his Datsun, but he feared it was too conspicuous. His goal had been to establish himself on the island as unobtrusively as possible, and he felt he had succeeded.

He remembered how all that had started. June 15, 1987—almost a year ago now to the day. Three months before Charley Frost had died again.

———

"Senator?" he'd asked into the phone when Owen had finally come on. "This is Ben Scofield. I don't know if you remember me, but—"

"Of course, Mister Scofield," Owen had cut in smoothly. "What can I do for you?"

They were in Denver. Charley always knew Owen's itinerary exactly, just in case. He'd rarely had to risk breaching their semi-annual liaisons in advance of their scheduled dates, but this had been an emergency.

"Well, it's about the highway issue we discussed. I was out here and I thought—"

"No problem. Why don't you look for me in the bar of the Brown Palace after dinner—say ten-thirty."

Of course, it wouldn't be the Brown. Nor would it be at ten-thirty. Their meetings were becoming more and more difficult to arrange, especially now that Owen had become so well known. Charley never had liked the cloak-and-dagger end of it but had long since accepted the necessity.

Donning his jacket, he'd taken a cab west on Colfax and had walked the last three blocks into a quiet residential neighborhood. When he came to the house he produced a key from his pocket, opened the door, entered, and sat waiting in the living room. When his eyes adjusted to the dark, he noted the room was well appointed. The deep, comfortable U-shaped couch on which he sat was opposite a full-walled fireplace about which many paintings were hung; other furniture groupings were just visible in the shadows.

He hadn't seen the house before and knew only that it was owned by Westview Investors, a real estate firm that specialized in buying relatively high-priced homes for speculation. Westview had four counterparts, all operating regionally throughout the country, and the homes they purchased would often sit for months before they were sold because they were never pushed aggressively. It was a risky business, but yet Westview and the others still turned a generous profit.

Not that it mattered. The firms were only a precaution, like so many others. This was the first time, in fact, Charley had ever needed to use this safehouse system, and he was glad now they'd established it.

He waited perhaps a half hour before he heard the soft tap at the door. He got up to open it quickly. As expected, it was Owen.

They shook hands warmly, sat on the couch, and talked quietly in the dark as a soft spring rain began to pelt the shuttered windows.

"What's going on, Charley?" Owen asked, quickly coming to the point after the brief amenities were over.

"I think someone's on to me. And I think maybe he wants me to know it."

Owen fixed on Charley's eyes, which were merely black holes in the darkened room. He took a cigar from his inside pocket and shielded the flare of the match as he lit it. Only then did he ask, "What makes you think so?"

"There was someone around talking about buying my company. We've never discussed selling, of course, but people make a pass from time to time. Nothing I've ever been concerned about, but this time I felt the emphasis was on me—not my expertise but my background. There were some off-hand questions that seemed unimportant, almost polite, but I got the feeling the man was probing."

"That's it?"

"No. There's more. A lot more. He spent some time with a few of my managers, and one told me later he—Miller, the one who came around—seemed surprised my people didn't know I'd grown up at St. Mary's. He said Miller thought it was quite a success story. And then Miller asked him if I'd ever mentioned an old friend of mine—a Richie Peters."

The name hung in the silence that suddenly dominated the darkened room.

"You checked him out?" Owen said finally. "This Miller?"

"Of course. And he's legitimate. But that doesn't mean anything."

Charley watched as the glowing tip of the cigar moved up and down in a slow nod.

"I wish I could help somehow," Owen said carefully, after a moment, "but I can't." He paused a moment, then cursed softly, "Damn! It's going to be tough for you."

"I know." Charley had long since reached that inevitable conclusion. He'd been prepared for the eventuality for years—twenty-four years—but the fact of it was far more painful than he could have imagined. Despite his caution, despite holding something of himself always in reserve, he'd still allowed himself to become overwhelmingly close to his family.

And now—now he had to pay the price. They would all have to pay the price the power demanded, he cursed silently.

He and Owen had sat in the darkened room and worked out most of the details of the kidnaping over the next hour. They had met again once more in Baltimore in August. That was when they had developed the telephone trap for Masters and decided the man's ultimate fate.

"There's no other way. I wish there were, Charley, but we can't leave any possible link to me," Owen had reiterated with finality.

Charley reluctantly agreed, glad at least Owen had offered to take actual responsibility for the act.

They'd also worked out the timetable for Charley's own jump from the plane.

"I figure three minutes after they go is about it—far enough so they can't see my chute and enough time to get clear before the blast."

"You'd better free fall as far as you can, just to be sure."

"Don't worry."

"I mean about not being seen."

"I know what you mean."

Owen reached out and touched his fist to his friend's chin.

"Poor old Charley," he said.

Then they'd discussed the tough part: what would happen after.

"No contact with them, Charley. Not now. Not ever." Owen's tone was almost harsh as he told him what Charley already knew. But it had to be said.

Charley sighed deeply. "I know." He walked to the window and looked out toward the lights of Baltimore's harbor, which beckoned throngs of pedestrian traffic on the balmy summer evening. The stylish townhouse from which he watched was owned by Paramount Properties. He wondered where they'd meet next, knew that would become increasingly difficult when the primary elections began next year. Many of the people who didn't already recognize Owen on sight would be certain to do so then. And after November—

He broke off the thought and turned back to his friend. "I know," he repeated. "I guess I always knew this could happen. But still. So many years...."

"You gave them a lot, Charley. And got as much and more in return. You have a wonderful family. I envy you that," Owen said sincerely. "But you're going to have to put that behind you now."

Charley nodded slowly and took a deep breath. "Let's work out the rest of it," he said.

They made and discarded various choices.

"It has to be someplace that won't put you in contact with people who might recognize you, but it's still got to be large enough—and American enough—so you won't stick out like a sore thumb."

Charley remembered the trip he and his family had taken four years before. He recalled painfully for a moment how he'd shared his son's pride when Mike had pulled in the large hammerhead after a two-hour struggle.

"St. Thomas," he'd suggested. "I can get a place up in the hills, away from Charlotte Amalie where all the action is. Around Red Hook, maybe. Not a condo, maybe a small home. A lot of Americans live there year-round—that's no oddity. I can blend in pretty well there, I think."

They'd settled on it then, and Charley's first priority after arriving on the island had been finding an acceptable place in a reasonably but not oddly remote location. He wanted something he could move into immediately, preferably furnished. He had been fortunate to find exactly what he was looking for on the second day.

"It's a beaut, Mister Cavanaugh," the eager young agent had said, and he'd been right. "And the price is reasonable." That had been true, too, but it was of little concern to Charley, who moved in within the week.

His major consideration had been in getting out of the condominium he'd rented for the week. It was October, off-season for the island and its rainy month. Tourists were at a minimum. And he was sure he wouldn't be recognized, anyway, not with the gray-streaked hair, beard and mustache, and the nonprescription blue contacts that matched the passport Owen had provided identifying him as Lawrence Cavanaugh.

It was only after he'd moved into the house he truly understood his haste. He had needed to be cautious, but he realized later the new home symbolized the final break with his past life and admitted to himself only then how desperately he had needed that amputation.

The three previous weeks in hiding had been hell.

He didn't know what withdrawal symptoms were like for an addict, but he imagined they must be similar to what he felt in coming to deal with the fact he'd never again be with his family.

He'd had a long time to think about that, of course—those three long months before the kidnaping. And he'd thought he had dealt with it reasonably well, always understanding that in the end there could be no other way for him. But it had been one thing to accept that on an intellectual level, and quite another to come to grips with it emotionally as he'd had to when he left the house in Maine that Saturday morning.

He'd almost weakened at the door as he looked back at them. He even had thoughts of turning it around those two days in Canada. Even after the explosion, he could have reversed it. He remembered thinking, "It's not too late," but he knew he was wrong. It had been too late for a long, long time.

Maybe I should have taken the advice I gave Owen, he'd thought. Not have any kids. Losing Kate was painful, but the kids—Mike? If what he suspected was true, Mike would need him more desperately than ever.

He'd wallowed in that those three weeks in the small West Virginia cabin. Alone. That was the worst of it. At least an addict had professional help when he went "cold turkey," but Charley had to do it on his own.

"It'll be tough on you, Charley," Owen had said that Monday night in September after they'd disposed of Master's body by simply leaving it to be found in Rock Creek Park. Both of them had been anxious to be done with that part of the episode. "I wish I could help make it easier, but—" They both knew the words were unnecessary, couldn't change things.

So he'd struggled with the loss of his family—his betrayal. He wanted so much to comfort them in their need, to take away the pain he had so cruelly been forced to inflict.

The liquor hadn't helped; it had only made him drop deeper into the whirlpool of self-pity and recrimination that was going nowhere. So he'd cut down the drinking and sweated out the three weeks in the

West Virginia hideaway as he grew his beard and mustache and let his hair grow long.

But the pain was as sharp as ever when he boarded the plane to Miami, and it became almost exquisite when he'd first moved into the house above Nazareth Bay, over the hills from Sapphire. How they'd love it, he thought, and abandoned himself to that agony for days, consciously exposing all his nerve ends as nakedly as possible, sucking in the loss and sorrow through every cell of his body until finally, unexpectedly, it began to abate. He felt at last a deep exhaustion that soon leveled out into a dull ache of which he was generally, but not always, conscious.

The amputation was finally completed. He was aware always of the stump—he had "phantom pains" at times where the severed limb should have been—but he could live with it. He *was* living with it—better than he cared to admit, he thought now, as sitting on the rock Owen had so recently vacated, he watched a small power boat careen out of Sapphire, come out past the long jetty and turn a course for St. John, whipping a curl of white water in its wake. He glanced at his watch, saw it was one-fifteen, and looked back across the water. Was he really so shallow? he asked himself. Had he simply hidden behind a lifetime of sacrifice to high purpose? For the truth was, he was actually enjoying his life at times—a *lot* of times, especially of late.

The house itself was a treasure once he'd allowed himself to appreciate it. Set high in the hills overlooking Nazareth Bay, its master bedroom deck faced directly west. Often in the evenings he would sit out and watch as the sun's deep red slowly fanned and diffused as it was swallowed by the ocean. In the mornings he got the sun from the east on the patio by the small pool in the walled tropical garden, and often he'd read there for hours, in seclusion.

Then two months ago he'd met Janine. He wouldn't have discussed that with Owen had his friend not guessed.

Charley finally rose and made his way back to the beach, squelching both the resentment and the guilt that had begun to rise in him. After all, he reminded himself, he'd understood how it would have to be for a long time. In fact, it had all been his idea in the first place.

CHAPTER 12

"Can I help you?"

The young woman in the bright yellow and white dress who looked up at Mike seemed, at first appearance, several years his senior. When she removed her black-framed glasses and smiled inquiringly, however, the studious look disappeared altogether and Mike saw she was no older than eighteen. He also noted she was very pretty.

"I hope so," he responded, placing his hands on the center of the information desk and returning her smile. "Although I'm really not sure what I'm looking for."

She appeared to blush and Mike realized she'd mistaken his remark for a double entendre. That was the last thing he wanted, at least at the moment. What he needed right now was help, and he cursed himself for the cockiness that was so quickly growing in him since he'd left Boston and was on his own. That was less than a week ago, and he was already acting like Mr. Sophisticate. Keep your perspective, Mike, he cautioned.

"I wanted to speak to someone from the parapsychology clinic," he went on hastily, hoping to allay her doubts.

"I'm sorry, but there's no one here now. The clinic closes at six." The voice was cooler now, almost officious.

Mike nodded. "I figured it would be closed. I just got into town and thought I'd give it a try, anyway. Thanks." He started to turn away, then added, "What time will someone be here in the morning?"

"Well, the clinic usually opens at eight-thirty. But no one will be here tomorrow—or for the next two weeks, for that matter. At least not officially. The university programs are all shut down until the summer session and that doesn't start until after the Fourth. So the staff's on vacation."

"Damn," Mike said softly. He'd thought about calling ahead but had decided not to take the time. Now he cursed himself for his impetuousness. Mr. Sophisticate indeed.

"Well, thanks again," he mumbled, feeling foolish as he walked down the short corridor and out through the double doors. The evening air was hot, almost palpable as it hit him, even though he only wore a short-sleeved blue shirt above a pair of khakis that had been fresh that morning. Durham must be a real sweat box in August, he thought.

He seated himself on the highest of the steps that led to the building's entrance and looked back to the large bronze plaque engraved "Duke Medical Center." The brick and stone building that had seemed so inviting when he arrived only moments ago now seemed cold and institutional.

Damn, he thought again, and faced out across the campus to the lights of the Hilton Inn that beckoned beyond. He looked at his watch. Eight o'clock. He had to stay somewhere. And besides, he realized suddenly he was very hungry.

Rising slowly, he'd just begun to walk down the steps when he heard the door open behind him and footsteps come quickly. He turned and recognized the girl from the reception desk.

"Hi," he said as she came abreast of him.

"Hi," she returned. Her glasses were off, and her features appeared very soft in the late twilight.

They walked down the steps side by side.

"I'm Mike Frost," he offered, stopping as they reached ground level.

"Susan Mallory," she responded, extending her hand after a brief hesitation.

They started walking again down the long path toward the parking lot. She was very pretty, Mike thought again, and quickly gave in to the "Why not?" that bubbled in him.

"If you'd just driven three hundred miles nonstop," he said, "looking for something twenty-five years gone you don't know why you're looking for, anyway—if you did that and found the place was closed for two weeks and you knew you could have called ahead and saved yourself the trip—if you did that and were feeling really hot and stupid and tired—and if on top of everything else you didn't even have a place to stay yet and suddenly had the brains to figure out you were really hungry, too—if that was you, where would you go for dinner?"

"Two questions," she said, blue eyes mischievous.

"Shoot."

"First, can you hold out for twenty minutes?"

"Sure."

"Second, was that an invitation?"

"Absolutely," he grinned. "I'm not all that sure about the twenty minutes, though."

"You'll like this place."

"You're on," he said, taking her arm and hurrying her toward his car. He did feel hot, tired, and stupid—but also good, excited for the first time in months.

"Wow," she said as she saw the Porsche. "If I'd known this I'd have suggested another place I know. It's about—"

"I know," he cut in, laughing. "A good half hour, right?"

"Well, not quite—but close. And they've been known to serve wine sometimes without carding you."

"Get in," he shoved her playfully. Closing her door he walked around the car and seated himself. "Where to?" he asked as he started the ignition. He reached over, took her hand, and faced ahead as he swung out onto Irwin Street, crossing in front of the Hilton and tooting his horn at the bright lights as he passed. A few blocks down he picked up Route 70, as she directed, and headed toward Raleigh.

* * *

"Tell me about your father, Mike."

She was gazing at him across the candlelight, elbows on the wooden table, her small chin resting on her clasped hands. The flame that flickered in her blue eyes gave them an almost haunting look. They seemed extraordinarily large and moist, those eyes, warm and compassionate and interested, and Mike realized some of that came from the wine she had drunk, but that part of it, too, was because she was very, very nice.

99

He considered her statement for a moment. Finally, he said, "I couldn't even begin, Susan. He was such a hell of a guy. I could say he played tennis, owned a plane, loved his family, made a lot of money—but that doesn't tell you about a person. It doesn't tell about walking in the woods, or watching a ball game, or—" he broke off, suddenly caught up in the emotion that came unbidden as he spoke the words. He was afraid he might cry and realized oddly that wouldn't have bothered him with her, not then, not this night. Somehow, it would have been okay.

But he blinked back the tears anyway, still feeling an immense comfort knowing he could have gone the other way. And also in knowing beyond doubt that whatever suspicions had plagued him, he *did* love his father without reservation. It made Mike feel very good indeed, and his search suddenly took on a brighter, almost knightlike dimension.

"He was just a helluva guy," he repeated.

Mike felt full—contented full—and drained simultaneously. It was the first time he'd really talked about his father to anyone. It had given him an enormous sense of relief he hadn't been aware he needed.

Almost before he realized it, he had begun spilling out his tale, all of it. He had started slowly but the words were almost rushing out of his mouth as he concluded. He didn't know if it was his disappointment at finding the clinic closed or the warm southern air as they'd driven down. Perhaps it was the restaurant itself, where they sat beneath the immense rafters and lofts that still managed to provide a feeling of intimacy. Maybe it was the wine. Or simply Susan. Possibly it was a combination of all those things, or maybe it was just that he had finally been ready to talk about it. Whatever it was, he was glad it had happened.

And now she was asking about his father, about Charley, not as a kidnap victim but as the man himself.

"I miss him a lot," he added, and she nodded as if that told her all.

"And this Richie Peters? He was your dad's best friend?"

"Once. A long time ago. But he's been dead now for twenty-five years or so, like I told you."

"What is it you expect to find?"

He shrugged. "I have no idea. It's probably ridiculous for me to even be here, but I was already so close. I mean, it's not like this thing with Richie had anything to do with my father. But—I don't know—

it's just that when Anderson—their coach—was talking, I felt like—I don't know," he ended lamely.

"Do you know what tests they gave him?"

Mike shook his head. "Only that he was here in the spring of sixty-three. I thought maybe if I could see the records...." He looked up and grimaced. "I know it was a dumb idea. Even if the clinic was open."

"Poor Mike," she said, gently chiding him. "Don't get so down on yourself. It won't be hard to work out."

"Oh?"

"Sure. Even though the staff is on vacation, a lot of them are still around. They live here, you know. I'm sure you can see somebody, get to see the records. As a matter of fact," she snapped her fingers, suddenly animated, "Doctor Kreiger! I just saw him yesterday! He runs the testing, but more important, he's been here for over thirty years—ever since they started the program. He might even have met this Richie."

"Hey! Great. Will you introduce me?"

"Can I have some coffee?"

"Sounds like a fair deal," he said, signaling the waiter.

"If I go you one better can I have some cheesecake?"

"Sure," he said, as the waiter nodded and left. "What's one better?"

"We can go see the records tonight."

"But they must be locked!"

"Sure. But I can get the key."

"But this Kreiger you mentioned—he'll have a key. I can go with him in the morning."

Her face had been bright and now it dimmed with disappointment. Suddenly he realized that in the telling he'd made her part of it. Of course he could go tomorrow, she knew that better than he, but tonight it was theirs, no reason more important than that to do it. He felt abashed at his insensitivity.

He remembered cursing himself earlier about not growing up and wondered now why he wanted to. He felt his excitement rise. Feeling young and carefree suddenly, he brought his fist down on the table. In mock ferocity, he said, "Eat up, fair lady. It's time to buck the establishment."

* * *

The excitement held during the hectic drive back and heightened when the door to Entrance One finally opened. She emerged briefly, ushering him quickly inside the clinic.

"Shh," she whispered, but the warning was unnecessary. The long dark corridor lent itself to silence.

He followed softly, taking the key from her hand when she stopped in front of a door. He opened it quietly and they stepped inside. Mike and Susan now stood in the room that housed the records of the parapsychology clinic. He took the flashlight from his pocket, turned it on, and shielded the beam with his hand. In the dim light he could see rows and rows of gray filing cabinets.

"Where do we start?" he whispered.

"How about with the Ps?" she responded, and he had an urge to giggle but kicked her lightly on the ankle instead.

"Smart ass," he hissed.

"Dumb ass," she came back, and he switched off the flashlight and tilted up her chin. He kissed her lightly, just a promise, and switched the beam on again.

"Where are the Ps?"

"I don't know. I've never been here before, either. After the Os, I guess."

He realized she must be as nervous as he, more probably, since she had more to lose if they were discovered, and he marveled at her cool. You are some gal, Susan Mallory, he thought.

There were three complete cabinets of Ps, and the drawer they were looking for was at the bottom of the first.

"Here it is," he whispered, kneeling and letting the light shine through his fingers. The label read, "Pessaro–Pettijohn." Quietly, he pulled out the drawer and scanned the names at the top of the folders. There were two Richard Peters: Richard A. and Richard L.

Richard A. showed a rating of 42.6 percent and had a red star next to his name on the information sheet Mike removed. He was from Atlanta, Georgia, and had been born on August 14, 1954.

Richard L. rated 32 percent and had no stars. His birthrate was registered as May 9, 1965.

Mike had calculated Richie Peters would have been born in 1945 or 1946.

"Shit," he swore softly.

"Try the plain Rs," Susan said at his ear. "You know. Just the initial."

But R. Langley Peters and R. Howard Peters were wrong, too.

"How about Ricardo?" she offered, but he turned quickly and she saw he was in no mood for levity then.

"Well, are you sure it's Richard?" she said, quickly serious.

He nodded. "What else would Richie stand for?"

Nevertheless, he checked every Peters in the file, but came away with nothing. The only one who had been born in 1945 had been named Mary Ellen.

"Damn," Mike exhaled as he closed the drawer.

He looked up at her, and her face mirrored his own disappointment. Suddenly her eyes widened.

"Wait a minute," she whispered. "There are probably cross files. There have to be!"

Reaching down, she took the flashlight from his hand, shielded it with her own as she quickly moved down the room.

"Here it is!" she hissed through the darkness, and he came up to see her pointing at a file cabinet. "See," she said excitedly. "I told you. Nineteen sixty-three. That's when you said, right?"

He nodded, impressed at her determination.

Opening the drawer, he quickly ruffled through the files, Brian Peters, 39 percent with a blue star, born in 1905 was followed in the drawer by David Peterson.

He checked 1962 and 1964 just to be sure, but when they revealed nothing it was only anti-climatic. He pushed in the last drawer and turned off the flashlight. He rose and took her hand. In the aftermath of excitement, he felt her disappointment almost as sharp as his own.

CHAPTER 13

Mike drove slowly along Campus Drive, looking for South Gregson as Susan had instructed.

Susan. The thought of her brought a soft smile to his face. That, at least, had ended well. He'd felt a strong attraction to the girl he'd known had been reciprocated and which had accelerated for both of them as the adventure of the night before had developed. His desire for her had become so intense, in fact, that in the records room the night before, as they'd searched the files, he'd had a difficult time keeping his hands off her.

And he'd known with a certainty that, had he pressed it, so great was the electricity between them, she would willingly have acquiesced. The thought of them together on the floor of that dark room had crossed his mind more than once during their hushed endeavor.

But that mood had shattered, at least for him, in the failure of their quest. From giddy expectation he had plunged to morose disappointment, and he'd felt whatever it was they had together was irrevocably dampened by his subsequent withdrawal.

So it had been with great surprise when, at the door of her apartment when she'd unexpectedly reached up to kiss him as they said their goodbyes, he'd felt himself respond with his earlier eagerness, a desire in him stronger than any he'd felt since before—

He'd cut that thought off and just let himself go with the moment, holding the kiss tantalizingly as their bodies strained at each other.

In bed, however, they'd been quiet, joining together with a gentleness that brought him a relief he had desperately needed. As he softly stroked her hair afterward, he knew somehow, despite their only having met that evening, Susan was not an "easy" girl. That realization was surprisingly important to him.

Over coffee that morning, they'd lingered at their goodbyes. Maybe when this was all over, he'd—

Mike spotted South Gregson and turned left. Susan had told him Dr. Kreiger's place was on the right, two blocks down.

The homes along the avenue were lovely, he thought, very different from the New England solidity to which he was accustomed. The mansionlike houses he passed now were smaller than many of the estates in his section of the country, but there was a softness here he liked, a gentleness in the architecture that seemed more in character with this easier climate than the stark grandeur of those northern monoliths would have been.

Looking to his left he saw the plaque on the stone gatepost that read "Dr. Theodore H. Kreiger," and he turned into the circular driveway that fronted the white colonial. The small gardens were in full bloom, the scent of hyacinth sweet as he mounted the steps, and he thought briefly how nice it must be to sit on the wide verandah some April evening just after a spring shower.

The elderly black maid with the shiny moon face who answered the door was dressed in a bordered apron and matching cap, both gleaming white. She ushered him into the cool, subtly lit study where the doctor rose from his desk and came forward with extended hand. He was dressed in faded blue coveralls, the hint of fresh sweat stains at the armpits suggesting he may have just come from tending his gardens.

"Mister Frost? I'm Doctor Kreiger."

Mike took the man's hand and tried not to appear to be looking down on the doctor, which was difficult since Kreiger was a good head shorter than Mike.

"It's nice meeting you, doctor," he said, trying not to sound too officious. "I appreciate your time."

"Not at all. Only too happy to talk to someone who's interested in our work here. Sit down," he said, indicating a leather armchair positioned before a paper-strewn desk. An array of framed diplomas hung on the wall behind him. "Would you like something to drink?" Mike shook his head negatively.

"Well," the doctor continued, reseating himself and reclining slightly as he regarded Mike, "what can I do for you? Miss Mallory said it was something about your father, I believe."

"Well, not my father, actually. Someone who was my father's best friend. A long time ago. Richie Peters. He would have been tested here in nineteen sixty-three, I think."

"Richie Peters," the doctor mused, running his hand thoughtfully over his graying hair. Kreiger's hair was bushy, wiry in a way that made Mike think of the stuffing in a sofa. The man's eyes were a soft brown and seemed weak but kindly as they peered at Mike through the thick glasses perched on the wide nose.

"Richie Peters," Kreiger repeated, frowning slightly. "The name rings a bell although I'm not sure why. I've been involved in the testing of so many thousands over the years, here and elsewhere—and I generally don't know their names, unless they turn out to be special, which of course is rare. They're all in the archives, naturally, in the records room." He paused and said again, "Richie Peters."

"Yes, sir," Mike prompted as the doctor seemed to ponder. "He would have been about eighteen years old. He was an orphan, lived at Saint Ma—"

"Of course!" said the doctor, bringing his chair forward quickly and placing his hands on the desk. "Of course," he repeated. "Richie Peters. I knew I remembered the name. How could I forget? I tested him myself early on. Odd case. Incredible, actually." He regarded Mike, shook his head ruefully. "I wish we'd understood what it meant when he was down here. We were looking for one thing and we came up with quite something else, and by the time we understood it…" He shrugged and Mike nodded encouragingly.

"We'd pick it up today, of course, because we understand so much more. But the clinic wasn't very old then and our thrust was primarily ESP in the more conventional sense of that expression. You know—thought transference, that sort of thing. What the layman might call mind reading."

"And today?" Mike asked.

"Today?" the doctor smiled kindly, wisely. "Today, Mister Frost, we're involved with everything. Everything and anything that has to do with psychic phenomenon. You'd be amazed at some of the things we've accomplished here. You might even find them—" he hesitated at the word deliberately"—unbelievable. Many people do."

"And Richie Peters? What about him? What made his case so odd, as you put it?"

Dr. Kreiger seemed to study Mike for a long moment, but Mike sensed the man was really going back over the experience, reliving it privately before he spoke.

"There's never been another one like Richie Peters," the doctor finally said, softly. "Not before or since—at least as far as I know."

"But what was so special about him?" Mike pressed again, intrigued by the doctor's statement and becoming impatient at the dialogue although he tried not to show it.

Dr. Kreiger looked closely at Mike.

"How familiar are you with what we do here?"

Mike shrugged. "I've heard of the clinic, of course, and I know you work with people from all over—your own students, but other people, too—testing them to see if they have a 'sixth sense' I'd guess you'd call it," Mike said. "You test them with cards that have symbols they can't see, and they try to guess what the symbols are. That's about all I know."

Kreiger nodded, picked up a pen and rolled it idly between the stubby fingers of both his hands. "That's accurate so far, although a great over-simplification. Everyone, you see, has ESP, or is at least capable of it to some degree. In some, however, the sense is much more highly developed. And in others—" the doctor trailed off, rose, and walked to the window.

He looked out for a moment before turning back to Mike. "Let me explain the test we gave Richie. It was really quite simple. It was the test we give everyone in our initial selection process for potential subjects.

"The individual is seated at a desk, and the test administrator stands at the front of the room and holds up cards one at a time. These cards have either a plus or minus symbol or a zero printed on them, but the subject can't see that. All he sees is the blank front of the card, and he writes down the symbol he thinks is printed on the back.

"In Richie's test, we used one hundred cards. Do you know what the statistical probabilities of "guessing" correctly would be?"

"Thirty-three and a third percent, I guess," Mike responded.

"Slightly more, actually, but I won't go into that. Thirty-three and one-third percent is close enough. Forty percent is significant, and at fifty percent we have a find."

"What did Richie score?"

"Eighteen percent."

"Eighteen percent!" Mike exclaimed. "But that would be incredibly low!"

"Incredibly," the doctor repeated, looking closely at Mike. The man was obviously enjoying the suspense.

"But—" Mike began.

"I'll tell you what," Kreiger cut in. "Let's go over to the records office. There's something I'd like to show you. I'm sure you'll find it very interesting."

Mike became immediately uncomfortable. "You don't have to do that, Doctor Kreiger. I appreciate it, but I know you're busy. You can just tell me what happened if you'd rather."

"Nonsense," the man beamed, brushing off Mike's demurrer, obviously caught up in the retelling of the incident. "I wanted to go over to the clinic today, anyway. Do you know where Entrance One is?"

The shadowed door flashed in Mike's mind.

"I'll find it," he answered reluctantly.

"Good. Let me change out of these," he gestured at the stained overalls, "and I'll meet you there in fifteen minutes."

* * *

The records room hadn't changed in the twelve hours since Mike had been there last. Not that he'd expected it to. The only difference was that the fluorescent lights made the rows of file cabinets seem less menacing than they had in the flashlight's beam.

But Mike felt very apprehensive as the doctor made for the 1963 files. He watched as the man opened the drawer, held his breath as he anticipated Kreiger's confusion at not finding Richie's records inside.

Kreiger lifted a folder out slightly and Mike read the label—Brian Peters. He remembered the blue star pasted behind the man's name and the file behind it being Peterson. Kreiger slipped his finger back further, withdrew the next folder, looked at the label, and straightened.

"Here it is," he said cheerfully, and walked to the long work table at the end of the room. Opening the folder, he motioned Mike to come up beside him.

"Look at this," Kreiger said, indicating the information sheet in his hand. Mike looked, but not at the sheet Kreiger held. Instead, he quickly checked the label on the folder that lay open on the table.

Peters, Richard.

Mike was certain he'd been thorough in his search the night before. He felt a sudden, vague alarm.

"See here?" Kreiger prompted, and Mike followed the man's finger. May 26, 1963. "Note the results."

"Eighteen percent. Like you said," Mike managed.

"Ah," Kreiger replied, turning to look at Mike with approval as if Mike had indeed discovered something monumental. "Eighteen percent. Correct."

The man paused for effect. "Now," he went on, "look at this."

Carefully, as if it had incalculable value, he removed a second sheet from behind the first. "See the date?" he asked.

June 18, 1963. "But I thought he'd only been tested once," Mike said, somewhat confused.

"We thought so, too," Kreiger responded enigmatically, excited now as he sprung the rest of it. "But look. See—here," he moved his finger down to the score written below the date.

Mike's eyes rounded in wonder. "You're kidding!" he exclaimed. "But that's impossible!"

"It would seem so, wouldn't it?"

"One hundred percent! That's incredible."

"Incredible, Mister Frost, is a poor choice of words in my profession." Kreiger's voice was gentle now, understanding. "However, I must admit we, too, were surprised. To put it mildly."

"But I thought he did so badly the first time," Mike put in.

"He did. Just as you saw."

"Then what—"

"Let me explain," the doctor said, seating himself on one of the hardback wooden chairs and indicating Mike do likewise.

"The first test went exactly as I described earlier. Richie scored eighteen percent, which is extremely low, and of course we were disappointed. After all, he wasn't just a routine subject, but rather had been sent here by one of his teachers, I believe, or his coach, who had noticed some significant incidents.

"So, as I said, we were disappointed, but of course that happens—often. We sent him home. I was intrigued by his test, however, because to score so low seemed somehow significant to me, since the laws of probability are against that, too. So I studied the answers, looking for a pattern or something—I didn't know what. I came up with nothing. I put the file away and thought no more of it."

Kreiger paused for a long moment, and Mike was about to prod him when the man suddenly continued. "I thought no more of it, that is, until some three weeks later, when I had occasion to administer a similar test. There were the same hundred cards, patterned at random, and as I scored the dozen or so subjects, something kept nagging at the back of my mind. Suddenly I had it," the doctor snapped his fingers as if he were there again, "and I went to the files and checked Richie's answers. They exactly matched those for the test I gave that day three weeks later. Exactly," the man added softly, and his eyes took on a far away expression.

"I'll never forget my excitement," he went on after a brief pause. "I didn't even phone ahead. I just jumped in my car and drove up to Mills River. It was his coach, I remember now, but I went directly to the orphanage, Saint Mary's, and they told me when I got there. He'd been dead for a week. Dead. A ridiculous, wasteful accident," Kreiger ended, an old bitterness sharp in his voice.

"But a hundred percent!" Mike said. "I mean, what are the odds on that?"

The doctor's voice was flat. "There are no 'odds' on that, Mister Frost."

"Then what does it mean?" Mike went on in bewilderment.

Kreiger's voice seemed almost weary now. "It means Richie Peters had the ability to foresee the future. Perfectly. And I don't believe he ever knew it."

CHAPTER 14

The drive back to Mills River seemed endless to Richie that day in 1963. It was not merely his own disappointment he had to deal with but that of the others as well.

"Good luck," Owen had called out as Richie had driven away the morning before, eager to be away in the sleek Mercury they'd so recently won in the raffle. "Knock 'em dead," Charley had hollered after him through cupped hands.

Both his friends had been excited at the prospect when Mr. Anderson had first brought it up to Richie and had built it to Lord-knows-what by the time he finally agreed to go down to Durham.

Charley especially.

"I knew it, Richie!" he exclaimed. "I knew it all along, through the basketball things and all. You got some kind of power, that's what it is. I'm telling you, we'll be famous! We'll make a fortune!"

Owen regarded Charley quizzically. "What's this 'we' business, Charley? It's Richie's thing—if it is anything."

"Well, I know," Charley toned it down. "But still—can you imagine! I mean, suppose you really can read minds and stuff like that? Think about what that means!"

Richie *had* thought about it, caught up not only in Charley's excitement but by his own feelings as well. He didn't know why he'd been such an asshole about the raffle ticket; he only knew he had to go through them all until he found the right one. And the basketball games, the

111

fight that time—he'd seen them clear as day, not seen them actually, but—

And he had certainly seen the headlines in his dream. That was no figment of his imagination, and there were other things, things he'd hesitated to share, even with Charlie and Owen.

He had fought the visions for a time, frightened that they led to some strange arena of which he wanted no part, and for that same reason had resisted the trip to Durham. But in the end he had succumbed, not only out of an overwhelming need to find out the truth, but also because of a dawning realization of what he perhaps possessed.

Suppose he *did* have the power? *Could* foretell the future? There would be no stopping him! The implications were limitless, and at times he became obsessed with them, knowing the fantasies he allowed himself to develop could be painfully shattered but unable to resist the temptation of hope.

Because that was what it became.

A hope.

A way out.

They were all eighteen, and the bravado with which they'd talked about the future would soon be put to the test. They'd be leaving St. Mary's within a few short months, and although they'd hoped and dreamed for years to finally have their chance, Richie knew deep down he was afraid. He knew Owen to share his fears, and suspected that of Charley as well, although he tried the hardest not to show it.

"You just wait, guys! When we're out of here we'll knock 'em on their ass! There'll be no stopping us," Charley would say.

Richie and Owen would agree, but their proclamations seemed more hollow as the time narrowed. The world was tough, Richie knew, and they were starting out with very few advantages. It would be easy to get swallowed up.

That was Richie's greatest fear, even though he'd never expressed it.

But it paled beside that same fear in Owen, which *had* been expressed. Or rather, exposed—humiliatingly so.

Richie could have killed Charley that day, he remembered in retrospect. Even now, nearly a year later, he could feel the anger rise in him when he thought about the incident.

It had been September, a muggy, late-summer day. The thick over-cast sky trapped the heavy air as if in some enormous box. Only the flies, fat as ripe berries, seemed to have the energy to move about, and even they appeared sluggish, coming to rest on the boys' bare arms and legs, buzzing off only when a swat came their way.

Charley, Richie, and Owen were down at the creek, pants rolled above their knees, dangling their feet in the water as they sat on a long, flat rock that bordered the slow-moving stream. School had begun ear-lier in the week.

Their senior year.

In June—a mere nine months away—they would graduate.

They sat mostly in silence, Charley idly tossing pebbles at some drifting twig, acting somewhat distracted as he had all afternoon. Sud-denly he turned to Owen.

"You got some mail today," he said. His voice was casual, but some-thing in his tone alerted Richie and he was not surprised to see Owen stiffen.

Mail—any sort of mail—was a rarity at St. Mary's, almost an event in itself. But somehow Richie knew whatever this was, Owen had been expecting it.

Privately.

"I stopped in the room before and saw it on your bed. Figured you'd want it as soon as possible, so I brought it down. It looks important." Charley was still straight-faced, but there was a glint in his eye Richie had seen all too often. There was a malicious streak in Charley, a Siamese appendage of his bravado Richie felt sometimes went too far.

And he was certain this would be one of those times.

"Here you go," Charley said casually, reaching into his back pocket and removing a letter. It had been folded over and was now rounded and wrinkled. He held the letter out toward Owen, who looked at it with guarded eyes.

"Charley," Richie began, but in that instant Owen reached for the letter.

And Charley pulled it away.

"You really want this letter, don't you?" he said, mockery clear in his voice. "I mean, you really *want* it!" Charley rose, turned to face them, and held the letter above his shock of black, curly hair with an

113

insolent gesture. But it was Richie to whom he spoke, and there was disgust in his voice.

"The United States Army, Richie," he spat the words. "Recruiting Office. How about that, buddy?"

Richie looked at Owen, surprised. He would never have guessed that to be on Owen's mind and wondered that the other had never shared the thought.

"The United States Army, Richie," Charley repeated. "That's what old Owen wants for himself. To be a fucking dog face."

The draft had long been abolished, and the three had often discussed with disparagement the high percentage of St. Mary's boys who volunteered for the military immediately upon graduation.

Or upon turning eighteen, as Owen would shortly.

"From one institution to another," Charley would say, shaking his head in wonder. "Gutless copouts. Afraid to be on their own without somebody to take care of them."

And Richie had agreed with all of that. As, he'd believed, had Owen.

But here was his friend, looking with humiliated eyes at the letter in Charley's hand.

"Give him the letter, Charley," Richie said softly.

"Sure," the other responded, but his eyes now glittered at Owen. "Sure. Here, Owen—come take the letter," he taunted.

Owen sprang up with a fury that took both the others by complete surprise. He was strong, perhaps stronger even than Charley, but Richie would never have believed the quiet boy would take the challenge. There were tears in Owen's eyes, and he emitted what sounded like a sob as he went for Charley's upraised arm, grabbed his wrist with both hands, twisted hard, and swivelled his hip sharply, sending the other off balance. Charley stumbled and, when Owen gave a final wrench and released his hold, sprawled backward to land with a splash in the creek. He spluttered, rose, and quickly hoisted himself back onto the rock where Owen waited with clenched fists.

Richie stepped between them, grabbing Charley's arm roughly, trying to hold him in check.

"You asked for it, Charley," he said. "Don't make it worse than it is already."

The other boy was breathing hard. He seemed to debate pulling away from Richie's grasp, but instead took one deeper breath that, when finally released, took with it the animal tension emanating from him.

"I'm sorry, Owen," he said in the mercurial change of mood he showed frequently. His black hair hung in wet ringlets on his forehead and water ran in rivulets across his crooked nose. Beyond him, the unopened letter drifted toward the current.

"I'm sorry," he repeated, and Owen nodded, unclenching his fists. Only then did Richie release his hold on Charley's arm.

They stood a moment, still caught in what had transpired, and then Charley spoke. But when he did, it was with an intensity, a concern, that surprised Richie. Charley was never easy to figure, even after all these years.

"Owen," he said, "I shouldn't have teased you. And the letter—" he gestured to the creek, "I'm sorry about that. But Jesus, Owen. The army! I was so shook I nearly tore that damn letter up when I saw it. You *know* how we feel about that. What it stands for. What we talked about. You're better than that, Owen."

"Am I?" Owen raised his head now and faced both of them with belligerent but questioning eyes. "Am I? And what does the army stand for, anyway? Really, Charley, without the bullshit," he challenged.

"It's a dead end, Owen. At least, for guys like us it is. Orphans. It's the same as Saint Mary's, but when you choose it—" he broke off, shaking his head. "When you deliberately choose it, you're throwing in the towel. You're saying you can't make it on your own, that you need somebody to take care of you, that you're willing to sell out your freedom—your chance—in return for guaranteed room and board.

"It's running scared, Owen. That's what it means."

"Well I *am* scared!" Owen almost shouted the words and balled his fists as he looked at his friends in defiance. "I'm scared. How do you like that, Charley? I'm scared. Owen Reid is scared. Your good buddy is scared.

"And I'll tell you something else. I've been scared for a long time— as long as I can remember. Really scared. We talked about graduating, getting out of here," he flung his arm out wildly, "but what's out there, Charley? What's out there?"

"Come on, Owen," Charley began, but the other cut him off quickly.

"Don't give me that 'come on, Owen' shit, Charley. Not now. Not when we're finally talking about it. I've listened to you—to both of you—all these years, talking about what we'd do once we got out. And I agreed—or pretended to, anyway," he admitted. "But what *is* out there, really? For us. What chance do we have?

"You said it before, Charley. We're orphans. In the end, that's all we are—three fucking orphans!"

The anger—and the shame—was so evident in his voice no one could not respond.

"Tell the truth, Charley. Just this once." Owen's voice was soft now. "Aren't you scared sometimes? I mean, with all your devil-may-care crap—aren't you really scared of it, too?"

Charley looked at Own but said nothing.

Richie had been glad Owen had not directed the question to him. For he *was* scared of the future, scared of getting swallowed up, scared of not being able to make it. Maybe not as scared as Owen finally admitted to being, but scared nonetheless.

And so was Charley, Richie sensed, although the boy would never admit to it. Charley had to be scared despite his bravado.

That's why the power had become so important to Riche and why he'd allowed the possibility of its existence to grow in his mind. Why he'd permitted the hope of it to blossom.

If it was so, it could be a way out. And that was why the invitation to Durham had loomed so large, why it had become more important for him than he'd let the others realize. There *was* something in him. He could feel it growing, solidifying. And now other people would help him to understand and develop it. Or so he'd thought.

But he'd failed the test, he reflected bitterly again as he swung the car onto the dirt road that would dead-end at St. Mary's. Failed, no matter what the polite little interviewer had told him afterwards about "a particular and unusual quality we're looking for that few possess." And as he related the story that night to Charley and Owen, he could see how far their own imaginations had run.

"Shit," said Charley, turning away in frustration.

"I'm sorry, Richie," Owen had offered, naked disappointment apparent in his gentle brown eyes.

Whatever the "thing" was, the "power" as Charley had called it, their "edge" as Richie had hoped it would be—whatever it was simply wasn't. They were merely three orphans as they always had been.

"Let's go out for a beer," Charley said disconsolately.

Richie looked to Owen who shrugged.

"Why not?"

It was against rules for them to leave on weekday evenings even though they had the car now. But school would be over in ten days, they'd graduate, and then—what the hell. Old Man Winter held few threats for them anymore, whatever their future.

Charley tried to brighten their mood with wisecracks as they drove up to Mills River but eventually tired of his monologue. They drove the last few miles in silence, basketball windbreakers zipped tight against the crisp mountain air that washed the open convertible.

The parking lot at Barney's was almost empty, just a few cars and two or three pickups that were etched in the eerie red glow of the blinking sign that proclaimed "BAR EY's T ERN." A "Schlitz" sign shone in the window like a drunken Halloween pumpkin.

To Richie the scene was prophetic. He could see their lives stretching ahead, nothing more than a broken neon joke.

"What'll you boys have?" Barney asked as they opened their jackets and hunched themselves over the scarred wooden bar. He knew them from the basketball team. He had not asked for an I.D. when they'd first come there months earlier and did not now.

"Three Millers," said Charley.

"Well," Owen said, raising his glass when the beer arrived, "here's to us."

They solemnly clinked their glasses and drank.

Since their growing excitement about Richie's power, the subject of the army hadn't come up again. But Richie wondered now what Owen was thinking about the future.

He watched as Barney wiped up some wet spots from the bar in front of them with his stained apron before walking down to the end of the bar where two men and a brassy-haired woman had signaled for another. Barney wasn't tall but he was built powerfully, and Richie noted the thick neck below the bald head as the man walked away.

"Shit," Charley said, staring straight ahead.

Owen merely looked down at his glass, and Richie grew even more depressed as he saw their images reflected dimly in the mottled glass of the mirror that backed the rows of whiskey bottles behind the bar. Breaking his eyes from that sorry tableau, he noticed a folded section of newspaper on the barstool next to him. He picked it up, unfolded it on the bar, and saw it was the sports section of the *Asheville Gazette*.

Charley glanced over and said sourly, "You won't see any headlines in there about us, old buddy. Not anymore. Those days are gone forever."

Richie, feeling down himself, was irritated at Charley, who as usual, was pushing it too far. He turned back to the paper and began to read as Hank Williams poured his heart out to the solitary couple on the dance floor.

He saw Koufax had won again, already had six victories even though it was very early in the season, figured he'd hit twenty for sure by September. The Dodgers led the Giants by two games, and the Yankees were one on top of Cleveland. That's your World Series right there, he thought, wondering how many strikeouts Koufax would end up with.

He studied the box scores, then glanced idly at the racing results, although they held no particular interest for him. The third at Pimlico read:

Exterminator:	6.20, 4.60, 3.10
Mark's Cross:	4.80, 3.40
Billy the Kid:	5.60

Richie's eyes riveted on Billy the Kid and the room seemed suddenly silent. Finally, he pulled his eyes away from the name and looked lower, stopping at the sixth race.

Bob's Fancy:	10.00, 6.20, 4.10
Wunderbar:	3.20, 2.80
Silent Sam:	3.60

Wunderbar held him like a magnet.

He skimmed the seventh race, went to the eighth. Pajama Tops had won, paying $9.20. The named burned itself into his brain.

He quickly reviewed the first two races, which he'd skipped before, finding Irish Lass and Harvey One, both also-rans.

Closing his eyes, he sat still.

"Headache, Richie?"

He shook his head, opened his eyes and regarded his friend. Owen was so quiet, so vulnerable. Richie worried about him. Charley had the balls, and Richie felt he himself would make it okay. But he feared for Owen.

"Just thinking," he responded. He went quiet again, then asked, "Owen, how much money do we have saved?"

Owen was their treasurer and kept track of their meager savings account at Southland Trust.

"Twelve hundred, eighty-six dollars," Owen answered, trying to make the sum sound significant.

Richie nodded as if it were. He thought of all the sweaty hours of odd summer jobs the sum represented, extra jobs that had been hard to find and even harder to fulfill within the framework of their commitments at St. Mary's. Backbreaking jobs often, three hours walking to put in two hours of work on occasion, but they'd been determined to build their stake. And after four years—all of twelve hundred, eighty-six dollars to start them on their way.

"Another one, boys?" Barney asked, coming up and wiping the counter with his apron again.

"Why not?" Charley answered as Richie and Owen nodded, too.

"Barney?"

The man looked back and came to the bar in front of Richie. The boy turned the paper toward him.

"How often do these horses run?"

Barney shrugged.

"Every ten, twelve days maybe. Why?"

Richie took a deep breath and said slowly, "Well, if I wanted to bet on one of these horses the next time out—how could I arrange it?"

The bartender threw his head back, gave a short laugh. "Jesus Christ!" he exclaimed. "Not even out of high school and already goin' for the big leagues. That fancy car sure went to your head." He chuckled.

"No, Barney," Richie persisted, intense now. "I'm serious. How do I bet on them? You know how, I'm sure you do."

Barney smiled and narrowed his eyes slightly, but his expression was open and friendly as he placed his hand on Richie's arm and said,

"Hey. Calm down, buddy. I can work it out for you, sure, but don't be so uptight about it, you know? Betting's okay, everybody does it—but don't look so damned desperate. You're way too young for that."

"I'm sorry, Barney." Richie relaxed, met the other's eyes. "It's just I've never done it before."

"Sure, sure. I understand. Anyway, what is it you want to do?"

Richie looked over and saw Owen's face held a touch of fear whereas Charley's eyes glistened almost wildly. He paused just a fraction of a second. "I want to bet on these horses the next time out. These five," he said, taking a pencil from his pocket and writing the names down rapidly on a napkin.

Barney looked at the list, said, "Sure, Richie. Sure. I'll arrange it. How much? Two bucks apiece?"

Richie could feel his heart pounding but tried to keep his voice level as he said, "Two hundred apiece, Barney."

The voice of Patty Page, which had seemed so loud in the bar only a moment before, failed to penetrate the silent vacuum in which the four of them were suddenly transfixed.

Richie finally expelled the rest of his breath, and Barney gave a low whistle. The other two were motionless, although Richie noted Owen's eyes had widened and Charley's had narrowed.

"Two hundred apiece, Richie?" The bartender's voice was soft, incredulous.

"Two hundred apiece, Barney." Richie's tone was firm now as, without turning his head, he raised his left hand to silence Owen before he could protest. "Can you arrange it?"

"Well, sure I can, sure, you know"—the man hesitated. "But it's gonna' have to be cash up front, Richie. You understand that."

It was not a question and Richie held the man's eyes and nodded.

CHAPTER 15

"Richie," Owen said repeatedly, as they drove to the tavern the following Wednesday. It was two days before graduation. "I don't like it. We worked so hard for that money. It's all we've got for our start."

"Yeah, Owen. We worked hard. And what have we got to show for it?" Charley's voice was gruff as he drove. "Twelve hundred and eighty-six dollars. Big deal."

"It's better than nothing."

"Not much.' Charley turned briefly to look at Owen and his eyes glistened with a nervous anticipation. "Listen, this is our chance, our shot. Right, Richie?"

Richie merely nodded, but was disturbed at the hint of desperation he'd felt in Charley's voice. It was so important to all of them, and he didn't want their hopes dashed again like Durham. But somehow he was sure it *was* their shot, as Charley said.

Their nervousness was so obvious Barney laughed when he saw them. He set down three shot glasses and filled them with a good bourbon.

"On the house, boys," he said and laughed again as they self-consciously toasted each other silently before downing the whiskey. They were relatively unfamiliar with the harsh taste, and Richie choked back a cough but managed to keep the liquid down. Owen's face got very red and Charley managed a brisk, "Whew!"

Barney hunched across the bar, eyes level at Richie. "Well?" he asked.

Richie reached into his pocket, took out a slip of paper and handed it to the man.

"Pajama Tops," Barney read. "Fifth at Pimlico tomorrow. Two hundred dollars to win." He looked up at Richie, who handed an envelope to him.

"Two hundred," Barney confirmed, counting out the twenties.

"What'll the odds be?" Charley asked.

Barney shrugged. "The paper says five to one, but who knows? Whatever he goes off at, that's what you'll get. If you win," he added. "We'll have the results tomorrow night. Stop in around the same time."

"Suppose we lose, Richie?" Owen asked on the way home. "Are you still going to bet on the others?"

"We'll see," Richie said. "We don't even know when they're racing again."

They'd already invested three dollars going over to the drugstore after school to buy the *Racing News* so they could see who would be running the following day. Pajama Tops had finally come up on Wednesday.

They tried to remain calm as they poured over the *Racing News* on Thursday, knowing Pajama Tops had already run by that time and wishing Pimlico was in North Carolina instead of Maryland. They were frustrated they'd have to wait until evening to get the results of the race.

Slowly, Richie ran his fingers down the list of Friday's entries, stopping at the second race. "Wunderbar!" he exclaimed softly. "He's the favorite, two to one."

Glancing lower, he pointed suddenly to the sixth race. "Billy the Kid," Charley said excitedly over his shoulder. "And he's listed at ten to one!"

Richie nodded, still looking. He placed his finger next to Irish Lass in the eighth. "Twenty to one," Charley whistled. "The long shot!"

"He was an also-ran last time, remember?" Owen stated.

"Three of our horses going tomorrow!" Charley couldn't contain himself. "At two to one we win four hundred dollars! Then two thousand on Billy the Kid if he stays at ten to one and with Irish Lass—we'll be rich!" Charley said it in a way that left no room for doubt.

Owen reminded him gently, "We don't even know if Pajama Tops won today."

Richie could see Owen was highly nervous, and he himself felt a vague nausea. Both picked at their dinner while Charley wolfed his down. As soon as they'd finished clearing the tables they were off.

"Well?" Charley exclaimed as they exploded into Barney 's. "Well? What happened?"

Barney turned from the couple he'd been serving and walked to the end of the bar where the boys stood. The look on his face gave them their answer before he reached them.

"We won!" Charley shouted, and the few patrons in the place turned to look at him as he jumped in the air. "We won, Richie!" he repeated, clapping his friend on the back and hugging Owen with his other arm.

Owen's face appeared drained and he didn't move until Barney finally gave an affirming nod. He signaled with his hand and they followed him into the back room where they crowded into what small space was not taken by the bill-laden desk with its rickety chair and the surrounding cases of liquor that were piled to the ceiling. The light from the swinging bulb glistened on Barney's sweat-tinged bald head.

"Here you go, boys," he said, taking a large roll of bills from his pocket. "He went off at four to one. One thousand and sixty dollars."

He handed the roll to Richie who felt it for just a moment before handing it to Owen to touch. Charley took his turn; his face was bright as he passed it back to Richie.

"That's quite a payoff," Barney said. "My man ain't used to that kind of action here in Mills River. Asheville, maybe, but that's a bundle for down here."

"Wait until tomorrow!" Charley said. "We'll really put him on his ass!"

Owen looked to Richie who nodded, took the bills, and counted out six hundred dollars.

"Here, Barney," he said, handing the man the money. "And here's our picks."

The man looked at the bills, then at the list. He walked over to his desk and picked up the *Racing News*.

"Irish Lass is twenty to one, Richie. And Billy the Kid is ten." He put down the paper and looked at Richie.

"Bet it, Barney," he said, and the man nodded.

"What about the rest?" Charley put in. "There's another four hundred here. We could put a hundred down on each!'

"For Christ's sake, Charley!" Owen was angry now, his dark eyes blazing uncharacteristically in his pale face. "We were lucky. We won—and that's great. But let's not blow it all!"

Charley looked at Owen with ill-concealed disgust, then turned to Richie.

"Well?" he challenged.

"Let it stand, Barney," Richie said, turning away.

* * *

Friday dawned bright and glorious, the sun rising slowly above the pines and glistening on the dew as they sat on the hill and looked unseeing to the distance.

They'd been out of their beds at five but awake hours earlier. Charley hadn't slept at all, the other two barely.

It was June 5. The most exciting day of their lives.

Graduation day. They'd looked forward to it for so many years, the opening of the gate to freedom from St. Mary's and the chance to get on with their lives, despite whatever varied doubts they might have.

It was hard for Richie to believe that after all these years the event seemed hardly noteworthy. He wanted the ceremony to be over; he wanted it to be evening so they could go to Barney's. Looking over at his friends, he knew they shared his feelings. Charley's face was aglow with uncontained excitement, and Owen's expression was far away and preoccupied.

They had tentatively planned on leaving sometime during the following week to head out West, probably Colorado. Charley kept opting for Las Vegas—"Just one quick spree," he implored—but the other two nixed that suggestion. Now, however, they'd be leaving earlier, although they hadn't discussed it. They hadn't had to. The outcome of their appointment at Barney's would mark a point of no return; everything—perhaps their very lives—depended on what happened that day at Pimlico.

So they spent the day trapped in their own private hourglasses. The ceremony dragged and when they heard their names called each rose and accepted his diploma with a perfunctory nod. Richie was president of the class, a bright student in addition to his athletic prowess, but his speech that day was flat and uninspired. He was glad he'd brought his notes even though he'd memorized the text weeks before.

It was eight o'clock when they finally got to Barney's, and the parking lot was already crowded because it was Friday night. So giddy were they in their nervousness that the broken neon sign atop the tavern actually seemed inviting above the dusty pickup trucks as the sweater-clad boys walked across the gravel.

"I gotta pee again," Charley said as they approached the door, and the others laughed because they knew what he meant.

The bar was crowded. It was a moment before they caught Barney's eye, and his look when they did told them nothing.

"Shit," Owen said under his breath, and Richie understood only then the boy was as hooked as he and Charley.

Barney spoke quickly to the other bartender and motioned them toward the back room, wiping his hands on a towel as he made his way behind the bar.

His eyes were flat and his face was all business as he closed the door behind him and faced them under the harsh glow of the naked light bulb.

"Well?" Richie finally managed as Barney's stare continued. "How'd we do?"

Barney paused a few moments longer before he said, "You won."

"We won!" Owen and Charley said it in unison, but it was more a question than an exclamation, the two of them obviously unable to accept the pronouncement unequivocally.

"All three?" Owen got out after a moment.

"All three." Barney's voice was quiet and he never took his eyes from Richie, who'd said nothing.

"How much, Barney?" this from Charley.

There was another pause and the man's look never wavered from Richie before he said flatly, "Seventy-eight hundred dollars. Six forty back on Wunderbar, nineteen sixty on Bill the Kid, and fifty-two hundred on Irish Lass."

"Seventy-eight hundred." Owen's voice was a whisper. With what they had left in the bank, they had over nine thousand dollars!

Barney stood looking at them, eyes giving nothing, and Richie knew there was something wrong.

"The money, Barney. Where is it?" he asked finally.

"Here," the man said, reaching under his apron and extending an envelope. Richie took it, grinned broadly as he felt the weight, and saw Barney's eyes narrow slightly as he did so.

"Count it," the tavern owner said. Richie detected anger in the voice, looked up sharply.

"But it's the bookie's, Barney," he offered, knowing even as he said it he was mistaken. Oh, Jesus!

"Just count it," the man commanded, and Richie broke his eyes away from the cold narrow slits that bored into him. He opened the envelope and removed the thick wad of hundred-dollar bills.

"Holy shit!" Charley exclaimed when he saw the bills.

"Just count," Richie said quietly, dividing the pile into thirds.

"Twenty-four hundred," Charley said after a moment. "Twenty-nine here," Richie said, looking to Owen.

"Twenty-five. That totals seventy-eight. Hundred," he added.

Richie took the piles back, put them in the envelope, and handed it to Owen.

"Barney," he began, but his voice trailed off.

Barney said nothing.

"What about tomorrow, Richie?" Charley broke in. "Harry One is running. Aren't we going to—"

Barney's head shifted quickly and his glance knifed through Charley.

"Well, I mean," Charley started to push on lamely, but Richie stopped him.

"No more, Charley. This is it." He turned to Barney, met the man's gaze again.

"Thank you, Barney," he said quietly, understanding now the man's loss and uncomfortable suddenly in his presence.

The man nodded almost imperceptibly and opened the door without a word. Charley and Owen filed out but Richie suddenly found his way blocked as Barney thrust his powerful arm across the doorway at chest height.

The bald head was very close and the proximity was distinctly menacing as the man said quietly, "How'd you do it, Richie?"

Richie looked into the tavern owner's eyes for a last time, saw a threat there, too, but something else as well. Fear—or perhaps respect? He wasn't sure.

He thought a moment on the man's question, then slowly shook his head. "I don't know, Barney," he said truthfully.

The arm was withdrawn slowly and he walked out the door.

"Don't come back, Richie," he heard softly behind him. "Ever."

* * *

"Whooee!" Charley yelled again, throwing his head back and sending his voice off into the wind. The top was down and the night air brushed their faces as they sped down the back road. Above them, the full moon seemed especially bright, in concert with their exuberance.

"Slow down, Charley," Owen cautioned, but he was laughing. "Don't get us killed now we're finally rich."

"Hey, Richie, whadaya say! How 'bout that?" Charley called back to his friend who remained quiet in the back seat. "Seventy-eight hundred! I'm proud of you, buddy. But you know," he said seriously, "we really should have gone on Harry One tomorrow."

"It doesn't matter," Richie said quietly, the wind taking his words.

"What'd you say?" Charley came back.

"I said, 'It doesn't matter'," Richie repeated loudly.

"Doesn't matter? That damn horse will go off at ten, fifteen to one. And you're saying it doesn't matter?"

"No, Charley, it doesn't," he repeated, shouting almost angrily.

Owen turned at the sharp tone and looked reflectively back at Richie.

He looks older, Owen thought in sudden surprise.

"Well, what the hell then," Charley rejoined, eyes on the road. "Let's get on our way tonight. Nothing to keep us here now."

"The bank doesn't open 'til Monday," Owen reminded him.

"Screw the bank. We can always send for that money, and we sure don't need it now. By Monday we can be half way across the country."

Owen looked back to Richie who nodded. "He's right." Richie smiled for the first time since they'd left Barney's, said, "Hell, Owen, let's get goin'." His smile broadened into a wide grin as he finally let himself go and yelled, "Whooee!" himself.

Charley laughed and tooted the horn, then slowed down a moment later as he made the turn off to St. Mary's.

"We should stay 'til tomorrow, though," Richie said as they moved up the dirt road. "To say our goodbyes."

"Goodbyes? To who? Old Man Winter?" Charley mocked.

"To Anderson at least, if nobody else."

Charley sobered and nodded after a moment.

"We'll pack tonight then and leave first thing tomorrow. Agreed?"

"Fine with me. Owen?"

Owen hesitated a moment, then grinned. "Are you kiddin'? I'm just as happy to be out of this fucking place as anybody! Whooee!" he yelled and Charley reached over to punch his arm.

"Goddamn," Charley exclaimed, hitting the horn in three short bursts. "We are going to be the three biggest livers you ever did see. Can't you see us now, strutting in Vegas—we got to hit that first now. We'll win a bundle! Then Hawaii—"

"Charley—Charley, stop the car," Richie commanded.

"What the hell—"

"I said stop the car, Charley."

"Goddamn," Charley grumbled, but he pulled to the side of the narrow dirt road. "Yeah?" he asked querulously after he'd killed the motor with a twist of the key.

"It's not going to be the way you said, Charley. We're going away—but not like that."

"Not like that?" Charley turned, arm on the back of his seat as he faced Richie. "What do you mean not like that?" he repeated, amazement frank in his voice.

"Just what I said. Not like that. And I think we have to get it straight right now. About how it's going to be."

"And how *is* it going to be?" Charley asked sarcastically. "For Christ's sake, Richie, we've never had anything, *any*thing, and now all of a sudden we can own the world, and you—"

"That's right, Charley. That's it exactly. But not that way."

"What way, then?" This from Owen, who had sat silent beside Charley during the argument. The cascading moonlight cast his narrow face in long shadows and glanced highlights off his straight black hair.

"I've been thinking about it—a lot," Richie began, and his voice was firm and earnest. "And I have a plan."

"Okay." Charley was calmer now, interested. "Shoot."

"Well," Richie began, improvising, for he really hadn't thought it out that well. He had only a vague idea of what he wanted to do. "Well," he said, "first we have to agree on our long-range goals." He paused significantly. "And I'll tell you flat out I intend to use this 'power', or whatever it is I have, to help people. As many as I can and as best I can." The simplistic fantasies of his childhood nights flooded back in that moment—stop war, cure disease—and Richie repressed a private smile for the child still in him.

"Well, sure, Richie," Charley agreed. "But what about us? Don't we deserve anything?"

"Of course we do, Charley," Richie reassured him. "And we'll have everything we need—and more. But we'll do it in a way that helps us achieve our other goals."

"Like how?" Charley asked, suspicion in the words as he faced the rangy boy whose soft dark hair blew gently in the night breeze that washed the rear seat of the open car.

"Well, the main thing is, we keep a low profile—a very low profile, at least for a long, long time." *That* was clear enough to Richie now. "Because the important thing is nobody else knows I have the power. What do you think would have happened at Barney's tonight if he really understood?"

"That makes sense," Owen put in, and Charley grudgingly nodded agreement.

"The first thing is college. We'll each specialize in something so we have a professional career that will help—"

"Richie." Charley's tone was flat as he cut the other off. "Richie," he said, "I'm not going to college."

"Charley, listen to—"

"Bullshit! Listen to nothing! Goddamn it, Richie, we've spent our lives with nothing. Nothing!" The voice rose in anger. "Now we've got the world at our feet—broads, cars, clothes—anything we want. Right now! And you want to wait through college—and careers? Not me, Richie," he shook his head vehemently. "I want mine now."

"Charley—" he began tentatively. The truth of the matter was he'd had those same thoughts himself. Even now he felt the exhilarating lure of "Why not?" although he was determined to overcome it. "Charley," he went on, "we can't just—"

"I mean it, Richie—now. You go off and do whatever is it you want to. And you, Owen—" he looked to the other boy.

Owen hesitated a moment, then nodded. "I'm with Richie."

"Good." Charley spat the word. "You two do whatever you want. Just give me my share of the money now, and I'll do what I damn well please with it!"

"And how about the future, Charley? We'll give you your share, sure, but that's not enough to get you far."

"It's enough for now. And there'll be plenty more later."

"How, Charley?" Richie's tone was such that Owen felt a sudden apprehension that was immediately confirmed by Charley's broad grin flashing electric-white in the moonglow.

"Why that's easy, Richie," Charley said. "I've been thinking, too. Just now. I've got Harry One to bet on tomorrow, at maybe fifteen to one. And after that, there'll be more."

"From where, Charley?" The question came quietly.

"Why, from you, Richie." The words were slow and saccharin sweet. "All you have to do, every once in a while, is give me the names of some winners. That's all you have to do. That's not asking much, is it? For an old friend?"

"And if I don't?"

"If you don't—come on, Richie," Charley's voice changed suddenly, the singsong sarcastic cadence vanishing as the words came now in angry exasperation. "For Christ's sake, don't make it like I'm threatening you. You're my best friend—both of you," he said, turning to include Owen. "There's nothing I want to do more than stick with you guys. You know that. You think I want to split?" He shook his head, then caught Richie's eyes directly.

"It's just that I can't do it your way—and you meant what you said, didn't you?"

Richie nodded a slow confirmation.

Charley shrugged in resignation, shook his head again, and rubbed his fingers along his broadened nose at the point where it had once been broken. There was a plea in his voice as he continued. "Richie, I'd never do anything to hurt you—either of you. But college, careers— that's not for me. Hell—the truth is, I was lucky to get through Mills River. You know that." He shook his head dejectedly. "Nope. That's not for me. I can't swing it. I'll go out West with you, but then I'll take my share and split. Okay?"

Richie nodded, and Charley brightened suddenly. "Hey, you guys!" he exclaimed. "It doesn't have to be the end of the world, you know. I'll catch up with you—a couple years, maybe, but I'll be there. Just not now," he ended it, sobering again. "But you got to help me, Richie— you owe me that."

"Sure, Charley," Richie said as positively as he could manage. "Well," he added with a deep sigh, looking to Owen, "we'd better be going if we're packing tonight."

Charley kept his eyes on Richie's face a moment longer, then turned and started the car. The headlights picked up motes of dust as they continued on to St. Mary's.

* * *

Richie threw the last of his shirts on top of his battered valise. He looked once more out the cracked window with its torn and limp shade and turned to look at Owen.

The other boy stood by his bed, staring down at his packed and meager belongings that rested on the faded khaki blanket that matched Richie's own.

"That's it," Owen said. "Not a helluva lot, is there?"

"Don't worry, Owen. I mean it. You don't have to worry—ever again."

Owen met his eyes. "Well," he began, turning to the bureau atop which he'd placed the packet of money—their stake.

The bureau that now lay empty.

The bureau against which Charley had been leaning only a moment ago, just before he left the room.

Owen turned back quickly to Richie, but before he could speak the sound of a car starting could be heard from the driveway below.

131

CHAPTER 16

"Owen—stop talking about the money! And the car." Richie knew his exasperation with Owen was misplaced and stemmed from his seething anger at Charley. He repeated, more soothingly now, "Don't worry. About any of that."

They were seated on their beds, as they had been for those long moments since they'd heard the car squeal off down the road, long moments during which Owen had again and again bemoaned their loss. The gangly boy sat hunched forward, elbows on knees and hands supporting his head as he stared at the paint-flaked wall where the mottled mirror hung.

He doesn't understand, Richie said to himself. He really doesn't understand.

But Charley does, he reminded himself.

And that was where the danger lay.

"Owen—we're not stuck. We can always make money. Believe me, that's not our problem. That will never be our problem."

Owen nodded and said, "Okay, Richie. That'll never be our problem. But if you believe that, what are you so agitated—so worried about—yourself? That Charley left? If he could do that to us then the hell with him! We're better off without him."

"That's not it, Owen. I agree. I'm as pissed at Charley as you are. I'd strangle him right now if I could get my hands on him, but that's not what worries me. What worries me is he's out there—he knows."

A dawning grew on Owen's face, and he looked at Richie now with a mixture of both fear and wonder. "You mean he knows you really *can* predict the future," he whispered as full understanding came to him.

"That's right, Owen. He knows. And you heard him. You heard what he said on the road. He threatened me. And you saw what he just did.

"We can't just let him go, not like that," he went on. "We'll never know. He'll always be out there, and sometime, when we least expect it....." Richie trailed off. Owen nodded.

"Where will he go, though?" Owen asked. "Can you foretell that, great leader?"

Richie chose to ignore Owen's sarcasm as he responded seriously, "No, Owen, I can't. But I can make a damn good guess."

* * *

The Tropicana Casino was crowded, as all the others had been. Richie thought the stifling heat of the Las Vegas summer would have discouraged visitors, but the city was packed.

There were throngs of people everywhere, especially in the casinos. Under bright, flashing lights, customers vied for seats at blackjack and roulette tables. Boisterous groups crowded the crap tables where their shouts carried clearly above the high decibel level of the room. Everything seemed to be in constant motion, a subtle, seductive churning of clusters of bodies. Long-legged, briefly clad cocktail waitresses glided like magic spiders from table to table in exaggerated walks, trays held high above their heads.

Richie and Owen had left St. Mary's the same night Charley had deserted them. They'd written farewell notes saying the three of them were "off to make our way." Carrying their bags, they walked the ten miles to Asheville where they paid for a room at a cheap hotel from the remaining four hundred dollars of their winnings Owen still had in his possession.

The next morning they bought bus tickets for Las Vegas. And now, four tired days later, they had arrived in the glittering desert city.

This was the eighth casino they had searched in the six hours since their arrival. The eighth and last—the Tropicana, at the bottom of the gambling capital's "strip."

133

"I don't see—" Richie, standing at Owen's elbow, began, but he stopped abruptly as he became aware of the other's almost frozen stance. Following Owen's gaze, Richie looked to the farthest blackjack table.

There, at the first seat, his profile to them, sat Charley. He wore a lightweight sportcoat that, although it struck Richie as ridiculously loud, was obviously expensive, as was the open-necked silk shirt beneath it. Next to him, her arm on his shoulder, stood a voluptuous blonde in a low-cut black dress. The brittle-featured woman's alert eyes roamed the room as Charley kept his gaze riveted to the table.

Richie stood a moment, then walked nearer the table where he stopped to watch.

Charley's face was tense as he watched the dealer turn a card for him. He grimaced immediately when he saw it, hit his fist in ill-controlled anger against the leather cushion that edged the table where he sat as the dealer reached out and swept away the stack of chips in the box before him. Charley reached over, picked up a glass at his side, and took a long swallow. Then he took a cigarette from his pocket and lit it. Richie knew Charley smoked on occasion, as he himself did, but the overflowing ashtray on the table gave evidence of far more than that.

The dealer seemed to be waiting for Charley and, after a brief hesitation, the latter pushed an entire stack of chips—his last, Richie noted—into the box before him.

The swarthy man with the green eye shade proceeded with the deal, quickly flipping cards to each of the six seated players. He completed the cycle and, with deliberation, finally peeked at his own hole card. He raised his head, seemed to look directly at Charley, and slowly turned his card.

A groan came from the table, over which Richie could hear the dealer say "blackjack" before he quickly raked in the players' chips.

Charley stood slowly. He seemed oblivious to the girl next to him whose hand fell from his shoulder. But, as he reached into his pants pocket, he turned and gave her a sudden, confident grin she returned brightly. He removed a small wad of bills and without hesitation peeled off five. Even from that distance, Richie could tell they were hundreds.

Charley put the money on the table. He spoke to the dealer, who turned his head and called "money plays" to some unseen authority and began to deal the cards.

Charley stood as the cards went around, then looked at his own cards with the same tense expression he'd had earlier. The cocky grin was gone now, as quickly as it had come, molded into lines of grim concentration that etched his face. He hesitated, then made a quick motion with his hand and the dealer turned a card for him.

Charley seemed frozen as the card fell, and the dealer, too, appeared caught up in the drama as he stood still and looked at the jack that lay exposed on the table. The man reached out, picked up the bills in front of Charley, tapped them twice, and held them up before sliding them into a slot in the table.

Charley stood and turned angrily from the table. The girl at his side seemed about to say something, looked at his face, shrugged indifferently, and walked off. Charley's eyes lingered on her briefly before he wrenched them away, and raised his head with a glare to face the room behind him.

His eyes locked with Richie's. Neither of them moved.

Something changed in Charley's face, a softening that surprised Richie and made him wary. But the hard set of Charley's jaw was suddenly gone and he took a deep breath and came forward. Stopping a pace in front of Richie, Charley seemed about to extend his hand, thought better of it as the other stood stock still as he had throughout, and offered instead a simple, "Hey, Richie."

"Charley," Richie said between clenched teeth. His eyes bored into Charley's, and it was only through the greatest effort he could restrain himself from striking out at the other boy. Especially when Charley suddenly grinned that easy grin of his and tapped Richie lightly on the arm.

"How's it goin'?" Charley asked breezily.

"Fine." Richie could barely get the word out.

Charley motioned with his head toward the doorway. "Let's get outta here. We've got some catching up to do."

Richie forced a nod. After all, wasn't that why he'd come? To talk to Charley, painful as that would be?

Charley grinned again, then seemed to notice for the first time that Owen stood a few paces to the side. He acknowledged the other boy now with a casual, "Hey, Owen," turned and threaded his way through the crowded casino toward the yawning glass-door entrance to the hotel.

Richie and Owen followed in silence.

135

Once outside, Charley gave a ticket to the doorman. When the yellow Mercury pulled up to the curb the top was down and a husky, well-tanned blonde boy about their own age leaped out gracefully and raced around to open the passenger's door for them.

Richie noted with annoyance Charley's easy air as he reached into his pocket, removed his thin wad of bills, and extracted a dollar, which he casually handed to the appreciative attendant.

Big shot, Richie thought to himself as he climbed in to sit beside Charley. Fucking big shot.

Owen sat in back.

Charley pulled out of the curving driveway lined with shining cars, turned away from the strip and drove out toward the desert. The glittering lights were quickly behind them, and in the near distance rising mountains could be seen under a bright moon.

The night air was hot, but its breeze was welcome as they sped in silence along the dark, deserted road in the open convertible.

The mountains loomed closer, etched clearly in the velvet desert night beneath a sprinkle of stars.

Richie closed his eyes and leaned his head back against the leather seat.

Their car. The sleek convertible they'd won only months earlier in the raffle, the vehicle of which they'd been so proud. The lucky talisman that had seemed to presage all sorts of bright and wonderful things for their future. Richie tried to recapture those good feelings as, eyes closed, he sat beside Charley and felt the night breeze rush by.

He remembered the day of the drawing; he could feel even now a thrill of excitement as he pictured the photo that had been run in the *Mills River Gazette*. The three of them grinning widely at the camera as they stood beside this very car.

The photo was clear in Richie's mind. He could see it on the bottom right of the newspaper's front page. He held the image.

Suddenly Charley was speaking, but Richie was hardly aware of that as his mind froze and focused on the news page he *now* saw. It no longer contained a picture of the car but rather a picture of himself.

Beneath the terrible headline.

"...sorry, Richie," he heard the words as from some dark tunnel. "Really sorry." Charley had stopped the car and was speaking to him.

With great effort, Richie opened his eyes and let the shattering image in his mind disappear.

Charley was turned to him, his arm resting on the top of his seat, dark eyes like coals as they searched Richie's through the dim light cast by the dashboard.

"I couldn't help it, Richie. You got to understand that. I cursed myself the whole drive out here. I wanted to turn back a thousand times, but I didn't know what I'd say. I asked myself, 'How the hell could you do that to your best friends—your only friends?'

"I said that over and over, Richie, because it's true. You two guys are my only friends—the only people I've got in the world."

Richie could see Charley's eyes now, noted vaguely they were moist as they looked at him and beseeched understanding.

And Richie might have spoken, might have in fact bestowed that unwarranted forgiveness, had not the terrible vision so paralyzed his mind.

So he held Charley's gaze, heart pounding, not in silence but rather unable to speak.

"Richie," Charley went on, misunderstanding, "c'mon Richie." He was pleading now and a touch of hysteria tainted his words. "Richie— you were right. We should stick together. We gotta stick together. And Richie—I'll do anything you want—anything you say. Just take me with you.

"Please, Richie." Charley's voice rose higher as the other maintained his silence. "Please! I know I come off like a big shot, like I'm not afraid of anything, but the truth is, I am. I am! Just like Owen said that day, down at the creek, about the army.

"Well I'm scared, too, Richie. I admit it. I'm scared of the future, scared of what's going to happen to me. And I'm broke now, Richie— broke! I lost it all, Richie." Charley was openly crying now as he reached out to touch Richie's arm. "I lost it all!

"I'm scared. You got to forgive me, Richie. You got to take me with you. You can trust me, Richie. I'll never hurt you again, never cross you again. I'll do anything you say, Richie. But you got to take me along. You got to take care of me. I know you can. *You* know you can. It's nothing for you. But for me...." Charley trailed off and the last of his words drifted away in the night air.

Charley had parked on the shoulder of the road beside the first of the desert cliffs. He had turned the motor off but had left on the parking lights, and in the dim glow of the lighted dashboard they faced each other. Richie was only peripherally aware Owen sat witness in the back seat.

Charley's sweat-drenched face was distorted, his eyes wild as he waited for Richie's reply. The boy—his friend, if he was still or could ever again be that—believed his fate rested in Richie's hands, that Richie could make things right for all of them.

Forever.

The deep irony of that pierced Richie's shock, and his lips tightened.

"I'm going to die, Charley," he said. "I'm going to die soon. Right here in Nevada. What do you think of that?"

The words hung, and Richie took a perverse pleasure in the widening of Charley's already distended eyes.

"Where's your meal ticket now, Charley?" The words, the anger—the fear—spilled out of Richie as he faced the other boy aggressively. "Huh, Charley—tell me that. Where's your meal ticket now?" Richie was aware his voice had risen, but he didn't care as he yelled the words across at Charley.

"Richie." Owen's voice, sharp with concern but rational nonetheless, cut through from behind. "Richie—what are you talking about? What are you saying?"

Richie turned slowly and looked at Owen's anxious face. He loved Owen and wanted to protect him, but he knew now he never would. He would never do any of the things he'd planned. He felt a great, sudden surge of remorse that overrode even his desperate fear, and said, "It's true, Owen. I'm going to die."

His voice was hardly more than a croak, but he pushed himself. He felt an urgency to continue speaking, to say it all as if the telling of it would change what he knew was to come. "I'm going to die, Owen. Here. Like I just told Charley. I saw it in my mind, just now. In the paper, in the *Gazette,* at the bottom of the front page. Just where the car was," he put in, as if that were relevant. "Just there—an article that said, 'Former Cage Star Dies in Nevada'.

"And my picture was underneath."

Richie stopped, and it was a moment before Owen could whisper, "Jesus!"

Richie turned to Charley, all the anger gone now, everything, even his fear drained from him in that moment, as he thought of the impending loss they were all to incur. So many things, he thought to himself, and the idea brought tears to his eyes. He looked at Charley, fondly now. Charley, who was still wearing that ridiculous sportcoat despite the oppressive heat. Richie remembered the good days and wished things had turned out differently. He wished they could yet turn out differently, but wondered how that could be now. He felt a sudden rush of feeling, a need for Charley—the old Charley—to help him now. Richie reached his hand down to touch his friend who sat frozen like stone.

"Charley," he managed, but the other sat stiff, only his eyes alive, wilder than they had ever been as they glittered at Richie.

"Charley," Richie repeated, but the other didn't seem to hear him. Charley cut him off with a voice so intense Richie was shaken from his deep malaise.

"No, Richie. No! You can't die!" Charley almost screamed the words, and in a sudden move gripped Richie's shoulders in anger. "You can't die, Richie. You can't!" he repeated, shaking the other. "I need you! What the hell will I do? What'll happen to me? You *can't* go, Richie."

Richie felt a wave of revulsion. He forced down the urge to place his hands at the other's throat. Then he saw the change in Charley's eyes, the subtle change from semi-madness to brittle, animal cunning. Too late he realized Charley had stopped shaking him. Charley had removed a small gun from his jacket and held it tight in his hand. It was leveled directly at Richie.

In the rear, Owen made a quick movement, but Charley motioned with his head in such a way the other sat back.

The gun looked obscene in Charley's hand, but somehow Richie was not really surprised. Yes, Charley would have gotten a gun, along with the flashy clothes. There always had been that potential lurking in Charley, Richie admitted to himself.

"Now, Richie," Charley said in an overly calm voice and a smile seemed to touch his crazed features. "Now, Richie, you know you're not going to die," he reasoned, as if with a child. "No, you're not, Richie—you just said that. Right?"

139

Charley didn't wait for a reply and Richie realized he was essentially speaking to himself. "No, Richie. You just said that. To fool me. To get even with me. So you can leave me here—out here—" Charley indicated the silent desert, "—stuck while you go on your merry way.

"Oh no, Richie," Charley laughed. "I'm not falling for that. Not Charley. No, sir. You didn't think I'd believe that one, did you?"

But as Richie searched Charley's eyes, he realized that on some level the other did believe it, despite the hysterical words, and Richie felt a rise of sharp panic. He thought of the article, the headline that had burned in his mind, and looked at the steady gun.

Was *this* how it would be? he thought suddenly.

Here, in the car—from a Charley with a sly smile and crazy eyes?

"No, Richie, you couldn't fool me," Charley was going on. "You're going to leave me. Okay. Do it. Do it, Richie!" Anger sparked in Charley's voice, but he reverted quickly to his smoother, cunning tone. "Do it," he hissed. "But first, Richie, you're going to tell me things. Tell me what's going to happen. Things that can help me, things I can score on. Yeah, Richie—"

But Charley never finished the sentence. Richie jerked his knee up sharply, felt the firm contact with Charley's forearm, and heard the gun go off. He thought that was accidental but knew nevertheless the bullet flew somewhere in the air above his head. He didn't give himself time to think about it, instead vaulting over the door. He was lucky the top was down but he didn't have time to dwell on that either. Instead, he hit the ground running and fought his panic down as he raced for the shadow of the rocks ahead.

In the car, Owen, who had grabbed at Charley's arm during the swift and unexpected exchange, now sat still in the rear seat of the car and looked at the barrel of the gun, now pointed at him.

* * *

Richie reached the shelter of a large boulder and knelt behind it. His breath was coming in quick gasps he was sure could be heard yards away.

Calm down, he ordered himself angrily. Calm down! he commanded, and somehow he managed to bring his breathing under control. But he was still shaking, the terrifying implications of the situation crowding his mind. His vision, the terrible thing he'd seen in the paper. Charley's gun.

The black, deserted wasteland in which he crouched hidden behind some boulder.

Yes—it would be now, here, in this desert. Richie Peters dead, here in Nevada, as the headline had said.

An anger born of impotence rose like bile in his throat as the weight of premonition pressed him. He'd fight. Oh Lord, would he fight! He didn't care if it was written or not. He wasn't some horse slated to win. He was Richie Peters, the boy with the vision, the boy with the power, and he'd fight to stay alive no matter what the paper had forecast.

He thought of Owen, still in the car, and wondered what was happening to him. He wrestled with the thought of going back to help his friend. He had almost gained the courage to attempt that when he heard a muffled cry and a low curse he knew was uttered by Charley.

He heard the car door open and footsteps come across the gravel that shouldered the road, and he pressed himself tight against the shelter of the boulder.

The sound of the footsteps disappeared.

Charley was on the sand now, coming toward the rocks.

Coming for him.

Part of Richie wanted to stay and wait for Charley. To reason with him. Charley was panicked, Richie knew. He was out of control, frightened and shaken—terrified—beyond anything he'd ever anticipated. He'd admitted it in the car.

Richie felt he could reason with him. There was no murder in Charley, he told himself. Despite the gun. That was just bravado, part of the tough-guy image Charley found it necessary to project. But there was no *murder* there. Certainly not against himself.

The gun had gone off accidentally. Richie was certain of that.

But what had that cry meant? What had happened to Owen?

And the article: The thing that had sprung clear in his mind?

Former Cage Star Dies in Nevada!

With his picture below!

The panic rose again, bubbling inside him, churning to break loose, to explode, to propel him into some screaming rush—

Where? He forced himself to think.

Where?

From the article?

Or perhaps—and this thought was the worst of all—*to* the article?

The questions swirled, but Richie forced them away. He took deep, silent breaths and finally, miraculously, felt himself become calmer.

When the pounding that had filled his eardrums receded, he listened, and in the silence of the desert night he heard a pebble move scant yards away, on the far side of the boulder that sheltered him.

Charley was coming.

He would fight for his life, Richie vowed again. Whatever the paper said.

Another pebble scattered, closer yet, and Richie rose quietly. The boulder still blocked him from view, and he inched back cautiously to the wall of rock behind him.

"Richie—" Charley's voice came softly, but with the same mad cunning of before. Lord, if he's hurt Owen, Richie thought, but cut that off quickly. He couldn't concern himself with that now; he couldn't be distracted by anything in what he was now certain would be a test of his ability to survive.

"Richie," the insidious whisper came again. "Come on out. I only want to talk. It's just me, Richie. Charley."

A part of him yearned to go. A part of him wanted that more than anything, to talk to Charley, reason with him, help him. He couldn't believe Charley wished him harm, despite the other's state. But the article—

Richie felt the rocks at his back, a clumped wall he realized was a cliff of some kind, and he reached up his arms on either side. To his right, away from the boulder's edge—away from the place Charley would come—he felt a narrow ledge. It was perhaps four feet from the ground, deep enough for him to stand on.

"Richie," the voice came again, and as it did Richie turned, placed his hands on the ledge, and hoisted himself up. His knees landed on the rocks, and some sharp corner cut him so painfully he almost cried out.

But he kept his control. He hadn't made a sound. He had managed to get to the ledge in utter silence, and he cautiously rose to his feet.

He had to move quickly. He had gotten a jump, but Charley would be just below him in a moment. Speed was the thing now, not caution, he realized instinctively, and in the darkness he reached up in hope of another hold.

It was there! A deep niche just above his head, a firm hand-hold he gripped. Without stopping to consider where it might lead, he leaped up toward it, kicking out and scraping his body against the cliff face. He was vaguely aware of the clatter of stones, but he didn't care as he scrambled up over the edge and rolled onto his side. His body was pressed tight to the wall of rock at his back.

The ledge was perhaps two feet wide, but it was shrouded in darkness, and he knew he could not be seen from Charley's vantage. But he could hear the other breathing. Charley's head was a mere four feet below, he estimated, and he wedged himself back tighter still.

And waited.

Moments passed, how many he didn't know, but at some point he could no longer hear Charley's breathing.

Perhaps he had walked away, so quietly Richie hadn't heard him.

But why would Charley walk away? Richie knew he was trapped, wedged on a narrow ledge against the cliff face. Suddenly, he realized Charley didn't know that. For all Charley knew, Richie might be anywhere above in the darkness.

Perhaps that's what Charley had reasoned, he thought. If so, maybe he'd gone around and tried to find some other way up himself.

In which case Richie should scramble down and make for the car.

But if he was wrong—if Charley were down there waiting, not beneath him perhaps, but beyond the boulder or by the car—

Yes, that's where Charley would be, Richie decided. Owen was still there, and that would finally bring Richie down.

That's how Charley would think, Richie knew, and he'd be right.

Except Richie wouldn't come from behind the boulder. No, he'd get up the cliff somehow and find some other way down, some way that would bring him around, some way that—

He was on his feet then, already up and moving, pressed close against the cliff and reaching upward for yet another hold. He found one, hoisted himself easily this time, and realized the cliff angle was receding, leveling out to a steep but negotiable embankment. Richie moved higher. He crawled on his stomach, for once on this slope he found himself exposed in the moonlight. There were no trees, and the shadows cast by scattered rocks and boulders formed a silent and eerie landscape in which a single bush crouched ahead like some waiting supplicant.

He stopped every few feet, listened—and heard nothing in the desert silence.

He turned cautiously toward the road, but from where he lay he could not see the car. He had to get to some higher vantage point. He looked to his left and saw the cliff face rising sharply again, perhaps another twenty feet. He would be able to see the road from the top.

Inching his way over, Richie reached the base of the cliff and rolled into the shadows. Shielded, he rose and began to climb. It took perhaps five minutes for him to reach the top. When he did, he came up in a semi-crouch and could indeed see the car some fifty feet below, etched clearly in the bright moonlight.

Was someone moving in the car? He could see someone moving, and it was as he crept closer and strained his eyes that he heard the footsteps come quickly slithering from behind.

* * *

Owen tried to raise himself but couldn't and fell back again. His head was wracked by a blinding sheet of pain, and he wanted only to succumb again to the sweet blackness.

But he couldn't let himself.

Richie was out there somewhere.

And Charley.

That knowledge was clear even through the pain, and Owen willed himself not to black out again.

Charley, he thought as he forced his eyes open, only to close them involuntarily as a sharper pain struck.

Charley.

He remembered being mesmerized by Charley's wild, bright eyes as they'd locked with his across the black barrel of the gun.

He wouldn't use it, Owen had thought.

He can't. Not Charley. Not against me.

But the eyes had held him in check as Charley seemed to consider, and suddenly Owen had believed he would use it.

But whatever had been there, lurking in Charley's mind, had somehow receded as their eyes held, and the last thing Owen remembered was the swift and unexpected rise of the weapon and the violent downswing that brushed aside his upthrust arm and exploded against his skull.

How long ago that had been Owen didn't know, but he pushed himself upward now into a seated position. He rested a moment before trying to open his eyes again. The pain was back instantaneously, as brilliant as before, but he fought to keep his eyes open and somehow succeeded.

It was only when the pain began to recede he could concentrate on focusing. When he did, he looked up, and there far above him, on the edge of the cliff—there, etched against the velvet desert sky, he saw some phantom nightmare being played out.

Two figures, drenched in silver moonglow, struggled. Arms raised, hands entwined, they seemed to twist and turn in some sinuous, exaggerated, slow motion dance.

The figures were like cardboard silhouettes as Owen tried to focus through blurry eyes.

His vision cleared just as the gunshot rang, the noise of it reverberating from the rocks. It was an echoing accompaniment to the body that seemed to float down from the heavens, the body that seemed as if it would land right on Owen as it accelerated quickly, more quickly than anything he had ever seen, blocking out the night sky as it closed on him.

Oh my God, he thought, closing his eyes and covering his head with his arms to protect himself.

Oh my God—Richie! Just as he said! Owen thought as the body struck just in front of him, landing on the hood of the car with a thudding sound more awful than anything Owen had ever heard.

* * *

In the dim parking lights of the car, they stood looking down at the body. It appeared almost serene as it lay on its back, soft in shadows, arms folded at the chest where Owen had carefully placed them. A jacket lay across its face, as Owen had placed that, too.

They stood to the side of the cliff where Owen had driven the car. They were beyond some high stands of sage brush that would shield them from any passing car, although none had yet come down that deserted road in the early morning hour.

"Jesus," Richie said again, eyes riveted to the body. "I didn't mean it, Owen. It just happened."

Richie repeated the words as he had time and again since he'd scrambled stumbling down the cliff face to come and stand at Owen's side, over the body that had slid off the smashed hood of the car and sprawled on the two-lane macadam highway.

"He just came at me," Richie had said in an almost whisper, speaking to the still desert air. "He rushed me—at the top of the cliff. He had the gun, Owen, but I know he wasn't going to use it." Only then had Richie raised his eyes from the thing on the road. "I *know* he wasn't going to," he said, searching Owen's face.

"It was just that he was scared, like he said. Panicked. He'd lost all the money, didn't know what to do, and suddenly there we were—there I was—his last chance."

Richie had looked down at the body again, went on, "He rushed me, Owen. With the gun in his hand. But he didn't use it. He just wanted—what he said, I guess. For me to tell him things.

"And maybe I would have, if I could. But I was panicked too, Owen. And I didn't *have* anything to tell him. Only what I'd said in the car—what I'd seen written about me.

"So we wrestled. And then the gun went off—in the air, Owen—by accident. The bullet never hit him." This was obviously important to Richie. "But then somehow he went over anyway."

As Richie related the incident, Owen realized his friend was in shock. His eyes were glassy and his voice distant as he stood in the dim light with smudges on his face. His clothing was torn and disheveled. Despite his own impairment, his own shock and the pain that still shackled his mind, Owen had understood he needed to take charge.

He had taken the car around and carried the body from the road. Now they stood over it in its new resting place.

"It just happened, Owen," Richie said again. "And I was so sure it would be me, just like the paper said."

And standing there in the dim light that cast their bodies in long shadows blending into the black of the desert night—standing there looking down at the thing at their feet, the idea came to Owen.

146

A Long Way From the Creek

* * *

They were high in the mountains now; the stars were bright in the sky above them since the moon had waned.

Owen looked over at Richie and saw his eyes were no longer clouded. They seemed full of pain but alert.

"Can we talk now?" he asked.

Richie nodded wearily. "Yeah," he said, leaning his head back and looking ahead as Owen began to speak.

* * *

Owen pulled off the highway onto the overlook. Switching off the headlights, he sat for a moment and looked out at the river meandering far below. It was a black string in the moonlit, surrealistic landscape.

Here, he decided.

Looking back, he could see nothing through the trees that shielded the deserted parking area. They'd passed only one car in the several hours they'd been heading north. Now it was three in the morning, and Owen was exhausted. He wondered again if Richie had truly grasped all he'd said to him. But he didn't have time to worry about that now.

Opening the door, he got out of the car. From somewhere far off the call of a night bird drifted down.

"Come on, Richie," he said softly.

Richie nodded, the faraway look still on his face as it had been for most of the drive.

They walked to the rear of the car and lifted Charley's body from the trunk. His body was heavy, but they finally got it past the steering wheel into the driver's seat. Richie kept his head averted as Owen leaned in and positioned Charley properly.

Owen removed from the trunk the can of gasoline they'd kept there from the first day they'd won the car. Just in case. But who would have imagined this? Owen shuddered.

Opening the top, he spilled the liquid across the front seat and onto their suitcases resting in the rear. He poured the rest almost ceremonially on Charley's body, which sat hunched behind the wheel.

"Goodbye, Charley," he intoned to himself, as close to a prayer as he could manage. Tears came to his eyes but he blinked them back,

147

took a deep breath, pushed down the lock button, and closed the car door.

Finally he reached through the open window and pulled on the headlights that picked up nothing but a large green refuse barrel standing like a sentinel against the blackness beyond.

"Let's go, Richie," he said.

They got behind the car and began to push it toward the wooden railing ahead. As it rolled across the gravel and gained momentum, Owen ran to the open window, struck a match, ignited the entire pack, and tossed it onto the front seat. A small whoosh started just as the car broke through the guardrail.

They watched it tumble end over end through the trees and saw it finally roll to a stop a few hundred feet below. The fire was bright where they stood, but Owen was certain it couldn't be detected from the road behind, even if anyone had been there to see.

"Okay, Richie. Now."

Richie hesitated and Owen repeated, "Now, Richie. Jump!"

It was as much a command as he would ever be able to manage with Richie, and even so he wasn't sure it would be enough, for the other seemed rooted in place.

They faced each other and something suddenly shifted in Richie's eyes. He looked down at the burgeoning flames, then back to Owen, and in that instant Owen realized some transformation had taken place.

Richie's eyes were calm. Totally calm, Owen noted in wonder.

"I'm okay now," Richie said in such a way that Owen knew it was so. Richie was in charge again, as he would always be. As Owen wished him to be.

And so it was Owen, almost in relief and after only a moment's pause, who turned away, walked to the shattered railing, and jumped.

Richie saw him hit the ground below, go into a roll.

He's clever, Richie thought, as Owen came to a stop and looked up at him, silhouetted on the brush-covered slope against the fire below. He was on his hands and knees, waiting.

Owen's very clever, Richie said to himself again. Richie *had* understood everything his friend had put forward, and saw now Owen could be of far more help to him than he'd ever anticipated. He'd only thought to take Owen along, to take care of the other boy. But now—

148

Owen's plan was a good one, well conceived.

He just hadn't taken it quite far enough.

Richie looked down one last time, then leaped out into space himself.

As the ground came up, he thought of Barney's words. He could see the menace in the tavern owner's face as he'd said, "Don't come back, Richie. Ever."

* * *

The nurse in the emergency admitting office regarded the two disheveled young men seated opposite her in open sympathy. Fortyish and heavier than she wanted to be, Amy Caruthers had a gentle nature. Despite her job of the past ten years, she still managed to maintain the compassion that had led her to her profession in the first place.

She felt sorry for all the accident victims she processed, the endless, bloody parade that passed through her doors. She always projected what warmth she could.

"Where are your families?" she asked, pen poised to write the information on one of the forms in front of her.

There was a pause, and the one with the swollen wrist said finally, "We have no families. We're orphans. All three of us. No relatives at all."

"Oh," she said involuntarily. She felt very motherly as she looked at the dirt- and mud- streaked young faces. She was especially sad for these boys because the state trooper who had brought the boys in had informed her their companion had been killed in the crash, his body burned beyond recognition.

"Your names?" she asked gently.

"Owen Reid."

"And yours?"

The dark eyes that looked at her from above the smashed and bloodied nose seemed far too old.

"Charles Frost," the boy said. "Charley."

CHAPTER 17

Two days later, an article appeared in the *Mills River Gazette*. It was dated June 12, 1963, and the headline read: "Former Cage Star Dies in Nevada."

Beneath it—on the bottom right of the front page—was a picture of Richie Peters.

Part III

CHAPTER 18

Charley pulled the mainsail tighter, secured the line into the cleat, and leaned back against the flotation cushion lining the richly polished slats of the mahogany bench. Resting his forearm lazily across the tiller, he stretched out his legs and reached down with his free hand to retrieve a beer from the ice-filled cooler he'd stashed beneath the bench to shield it from the high tropical sun. He took a refreshing swig and wiped his moustache with the back of his hand and proceeded to rub the chilled can rhythmically across his forehead. It was hot even in the strong wind, and he'd worked up a sweat although clad only in his blue denim shorts.

Eyes closed to the cloudless sky above, he leaned back and listened to the waves lap the boat as it pressed through the translucent blue of the Caribbean waters. The occasional spray felt delicious on his body.

"Larry."

The soft voice drifted across the wind, interrupting his reverie. He looked up to the bow and saw Janine had sat up, arms folded across her updrawn knees as she regarded him with serious green eyes. Her tan face glistened in the sun and the wind whipped her long black hair about her shoulders.

He blew her a kiss and was rewarded with a quick white smile of obvious contentment.

They held the moment briefly—wind, sun, and surf—before she again stretched out on the deck, her face to the sun, and removed the top of her bathing suit.

Instinctively he looked around but laughed at himself as he did so. They were two miles off-shore, the nearest boat a large three-master nearly half a mile to their stern. Charley lingered on the graceful vessel as it drew rapidly away from them; he sensed its churning wake and the strain of its tilted sails. He thought she'd probably make port in Charlotte Amalie for the night, and he visualized the town that rose steeply above the deep harbor, its narrow streets and shops bustling with visitors from cruise ships.

He looked further to his right, past the schooner, and saw the green tip of the island jutting out, then turned his eyes back to the open sea ahead. The wind came up even stronger and Janine's hair trailed across the deck toward him like tendriled weather vanes as the boat pushed forward.

Charley closed his eyes, breathed the salt air in deeply through his nostrils, and gave himself up for the moment to the hectic spray that coursed across his body in hypnotic rhythm.

I'm actually enjoying myself, he thought guiltily, still deeply bereft of his family, but acknowledging by the way he'd adapted these past months he would not only survive but would in fact thrive in this new and pressure-free atmosphere.

The simple life. He smiled to himself, thinking of the irony of the statement. Fate had its ways. He'd been marked early and he'd never had a choice, not really. He'd grown so tired of it all at times. But now that Owen was almost there and he himself had no option but to flee—

The soft motion of the boat nearly lulled him to sleep and he opened his eyes abruptly, searching the horizon to ascertain there was no danger, then narrowed his lids in the contentment of the moment as his mind drifted back to his first sail, a lifetime ago.

———

The wind on Lake Mendota still carried a chill even on the sunny May morning as it whipped toward them from the dense forest making up the far shore. Spring came late in Wisconsin, and Charley was grateful for the heavy crewneck sweater he'd worn under his windbreaker.

Looking at the small whitecaps as the boat plowed ahead, he marveled that only two months before the lake had been a mass of ice so solid you could drive a car all the way across the two-mile stretch that fronted the Phi Delta house. They'd done it themselves, he and Andy along with the rest of the pledges on the night of their initiation. It had been a mad exercise that had seemed at the time a logical extension of their celebration in having the long pledge period finally end. That mood, coupled with the rousing toasts at the beer party, had demanded some display of sheer bravado. Charley had heard several students had drowned in the past by attempting the stunt, and although he'd known they would come out all right, he still hadn't relaxed until the escapade was over and they were back on shore again.

Other than that, he'd never actually been on the lake before, and he enjoyed it now as it was meant to be enjoyed. Heretofore it had merely been a glorious backdrop for the tree-lined shores that edged the campus, but he was beginning to understand its deeper function as the fine spray brushed his face and the wind stung his eyes.

Charley was exhilarated, more at peace than perhaps he'd ever been. His life was a far cry from an orphan in North Carolina, further already than he would ever have dreamed. He reached for Alice, put his arm around her shoulder, and drew her close. As she snuggled into the embrace he felt her shiver. He looked down at the light brown hair framing her oval face, reached in gently to lift her chin, and kissed her full lips softly.

Over her shoulder he saw Andy grin his college-boy grin. Charley smiled himself, feeling good about all of it as his roommate turned them a shade further into the wind and he felt the boat surge faster.

Charley was reasonably fond of his roommate. Lithe and classically Nordic, Andy was pleasant and easygoing, but at times he was a little too rah-rah as far as Charley was concerned. His University of Wisconsin pennants were one thing and even the stickers on his car were okay. But the Wisconsin labels with which Andy sealed his letters Charley thought a bit much.

Still, he reminded himself, he could have done a lot worse for a roommate. If Andy asked a lot of questions, at least they weren't deep.

"Want to try it?" Andy called now, and Charley nodded, releasing Alice who joined him as he made his way back to the tiller. She looked perky in her yellow slicker, dark eyes exhilarated, fair skin flushed by the gusty breeze.

155

"Hold this," Andy said, placing the tiller in Charley's hand. "Now," he went on, "do you see that string?" Charley followed the pointing finger and noticed the small piece of string tied to one of the wires descending from the mast.

"That's the tell tale," Andy continued, pulling his Greek captain's hat tighter down over his blonde hair. "It lets you know the wind direction. What you want to do is keep the tell tale pointed at the sail at about the angle it is now. Too far into the wind," he placed his hand over Charley's and pulled the tiller slightly, "and this happens." Charley felt the boat stall slightly before Andy made the quick readjustment.

"Understand?"

Charley nodded.

Andy's blue eyes sparkled, and Charley could picture him ripping the waters of Green Lake where he'd been raised. "The danger is," Andy went on, "if you let it come about too far without warning, the sail can get taken and..." Andy's voice trailed off, alluding to the possibility of capsizing and the necessity of properly coming about.

"I'll teach you that later. For now, just hold her steady and get the feel of it. Make for that cove over there," Andy said, pointing to a small inlet on the tree fringed far shore, "but remember—watch the tell tale."

Charley nodded, perched himself on the gunwale, held tight to the tiller, and looked ahead. After a moment he remembered to check the tell tale and realized he could sense the wind direction from the tautness of the sails and the general feel of the boat's speed. He pushed the rudder left a hair, felt the quick fall off, then pulled it back and felt the boat tip sharply before he adjusted again.

Andy looked back quickly but Charley grinned a reassurance. He held her steady and relaxed, eyes ahead on the cove. After a bit he looked over at Alice, reached out and touched her hair.

The year had flown, he thought, had swept by as pleasantly but inexorably as the wind on his face. Charley smiled at his use of the metaphor, realized how much he'd changed in his perceptions and so many other ways as well.

He enjoyed all of it, the entire college theme. He was amazed at how well and quickly he'd adapted; he hoped Owen was having the same experience in Colorado. It had all gone smoothly—remarkably as they'd anticipated.

Charley and Owen had been released from Sunnyside Hospital on the morning following the accident. They had spent an hour answering more questions at the police station, but had finally been allowed to go their way. They had only the khakis and T-shirts they wore, newly washed at the hospital but with a tear here and there from their slide down the rocky slope the night before.

"How much money do we have left?" Charley asked. His voice sounded nasal because of the thick bandages covering his nose. Both eyes were blackened and so deep-set they were little more than slits.

Owen counted. "Three hundred seventy-two dollars." He turned to Charley. "Does it matter?"

They'd eaten at a diner and later, passing a liquor store, they'd impulsively purchased a bottle of bourbon and taken it to their hotel room. The twin beds and dresser were not appreciably different from those they'd shared at St. Mary's. Only the upholstered green chair into which Owen sank with the lamp and table beside it made the room less than spartan.

Charley poured some of the whiskey into water tumblers, raised his glass, and said, "Here's to Charley."

"To Charley," Owen said, reaching up to touch the other's glass.

Owen made the next toast. "To Charley and Owen," he said, and there was a resolution in his voice that made them both feel better as they drank to themselves. Oddly, it seemed a more fitting farewell to their friend.

"To the future," Charley offered from the edge of the bed where he sat, and they drank again.

Somewhere in the process they left the real Charley—and Richie, too—behind.

Then they sat and expanded on the plan they'd discussed during the long ride north from Las Vegas, the plan Richie had quickly embellished as they'd stood on the slope above the burning car in which Charley's body was being consumed.

The plan on which they had finally agreed.

By ten o'clock, they'd worked out most of it, at least the long- and short-term goals. College was the first, obvious step. They still had to work out the rest of the process that would lead them through to their ultimate goals, but they were excited at the challenges ahead.

The next day they had taken a bus to Denver and had built their stake by following the tracks, flat or harness racing—quarter horses on occasion. It didn't matter so long as there were wagers to be made.

Charley remembered the small half-mile track in Navasota, Texas, where they'd won eight thousand dollars one Thursday afternoon while thundershowers had plagued them. He doubted he could find the town again if he had to.

But the Racing Form was their Bible, and they followed wherever it led them.

The important thing was they move around, never stay long enough to be noticed. They were careful not to win exorbitantly. And they'd never again go through an intermediary. Barney had taught them that lesson all too well. Whatever would be accomplished they would always have to do on their own.

They bet at the two-dollar windows, purchased their tickets from several, cashed them in similar fashion by dribs and drabs. But the dribs and drabs grew quickly. By early September they had over three hundred thousand dollars.

The base they'd need would have to be far larger to support even their initial plans, but they certainly had a good start, and amassing the rest was only a matter of decision and discretion. Charley was relieved when Owen agreed with his suggestion they begin dealing in the stock market in the future. The races were quicker but speed was not a major consideration anymore, especially now that they understood they could trust the power. But how they got the money was something else again, and Charley had felt almost as if they'd taken it personally from the harried lines of humanity that joined them daily at the teller's windows. The stock market, on the other hand, was impersonal.

There were problems with the market, of course, the most notable being the profits could then be traced and accounted for. To amass what they needed could well bring attention to them, which was the last thing they wanted. But they'd have to figure a way around that in any event, so for the time being they decided to make a few small investments and begin to learn about the system.

That would really be Charley's job—not only the making of the money, but more important, the hiding of it.

So he was majoring in business and finance.

Owen's future was in politics, so he'd go after law school.

The future was clear now and, all in all, the summer that had begun with the tragic and shattering experience in Nevada had in fact turned into one of excitement and growing promise.

Their stake was set, they had learned to trust the power and what it would do, and perhaps more important, their long-term plans had jelled. What had initially been a basic but undefined vision of the future, as hastily conceived as their flight from Carolina had been, had congealed over the long, hot southwestern weeks into a blueprint of the future whose precise dimensions they could now examine in clarity.

Charley would become the ultimate entrepreneur/philanthropist. He saw exactly how that could be accomplished.

And Owen was to be president of the United States, but a far more effective, far-sighted—and powerful—president than had ever existed before. And he knew exactly how that would come about.

Yes, the blueprint for amassing power, both financial and otherwise, had been carefully drawn and edited. The motivation behind the plan would be essentially altruistic, infusing both Owen and Charley with a sense of purpose that welded their entire thoughts and beings to their project.

As the plan had matured, so had the boys. No longer were they two orphans on the run with an awesome secret that might bring them riches. Rather, they were now young men with a plan that had not only been well thought out over the long summer nights, but one of which they were absolutely certain.

"It works," Charley said one night, for perhaps the tenth time, shaking his head in wonder.

And Owen nodded again, confidence clear in the set of his lips as it had been all evening since they'd put the last piece in place. That final master stroke had been Owen's, and Charley marveled again at the emerging facets of his friend's mind. His respect for the other had grown beyond any point he would ever have imagined, and in fact, he found Owen's ready acceptance of even the most far-reaching of concepts to be almost frightening at times.

"It really works," Charley said one last time, almost matter-of-factly as the idea took further hold.

The swelling of his nose had disappeared leaving it permanently thicker and as obviously broken as the real Charley's had been. He'd filled out a bit, too, and his white T-shirt stretched almost uncomfortably across his chest. He could feel the perspiration damp under his arms as he stood by the cigarette-burned coffee table of yet another hot, dead-aired motel room.

Owen had fleshed out as well, looked more the large man he would be than the gangly boy Charley had known as he sat on the cracked vinyl of the orange couch. "We can do it all, Charley," he said, indicating the small stack of handwritten note paper that lay on the table, the culmination of those long conversations that had run deep into the night, the final blueprint he no longer needed because it was etched indelibly in his mind.

"Think of it, Charley—two orphans making the Great American Dream *really* come true."

Owen was speaking more and more like that of late, full of his own importance, Charley thought, although it didn't grate on him now as it sometimes did. Because what Owen had said was right—absolutely right, despite the high-sounding words he'd chosen.

Making the Great American Dream really come true. When he considered it, Charley could find no fault with the phrase.

He would become Charley Frost, the man of quiet but incalculable wealth, the man who, in total anonymity, effected philanthropy on a scope such as the Rockefellers would never have dreamed.

And Owen as president. With that power, too, in hand what couldn't they accomplish?

The Great American Dream

The words seemed to echo in the flat air of the stifling motel room, against whose exposed and rusted screens rather than the rush of some sweet night breeze only an occasional insect struck.

The room in which Charley met Owen's eyes and extended his hand.

The room in which their final, unalterable commitment had been made.

They'd parted a few days later in Albuquerque, and Charley had taken his share of the stake and headed north. Arriving in Madison, he opened an five-thousand-dollar account at Northland Trust, stashed the rest of the money in a safety deposit box, and registered at the University of Wisconsin.

That had been eight months ago, he thought now, as the sailboat surged the waters of Lake Mendota and the cove ahead drew closer. Eight months. But it seemed to Charley as if he had always been a college student, a member of Phi Delta for a lifetime. He was often so immersed in that self-image he had to forcibly bring himself back to his other purpose.

But not today. There were no purposes today other than the pure enjoyment of the sail, the feel of the wind and the spray and the motion. The feel of life and excitement stretching ahead.

Alice was seated on the floor of the boat with her back resting against his legs as he steered. Reaching down, he touched her cold cheek, felt exuberantly young as she turned her face to him, eyes crinkled against the wind, and covered his hand with her own.

CHAPTER 19

Kicking the snow off of his boots, Charley bent and loosened the laces before entering the Student Union. The immense, high-ceilinged room with its massive wooden rafters was charged with noise and energy, and the trees showed gray and cold through the huge windows facing the lake. He looked above the milling students who crowded the room, saw the sign that read "Econ," and headed for that table.

Although he picked the shortest of the four lines, he counted at least a dozen students ahead of him and estimated it would be a good half hour before his turn came. With five courses for which to register, he would probably be there at least three hours. Registration day was always a pain in the neck, but at least this would be his last.

Resigning himself to the line, he idly flipped through the spring course catalog as he waited. He paused at the last page, noting the simple announcement:

Commencement Exercises
9:30 A.M., Friday, June 7, 1967
Langdon Hall

His last graduation day had been June 5. He wondered how many college seniors would remember the date of their high school graduation and figured not too many. But he'd never forget his. It was the day Charley had betrayed them and the long odyssey had begun.

He leafed backward through the catalog as the line inched forward. Here was a picture of last year's Hare's Foot production group, flushed and excited faces caught by the camera as the cast took their bows after the final performance of the original student musical. Charley had wanted to try out for the show. He thought he had a fair chance because his voice was good and his height gave him an advantage, but he had not wanted to risk the publicity. Or the photographs. He managed to miss the first two fraternity groupings in the Badger yearbook. He finally showed up in the third one, but his head was turned enough so you couldn't really recognize him. The graduation pictures would pose a problem but with his long hair, broken nose, and the fact that his face had filled out these past four years, he hoped it wouldn't be a giveaway. Anonymity was his watchword, but he nonetheless rankled at the limitations it imposed. There was so much he was missing in his young life, he frequently reflected.

He remembered his first intrafraternity basketball game the winter he'd been a sophomore. Going high, he'd blocked the opposing player's shot in the final minute of play, had raced down court to take the lead pass as the ball was rebounded by a teammate, and had scored on an easy lay up the last of his twenty-one points that led Phi Delta to a three-point victory over arch-rival Sigma Chi.

"You ought to go out for varsity," Skip had said to him in the locker room following the game. Skip was the team captain, a powerful senior with an exceptionally hairy body who used his muscle well under the boards.

Charley had shrugged deprecatingly, implying he really wasn't all that good, but Skip had known better and had shown his resentment of Charley's wasted talent by treating him with aloofness even though together they were responsible for Phi Delta's championship season. A Phi Delta on varsity meant more to Skip than the fraternity championship, and he never understood Charley's reluctance.

He doubted anybody was looking anymore, if they ever had been. Still, the less tracks he left behind the better. He regretted the fire at St. Mary's, but he had known Owen was right. The records were just too dangerous. But he'd make it up to them in a year or so, just as soon as he could legitimately send the money.

They'd have to go after Anderson's office too someday to destroy his collection of basketball photos. But that would have to wait long enough so the two events wouldn't be connected. Maybe the newspaper files also, although those pictures weren't all that clear, and the crewcuts they'd worn in those days made them look different than they did today.

You couldn't cover all the bases, he thought. The trick was to destroy as much of the past as they could and to keep it low key for enough years until fading memories and their own changing appearances blunted the risks. But Charley knew well the chance of exposure, however slight, would always lay waiting.

The girl ahead stepped aside and Charley found himself before the registration desk. Handing his card to the freckle-faced student who was filling the schedules, he watched as the young man entered his name on the list and stamped his card.

Charley turned away and saw beyond the great windows of the crowded student union that the light snowfall was beginning to grow heavier. He glanced at his watch. It was already ten-thirty. If the lines didn't move, he'd be late for his lunch with Alice.

* * *

The lunch in the crowded, steamy Brat House had not gone well, but he hadn't expected it to. Alice was getting more impatient with him as time went on, and he couldn't blame her.

They'd been invited by Andy to spend a weekend up at his folks' place on Green Lake—just two couples, Andy had said—while his parents were vacationing in Florida. Alice had been excited at the prospect, then hurt and angry when Charley had declined.

"For God's sake, Charley, we're twenty-one, almost twenty-two. We've been going together for three years and—" Her voice broke and tears sprang suddenly in her fawn-colored eyes. She released his hand, picked up her books, and moved quickly from the table.

He watched her weave her way past the overflowing tables and search out her coat from amidst the tumble of the rack. He thought how small she looked in her fur-collared storm coat as she opened the door and pushed out into the snow.

He loved her more than she knew and wanted her in ways she would never believe. She thought him cold, disinterested, and she would have been amazed to know it was her face in his dreams, her body in the erotic fantasies with which he relieved himself when he felt the need.

164

She would never have understood that, either, since both of them knew he could have the real thing if only he'd ask.

But he never did.

Sighing, Charley rose, dropped a tip on the table, and gathered up his things.

There was a lot she didn't know. Including the fact he was leaving in June for good. And the fact he wasn't slated to marry, at least not for a long while.

Those were the plans as he saw them now.

He pulled his collar high against the cutting wind that ripped through him when he stepped outside. There was ice already beginning to form on his lashes as he squinted into the driving snow. He could just make out Alice's small figure almost a block away.

The privilege of knowing the future isn't always a blessing, he thought not for the first time. There was something almost evil in a calling so overwhelming it left little room for the natural embrace of personal feelings and desires.

The small figure had long since disappeared into the snow before he finally turned away and walked thoughtfully up Henry Street toward the lake.

* * *

"Hey! Owen!"

Owen snapped the rack lock around his skis and turned to face Jerry.

"How was it today? Great, I bet," the sandy haired boy went on, eyes glittering.

"Best day all year," Owen replied, unzipping his bulky ski jacket. The warmth of the fraternity house enveloped him, and he quickly peeled down to the black cotton turtleneck he wore beneath his sweater. "Pure powder and the slopes were empty."

"Damn. I knew it. Wish to hell I could have gone." The eager boy was at Owen's heels as he mounted the two-tiered stairway.

"Come on, Jerry. You go more than anybody I know. If you don't slow down, you'll be skiing every day, because you sure as hell won't be in school anymore."

Jerry laughed.

"Hey, by the way, you had a phone call before. Guy named Charley, said you knew the number. Sounded like long distance."

Owen stopped on the landing.

Charley. What was he calling for? They'd met at Sun Valley over Christmas and had skied and talked for the better part of a week. And that had been only three months ago. They weren't scheduled to meet again until July in Vancouver.

Charley had never had cause to breach the precautions before, and Owen was concerned.

He went up to his room, closed and locked the door, sat down at his desk, and picked up the phone.

"Owen," his friend said when he came on. "I have to see you right away. I want to change our plans."

* * *

Alice looked out and saw the boys below her, already at work at the hoist in the boat house. They'd only arrived at Green Lake a few minutes earlier, and she hadn't even unpacked yet.

Opening the window, she leaned out and heard their voices drift up through the crisp April air.

"Easy," Andy said, cautioning with his hand as she watched Charley bring the handle almost to a standstill.

"That's good. A little more now," the hand circled encouragingly, and Charley responded with a quickening of his motions, his sweatshirt hiking up on his back. Through the slats of the boathouse she could see the sleek lines of a white hull dropping gently downward.

"That's it," Andy's hand shut off with a snap. "Just let her sit and we'll get the mast."

Charley straightened, turned, and caught sight of her. His grin was instantaneous, and he waved with delight.

It was hard to believe how much he'd changed in the past few weeks, how much like the old Charley he'd become again, she thought as she waved back at the tall, slender boy who stood on the dock.

Charley had a way about him, the ability to make things seem fresh. She smiled to herself as she remembered their first kiss.

166

They'd met at a beer party which Phi Delta had thrown to celebrate the initiation of their pledge class. She herself had recently become admitted as a Gamma, the Phi Delta's sister sorority, and the girls had been invited en masse.

She had thought she looked especially nice in her black cashmere cardigan and tartan plaid skirt, and had arrived at the party in high spirits. She'd never been at the Phi Delta house before; she recognized none of the sweatered boys milling about with a beer in one hand and a cigarette in the other and was feeling a little left out in the midst of the chatter when she suddenly heard her name called.

"Alice! Alice Winslow! Son of a gun."

Turning, she saw Andy Billingsly coming toward her, a wide grin on his face.

"Alice," he said again, giving her a quick embrace. "It's been years. I didn't even know you were here at school."

"How are you, Andy? You look great." She held his arms, felt good as she looked at the familiar face. She and Andy had known each other as kids. They had gone to the same summer camp together for years.

"You still going to Algonquin?" she asked.

"I did last year. I was a counselor."

She laughed. "You look like a counselor." And he did, his athletic frame and open good looks almost a walking poster proclaiming the advantages of a glorious summer in northern Wisconsin.

"You look great yourself," he returned, still preening at her remark although she hadn't meant it quite that way. But she forgave him, not only because he was a friendly face, but also because no matter how affected Andy was at times, she still knew him to be basically a very nice guy.

"You here alone?" he asked, and she nodded.

"Well, I've got a date myself. Patty Fleming, girl from New York. But I do want to talk to you, go over old times. Gamma, huh?" he said, glancing at the pin on her sweater.

"Just."

"I was just initiated, too," he squeezed her arms with affection. "Hey," he went on, looking over her shoulder, "here comes somebody I'd like you to meet. Hey, Charley!" Charley looked over and came to them.

"Charley, this is an old, old friend of mine. Alice Winslow, from Portage, about twenty miles from my home town. Alice and I spent a lot of summers together—but we were just kids, then," he winked. "Alice, this is Charley Frost, my roommate and a helluva guy."

"Pleased to meet you," she said, extending her hand.

"Me, too," Charley responded as he tentatively shook her hand.

"Well, I'll leave you two for a bit. Got to minister to Patty or somebody else will. Don't ever trust a Phi Delt, Alice," Andy winked again and walked off.

She looked up at the tall boy who stood uncomfortably in front of her. He was neatly dressed in a navy blue pullover, khakis, and bucks. His broken nose added character to a face that might otherwise have seemed too thin, and his dark brown eyes seemed vulnerable in a way that made her suddenly feel motherly toward him. "Does that apply to you, too?" she asked.

"Me?"

"Never trust a Phi Delt."

"Oh," he relaxed. He seemed to ponder the question seriously, answered in that vein, "No, I don't think so."

She liked the soft voice, noted the southern accent.

"Where are you from, Charley?"

"North Carolina."

"That's a long ways away. How'd you get here?" she prodded gently, not wanting to appear aggressive but knowing instinctively she'd have to help him along.

The dark eyes seemed to cloud at the question, but he smiled a little boy smile and said, "That's a long story and it calls for a beer. Okay?"

"Sure," she said, and he took her arm and forced their way through the press of young bodies milling about the scarred mahogany bar that stretched half the length of the dining room wall. The Phi Delts took great pride in that bar, and the boy who placed their overflowing mugs in front of them did so with great flair.

They sat in the quietest corner of the large brightly lit room but still had to speak loudly to make themselves heard, laughing often as they shared with one another the foibles and triumphs of their first college year.

168

He had asked to take her home, his expression so tentative and his relief when she nodded so obvious she had to stifle a laugh. They'd held hands on the way to her dorm, and she felt a gaiety in the awkward intertwine of their fingers through their thick leather gloves.

She'd turned at her door and he'd held her with serious eyes, leaning down finally and touching his lips with hers, not really a kiss so much as a discovery not to be damaged in the handling, a tenderness there so unexpected as to make her knees go weak.

She'd known without asking it was his first kiss, and somehow it became hers as well even though she'd been kissed often before. But that's how it was with Charley—everything had been fresh and new, beautiful in its innocence, reduced to some pristine simplicity.

Their kisses had advanced rapidly from tender to passionate. They had never gone beyond that, but she hadn't minded. Sometimes she could feel him straining at her as they embraced, welcomed the feel of his body, wondered that he didn't push it further. But she thought that was his way and was willing to follow his lead, trusting things would go somewhere.

At least, that's how it had been for two years. But now, in their senior year, things had begun to change. The reaching boy she'd known had subtly taken on a more somber air and was reserved in a way somehow different from his natural shyness. She sensed a holding back that was deliberate and wondered about it. She found his physical reticence suddenly threatening and reacted by challenging him. She was baffled by the hurt look in his eye when she did so. She knew he wanted her, knew he knew he could have her, but felt him slipping away more and more as the year moved on.

Until two weeks ago, when an abrupt transformation had taken place. Charley had gone away for the weekend. When she asked him where he was going, he seemed so mysterious in his vague explanation the thought had crossed her mind, irrational as it seemed, that he was never coming back.

But he had, and when he called her that Sunday night it was as if he were rejuvenated. His voice held an excitement she hadn't heard for a long time, and when he kissed her at the door, there was an abandon in him she'd never felt before.

Her arms were about his neck, and he'd placed his hands at her sides, gently moving his thumbs up over her breasts as he looked deep into her eyes. It was the first time he'd touched her like that and she shuddered involuntarily but held his gaze, heard him say, finally, "I love you."

A thrill had gone through her then, the same feeling she had now as she looked down at the waiting figure on the dock by the boathouse.

She tossed a kiss, turned away, and walked to the closet of the small guestroom, wondering what the next two days would bring.

* * *

She didn't wonder long.

By noon they were in bed together, and as she lay cradling his head against her breast a long hour later she marveled when it finally happened it had happened so fast.

She'd gone down to help the boys set the mast and had followed Andy's instructions with the ropes and wires, although she knew as well as he where to place them. They had just attached the sheets when a resplendent Sally finally appeared on the dock.

Sally was tall, almost Andy's height, and she moved with a grace Alice envied. Everything about Sally appeared perfect, from the casual elegance of her clothing to the long blonde hair that blew sensuously in the wind but always managed to drop back into its stylish cut.

Alice wasn't jealous of Sally, although she might have been had not the girl's combination with the handsomely nordic Andy created an image of such perfection it was impossible for her to take seriously.

She thought of her own slight figure, her oval face, her dark but pleasant features, the touch of sloppiness she shared with an average-looking Charley, and felt very good as she looked at the beautiful people.

Andy hoisted the main sail and they moved out onto the lake. Small whitecaps rippled toward the far shore, and the summer house shone bright in the sun behind them.

"Charley?" Andy questioned, nodding his head to the tiller in his hand.

"Not today," Charley responded with a look that told her all.

Taking her hand, he'd led her to the bow, and they sat with their backs to the cabin and the wind, his arm close about her shoulders as the light spray played on their faces. His leather cap was pushed back on his head and he looked rakish indeed.

They'd docked late in the morning, chilled but exhilarated from the water.

"Let's go in town for lunch," Andy suggested.

"Can we get a drink there? I need one."

"Sure thing, Sal. Charley?"

Charley looked to Alice for confirmation he didn't really need and shook his head after catching her eye.

"I think Alice needs a hot shower more than anything." She shivered in affirmation, and he put his arm around her. "See you guys later."

Leading her into the house, he'd held her close for a moment as she shivered again.

"I meant that about the shower," he said, tilting up her chin and kissing her lightly. "Go."

She nodded, went up to the guest bedroom, stripped, and put on her flannel robe. She could hear him in the kitchen as she entered the bathroom.

She stayed under the shower longer than she'd intended, but the luxury of the hot water as it dissipated the chill was too delicious to surrender. When she entered the bedroom he was waiting, as she knew he'd be, under the coverlet he'd folded to his waist, black hair on his chest glistening in the sunlight that came through the window overlooking the lake. She stood silently for a moment, then opened her robe, dropped it to the floor, and went to the bed.

Whatever problems she'd thought there might be, whatever doubts, had quickly vanished when they came together. Suddenly, it all seemed so simple.

"You came," he said after, a pride and a wonder in his voice.

She nodded, a soft smile on her face as she turned to him.

"You're not supposed to do that. Not the first time."

"That's what they say," she said, taking his hand and turning it so she could kiss his palm, understanding fully what his own doubts and fears must have been.

171

He pulled her close and she felt him hard against her thigh. Reaching down she touched him, moved her leg over his hip, and guided him inside.

"Oh my God," he called softly as his hands moved to her buttocks and pressed her further down.

* * *

"Let's talk, Andy."

Charley was the picture of comfort that evening as he sat settled into the deep-pillowed sofa. His checked wool shirt was open at the throat, his legs stretched out on the coffee table before the blaze roaring in the stone fireplace, brandy snifter cupped in the palm of his hand. Relaxed as he seemed, there was an air of command in his voice she'd never heard before, a surety that made her suddenly alert.

"Sure, Charley." Andy, in contrast, sounded the slightest bit uncertain, and she knew he'd picked up on Charley's tone as well. "What about?" Andy added after a moment.

Charley paused, and if she hadn't known him better she'd have thought it was for dramatic effect. Then, looking into the fire that highlighted the antlered trophies set on the paneled wall behind it, a private expression touched his face, and he said quietly, "About the future."

CHAPTER 20

Mike stood in the massive Phi Delta living room. He took in the beamed ceiling, looked at the settings of sofas, tables, and chairs, noted the grand piano in the corner, the stone fireplace on the far wall, the large windows with the view of the lake, and tried to picture it as it must have been twenty-five years ago.

Charley had been eighteen then as Mike was now, an unsophisticated boy from a southern orphanage who was out in the world for the first time in his life. Mike knew the bustling university setting must have been frightening for a shy boy who'd spent his life cloistered in the structure of the institution.

It was funny he perceived his father as a shy boy, Mike thought, because that was certainly not the picture Coach Anderson had drawn of the spirited teenaged hell-raiser out to shake the world. But in all the stories Charley had told him about his college days, Mike had detected a sense of separateness there, a sense of his father being an outsider looking in, even when he'd recalled with obvious relish the excitement of fraternity life.

Mike pictured Charley at beer parties; he saw his father involved but still holding back, a quality he had retained as an adult. Although his father had many interests, there was still something lacking in his participation, and Mike suddenly identified what it was.

Passion.

Charley had been curious, interested, appreciative, and certainly loving in the varied aspects of his life—but Mike realized now he had never been passionate.

Funny, he mused, but his train of thought was interrupted as he heard someone come up behind him. Turning, he saw a fair-haired young man almost his own height wearing jeans and a gray sweat shirt which read "Phi Delta." Mike, in khakis and T-shirt himself, felt immediately at home.

"Hi," Mike offered.

"Hi," the slender boy came forward, extending his hand. "I'm Jeff Shore. Can I help you?"

"Mike Frost. Just looking around. My dad used to belong here."

"When was that?" Jeff asked, appraising Mike as he did so.

"He graduated in sixty-seven, but he stayed around Madison for a couple of years afterward. Charley Frost."

The boy shook his head. "Don't know the name. I thought I might, because some of the alumni still come back every year for Homecoming and even more often than that sometimes. You ought to see them when they get soused and start singing the old drinking songs. You'd think there was nothing better in the world than good old Phi Delta." Jeff laughed. "They get pretty sloppy sometimes, and you've sure got to watch your date."

"I'll bet."

"No kidding. It's funny sometimes, but sad too, you know what I mean? Like they can't let any of it go, like it was all downhill from here. Scares me sometimes when I think about it."

Mike nodded.

"But I never met your dad, and this'll be my senior year."

"I don't think he ever came back."

"Where you from?"

"Boston."

"That your car outside?" Jeff raised his eyes in appreciation as he motioned his thumb toward the window.

"Yeah."

"You planning to go to school here?" Jeff asked with obvious interest.

Mike shook his head, repressed a smile. He must look like a catch. "No," he said. "At least, I hadn't thought about it. Like I said, I'm just looking around."

"Where do you go now?"

"Nowhere. I just got out of high school, and I've sort of left next year open." That idea was suddenly appealing, Dartmouth notwithstanding.

Jeff nodded in agreement. "Good idea, if your folks support it. But when you go, you could do a lot worse than here. Summer school doesn't start for another week, but there are five of us in the house already. Great place to vacation." He paused. "You oughtta talk to your dad."

"My father's dead."

"I'm sorry," Jeff offered.

"That's okay. You couldn't know."

"Hey," Jeff said with a quick enthusiasm, "why don't I show you around the house?"

"I'd like that."

"Let's go upstairs first." He proceeded Mike up the wide staircase, taking the steps two at a time. When they got to the first landing, Jeff turned and said, "Any idea which room was your dad's?"

Mike was touched by the older boy's perception. Maybe he should think about Wisconsin.

"I don't know which one exactly, but he said it was on the end and he could look over the lake with no obstruction."

"There's a couple of rooms that could be, but most likely it would be the third floor. Let's go up."

They ascended another flight, and Mike followed Jeff down the long corridor to the end. "Could be either of these," Jeff said. "Let's go here first."

He opened the door to his left and they entered.

The room was adequate but not spacious, with two bare-mattressed beds against each of the inside walls and two desks positioned in front of the windows. There were several posters hung on the wall, but the one of Bo Derek in a soaked T-shirt dominated.

"It could have been here," Mike said, "because my father told me he could sit at his desk and look out across the water."

175

Mike walked to the window and stared down past the trees to the lake, which was calm in the summer sun.

"Want to be alone?"

Mike turned. "No. It's not that kind of a trip." Again, he was thankful for Jeff's thoughtfulness.

"What kind, then?" Jeff posed, and Mike thought about it for a minute before shrugging. He really didn't know how to respond.

They walked back down the corridor, Jeff stopping to open a door or two as they passed so Mike could inspect the unoccupied rooms briefly, then descended the three flights to the basement, which housed the dining room.

The ten long tables could easily accommodate a hundred students, Mike estimated, and the room could have handled more had it not been for the handsome mahogany bar that took up a good portion of the space to the rear.

"The pride of Phi Delta Theta," Jeff intoned as he walked Mike toward the bar.

They stood, each with a foot propped on the brass rail as they leaned against the scarred but well polished wood. The wall beyond was arrayed with photographs.

"You dad's probably there," Jeff said, and Mike nodded.

They walked behind the bar, and Mike quickly scanned the dates.

"Here it is. Class of nineteen sixty-seven," he said, excitement in his voice. Eagerly, he searched the young faces. He was sure he recognized Charley as the third from the left in the top row and was gratified when he dropped his eyes to the list of names below and saw the dark-eyed young man with the broad nose was indeed identified as "Charles Frost."

"Nineteen sixty-seven," he read aloud. "Twenty-one years ago."

His eyes were riveted to the serious face as Jeff said behind him, "A long time. But like I said, you should still see some of them today. It's like nothing ever changed."

Mike turned almost reluctantly from the picture.

"I wonder if any of my father's classmates still come back."

"Probably, from time to time, but it would be hard for me to tell. Let me take a look, though."

Jeff moved to the picture, looked blankly at the faces for a moment, before examining the list of names.

"Hey. Here's one. Andy Billingsly."

"Andy Billingsly!" Mike snapped his fingers. "He was my dad's roommate. He told me the name, but I'd forgotten."

"Well, he's still around, that's for sure,"Jeff said, enigmatically.

Mike looked at the other boy who grimaced.

"The kind of alumni you hope for, then wish you'd never gotten sometimes. Like 'The Monkey's Paw'. You know what I mean?

"Active, important, gives a lot of money and a lot of support. The only problem is, when he shows up himself, he can really be a pain in the ass. He's do damned rah-rah it can make you puke sometimes, and I'm a pretty intense Phi Delt.

"Drinks a lot," Jeff continued, "and that's when he's the worst, standing here at the bar going over all his old stories time and again like they meant something to anybody else but him. I was never sure what the word 'maudlin' meant 'til I met old Andy."

Jeff chuckled and Mike smiled encouragement.

"Still, he does help out a lot, and he gives Phi Delta a dimension no other fraternity on campus has."

"What's that?"

"Well, Andy's really well-to-do, and he lives around here, and Phi Delta seems to be one of the most important things in his life. He's got this super summer place up at Green Lake, about fifty miles north, and every spring he throws a real bash or two, invites all the Phi Delts up for a day of drinking and sailing, whatever you want. It's a real institution around here, and the girls really consider it a big deal to get invited to a 'Green Lake Break,' as we call it.

"But better yet," Jeff went on, "he owns the best ski resort around—Mohawk, up near Wild Cat Mountain. And would you believe it—every year he closes the place down for two solid days, right during midseason, and has the whole fraternity up, dates and all, for one big private party. Rooms, food, drinks, lifts—everything on the house. If you don't have your own equipment he lends it to you."

Jeff looked at Mike who shook his head in wonder. "Must cost him a fortune," he said.

"No question. I figured it out once, and came up with twenty-five grand—minimum."

Mike gave a short whistle.

"Doesn't seem to matter much to him though. They say he's got plenty. His folks had a lot to start with, but he made it big on his own anyway, too, right out of college. Had the first really successful resort around. Got in just at the right time at the right place. Skiing wasn't all that big here then, despite all the snow, but all of a sudden it boomed and old Andy was there."

Jeff shook his head. "Got to give him credit. He showed a lot of balls and foresight, although you wouldn't think him capable of it to see him now. Just seems like a good-looking college boy who never grew up."

"Where does he live?" Mike asked as Jeff went quiet.

"Well, in the summer he lives up at Green Lake."

* * *

"Mister Billingsly?"

The blonde-haired man in the Greek cap sprung lightly onto the dock and approached to where Mike stood waiting. Although his body was fleshy over the white shorts, there was no mistaking the athlete's frame that lurked thirty pounds beneath.

"Yes?" the man responded, stopping a few paces from Mike and standing hands on hips, tanned legs spread, his imperious expression touched with wariness as he examined the intruder.

"I called earlier, Mister Billingsly," Mike explained quickly, uncomfortable in the man's stare, "but there was no answer, so I thought I'd take a chance." He paused. "I'm Mike Frost. Charley's son." He didn't know whether to extend his hand or not, then decided against it.

The blue eyes narrowed for the briefest instant before the mouth widened in a smile that was so warm and welcoming Mike was put totally at ease.

"Charley's son? Mike, you said? I'll be damned!"

The man took a tentative step forward, then came with a certainty and put his arms around the boy.

178

"Let me look at you," he said, stepping back, hands strong on Mike's shoulders.

"Charley's son," he repeated and shook his head. "Been here long?" he added, as if suddenly remembering his manners.

"Maybe half an hour," Mike said as the man walked him toward the house, arm about his shoulders. "I saw the boat out and figured it was you."

Andy grunted good-naturedly. "Probably from what your dad told you, huh?" He didn't wait for a reply. "Your dad would have been out there, too, if he were here. I think—" He stopped, looked at Mike. "I'm sorry about what happened. I read it in the paper. He was the greatest guy I ever knew."

Mike nodded. He didn't trust his ability to respond as he was touched by the simple sincerity in the man's voice.

"Did he talk much about this place?" Andy asked as they entered the house. "I always felt he had a special feeling for it."

"Yes, he did, Mister Billingsly. I know he spent a lot of time here and he loved it."

The man nodded reflectively, and Mike was glad he'd told the white lie. He didn't remember ever hearing the name Green Lake before Jeff had mentioned it that morning, although his father had made occasional reference to a lake up north where he'd learned to sail.

"He was the best friend I ever had," Andy went on, and Mike tried not to show his surprise. "We were as close as two guys could be until he left."

"He spoke of you often, Mister Billingsly," Mike offered, and the wide smile came in a way that made the man seem boyish.

"Call me Andy," he said. "Everybody does."

"Okay, Andy."

"Beer?" the man asked, walking toward the kitchen.

"Thanks," Mike called.

As he waited for Andy to return, Mike looked around the spacious living room. The furniture looked expensive but casual and blended well with the deer heads mounted on the wall so as to give the feeling of a hunting lodge. The cathedral ceiling was beamed; two of the walls paneled, and a third, which housed a large fireplace, constructed entirely of stone. The fourth wall consisted of sliding glass doors, which were opened now onto the redwood deck beyond. Despite the fact that it was summer, the sharp breeze felt cool as it came off the lake.

The paneled walls were covered with photographs, and Mike walked toward them as his host returned.

"Thanks," Mike said, taking the cold can from Andy's hand and moving to the wall.

Andy came up and stopped behind him. "There's a bunch of Charley there."

Mike noticed the same picture he'd seen at the Phi Delta house and recognized his father and Andy in the photo next to it. The two young men were standing on the deck of a sailboat, clad only in shorts, Andy's arm on Charley's shoulder as they grinned at the camera.

Further along the wall was the same boat again. Charley was with a girl this time, his arms about her waist as she leaned back against his shoulder, the expression on their faces leaving no doubt they were in love.

"That was Alice Winslow," Andy said as Mike continued to stare at the picture. "Charley ever mention her?"

Mike shook his head.

"I always thought—" Andy let it drop, but Mike detected the disappointment in the man's voice.

There were some more fraternity pictures, another of Charley and Andy with Alice again, and one of his father on skis.

"That's Mohawk," Andy said with pride.

"I thought so."

"You dad told you a lot about that, I bet."

"No. He never mentioned it."

There was a look of surprise, almost shock on Andy's face Mike felt was out of all proportion to his answer. "I heard the name from a fellow at the Phi Delta house in Madison this morning," he continued. "He told me about the weekends you throw there."

"Never mentioned it?" Andy asked incredulously, ignoring Mike's last words.

"No," Mike repeated, puzzled by the look on Andy's face that had grown to one of bewilderment.

"But that's impossible," the man stated as an absolute matter of fact. "It was just as important to him as it was to me, maybe even more at first, because it was all really his idea. I would have thought he'd be so proud he'd have told everyone about it, even though he did walk out the way he did."

There was a trace of anger in his voice that confused Mike.

"What did that have to do with Mohawk? How my father left, I mean. I always thought he sort of hung around Madison for a while after he graduated, went into the investment business, and then moved to California where he met my mother."

"Well he did stay around for a while, but it wasn't like that. He got the idea for Mohawk just before graduation, picked the location, took me in with him—but it was really all Charley, although I was the one who managed the place. Even most of the money was his, although he insisted we split the profits fifty-fifty."

"You mean my father owned half of Mohawk?"

"Absolutely. Not only that, he could have owned all of it, because he didn't need me to start it. Not that I didn't help make it go," Andy added quickly, "because I was instrumental in promoting it and really getting it off the ground. That's why most people thought it was mine—that and the fact your father preferred to stay pretty much in the background."

Andy paused for a moment. "The real truth is," he said quietly, "he didn't need me in it at all."

"I can't believe he never told me. When did he sell out to you?"

Andy hesitated, an odd expression on his face. "Well," he said finally, "he never did sell out. Just took off and gave me his half."

Mike walked to the couch and sat down as he thought about what Andy had just told him. Charley was generous, more so than anyone he'd ever known, but it was incomprehensible to him that anyone—certainly a young man just starting out—would walk out on a highly successful venture and just give it away.

But he had no reason to doubt Andy, especially because he realized the man really would have preferred everyone to believe he himself was the catalyst in the success story.

"Why did you tell me?"Mike asked. "When I said I'd never heard of Mohawk—why did you tell me it was all my father's? You know everybody thinks you did it on your own."

Andy sank into the leather armchair opposite and looked frankly into Mike's eyes.

"Because I never understood what happened, I guess, and it always bothered me. I thought maybe you could explain things."

Mike said nothing. The older man stood and began to pace. "It was all so crazy. Here was Charley, this orphan from North Carolina. His folks had left him a little money, how much he never told me. Enough at least to get through college, but he sure wasn't independently wealthy for life, at least not as far as I knew.

"Anyway, we were the best of friends, close as two guys could be all through college." Andy reflected seeming to talk more to himself than to Mike. "Did everything together—sailed, skied, partied—he was like my brother. And it always bothered me he'd be leaving when he graduated. He never said where, and I knew he had no place special in mind, so I used to talk to him about staying, maybe the two of us would go into something. And I thought with Alice—"

He turned to Mike, a vague appeal in his eyes "But he always said no. And then, all of a sudden, toward the end of our senior year, he did a complete turnabout. Right here in this room, sitting right on that couch where you are, with his feet stretched out to the fire, he started to talk to me and he had the whole thing mapped out, the whole future, and it went exactly like he said.

"Nobody was really into skiing here. Nobody. But Charley guessed right and he picked the right place, too. We had two great years. We were the only resort I ever heard of to make it so fast.

"And it was easy, too. The operation was so smooth your father wasn't even around half the time. He'd go off skiing to Sun Valley, which was big then, or Aspen—places like that—to get ideas and to have fun, of course. He went everywhere—Switzerland, Austria—any place with slopes. Even went to Liechtenstein a couple of times, and nobody ever even heard of that place." Mike smiled to himself, liking that image of his father.

"It was a good life, a great life, and I know he was happy. I know it," Andy repeated almost angrily, a challenge naked in the glare he fixed on Mike.

"What happened?" Mike prompted.

"What happened? I don't know what happened. All of a sudden he leaves, just like that." Andy snapped his fingers. "Calls me from California and says he's not coming back. Says he's met a girl out there and gotten married—that was your mother," Andy's voice softened, but hardened again as he continued. "He was only gone a week when that call came and he left me high and dry, right in midseason. Never even said a word to Alice, either. Just asked me to tell her.

"That wasn't like your father, Mike." Andy's eyes were pained. "He was the most considerate man I ever knew. I'm sure he loved your mother, but he should have at least called Alice or come to tell her himself.

"And all I ever got from him were the papers giving me his half of Mohawk. Never heard from him again."

Andy looked at Mike apologetically. "I'm sorry. I didn't mean to knock your father. He did a lot for me, gave a lot to me, put me where I am today. But dammit, don't you see? The friendship was more important than the damned resort. I thought he understood that."

Mike was silent for a moment. "You say he left in midseason?" he asked.

"That's right. Just before Christmas. Nineteen sixty-nine."

"And he went to California. Had he ever been there before?"

"Not as far as I know. Just went out and got married, and I never heard from him again. I read about him once in a magazine a couple of years ago, so I knew he was in Boston. And then, of course, the thing last year," Andy ended lamely.

"But I know he didn't forget me," he went on, his face brightening. "I mean, he talked to you a lot about me, about this place." He included all of it with his hand—the house, the boat, the lake. "And he talked to other people, too, so it must have been important to him.

"Why, just a couple of months ago a fellow came up here to interview me. Asked me if I remembered Charley Frost and I said sure. I knew what had happened from the papers, but I was really surprised somebody came by here after all those years. But he was doing an article on Charley's life, a 'success story' he called it, and he was looking for some angles from way back.

"Spent a lot of time looking at those pictures, "Andy indicated the far wall. "I even gave him one, the two of us on the boat."

"Where's the article?" Mike asked. "I'd like to read it."

Andy shrugged. "I don't think it ever came out."

Mike rose and walked to the open glass doors and looked out over the lake, his mind working swiftly. When he turned back he said, "Thanks for your time, Andy. You've really been helpful."

"You're not leaving?" Andy said, and Mike pitied the plea in the grown man's voice. "Stay for dinner, anyway. I'll put some steaks on, or we can go to a place in town that's the best around."

Mike shook his head. "Thanks, but I've got a long way to go. I want to get started while it's still light. I appreciate your help."

"Where you headed?" Andy asked as he stood in the doorway, looking down as Mike got into the Porsche.

Mike hesitated. "Back to Boston," he replied, not certain why he lied.

In his rearview mirror, Mike saw Billingsly's solitary figure watching his car pull away.

CHAPTER 21

"Reid to Europe Before Convention."

Charley read the brief article, folded the paper, and stretched out on the chaise lounge by the small pool in the high-walled, tropical garden. It was noteworthy to him the insignificant bit of news had made its way into the small *St. Thomas Daily.* The local paper had reminded its readers, too, the senator had graced their island with a brief visit only the month before. Charley remembered that last meeting with mixed emotions.

Owen Reid. President of the United States. Charley thought about that. They'd worked for it for so long, planned so carefully, sacrificed— and now it was finally to be.

He hoped Owen would maintain his perspective, although he understood well how difficult that challenge could be. It was Charley's only real fear, but it loomed large. There was so much to be done. Although, he reminded himself, they'd accomplished a great deal already. Not as much as he knew they could eventually but enough to have made a difference. The mystery-shrouded corporation in Liechtenstein had seen to that.

Charley looked out past the gay tropical shrubbery surrounding the pool down to the occasional white sails that marked the blue Caribbean below. What a different setting this was, he mused , from the dark mountain beauty of that tiny European country.

"Another beer?" Von Horst asked, signaling for the waitress who was cleaning a nearby table on the open deck where they sat.

"*Nien,*" Charley answered, bending down to loosen the straps of his hiking boots. "Too much beer will knock me out, especially after all the exercise today. I want to be fresh for this evening."

August 15, 1974, marked the sixty-fourth birthday of Prince Franz Joseph II, and the capital city of Vaduz was prepared for a colorful ceremony to be highlighted by torchlight parades and fireworks.

"I could have a glass of local, though," Charley said as an after-thought.

"I'll join you," the barrel-chested man said. "A carafe of Vaduze, *bitte,*" he told the girl.

Von Horst watched as she walked away, long braids bobbing sauc-ily, the movement of her fleshy buttocks sensually evident even under the loose peasant skirt.

"Oh, my," he said, running his thick finger under the collar of his scarlet turtleneck, sighing deeply and with such regret Charley had to laugh.

"Come on, Klaus. You act as if your whole life were behind you. You're barely thirty. And Maria's the best-looking woman in Vaduz—certainly better than that girl."

"I know," the man responded, sighing again as wearily as a young man could and shaking his curly head. "But this one is so young, so...." He shrugged as his voice faded. "And besides," he added soberly, "Maria is my wife."

Van Horst said the last as if it explained so much; Charley laughed again.

It amazed him he could be in such good humor after having read the morning paper, because even in this tiny foreign country Owen's murder case in Colorado had made the news. Although he had known it was to come and they'd talked about it countless times, and in fact it was the event for which they'd been waiting to launch Owen's career, Charley nonetheless felt a deep empathy for the pangs of guilt he knew his friend must be suffering.

But that had been Owen's decision, only one step in the plan they had so carefully devised and committed to. Charley had his own ghosts to deal with, he had reminded himself as the day wore on until finally the mountains had lulled him.

He felt good now, relaxed, at one with life for a change. The August sun was warm even in the late afternoon, and he almost purred as he pushed up his sweater sleeves and stretched his arms luxuriously. It was all too rare he could indulge his need for simple quietude, and the hike above Steg, while exhausting, had left him with a lingering sense of exhilaration. The sight of the Alpine Valley stretching dramatically below, the quiet of the deep forests, the roar of the rushing mountain stream that had been icy cold when his foot slipped in—all had combined to give him the much-needed boost his soul seemed to require.

And besides, he enjoyed Klaus' company. The man could be quiet, enjoy things in their essence without comment, and Charley found that trait refreshing in anyone—especially a banker.

Although Klaus hadn't always been a banker, Charley reminded himself. In fact, the man had never intended to be one. He'd been a young lawyer when Charley had first met him some six years earlier, a graduate of The Haag who was then only in his second year of practice. Klaus Von Horst had not been a logical choice as his agent, but Charley had a hunch and had followed it. The years had proven him right.

Charley watched now as his friend's eyes shifted again to the dirndl-clad waitress who had reappeared. Placing the wine glasses on the table, she filled them with the delectable local rose from the leather bound flagon in her hand. As she leaned to her chore, the cleavage displayed under her colorful peasant blouse was such that Charley thought he might have to restrain the other man. Klaus's expression was rapt, his eyes as wide as the smile the girl gave him in her deliberate pause before leaving the table.

"*Mein Gott,*" Klaus exclaimed, rolling his eyes heavenward.

A Liechtenstein banker. Supposedly the stuffiest creatures on earth. Eighty years old at birth, if not older. And opposite him sat the wealthiest and most powerful banker of them all, although no one else knew that yet. But they would soon, and Charley hoped again Klaus would be up to it when the time came. Klaus was young, only two years older than himself, but there was a courage in the man, a spirit in his joie-de-vivre Charley trusted far more than the dour businesslike expressions of the lawyer-agents and bankers to whom he had been referred when he first came to Vaduz.

That had been 1968, he remembered. He recalled leaving Mohawk, telling Andy he was off on another ski trip, and mentioning Liechtenstein in his itinerary only by way of passing. His real trip would be Switzerland, he'd said, and the visit to the postage-stamp–sized principality adjoining it would be only a brief stopover.

"Liechtenstein, Charley?" Andy had exclaimed. "Jesus—whoever skis in Liechtenstein?"

"I'll find out." Charley had left it at that.

But Charley had already done his homework on Liechtenstein—not with regards to the skiing conditions but insofar as the economic climate was concerned.

Tax treatment for Liechtenstein-based corporations was excellent, and that was the prime motivation for most foreigners who established themselves there. But tax savings was a minor consideration to Charley. His concern was for secrecy and that was the lure with which the tiny country's laws beckoned. According to his source, an economics professor at Wisconsin, "Outside reporting on Liechtenstein corporations is strictly prohibited without consent of the corporate agent. Whenever the IRS or FBI has tried to pry something loose, they've been stonewalled in a way that makes Swiss bankers sound like fishwives."

So he'd come here himself and had indeed found what appeared to be stonewalls. Not that he couldn't get an agent—the list of men registered was available at any bank, or in the phone book, for that matter. The agents were locals, attorneys who would form your corporation and also act as "front man" if you so desired. Anyone wishing to find out the true ownership of a Liechtenstein corporation would invariably end up with the agent's name and no more.

But finding the right man was not as easy as obtaining the list, at least for Charley. Because of his intentions, he needed someone not only whom he could trust, but also to whom he could relate, and the stern businesslike visages in the stuffy offices he visited left him cold.

He knew he had to decide on one, because Liechtenstein was where it would have to be. But the capital city of Vaduz with its population of four thousand had not provided a choice with which he was comfortable.

Maybe it's my age, he thought. He was a lot younger certainly than most individuals the agents he'd met were used to dealing with. Still, it was discouraging, because the man he chose would be vital to his and Owen's future goals. After exhausting the short list in a second day of bland interviews, he said the hell with it, deferred the choice, and decided to take the next day off and just go skiing. Maybe another option would come to mind during a day of relaxation.

* * *

The slopes of Malbun were already crowded even though he got there early. Despite Andy's jest, a lot of people did ski in Liechtenstein and with good reason, he found. The powder was excellent, the slopes wide and challenging, and by the time he'd done four runs from the top he found himself tiring. Breaking off midway down the next run, he skied over to the hillside chalet that served as a restaurant, went inside, and got a hot meal from the cafeteria line.

The tables were crowded, so he took his tray out onto the porch and sat at one of the long wooden tables that were largely unoccupied. Reaching down, he unsnapped his boots, luxuriating in the feeling of release.

"*Es gutt, ja?*"

He hadn't realized that in easing the pressure on his ankles he'd closed his eyes in contentment. He opened them now to see a man standing beside him, tray in hand.

Charley returned the friendly sally.

"*Es gutt,*" he managed, trying the copy the other's accent.

"*Zetzen?*"

"*Bitte,*" Charley said, indicating the empty bench.

He'd about exhausted his vocabulary. He knew he'd have to learn more than a smattering of the language soon—but not today.

"I'm Charley Frost," he said. "I'm American."

"Klaus Van Horst." He took Charley's extended hand. "Don't speak German?" the other said in more than passable English. "That's okay. My English is pretty good."

189

"Better than that. You sound as if you'd spent time in the States," Charley said as the young man seated himself and loosened his own boots. He wasn't tall, but his bull neck and barrel chest made him seem a very big man. When he removed the goggles from his forehead and shook his hair to free it, the wild cascade of black locks accentuated that impression.

"Never out of Europe," Klaus said. "But I needed English for The Haag. And it comes in very handy with the lovely American skiers. The ladies, that is," the man added, laughing heartily, as he noted the subtle change of Charley's expression.

Charley felt immediately comfortable with Von Horst; he liked his easy, open manner.

"I saw you skiing earlier, alone," the young man said, "and you seemed to go about my level. I'm alone too. Shall we ski the afternoon together?"

"Sounds good."

During the afternoon, Charley learned Klaus was in fact a better skier than he, though not by much, and he enjoyed the extra challenge the man's ability placed on him. He also learned Klaus was an attorney, in his second year of practice, and he hated his work.

"This is what I was made for," Klaus said as they stood at the top of the mountain, parkas zipped tight against the sharpening wind, poised to begin their final run of the day down the slope whose moguls cast deepening shadows. Charley had understood the man to mean life, not merely skiing, and nodded agreement.

Later, they dined together in a quiet restaurant on the Triesenberg Road a few miles south of Vaduz. As they sat before the roaring fire over brandy, Klaus sighed deeply.

"I should never have become a lawyer," he said, eyes to the large picture window beyond which mountains rose bright under the clear moon. "But then—" he turned to Charley and the question that came was distinctly resigned, "what else would I be?"

"You could work for a business concern, perhaps—maybe something involving travel."

"But then, don't you see, I'd have to answer to them. Today, for example, I'd have had to work, instead of catching this glorious day that won't come my way again." The last words could have sounded banal, but Charley knew Klaus meant them sincerely.

"Have you ever thought of becoming one of those agents, the men who form the foreign corporations here?"

Klaus shrugged. "Not really. There's money to be made there sometimes, of course—but mostly it's just another boring job. And besides, why would anyone search me out as agent? My background is litigation—accidents mostly, that sort of thing. I'm not expert on corporate law or taxation."

"But you could learn," Charley stated.

"I could learn," Klaus affirmed, turning to Charley with a look of curiosity and interest dawning on his face.

"Why?"

"Because I'd like you to be my agent."

There was a long pause as Klaus considered, his dark eyes searching Charley's. Finally he said, "Will it be exciting?"

"You have my word on it, my friend."

* * *

Charley hadn't been mistaken. The next six years had been truly exciting, especially for Klaus. They would have been for anyone, Charley thought, because of the risks they'd undertaken. The dramatic leverage they'd employed at times left them stretched so dangerously thin that one bad day on the market could have caused their complete collapse. The pyramiding of the initial ten million dollars in capital into nearly two billion within six years created an atmosphere of tension and excitement that was almost heart-stopping.

Charley regretted deeply at times he couldn't truly partake of the enjoyment, but for him it was like having read in advance the last chapter of a particularly taut thriller.

They'd started in the European market, bought and sold recklessly, moving from issue to issue always just right it seemed. They also dealt heavily in foreign currency exchanges, picking up quick and enormous profits as the mark rose and the pound fell. The only thing they held were their investments in precious metals, gold and silver, which continued to soar and against which they always borrowed to the limit.

Klaus had been amazed at first, unable to believe their remarkable string of luck. Initially he'd been cautious and had tried to talk Charley into holding back, taking his profits and retrenching. But as success continued Klaus had changed, and within a few years the incredible luck that had once awed him he now took as their normal due.

"Let's see," he said, working at the calculator as Charley detailed the instructions for the coming six months. Charley came twice a year for such a meeting.

"By investing in Sony now at five dollars," Klaus went on, "we purchase two million shares. On margin, we get that up to four million. Then, next year at fourteen dollars, even selling out slowly to avoid collapsing the market, we should average twelve anyway. Which gives us a net of seven dollars per share times four million, which equals twenty-eight million dollars profit."

He tore the sheet from the machine and handed it to Charley as if it were a report of a transaction that had already been completed.

Ah, Klaus, Charley thought. He understood well by now that the unquestioning acceptance of good fortune was in everyone, that after a while it invariably became considered a right. And how about me? he wondered, knowing the answer already. He knew that he least of all could ever go home again; he understood too how important to him was the fact he was safe from the threat of that. Accepting, but not liking that in himself. He never had.

Watching the banker's confident, unquestioning eyes, he also knew in Klaus' case as well there would be no comeuppance. But he wondered how the other would have felt about his success had he really understood, as Charley did.

He'd probably adapt to it as readily, as willingly, as I, Charley concluded sadly.

Charley came to understand how true was the axiom money came to money. Once their base was large enough, Klaus could have pyramided the fortune even without Charley's guidance. The man had become an astute investor and tactician, and even though he had learned to plunge recklessly, there was still enough of Liechtenstein in him to ensure he would cover things well enough to prevent any severe loss.

Charley would turn that function over to him soon enough, although Klaus was unaware of that fact. For now, the man was busy with his other duties—following Charley's instructions and running the Alpen Bank. Although only three years old, the bank was one of the largest in the principality, exclusively due to the fact it counted among its depositors the Eur America Corporation.

It was the next move of that corporation Charley wished to discuss with his agent now as they sat on the deck over their carafe of rose, watching as twilight settled in and waiting for the parades to start.

"United Motors, Klaus?" Charley was happy he could still shock his associate.

Klaus' eyes were wide in the candlelight. "United Motors," he repeated.

Klaus pondered the thought so deeply he did not even notice as the buxom waitress leaned to refill their glasses. She walked away with a toss of her head.

"They're the fourth largest automobile manufacturer in America. It will take years to acquire controlling interest," Klaus said finally. "And then, as majority shareholders of a public company registered in the United States, Eur America's books would have to be made available to the U.S. government."

His look was sober and cautious as he awaited Charley's answer. Low key had been their style, anonymity their watchword. Although it was impossible to build the fortune they'd amassed without drawing some attention, there were still very few who had heard of Eur America. Fewer still who could even guess at their assets, and even those estimates would have been woefully short. And most important, there was no one at all except the two of them—to Klaus' knowledge—who had any idea of the company's ownership.

But now, all of that stood to become public knowledge if Klaus understood his friend correctly, and the possibility made him wary.

"I want you to buy United Motors, Klaus," Charley responded levelly. "Not take control of it."

"Buy it?" The whisper was so incredulous, so out of character for the person who emitted it, Charley almost laughed.

"Buy it," he repeated. "Cash deal."

"Cash deal?" Klaus' voice was becoming such an echo Charley finally had to smile.

"Cash deal," he said, making his tone as businesslike as he could so as to bring his friend back to earth. "No other stockholders. It won't be a publicly held corporation anymore."

"But, Charles," the agent said, his voice almost normal as he began to cope with the idea. "It would take at least four billion dollars to do that, if that's really what you want to do. Half again the assets of Eur America."

Four billion. Charley knew the figure was staggering to Klaus. It would be a nearly landmark purchase for the 1970s. But how paltry it would seem when the megabuck deals of the eighties emerged, he reflected somewhat nostalgically.

"I know we're not fully funded yet, Klaus," he said. "We're a year away, maybe a little more. But I want you to begin with the first feelers soon." Charley paused. "About the rest of the money—I'll go over that with you tomorrow."

Klaus' eyes were cold sober as he regarded his friend across the candlelight. Below them, a band struck up and there was a loud cheer from the throngs that lined the street.

Charley reached across to touch Klaus' forearm lightly.

"Come on," he said, rising from the table and walking to the railing. "Here comes the prince."

He watched as the handsome figure stood waving in the open touring car as it moved slowly through the cobbled street. The prince's uniform was white, the sash about his waist a brilliant scarlet, and even from here Charley could see the rows of ribbon on his chest. His carriage was majestic even with the motion of the car, and Charley was moved as the shouts for "Franz Joseph!" all but drowned out the crash of the cymbals and the deep oom-pah-pahs that preceded the stately vehicle.

Behind at a respectful distance, the men bearing torches came.

Charley felt Klaus at his side, turned, and saw the man was looking not at the procession below but rather at him. He returned the other's gaze, put his hand on the man's shoulder, and nodded briefly to affirm he had indeed meant all he had said.

* * *

"Gentlemen, I'm sorry. I really have a lot to do, and I can't help you further." Klaus rose from behind his glass desk, signaling the end of the interview.

The men across from him remained seated in their slingback leather chairs. The modern offices of Eur America's president, dominated by huge and colorful abstracts, was considered almost a scandal by the other bankers of Liechtenstein.

"You mean you refuse to help us further, Herr Von Horst." It was the thin one speaking, McFarland, whose hatchet face and ferret-like eyes Klaus felt suited the man well for his job.

"Refuse, then," Klaus responded. "However you like. The point is, you have no authority in my country, no matter how much you might wish to have. The only obligation of the Eur America Corporation to the United States is to obey its laws in our dealings there, including the payment of taxes due, which is your department.

"Since those taxes have always been paid promptly and in full," he went on, "and since you have accepted our audited statements, I feel our business with your department is currently complete. Ownership of Eur America is none of your official concern, and the release of that information is securely protected by the laws of this principality since we own United Motors outright. As agent for Eur America, I can tell you that I cannot—*will* not," he amended, accentuating the word with a touch of sarcasm as he bowed slightly to McFarland, "help you further. Good day, gentlemen."

McFarland glanced to his companion. The younger, blonde-haired man shrugged, a look of resignation on his face.

The two men rose.

"Good day, Herr Von Horst," McFarland said in mock sincerity.

"Good day," the other man echoed.

They did not shake hands as they left.

Weasels, Klaus thought, seating himself again as the heavy wooden door clicked shut. The IRS men grated on him—or was it the FBI? He really hadn't been sure this time. He hadn't paid attention when they presented their credentials. It didn't matter; he resented both groups. For, although he understood their concern, would himself have felt the need to know who was behind the massive corporation that had suddenly invested so heavily in their country, there was still an arrogance in their approach he found personally affronting. It was as if it were incomprehensible to them a law from the tiny principality could stand up against the desire of that monolith they called the United States. They were so smug, so sure.

He decided again he didn't like the country at all and was beginning to resent he had to spend so much time there.

Reaching over, he pressed one of the buzzers on the panel at the side of his desk.

"Yes, sir," the soft voice came immediately.

"Come in, Inga, would you?"

The heavy door opened a moment later, and although the girl was large and full-bodied, she seemed dwarfed in the massive aperture.

His eyes took her in as she approached the desk.

"Get me a ticket to New York," he said. "Going Saturday."

"And returning?"

"Leave that open."

Her long red hair bounced as she turned to go.

"Oh, Inga," he called almost as an afterthought.

She turned back, and the curve of her breast was silhouetted against the open doorway. The dark eyes waited.

"Make that two tickets, why don't you?"

* * *

The blonde man watched as the girl picked up the phone. He noted her carriage and the confident sway of her hips as she left her desk and strode across the reception area toward the massive wooden doors. He stared thoughtfully as she entered Von Horst's office, then broke his eyes away and glanced down at the name plate on her desk.

"Come on, Williams. We're shot down here," McFarland's officious voice came from behind.

The man called Williams, who was sometimes known as Barnard, nodded his head slowly, turned, and followed his companion toward the elevators.

* * *

The plane made its final approach, dipped the left wing sharply so the whole of New York lay stretched beneath them.

Klaus looked past the girl beside him and saw the Statue of Liberty below. Just beyond, the endless range of steel and concrete began. He remembered his first sight of the city and how in its immensity it had both attracted and repelled him. There was an excitement here, he had to admit, but after a few days he always felt stifled, hemmed in, and could hardly wait to head for home where he could breathe again.

Charles had told him there were parts of the country he would love, places that would make him feel very much at home. He'd found that to be true on one brief visit to upstate New York. But he felt out of place whenever he was in New York City. That had been especially true in that first year, during the long and arduous and often frustrating negotiations.

His first problem had been to make the Board of Directors of United Motors understand he was to be taken seriously. Initially, he'd been dismissed almost out of hand. But when he'd deposited a half billion dollars in the Chase Manhattan, he'd got their attention. Rumors had started and United's stock rose sharply, then settled again when no concrete information could be gathered about a potential offer.

United was selling at forty-eight dollars when he made his firm offer of sixty dollars per share for all shares outstanding. The market was touchy anyway, the mood generally uncertain that year, and many felt privately United might not even hold at forty-eight, much less advance sharply in the near future. So when he guaranteed top management would not be changed and the board could remain intact if it so desired with only the addition of himself as chairman, the deal began to move quickly. They finally settled on sixty-two dollars a share, not much of a margin under what his final offer could have been.

There hadn't been much liquid cash in the Liechtenstein coffers when the transaction was finally completed, but the last two years had shown great profit and the vaults at the Alpen Bank on Englestrasse were bulging again.

The plane leveled off and began its approach. Reaching over, he took Inga's hand and squeezed it reassuringly as the ground rose up.

* * *

197

Charley entered the suite, noting appreciatively the subdued black and mauve decor. He said nothing until Klaus quickly nodded. The banker wore a scarlet smoking jacket, in accord with the mode of dress he had affected these past few years—well tailored, expensive, and just short of flamboyant.

"It's okay, Charles," the man said. "My men searched the room earlier. They're stationed on either side of the corridor."

"I didn't see them," Charley said, removing his top coat and loosening his tie. He himself wore a conservative blue suit of the type he generally preferred for business meetings.

"You weren't supposed to see them," Klaus sighed. "Ach, Charles— I get very tired of the precautions sometimes. You and your phoney passports. Just so you don't get tied to me. Me having to arrange always that we not be seen together. Life should have been simpler, I think sometimes," he ended, shaking his head.

"How's Maria?" Charley asked moments later as they sat on the couch over an excellent coffee which Klaus had poured from the silver samovar on the enameled sideboard.

"Fine. She often wonders what became of you."

"And the kids?"

"Good, too. Anton will be six soon. I've started him skiing this year, and you'd be surprised at how good he is already."

Charley caught the wistfulness behind the words. He looked at his friend and nodded, letting him know he shared his sense of loss.

It had been nice in the early days when they hadn't had to worry, could take off for a few days at a time and share the challenging slopes. But as the Eur American accounts grew, and particularly after Klaus started the bank, it had become necessary to pare their time together to brief and surreptitious meetings. Now with Klaus as head of United Motors, those meetings had become even fewer and more furtive.

Charley rose, walked to the window, and looked past the parted drapes down on Central Park. It wasn't raining, but the heavy mist made the headlights seem almost magical as they cut the darkness. The couple descending from the horse-drawn carriage in the square below seemed to belong in some other time.

Anton almost six, he thought. And Klaus thirty-four. How quickly it goes.

He thought of his own son Mike, approaching eight. They'd skied Vail together this past Christmas, and he'd delighted in the small blue-clad figure that did a remarkable job of following Charley's pace.

He wanted to share that with Klaus now but decided not to. He regretted his relationships always had to trail off somewhere along the line.

Turning from the window, he walked back to the couch and seated himself across from his friend. He noted a pocketbook on the far table that stood by the colorful batik and looked inquiringly at the other man.

"She's out," Klaus said. "Went to see a musical. She won't be back for hours."

Charley's gaze held and Klaus added, "It's okay, Charles. She knows nothing."

Charley nodded. "Let me tell you why I wanted to see you," he began. "But first, a question. How much do we have in reserve now?"

"You mean exclusive of United Motor's assets?"

"That's right. How much?"

Klaus reflected a moment. "About five hundred million."

"That's about where I put it. Now, how much more borrowing power do we have on United? Another three hundred million, would you say?"

"About that, yes."

"Total of eight hundred million give or take. So we could afford to have a few bad years without it breaking us."

"Certainly." Klaus looked concerned. "But why the questions, Charles? The company is in wonderful shape, and with the new line we have planned for next year I've no doubt our profits will be greater than ever."

"With the new line," Charley repeated in a way that caused his friend to sit up sharply.

"What are you thinking?" Klaus asked thinly.

"Of changing the line."

"But Charles!" Klaus stood abruptly, hands deep in the pockets of his smoking jacket, and began to pace as he realized the other man was serious. "The new concept will get us a greater share of the market than ever before. These cars are sensational, power and beauty combined, and we can deliver them at a price that will stun the rest of the industry."

199

"I know," Charley reminded him gently. "It's just I no longer want to deliver power and beauty to the American people."

Klaus' face went blank. "What, then?" he asked finally, staring down at Charley, bull neck tensed as if expecting a charge.

"Safety and economy."

"Safety and economy!" Klaus exploded. "Charles, our cars are safer than any, and our prices fairer as well."

"Not safe enough, Klaus. And not practical enough."

Rising, he walked to the coffee table and opened his briefcase. "Here," he said, handing some papers to the other man. "Look at these."

Klaus seated himself, placed the plans on the coffee table, and examined them. His face became more clouded with every page he turned, and when he was finished he looked up at Charley quietly.

"These are the ugliest things I have ever seen, Charles."

Charley nodded in agreement. "True. But the safest, my friend. And the most fuel efficient. And," he added, "the most environmentally pure."

"And probably the most uncomfortable as well. They might sell in Germany—might, I say—but never in the United States. At least, not today."

"We're going to build them, Klaus—today. Well, next year, at any rate." Charley took a card from his pocket and handed it to the other man. "Here's the man to contact," he said.

Klaus looked at the card, then shifted his eyes back to the drawings.

"We'll go broke," he said. "Two years, three on the outside, and United Motors will be out of business."

"Do it, Klaus."

He took his briefcase and walked to the door. Pausing, he looked back at his friend and his eye again caught the pocketbook that lay on the far table. He stared at it a moment as if lost in thought, then walked over and picked it up.

Klaus began to protest as Charley opened the bag and shut his mouth abruptly when Charley removed the small recorder spinning silently. He looked down at what he held in his hand, raised his head abruptly, and threw the object to Klaus who caught it stiffly.

The look in Charley's eye was something Klaus had never seen before, and a chill went through him when the other finally tore his gaze away and quietly closed the door behind him. Klaus looked at the recorder in his grasp, thought briefly of the succession of men who had tried to pry from him the real ownership of Eur America. He felt again the force of Charley's look and realized for the first time a blunder on his part might be fatal in a way he had never considered.

CHAPTER 22

"My God, Charley!" Kate exclaimed. "Look at that car. It's the ugliest thing I've ever seen."

He glanced again at the snub-nosed compact moving past on the outside lane of the highway. He'd caught sight of it already in his rear-view mirror as the car had approached, thinking again how it reminded him of some miniature tank. The square back now presented to him was insolent in some way, almost like a kid who dropped his pants and deliberately flashed his rear end at you.

Charley had to admit to himself, even with the saucy red finish, the car left a good deal to be desired aesthetically.

"That's the new Aquarius," he told Kate. "A radical approach by United Motors—geared to safety, economy, that sort of thing."

"Aquarius?" Kate snorted. "Scorpio, maybe."

Despite himself, Charley was stung by the remark. The car was his, he felt, and although he had no illusion as to its appearance, it still grated when others discussed the ugliness of his progeny.

The name "Aquarius" was designed to dovetail into the mood of the seventies, a concern and respect for mankind and the environment in which he lived. He knew his ungainly toddler would contribute toward that end.

Of all the things he had accomplished so far, the inception of the Aquarius was to him the most important. It represented the first really significant contribution that had been made, the first visible step in the plans they had drawn so long ago, the plans of bettering things for everyone.

"They're supposed to get forty miles per gallon," he countered, a bit lamely "even with the environmental innovations of the engine and exhaust. And they say they're the safest cars on the road—a lot safer even than this," he added, speaking of the midnight blue Mercedes of which he was so fond.

"Well, do me a favor, Charley," Kate rejoined. "Don't surprise me with one for my birthday."

He gave a short laugh, but the remark bothered him further.

The Aquarius hadn't caught on at all yet. It had been on the streets for a month now, and this was the first one Kate had noticed. He himself had only spotted three or four, and he was avidly looking for them.

Despite the vigorous advertising campaign lauding the merits of the radical newcomer, most critics panned the car vehemently. Even Ralph Nader's endorsement fell far short of championing the vehicle.

United's dealers were upset and rightly so. Their business was off drastically, and many were talking of negotiating with other manufacturers. Some had already done so.

Charley knew beyond question it would work out in the end, but the next two years would be painful, and he'd have to take a lot of flack from Klaus who would be under enormous pressure. The man was already having a difficult time coping with what one magazine had called "United's farsighted but suicidal innovation."

Oh well, he thought as the small red car pulled further away. No one ever said it was going to be easy.

* * *

Nor was it.

Even in 1981, when the company finally turned around and showed a profit for the first time in four years, Klaus was still disgruntled.

"I agree, Charles," he said in one of their rare meetings. Klaus was natty as ever in a subtle tweed jacket that flattered his bulk. Charley, in his conservative gray, felt bland in contrast. "United Motors will survive. Two years ago I would have sworn we'd go broke, but we did level off last year as you predicted, and we're in the black again. But," he added, in a tone that was as close to insolence as he'd ever come with Charley, "so what?"

Klaus rose, walked to the window, and looked out at Central Park. He always chose this same suite at the Plaza and he always came alone. Charley had never brought up the incident with Inga, but he was sure his friend had learned that lesson well.

But Klaus seemed anything but his friend as the man turned and faced him with ill-disguised anger.

"So what, Charles? So we survived. What does it prove, huh?" The man paused then plunged right in again. "United is worth no more than it was four years ago, perhaps less. And we'll never recover our losses, at least not for a long, long time. We've little borrowing power left on United, and less than three hundred million in other assets. And we could have had it all, Charles," he added wistfully. "With our new line in seventy-seven we could have overtaken Ford—or at least come close. United would be twice its size today and our other assets triple."

"But we are stable, Klaus," Charley said quietly, partly in question.

"We are," the other man agreed stiffly.

"And we do have five hundred million at the Alpen Bank."

"Almost."

"Five hundred million United won't need."

"Probably not," Klaus offered reluctantly, wary now but already resigned as he recognized suddenly Charley was circling in again.

"And another two hundred million in gold and silver."

Klaus nodded.

"Good." Charley's tone was all business now. "Here's what I want you to do. Sell the gold and silver off, and then go short. When the market hits these levels," he handed Klaus a sheet of paper, "sell out again and move into video and home computers." He handed another sheet to Klaus who glanced at it only briefly before putting it in his pocket. "As the market moves up, borrow as heavily as you can and keep buying. I assure you, Klaus," he added in a tone that was intended to alleviate the other's hostility, "within five years the Alpen account will be all you could wish it to be."

The other man nodded, unmollified because he knew there was more to come.

"And the other five hundred million, Charles?" he asked pointedly.

"That's what I really wanted to talk to you about."

* * *

The Quality Housing Corporation began quietly in 1982. The first two projects in Detroit and Philadelphia were lauded by city planners, although most of those people thought privately the firm would probably not survive long enough to see its bold and far-reaching concepts in inner-city redevelopment achieve fruition.

Improved inner-city housing for the lower income groups was certainly a noble aspiration, but few thought there would be profit in it.

Nor did there seem to be. But Quality Homes seemed somehow to survive, and by 1984 had additional projects completed in Chicago, Los Angeles, and Cleveland, and was beginning to move into New York and Boston.

The video and home computer stocks had been sold at great profit and the currency exchange now supported the effort, but, although the assets in the Alpen Bank were still healthy, Klaus resented the constant siphoning off of monies that could be used to pyramid the fortune faster as the strength of the dollar continued to rise.

He said nothing, however, because Charles had made it very clear he was in full command. It was not like the old days when Klaus had felt the two of them had amassed the incredible assets together. Even though the direction had always been Charles', Klaus had still been allowed to feel part of that.

But that was no longer true, and Klaus felt a great loss as he came to understand that in the end he was truly nothing more than a glorified "front man," albeit an extremely wealthy and powerful one. Charles had taken the gloves off finally, and Klaus realized whatever the man's ultimate aims he would never be privy to them.

He'd thought at first it was money, but events had proven him wrong. The United Motors purchase had been suspect, the initiation of the Aquarius almost suicidal. And the Quality Housing projects would always be a drain. Charley Frost's motives had begun to appear altruistic in a way Klaus could not fathom, because it was now beginning to seem to him the entire enterprise had been created for just that purpose.

So he had not been surprised when, in 1986, Charles instructed him to establish, through United Motors, a foundation whose purpose was to offer grants for the research of environmental improvement. It was not such an unusual request: Many corporations did such things with part of their profits, of course. It was good public relations.

What no one knew, however, was Klaus' instructions were to commit *all* of United's profits toward that project.

* * *

Klaus looked up at the clock, slowed his pace as he neared the short line in front of the ticket counter. He had nearly a half hour before his flight left Kennedy for Zurich.

In ten hours he would be in Vaduz and the thought delighted him. Two weeks in New York was far too long under the best of circumstances, but since Charles' death he was fearful of spending too much time away from the bank and the oversight of Eur America's other enterprises, despite the surprisingly detailed directives Charles had given him at their last meeting. It was almost as if the man had known, he thought, wondering again who would take his place and when that man would appear.

Klaus moved into the line and placed his well-traveled attache case on the floor beside him. Over his arm he carried the gabardine topcoat he'd bought for the late March weather. A floral tie graced the blue shirt he wore beneath the tweed sports jacket with its leather-patched elbows.

"Excuse me." The young man in the gray suit who touched his elbow lightly looked innocent enough, but was obviously on some mission. "Are you Klaus Von Horst?"

"I am," Klaus said, wondering what problem had arisen that might require his return to United's offices.

"Would you step this way, please?" the young man asked politely, flashing a government identification card so smoothly in his hand no one else in the line could have been aware of it.

Klaus' heart seemed to stop as he looked down at the official emblem stamped beside the young man's photograph, and he raised his eyes and stared numbly at the other.

"This way, please," the man repeated conversationally, turning away, and Klaus picked up his attache case and followed like an automaton. When they had cleared the line, the man slowed his step until Klaus was beside him.

"What is this?" Klaus began. "What do you—?"

"We'll be there in a minute, sir," the other cut him off politely, continuing on back up the ramp toward the main terminal until he came to an unmarked door at which he stopped, rapped twice, and entered.

He ushered Klaus inside and closed the door behind them.

The room was without windows, its beige walls broken only by another door to the side. Behind a gray metal desk sat a youngish man with blonde hair who was smoking a cigarette. He was wearing a tan suit with a striped tie. He seemed vaguely familiar to Klaus.

There were three gray chairs set about the desk, in one of which sat a man whom Klaus *did* recognize. He'd seen the long dark beard and full sideburns that dropped from beneath the high top hat only an hour ago on a busy Manhattan street. The man still wore the black coat that fell almost to his feet.

"Is this the man?" the one who had taken him from the line asked without preamble.

The bearded man nodded immediately, eyes gleaming dark as black beads under thick eyebrows. "That is him." The voice carried a heavy accent.

"My name is Miller, Mister Von Horst. Douglas Miller, FBI, if you didn't register my credentials," the young man said, turning to Klaus. "Did you purchase a diamond ring from this man earlier today?"

"I did." Klaus' numbness had faded, replaced by a rising anger. He thought he understood the situation now and was annoyed not only by the unnecessary fright he'd experienced as a result of the unexplained summons, but also by the fact he was now in danger of missing his flight. "I have it right here," he said, reaching into his pocket and holding the ring out toward Miller. "I purchased it for four thousand dollars and planned to declare it at customs as required. Why are you questioning me?"

"That ring is stolen property, Mister Von Horst. We can prove it. This man has admitted to it."

"So what does that have to do with me? I didn't know it was stolen. This man approached me on the street, a street filled with diamond salesmen, and showed me a ring. I was looking for one, that's why I was there. I have purchased such things there often and have always declared them. I paid his price, and if the ring was stolen I will gladly return it for my money so I can go on my way." Klaus contained his anger, but impatience was clear in his voice.

"I'm afraid it's not that simple, sir," Miller said calmly, taking the ring from Klaus' outstretched hand and idly examining it. As he turned it in his fingers, the large diamond sparkled in the fluorescent light that shone from the ceiling. "You see, Mister Ostroski—the gentleman there—claims he has sold such items to you in the past, many of much greater value, and that you were aware they were stolen goods and priced accordingly."

"A lie!" Klaus exploded, the cords on his bull neck bulging and his face flushed as he swivelled his body violently to face the seated Ostroski. "I have never seen him before today!" He pointed a trembling finger. "Never!" He began to advance toward Ostroski; Miller quickly grabbed his arm.

"All right, Mister Van Horst. All right."

Klaus stopped and controlled himself by taking deep breaths. "I don't know what this is about," he managed finally when he could speak.

"As I explained, Mister Ostroski has admitted to dealing in stolen jewelry. He claims you were a prime and knowing source in his disposition of those goods."

"And I deny it. I have never seen the man before today. I swear it. You cannot prove otherwise."

Klaus looked at Miller, who in turn looked at the blonde man in the tan suit who had sat silent behind the desk throughout. After a moment's pause, the man gestured with his hand toward the other door to the room. Miller walked over and opened it.

With red hair sleek above a simple blue coat that flattered her stunning figure, Inga stepped into the room. In her hand she held a pocketbook, which she handed to Miller when he asked for it.

She did not meet Klaus' eyes.

At the sight of his former mistress Klaus felt a fury rise, but he was becoming frightened. Despite his innocence, all his denials seemed futile, bouncing harmlessly off the implacable wall created by the bearded Ostroski's steadfast accusation, the display of jewelry taken from her handbag, and Inga's mumbled corroborations. How they got to her, Klaus didn't know, but his anger had slowly been replaced by a sense of some impending and unwelcome eventuality.

He must not weaken, he told himself, but felt his will eroding. They can make things very difficult for me, he thought, and they obviously intended to, although he did not understand why that would be.

Finally, the blonde man in the tan suit, who had yet to utter a word, rose and came from behind the desk. He stopped in front of Klaus, and as Klaus looked into the cold gray eyes he remembered where he had seen him before. This man had once pressed him recently at his office in Liechtenstein. Eur America, he realized with a start.

"Now," the man said calmly, "about the illegal drugs Miss Gersten mentioned...."

Inga raised her face as the man spoke, and her eyes, when they met Klaus', glistened bitter and worldly wise.

* * *

Four months later, Klaus sat in his office, waiting, oblivious of the colorful abstracts that so often drew his attention. He didn't know who was to come but knew he'd be contacted sometime during the week. The cryptic message he and Charles had worked out so many years ago had finally been sent in the telegram he'd received that morning.

He walked to the window behind his glass desk and looked south toward Triesenburg, where the mountains began their rise. On the other side one had a breathtaking view of the Rhine Valley; he'd often gone there with Charles.

Poor Charles, he thought as his eyes took in the Alpine beauty his friend had loved so well. He missed the man terribly, had not realized how deeply attached he was to him still until he'd read the article about his death in the Wall Street Journal. They'd grown apart in the past years, but the ache in Klaus' chest as he read of Charles' death was so painful he realized nothing could really overshadow the deep love he felt for the other man.

Charles Frost, he thought again, and the sense of loss seemed fresh.

He realized now he had come to appreciate the things Charles had insisted on, although he'd resisted them at the time. But today, there were nearly five million Aquariuses on the road, and Klaus knew in his heart the unattractive vehicle was really the better way.

And Quality Housing had improved life for thousands.

And, he reminded himself, the unfaltering rise in the dollar Charles had predicted still left Eur America with more assets than he would ever have believed.

He wondered who would be coming now, what this man whom he'd been expecting for nearly a year would be like. He wondered, too, what his instructions would be from the swine Barnard who had managed to spin a web of invented circumstance strong enough to hold Klaus hostage.

CHAPTER 23

Mike put a hundred-dollar chip on the red and watched as the wheel spun. The white blur became a ball as it slowed and finally settled after a tantalizing clickety-click bounce as the wheel wound down.

"Number twenty-seven," the croupier announced. "Black."

Shit, Mike thought, walking from the table.

That last bet was just throwing money away, because he'd been sure he would lose.

Still, he couldn't complain. His hunch had paid off, and he was five thousand dollars richer.

Pushing his way toward the crowded bar, he thought about how lucky he had been. He hadn't really planned to stop in Las Vegas. He had only done so because it was so near—and because his father had always promised to take him sometime but had never been able to.

That was really it, he admitted to himself as he ordered a beer from the willowy, scantily clad waitress. He wished his father could have shared his thrilling run of luck.

"All right, Mike!" Charley would have shouted, clapping him on the back as his streak at the wheel had continued.

Conjuring that scene made him suddenly think of Susan Mallory. He'd shared that heady type of excitement with her in their hushed midnight search of the files in Durham, and he wished now that she had been with him here, urging him on with unrestrained encouragements and looking at him with worshipful blue eyes as his number came again.

Susan Mallory. The thought of her brought a smile to his lips. He liked her very much. Maybe, when he went back east, he'd stop first in Durham and give her a gift, some expensive piece of jewelry, perhaps, from the winnings that number fourteen had brought him.

Fourteen. He had been born on the fourteenth.

Mike liked to gamble. He had played poker and blackjack often with his friends in addition to the increasing penchant he'd developed for following—and consistently winning upon—his hunches on ball games. But he had never before coped with the frenzy of a casino. He did, however, understand roulette was the sucker's game, second only to the slot machines in giving the house an edge against the bettor.

He'd planned to sit at the blackjack table, maybe even try to decipher the fast moving mystery of craps, but somehow when he entered he'd been drawn irresistibly to the roulette wheel about which a number of bettors, mostly women, were seated, each with individually colored stacks of chips before them. He pushed through some onlookers to the table, gave the croupier some cash, and received chips of his own color—green.

"Fourteen," he'd said, placing a five-dollar bet on the number. Seventeen had come up, but he'd persisted, feeling more and more as the wheel spun he was destined to be a winner. He decided he would invest up to fifty dollars.

Fourteen hit on the fifth spin, again on the seventh, and Mike increased his bets as the evening wore on and the number continued to fall. A small crowd had gathered behind him, murmuring from time to time. Mike felt sophisticated, important, and managed to keep a grin from his face.

"Fourteen," the tuxedo-clad croupier had said once more, and Mike had picked up his chips and counted his winnings. Fifty-one hundred dollars. He'd had the urge to run it up higher but felt somehow his luck had run out.

So instead he'd thrown the hundred-dollar chip on the red and lost, putting his gain at an even five grand.

It wasn't the hundred bucks that bothered him, he thought as he sipped his beer in the noisy lounge. It was more he had known he'd lose and had made the bet anyway in an act of perversity, as if it were a debt he owed, a token sacrifice to some unknown deity to acknowledge his good fortune. Like the French custom he'd read about, when they spilled a bit of their wine before drinking.

But that had been a hundred dollars he'd thrown out there, not a few drops of wine, and it annoyed him. Why did he have to thank anybody for his run of luck? It had been his doing. And his money.

Still, he was leaving Vegas a winner, which was more than most people could say. He finished his beer, overtipped the willowy waitress whose "thank you" was more than gracious, and, feeling larger than life, superior in some way, he rose to make his way to the cashier's window.

"Any markers?" the Asian girl behind the cage asked as he stacked his chips on the counter before him.

"Nope," he grinned, pushing the pile toward her. "All winnings."

She looked to a swarthy man behind her, who nodded slightly, and she quickly counted the chips, reached into a drawer and placed a bound stack of one-hundred-dollar bills before him, saying, "Five thousand even."

The words sounded a sudden alarm for Mike, and his euphoria, his grandiose picture of himself, vanished in a sudden chill. As he reached out and tentatively touched the stack, he was once again at home in Weston in the den, with the door of his father's safe yawning open before him.

Mumbling "Thank you," he turned from the cashier's cage and moved toward the exit.

He suddenly wondered what awaited him in Los Angeles.

* * *

"Thank you," Mike said, working hard to keep a tremor from his voice, astonishment from his face, as he handed the document back to the elderly lady who waited across the counter. "How can I get a copy?"

"I can have one made while you wait," she answered sweetly. "They're three dollars apiece."

"One, thanks," Mike said, handing her the money.

A moment later, he walked across the marbled floor, pushed open the glass door, and emerged into the brilliant Pacific sunshine. The smog he'd so often read about was certainly not in evidence today, his mind registered vaguely as he walked the block to where he'd parked the Porsche.

Unlocking the car, he got in and sat a moment. Then he opened the envelope he held, took out the photocopy, and examined it as if hoping it had changed from the original.

It hadn't.

The date December 28,1969, was irrevocably entered on the line.

* * *

The wave rose slowly and suddenly peaked, and Mike caught it just below the crest. For an instant he felt almost suspended before his body dropped sharply and he stiffened to take the force of the water above and below. He was buffeted by the turbulence but kept his body straight as his father had taught him to do so many years ago, and in a moment he was in the long, easy glide. His momentum was such that he was still moving when the rough sand scraped against his chest.

Rising, he walked well beyond the rough and tumble volleyball game to the quiet place on the beach where he'd stretched his blanket, and lay down on his back. The July sun felt good. He placed his hands behind his head, closed his eyes, shut out the drifting laughter and the pounding of the surf and tried to sort it out.

December 28, 1969. That was the day Charles Frost had married Ellen Kimball, Mike's natural mother. Charley had been twenty-four at the time, his mother twenty-two. He knew that from the copy of his birth certificate he'd procured earlier in the day. That document carried the other significant date.

May 14, 1970. His birthday.

His parents had been married less than five months when he was born.

He thought back on his conversation with Andy Billingsly, his father's old college friend. The date checked with what Andy had told him. "Your father left right in the height of the season, around Christmas—and never came back."

Mike thought the man might have been mistaken about the year, but he hadn't wanted to say anything. He had always believed his parents had lived in Los Angeles for a year or so before he'd been born. But Andy had been right. The marriage license proved it.

He remembered Andy had also said Charley had never been to California before. If he was right about that, too, it meant Charley had left Wisconsin with no explanation, met a girl four and a half months pregnant, and married her on the spot.

Mike couldn't imagine his father doing such a thing. It was completely out of character for the man he'd known so well to act so irresponsibly and recklessly. And the thing Andy had said about how Charley had left Alice Winslow without a word. Virtually abandoned her. There was a cruelty there that wasn't like his father either.

It didn't make sense.

Something else he'd heard during his odyssey didn't add up, either. He remembered Anderson, his father's coach, talking about Charley's spirit as a kid. "Some hell-raiser," Anderson had said a few times. That hadn't sounded like his father—as a man, at any rate. Although Charley had a real love of life and an adventurous spirit, Mike saw little if any "hell-raiser" in the man he'd known.

Still, things change.

That wasn't what bothered him about his talk with Anderson.

It was something else, something nagging at the back of his mind, and as Mike reviewed again that conversation, he suddenly realized what it was.

* * *

"What'd he do today?" Barnard's voice held its usual anticipation.

"Nothing more than we expected. Checked for marriage and birth certificates—then spent the rest of the day at the beach."

"So now he knows as much as we know. Good. If there is anything else...."

"Want me to stay on it?"

Barnard considered. "Give it one more day. I don't think he's picked up any more than we have, but you never know. My guess is he'll be heading home."

"Things set?"

"Rewired last week."

"Well, if nothing happens back there, it's a wrap. It's probably just as well, if you want my opinion. You and he seem to be the only two who doubt Frost is dead. Your suspicions I can understand, but why does the kid keep looking?"

"Well," Barnard paused, "he *is* Charley's son."

* * *

"Hey, Mom—how you doin'?"

"Mike!" Kate cried happily when she heard his voice. "How are you?"

"Great, Mom. How about yourself?"

"Fine, Mike. Just fine. Where are you?"

"California. Los Angeles."

"What are you doing all the way out there?"

"Just looking around. Hey, Mom, don't worry," he picked up quickly. "That's what I called to tell you. I'm leaving tomorrow; I'm coming home. I should be there sometime next week."

Kate questioned Mike about his immediate plans and was somewhat put off when he dodged the question of college.

"Well, we'll talk when you get here," she said.

"Yeah. Hey, Mom…," he trailed off.

"What is it, Mike?"

"About Dad—," Mike didn't know how to ease into this so he just plunged right in. "Did he have any scars or anything like that? Big ones, I mean. On his head."

She was silent for a moment. He felt badly for her, not just because the dredging up of the memory was painful, but also because his question would have to make her uneasy.

"No," she answered finally. "Nothing like that. Nothing big. And none on his face at all, besides his nose being broken."

Mike nodded, remembering it that way, too. But he pushed again, anyway. "Not just his face, Mom—anywhere on his head. His scalp, maybe." Jesus—he sounded like a six-year-old.

"Nothing, Mike." Her voice was testy now, held a touch of alarm. "Why are you asking?"

He hesitated, then said, "Just something that came up. I'll talk to you about it when I get home, okay?"

"Mike—you're sure there's nothing you want to say to me now?"

"Nothing that can't wait. See you soon. Love you," he added before slowly replacing the receiver.

He walked to the window of his motel room and looked out. Below him, the Pacific Ocean stretched in the afternoon sun and the cresting waves would have been inviting had he noticed them.

* * *

The Porsche was packed and waiting in the parking lot. Any thought of detouring through Durham to see Susan again was buried under the weight of what he now knew and must deal with.

All else had become secondary.

Taking a last sip of coffee at the counter in the diner, Mike picked up the newspaper again and leafed to the inside pages. A picture suddenly caught his eye and he looked at the article.

"Reid Vacations Before Convention."

There was a small picture of the distinguished-looking Senator Owen Reid smiling at the camera and giving a thumbs up salute as he boarded an airplane. The article noted the senator was off for a week of rest and relaxation in the tiny principality of Liechtenstein before the upcoming Republican convention in Dallas.

The article went on to review the senator's dramatic string of smashing primary victories and quoted the national polls, all of which ranked him far ahead of any of the possible democratic candidates. Although the conventions were yet to be held and the actual election was still some four months away, the tone of the article was such that those events appeared almost anticlimactic.

Mike put down the paper.

Owen Reid. The next president of the United States.

Mike would have to get to him and soon, because that was the only door left. Reid would know, Mike was certain of that now. Mike didn't know how he'd accomplish the meeting, and knew it would become even more difficult as time went on. Once the man was the official democratic candidate—

217

Liechtenstein. The name suddenly struck a chord and Mike tried to put his finger on it but couldn't. There was something that nagged though, something somebody had said maybe....

But not now, he reflected as he walked to his car. He already had enough to think about for now.

Because Mike had come to two overwhelming conclusions.

The first was his father was unquestionably alive.

And the second was he was Richie Peters.

CHAPTER 24

Charley checked the depth gauge on his wrist. Eighty-five feet. Reaching down, he grasped the pressure gauge that dangled by his side and brought it up to his face mask.

Four hundred pounds of air. He'd have to start up in five minutes at the most, he estimated. He always cut it close but didn't like to go under two hundred pounds that deep.

Swimming over to Janine who hovered motionless above a shadowed stand of coral, he checked her gauge and saw it registered over six hundred pounds. No matter how much he conserved his air, how well and shallowly he measured his breathing, she could always outlast him by a considerable margin.

"Women use less oxygen, Larry," she'd told him often, and he knew it was true. Still, it frustrated him at times, and he caught the elfin gleam in her eyes as she checked his gauge, turned her face mask up to his, and reached up playfully to tug his beard.

He took her hand, rose up the barnacled side of the corroded ship, and slipped over the top for the quick descent into the hole in the vessel's superstructure. It was dark as they made their way through the passage, and the lights filtering through the various apertures were eerie as they picked up a million dancing motes and an occasional drifting fish. They entered a room he thought to have been a cabin, carefully avoided hitting each other's apparatus as they looked about the cramped space, turned, and retraced the passage. As they came clear, he checked his gauge again, saw it was right at two hundred, and gave her a thumbs-up signal. He made his way to the anchor line and began his ascent, going slowly and taking care to keep the bubbles always above his face mask. The ship below faded to the barest outline.

When he broke to the surface, he took off his flippers, threw them into the boat, and climbed awkwardly up the ladder. The tank was heavy, and he reminded himself again to get a floating platform so as to ease this part of a dive.

Dropping his feet to the deck, he turned his back to the gunwale, positioned his tank on it, and knelt slightly as he eased the straps off. He placed the tank in its holder and quickly stripped off the rest of his gear. Walking to the small open cabin of the Ensign, he took a towel from the bench and rubbed himself down vigorously. He'd had a slight chill under water but the sun was strong and he felt warm again immediately. He reached into the cooler, took out a beer, opened it, and sat by the tiller to wait for Janine.

Charley rested his eyes on Salt Island, which lay only a few hundred yards to the east. He'd anchored there briefly when they'd dove the wreck of the Rhone some weeks earlier, a small patch of land inhabited by three blacks, an ancient man and woman, and another female of indeterminate age. There was something touching about the weather-beaten shack they called home and the goats and chickens that wandered freely. He didn't know how the three people existed. The salt they dredged from the great pond beyond the shack could hardly have brought them much income from the occasional boats that stopped with which they could barter.

"Dis mah home," the younger female had explained, in response to his question as to how long she'd lived there. "Ah born yeh," she offered brightly through a mouth of missing teeth.

She'd led him with pride to the small cemetery on the hill and had recounted as best she could the burial of some twenty-five or thirty bodies—he never was sure of the exact amount—that had washed ashore following the shipwreck of the Rhone. Few markers were visible, but she'd pushed aside the groundcover to show him where others had been placed.

He looked now to the cemetery hill on the small almost barren island, thought incongruously of Kate, and made the connection.

Jaffrey, New Hampshire.

They'd driven up for the day, no place special in mind, following the winding country roads and enjoying the sights and smells of the hilly countryside as an upstart Spring insisted on making its presence felt.

They'd stopped at the Cathedral of the Pines to walk in the silent woods, brown needles slick under their feet, and had driven on toward Jaffrey in search of a quiet inn for dinner.

"Oh, look," Kate had exclaimed, pointing ahead to her right. "There, on the hill."

Before a large, solitary oak tree was a rusted iron fence surrounding a small plot.

"Let's go see," she'd said, and he stopped the car. They held hands as they mounted the hill, stopping at the fence to inspect the weather-beaten stones.

"So young," she said softly as she noted the dates on the smaller markers that seemed so prevalent. The place was a silent monument to the Jenkins family, many of whom had not lived to see their seventh year. "It must have been hard here," she added with a catch in her voice.

Charley felt a catch in his own throat now as he remembered that day, recalled how close he'd felt to her and how happy he'd been when she accepted his proposal at dinner some hours later.

Kate, he thought now, eyes still on the nearby island. Would you be as touched by this cemetery as you were that other? Could you share this with me now as we shared that then?

Probably, he thought, for the woman who'd taken him and his infant son, who'd born him his daughter, had never failed him in all their years together.

Charley felt suddenly alone, more alone perhaps than he ever had. He was orphaned again, he realized, but in a far more permanent way. Never again to see Kate, Mike, Penny—Klaus, either—none of them. Not even Owen, he thought now, realizing for the first time how truly cut off he was. They hadn't discussed another meeting, and Charley realized there was no need for one, at least not for a long, long time. Owen's plans were set, the machinery there and in Liechtenstein well tooled and in motion, the backup secure. For the time being at least there was no real need for Charley. In fact, his existence ironically posed the only threat to the entire enterprise at this time.

He thought about that for a moment, but put it away as he heard the sound of the bubbles and turned to see Janine's head break the surface of the water.

CHAPTER 25

"Ready, Missus Reid?"

"I'll be with you in a minute, Bert."

"Right. I'll be outside in the car."

The man with the crewcut closed the door, and Nancy turned to Owen.

"You look lovely, Nancy," he said, openly admiring the green shift that brought out the color of her eyes.

She preened at the compliment "You sure you won't come along, Owen?" she asked again. She was leaving on the evening plane from Zurich and seemed a touch put out he wasn't accompanying her on their last holiday afternoon together.

He shook his head. "You go on, hon. I'm shopped out. And besides, I just want to sit and think for awhile."

"Anything special I can get you?" she asked, surrendering gracefully as she generally did.

He held her eyes and suddenly, unexpectedly, spread his arms. She came to him for the strong embrace that was so uncharacteristic of late; she placed her head on his chest and felt his face nuzzling her hair as of old.

Pushing away finally, he kept his hands on her shoulders, searched her eyes before nodding as if in answer to some very private question, then tilted her chin for a gentle kiss before ushering her to the door.

"Owen," she began, alerted to something.

He put his finger to her lips, shook his head, and said, "Bert's waiting."

He watched thoughtfully as the door closed behind her, then crossed the spacious living room of their suite, with its graceful archways and the high-domed ceiling from which a magnificent wood-inlayed chandelier descended. He reached the rosewood cabinet that housed the wet bar and poured some bourbon on ice, then walked through the open-latticed porticos out onto the balcony overlooking the Rhine Valley below. The quaint hotel in the small village of Triesenberg had been a good choice. They'd been there for five days, and Owen was as relaxed as he could be under the circumstances. The tiny principality was indeed a good place for rest and relaxation, although that wasn't why he'd come.

He sat on one of the cushioned chaise lounges, put his drink on the table beside him, and lit a cigar. As the smoke rose, he looked past it to the spectacular scene below, the deep shadowed valleys through which the rushing river curved. He remembered the other time he'd seen that view, the time on the precipice he'd argued with Charley when they'd met here a few years ago.

The thought pained him, and he pushed it away and let his mind go blank.

He'd told Nancy he wanted to think for awhile but nothing could have been further from the truth. He'd done all the thinking he could, all the planning he could, and now he could only wait out these next days as the game played out.

Taking a deep drag from his cigar, he exhaled slowly, leaned his head back on the cushion, and closed his eyes.

CHAPTER 26

Mike stripped down to his faded denim shorts. He stretched out on the blanket hands behind his head and rested his eyes on the cloudless sky. The salt air was heavy as he breathed.

Just beyond him, the small waves broke, rolled, and died in a last breath of white froth only a few feet from where he lay on the secluded private beach. Only the small sailboat moored at the bleached wooden dock attested to civilization. Several sandpipers darted spindly legged along the ocean's edge and an occasional gull drifted lazily. The rhythmic measure of crashing water combined with the pleasant heat of the noon Maine sun might have lulled him to sleep on another day.

But not today. He had too much to think about.

It was only the night before he'd come to realize what he had.

The power.

Now he had to ingest that fully and begin to learn how to deal with it.

He understood now why his father had often seemed to be searching his face, and finally identified the vague fear he'd sometimes felt about Charley. It was as if his father had always *known* everything deep down. More than ever, he wished he could see the man, speak to him.

The power.

It was going to be a difficult thing to handle, an awesome responsibility. And his father could have helped him greatly.

Suddenly, the world was at his feet, but the thought was so overwhelming it confused him. He could have anything he wanted. Anything at all. But there had to be limits and his father had somehow learned to deal with that.

Eighteen. That's how old Richie had been when he'd gone down to Durham for the test, when he'd purchased the raffle ticket, when he'd predicted the ball games as Coach Anderson had related it all to Mike. When he'd become Charley Frost, Mike added.

Well, he had an advantage over his father, because at least he understood what was happening. If not for what he'd learned in his search, however, he'd have no more inkling of the truth than Richie must have had, and he wondered when and how the realization would finally have come.

Mike didn't know where to start in sorting things out; he had made only one determination thus far—not to tell anyone any of it until he'd thought it out for a long, long time.

He realized now that's what must have happened to Richie. People had known, or at least suspected. Something had happened, something frightening probably, and that had accounted for the switch in identities. In order to live, Richie Peters and the power had to appear to die.

Mike pursed his lips. Even in his "death" his father had managed to teach him a valuable lesson—perhaps the most valuable of all, because Mike understood his very survival depended on his keeping the power secret.

He was sure, too, that's what the faked kidnap-murder was about, which is how he now thought of it. He knew it must have something to do with the power. Mike figured someone was on to his father, after all these years. He remembered Barnard, the FBI man who'd come to interview them months after, how he'd felt the purpose of the visit was really a search for Charley—Richie, he amended.

And the telephone tap.

He recalled then, too, what Andy Billingsly had said that day at Green Lake, how a reporter had come asking questions, had taken one of the old photographs, all for an article that had never appeared.

And he suddenly had the cold recollection of the records room in Durham. He could see in his mind's eye the gray file cabinet that had contained no file on Richie Peters in that quiet, dead-of-night search, but that had yielded those amazing test scores the following morning. No one could have expected him to search the files that night as he had done with Susan, and he now understood his surprise move must have upset someone else's timing.

So they were on to him as well, Mike realized, and his eyes narrowed as he looked out to the water. They'd probably been following him every step of the way in his effort to search for his father.

His lips tightened at the thought. He'd unknowingly led them on a cross-country chase, but in the end they could only have learned what they must have known—or certainly suspected—already.

But at least he hadn't led them, whoever they were, to his father.

Would they continue their surveillance of him? Mike doubted it. They couldn't know that he too had the power. They had likely only been interested in Mike for the possible results of his search.

And now that search had reached a dead-end.

His father might be anywhere. Mike had a quick vision of the open safe in Weston and saw again the fake passports carrying his father's picture. How important those implications had been then and how insignificant they seemed now. He was finally at peace with that now that he understood the need for Charley to have had to take such precautions. He felt enormous relief at least *that* suspicion of his father would no longer haunt him.

And the money? The nine hundred thousand dollars in stacks of crisp bills?

It all made sense to Mike now. The passports, the money, the kidnaping—and especially the bottom line. Charley's exposure had been threatened somehow, and he'd gone underground again.

If only Mike knew where to look.

He feared his father had disappeared for good and would never be back even though he was still alive. He understood that but knew too his father would want to help him learn to cope with the power because he was the only person who could.

Which brought Mike to another realization.

He sat up quickly, put his hands about his knees, and looked without seeing at the sailboat bobbing gently in the swells at its mooring on the weather-beaten dock.

Charley had not known the power was growing in Mike. He may have suspected it, with his searching gaze, but he hadn't known. If he had, he would certainly have spoken to his son, brought him into all of it, because they could have helped each other in ways no other two human beings could.

So Charley must not have known any more than Mike himself had. Which led to another conclusion.

The power, whatever it was, did have its limitations.

Mike wondered what those limitations were. He felt uneasy at the mere thought of learning to deal with any of it. It was all so new, so sudden. He'd never even suspected, or if he had, he hadn't realized it. Not until the night before when he'd returned home.

"Mom!" he'd shouted as he entered the house. "I'm home."

"Mike!" Her call had come from upstairs, and her footsteps sounded instantly as she ran down the curving staircase to greet him, face flushed with a deep summer tan.

Hugging him tight, she kissed his cheeks soundly, and squeezed him tighter yet.

When she broke away, she looked up at his face, searching.

"Hey, Mom," he said, a little uncomfortable in the long gaze. "I've only been gone a month."

The gaze held. "You've changed, though," she said thoughtfully. "You're older somehow. I can feel it."

The greeting was so intense, so out of proportion to the length of his absence Mike suddenly felt apprehensive. She was primed for something, he thought, and he realized what it was.

The scar.

He should have known better than to ask her about that over the phone, but he'd had to be sure. She must have spent these last days building up all kinds of images in her mind, some of them probably close to the truth, he added to himself. And now she could hardly wait to confront him.

He'd decided to share all of it with her, everything he'd learned about his father, but now the anxiety in her attitude put him off. It's my fault for ever bringing it up, he thought, but nonetheless found himself unwilling to take her into his confidence at that moment. He'd have to think about it some more, maybe even find a way out if he could.

For now, he decided to keep things light.

"Where's Penny?" he asked.

"At the club—swimming."

"Sounds like a good idea. I could use a swim myself after that drive."

Not waiting for an answer, he picked up his bag and mounted the stairs.

She was waiting for him when he came down moments later in his bathing suit, towel slung over his shoulder.

"Mike," she said, hand on his forearm as he paused in front of her.

"Not now, Mom," he said, an implied promise in the words. "Later, okay?"

Then he'd gone out to the pool and taken a lounge chair to the far end. He was asleep in minutes.

Kate had been her usual pleasant self as they sat down to dinner, and he relaxed, glad to be home.

"Tell us about your trip, Mike," Penny opened eagerly.

He glanced quickly to Kate whose face showed only interest. She's not going to push, at least not now, he thought, feeling reassured.

"Not much to tell," he began easily. "I went down to Saint Mary's, where dad grew up, then to Wisconsin where he went to college, and on out to California. That was more for me than anything else," he added.

"And?" Penny prodded, twisting her long hair around her finger.

"Nothing I didn't know already. Mostly it was boring," he said, wishing now he'd rehearsed this better. "Although," he said brightly, glad for the quick inspiration, "I did have some excitement in Las Vegas." He grinned broadly.

"And?" It was Kate now, rising to the bait.

"Oh," Mike shrugged. "Not much, really. Just won five thousand dollars, that's all."

"Mike!" Penny shrieked. "Five thousand dollars! You're lying," she went on, half in jest. "Let me see it."

"It's up in my room."

"I bet."

"Want to bet five thousand dollars?" he asked playfully.

"You really did," she said with wonder in her voice.

"Yep."

"On top of everything else! That's incredible."

Mike paused, fork halfway to his mouth. "What 'everything else'?" he asked.

"Mom didn't tell you?"

"I didn't have a chance," Kate said matter-of-factly. "Mike was in and out so fast I hardly had time to say hello." There was admonition in her voice he acknowledged with a brief nod.

"Well, tell me now," he stated, a bit annoyed at being caught in his own game.

"You won the state lottery," Kate said, eyes on him, unsuspecting, only pure excitement evident in the revelation.

"The state lottery," Mike's voice was a whisper, but they misread it.

"Uh-huh," Penny chimed in eagerly. "And guess how much?" She too was bound to repay him for his tease.

"How much," he managed.

"Fifty thousand dollars! Isn't that incredible! They only announced it two days ago, and everybody called and it was on TV and everything!"

"The state lottery," Mike repeated again, almost dazedly, putting his fork back on his plate. He remembered months ago applying for a special number, 51470, his birthday, and changing at the last instant to 14570 on a hunch he'd thought no more about.

But the connection struck, and Mike was suddenly alarmed.

"Tell him the rest of it, Mom."

Mike's head was buzzing so loudly he could hardly hear his sister's words, and he turned now to his mother. He almost had to read her lips to understand what she was saying.

"...stocks, Mike." The words came through somehow. "The ones you bought just after your birthday with some of your trust money. Well, Bill Chambers said it was the most unbelievable thing, but the ten thousand dollars you invested is worth sixteen thousand today, in less than two months. He said you went down the list and seemed to be just picking names from the paper, but every one showed remarkable gains, so he knows you must have studied up on them. Just like your father, he said," she added, a touch of pride in her voice.

Just like my father, Mike thought, remembering the haphazard way in which he'd chosen the companies.

Bill Chambers had prepared a list of recommendations along with a brief synopsis of each, but Mike had suddenly resented being spoonfed again—he was eighteen, after all, and the money was his own. Some part of him had known he was being foolish—reckless even—but the impulse to choose for himself overrode good sense. He had taken the newspaper from Chambers' desk, opened to the financial page, and randomly picked the stocks he wanted as the banker watched quietly.

Randomly.

So he had thought.

Random to the extent that ten thousand dollars had grown to sixteen thousand in less than sixty days.

He rose from the dinner table and said with great effort as Kate looked at him inquiringly, "I'm really tired, Mom. I'm going to bed."

He left before anything else could be said. It took all his self-control to keep from running up the stairs to his room, where he closed the door and turned off the lights.

He was shaking but stopped finally, and after a while the buzzing in his head went away too. He didn't respond to his mother's light tap at the door, which came sometime later, and had feigned sleep when the door opened softly.

He slept little that night and went downstairs early, a hastily packed bag in his hand.

"Where are you going, Mike?" Kate asked when she saw him, alarm evident in her voice.

"Up to Maine, Mom—for a day or two. I've got to be alone. Please don't ask," he added, not knowing what else to say, and the plea in his eyes was so naked she'd nodded dumbly.

Now he sat on the small beach watching the boat rise and fall with the waves and wondered how he'd deal with her. That was another problem he'd have to confront, ultimately.

For now, his major concern was how to get to Owen Reid, because the man who would soon be president had to know most of it, if not all of it.

* * *

Mike heard the scream and leaped from his bed.

His heart was pounding so loudly he hardly heard the cricket sounds syncopating the soft murmurs of the waves as they drifted up through the moonlit air from the Maine shoreline.

It was a moment before he realized the scream had been his own, and when he did, he sat on the bed until he stopped shaking.

The dream had been real, the image in his mind so clear it left no room for doubt.

Charley was in St. Thomas.

And Mike knew he was in mortal danger.

Although he was still shaking, he took the stairs in four jumps and raced into the den where he yanked the phone from its cradle.

Part IV

CHAPTER 27

"Another brandy, Mister Cavanaugh?"

Charley looked to Janine inquiringly, and she nodded.

"Two please, Walter."

The aging black waiter turned and made his way across the quarry-tiled floor to the small bar at the far end of the enormous open gallery.

At the grand piano that fronted the enclosed dining area, Leo began to play "When the World Was Young." Charley had tipped him five dollars to play the song earlier and had sent over a drink as well. The talented young pianist closed his eyes and swayed to the rhythm as he moved with authority into the minors.

Charley took Janine's hand and helped her rise from the deep rattan couch. There were seven or eight such settings in the huge open room, couch and chairs about glass-topped coffee tables. Most of them were in use despite the late hour. The exquisite after-dinner combination of view, music, and setting was an irresistible aftermath to the spectacular cuisine of the Harbor View restaurant.

They stepped to the waist-high wall that surrounded the edge of the balcony. He put his arm about Janine's shoulders as they looked out. Far below, past the spill of shrubs and trees, the lights of Charlotte Amalie shone, and in the harbor the circus lights of three cruise ships beckoned gaily.

"Happy, Larry?" she asked softly.

Charley pressed her closer almost absentmindedly as he gazed down at the water. Leo's throaty voice began the ballad, "Ah, the apple trees,

233

sunlit memories….", thought suddenly of Owen, the old days, "when the world was young…." Charley recalled with nostalgia the early, bright dreams of two eighteen-year-olds. He felt his mood darken as the soft music continued and his mind settled on the confrontation twenty years later with the man in Liechtenstein. It had troubled him beyond measure….

———

It was their usual winter meeting. Planning sessions, they'd called them these many years. A mixture of business and, more important to Charley, the chance to connect as the friends they were.

They'd spent one day skiing, but as excellent as the conditions had been, Charley had insisted on their last day they hike up the mountains that rose beyond the town of Triesenburg. He had wanted to instill in his friend a deeper flavor of the tiny country of which he'd grown so fond.

And Owen had indeed seemed taken by the view once the meandering trail they followed had cleared the thick forest. The wide valley stretched below in mesmerizing undulations of pine and snow, cut through its center by the graceful curves of the ice patched river. They sat at the edge of a precipice that bordered a dramatic drop and had been silent for some moments as they'd contemplated the spectacular panorama.

But Charley had sensed Owen was distracted rather than mesmerized. "What's the matter?" he'd asked.

Owen hesitated, then swivelled his body so he faced Charley from the rock opposite, hands in the pockets of his red-checked jacket, hiking boots planted firmly in the light groundcover of snow.

Charley himself had worn a navy ski jacket, and, noting the look on his friend's face, he reached into a pocket to remove a silver flask. Unscrewing the top, he offered the open container across.

Owen raised the flask to his lips for a swig and handed it back.

Charley took a short sip himself, dwelled on the rich aroma of the brandy, and felt the liquid warm him as it coursed his throat.

"What is it, Owen?" he prodded when he had replaced the flask.

"Charley—" the other began hesitantly, cautiously. "Charley, sometimes I wonder if we're right in stopping at the presidency."

Charley's deepest fear was finally realized, and he chose his words carefully before replying.

"Owen, I know what you're going through. I've had the same thoughts myself. I've seen your impatience, and believe me I've felt that way too. But the plan is a good one, and it's worked. Don't ever forget that."

"But we can do more, Charley. We can take advantage of the power on a level we've never used, change things in a very direct way. We can end up virtually reshaping the world if we want to go that far."

"Why would we?"

"Why not?" The phrase must have seemed cold even to Owen, who added quickly, "Charley, the Soviet Union is coming apart in a few years. We know that, and it's certainly not our doing. But we *do* know it, and more, we know the chaos that will come out of it. Bosnia, Chechen, Russia itself…." Owen ticked off on his fingers. "I'll be president then, and we'll have the perfect opportunity to step in and—"

"And what, Owen?"

"Make things better." He paused. "Reshape things." He said this last slowly, holding Charley's eyes.

"At what price, Owen? We've never dabbled with the future, not that way, not since the thing with the bus—we swore we never would again. Besides," he added, "manipulation of world events for some sort of universal good has been postulated before with tragic results."

"But dammit, Charley, it could be for their own good!"

Charley was surprised at Owen's fervor. He had expected the other to back off when faced with Charley's resistance but instead he found a naked determination.

"*Your* idea of their own good, Owen," he said, committed to hold firm on this. "Your idea—maybe not theirs. The Russians—"

"Charley, sometimes you're so damned . . ." Owen cut him off and rose to his feet to look down at Charley from full height. "It's not just the Soviet Union. Think about the squalor, the disease—Ethiopia alone! Think Charley," he commanded. "Think what we can do for them if we bring it all together!"

"But they may not see it that way, Owen," Charley answered quietly, remaining calm in the face of the other's passion.

"Goddamnit, Charley," he said, "the two of us—we can do it all! And we should do it, because it's right!"

"Owen," Charley said, rising and placing his had on Owen's elbow. "It's *not* right. The power—any power—has to stop somewhere. And remember, the bottom line of everything we've done, the way we've done it, has been to protect the power and keep it secret. We'd be throwing all that away and what happens then?"

They eyes were locked, but suddenly Owen pulled his arm from Charley with such violence he threw the other off balance. Charley stumbled toward the cliff edge, a sharp fear rising, but Owen reacted swiftly. Taking a step forward, he planted his foot firmly and reached out to grab his friend's arm. As Charley felt himself pulled to safety, to Owen, their eyes met, held, and suddenly they stood in a deep embrace. My God, some part of Charley thought, if only we could go back to where we once were.

"I'm sorry, Charley," Owen said, but Charley had long pondered, later and alone, exactly what those words implied.

Charley opened his eyes, yawned and stretched deliciously. The troubling thoughts he'd had of Owen the night before as he'd stood at the balcony overlooking the harbor had long since diminished, and he felt particularly good this morning.

Beside him, a rumpled sheet pulled to her waist, Janine still slept. The look on her face was peaceful, childlike, and he marveled their earlier passion had left no trace on her delicate features. Her long dark hair, which had brushed his face as she'd straddled him, now trailed softly over her shoulder, a few strands tracing her cheek.

He reached over to touch her, but thought better of it. She'd said she didn't feel up to diving and planned to spend the day just sitting at the pool, so he decided to let her sleep.

Rising silently, he walked to the window and looked out. Below him, the Caribbean pulsed blue as always. He noted the water was calm and saw from the tilt of the sails on the three-master that cut toward St. Johns the wind was relatively light.

It would be a good day to dive the caves at Dog Rock, he thought.

* * *

The girl in the brightly colored muumuu was walking briskly, swinging her purse. Mike could tell by the change in her direction she was headed for the door.

He looked at his watch. Nine fifty-five. He was impatient at the relaxed business hours evident on St. Thomas, but the girl was at least on time.

"Good morning," she said pleasantly as she unlocked the door. "Can I help you?"

"Yes, please," Mike responded, following her into the office.

He waited while she turned on the lights, noted the layout of two secretarial desks and banks of file cabinets set about a private office so as to maximize the space in the relatively small room.

"I've come to see about boat insurance," he said.

"Oh," the girl said. "Then you'll have to wait for Mister Wakely. He writes all the policies. I'm sorry, but he won't be in until noon today."

She was small and very pretty, with delicate, cinnamon-colored skin and Asian features. Mike decided his best chance lay with her.

"Well, actually," he began, "I didn't want to buy a policy. I'm really looking for some information, and you're the only people who can help me." He half shrugged in a helpless manner and was rewarded with a look of encouragement on her part.

"I'll certainly help if I can. What is it you want to know?"

"Well," Mike hesitated briefly, "I hate to unload personal problems on a perfect stranger, but like I said I really have no place else to turn. I'm looking for my father."

The girl's expression became quizzical, and he went on. "This is sort of embarrassing to me," he said, "but my father disappeared almost a year ago. Just left us, you know?" He paused, and she nodded sympathetically. "Anyway, a friend of the family heard from somebody who thought they'd seen him down here. It's a long shot, but we were here a couple of years ago, and he liked it, and it's the kind of place he'd go to…" That was all true enough, Mike thought, nervous nonetheless.

"The thing is, if he is here I know he's changed his name, and with so many new people buying on the island all the time, I could never track him down through the real estate offices. But my dad loved to sail, and if he's here I know he'd have bought a boat. I guess I could cover all the boat yards, but somebody told me your office writes most of the boat insurance on the island, and I thought maybe…" Mike's voiced trailed off hopefully.

She hesitated a moment, then asked, "When would that have been?"

"Probably last fall sometime. September to November—somewhere in there."

"And what's your father's name?"

"Robert Williams," Mike said, inventing the name in the instant. "But like I said, it's probably not under that name."

She walked to the line of file cabinets covering the far wall. Opening a drawer, she quickly leafed through the folders, pulled out one, examined it, and replaced it as she shook her head.

"No Robert Williams," she affirmed. "September to November, you said?"

He nodded.

"Let's try the renewal files."

She moved to a cabinet further down the line, opened it, and removed three thick folders, which she took to her desk. Pen in hand, she made brief notes on a pad as she riffled through the stacks of paper.

"You're lucky," she said when she'd done writing her list. "September to November is off season. There were only thirty new policies issued then."

"Let's see," Mike said, reaching for the list. Twelve of the vessels were power boats, and Mike crossed them off quickly. Ten of the others were sails, but under fourteen feet, and Mike deleted those also.

"These eight," he said, returning the list to the girl. "Could I see the applications?" He held his breath, and after a long pause she turned without speaking and went back to the files. "You can sit at the desk."

He found it in the third one.

There was no physical description of the man included—only that of the boat. But the owner's age was given as forty-six and that was close enough.

It didn't matter really, though, because Mike recognized Charley's unmistakable handwriting in the signature that read "Lawrence Cavanaugh."

* * *

"Mister Deering?"

The blonde-haired man turned, carefully placed the diving tank he was carrying down on the grass by the dock, and walked to Mike. His short beard was sun bleached and the lines surrounding the blue eyes in an otherwise young face gave additional evidence of long hours in the wind and sun.

"I'm Gary Deering," he said. "What can I do for you?"

"Mike Williams," Mike said, extending his hand. "I spoke to you over the phone about a half hour ago."

"Sure. Looking for Larry Cavanaugh."

"Right. Is he back yet?"

"Nope," the man shook his head. "Like I told you, he took off about ten. Went out to the caves, over by Dog Rock. It's only noon now," he said, glancing at his watch, which other than a heavy gold chain about his neck, was all he wore besides his tattered khaki shorts. "He won't be back for an hour at least."

"Mind if I wait?" Mike asked, indicating the chair situated in the shade by the door of the equipment room.

"Not at all. How about a Coke?" the owner offered.

"Thanks."

"Planning to dive while you're down here?" Deering asked as he returned with two iced cans.

"Maybe," Mike responded, seating himself and looking east toward Dog Rock.

* * *

239

The bell atop the church tower on the hill was just striking twelve when the door opened and Jim Wakely came in. He was in shirtsleeves and his ruddy face was damp with perspiration.

"Hi, Mary," he said, dropping his heavy briefcase on his desk. "Any calls?"

"These," she said, handing him a half dozen pink message slips.

He scanned them briefly. "Anybody stop in?"

"Nobody. It's been very quiet." She hesitated. "There was somebody in, Mister Wakely. Not for business. A young man who wanted a favor, and I did it for him. I hope you won't object."

Wakely looked at her curiously. "What favor?"

"He was looking for his father. The man deserted his family last fall, and the boy thought he might be here in St. Thomas, and if so thought he would have purchased a sailboat. I let him see the records for last September to November."

Wakely gave her an odd look. "That's incredible," he said. "What was the man's name, the one he was looking for?"

"Williams. Robert Williams."

Wakely shook his head.

"Did I do something wrong, Mister Wakely? He seemed like such a nice boy, so troubled. I'm sorry if—"

"No, Mary," he broke in quickly, patting her shoulder lightly to relieve the look of anxiety that had crossed the girl's face. "That's not what I was thinking about. I'd have done the same thing myself—did, as a matter of fact, just yesterday, while you were out to lunch. That's the amazing thing—this fellow told me exactly the same story, except he was thirty, maybe thirty-five, and was looking for his brother. That one's name was Henderson, though," he added.

* * *

The Ensign lay pulling gently at her anchor line, perhaps a hundred yards from the barren stand of rock against which sudden waves broke in fury. Her sails were down and loosely secured. The two men in the power boat passed close enough to ascertain no one was on board, then anchored about a hundred yards away. They'd been watching the boat for two hours, ever since it had moved out of Sapphire Bay, and they were positive the sailor had come alone. It didn't hurt to make certain, though.

The younger man donned his diving gear. His hawk-like face, while not handsome, was arresting.

"You sure you know this place?" the other asked again, wiping his hands nervously on his Bermuda shorts. He wondered if the currents below could really be as gentle as purported.

The first man grinned. "Like the back of my hand," he said. "Not to worry. You can come along if you like," he added, the look in his steel blue eyes challenging.

"No. You said you can do it alone," the older man put in hastily. He hadn't been down in years and did not relish the prospects under these circumstances. "We just don't want to blow it, that's all."

"We won't." The blue-eyed man looked at his diving watch. "He's been down for thirty minutes—should be along pretty quick. He'll end with another run through the passage."

"How do you know?"

"If you ever dove Dog, you'd know." Positioning his face mask, he placed the mouthpiece between his teeth, sat on the gunwale, and flipped backward into the water.

* * *

Charley checked his pressure gauge. Five hundred pounds. Enough for one more run through the passage before going up.

Breathing shallowly in a measured pattern, he followed the cliff to his right. A heavy school of Queen Angels skittered quickly as he approached, flashes of blue and yellow, and he noted a large grouper lurking in the darkness below a ledge. Beneath him, the sun played across the myriad coral clusters. The shadows seemed almost to pulsate as the rays of light filtered through the ripples of the waves above, and the effect was softly hypnotic.

He passed over a particularly lovely stand of stag coral and saw a school of about eight blue tangs that drifted majestically through some swaying fans.

The cliff edge ended abruptly and to his right was the opening of the passage. He checked his gauge again. Three-fifty. Easily enough to make the run and get back to the boat with plenty to spare.

Charley dropped about ten feet and rested for just a moment on the sandy bottom. He peered ahead. The darkness would have been frightening if he didn't know the narrow tunnel soon angled left and widened slightly, letting in light from the chimney that dramatically ended the run. The passage itself was exciting to maneuver, narrow to the extent you had to take care not to get your tank caught in some sharp rock that protruded from above. But the real thrill was the chimney suddenly breaking into the light. You could look up to see the slanting rays of the sun highlighting the brilliant fish that always hovered above, rising up those twenty feet of wall to break over the ledge not far below the surface.

Resting his stomach flat against the sand, Charley pulled himself forward with his hands, kicked his flippers carefully, and entered the blackness ahead.

* * *

The blue eyes waited, staring with intensity into the darkness of the tunnel. He knew in the light he would be seen by anyone coming through but by that time it would no longer matter.

The eyes narrowed, lids squinting, trying to pierce the murkiness as best they could. Suddenly there was something, a whiteness, and the man recognized it to be bubbles.

Right again, he said to himself, clamping harder on his mouthpiece as he entered his end of the tunnel with a strong kick of his powerful legs. He was glad he'd decided to do the job alone. Whoever had sent the urgent message down two days ago would be impressed. Alive, if possible, he'd been instructed. But dead if necessary.

He knew which was simpler and safest.

CHAPTER 28

Mike was seated at the edge of the dock, feet dangling as his eyes searched the shimmering open waters for the occasional boat that might be making its way toward Sapphire. Those few that had appeared to be approaching veered off about a quarter mile out, heading past the rocky point toward Cowpet Bay or perhaps Red Hook, the bustling native marina. Only one craft had actually entered the small channel where he waited, and it had been a power boat.

Mike took another sip of his Coke. It was his second, and he'd been nursing it for a long while now. He was only peripherally aware of the hot tropical sun and the sweat running in rivulets through the reddish matting of his chest hair. Glancing again at his watch, he saw it was nearly three.

He rose and walked down the dock to where Gary and his assistant Freddie were filling tanks. Gary would carefully measure that each contained a minimum of twenty-two hundred pounds, and Freddie would then seal the valve and place the tank along the white concrete wall in a line with the others.

Freddie was stocky, an islander with a pencil-thin moustache whose singsong accent made him always sound cheerful. His smooth black skin glistened in the sun as did the tight curls of hair that covered the powerful legs straining against his faded shorts as he bent to his task.

They were preparing to dive the wreck of the Rhone the next day, a two-tank dive, with ten passengers. It was the most famous dive in the

Virgins, and Mike hadn't been surprised when Gary had mentioned Larry Cavanaugh had accompanied him twice on the trip.

He approached the man now, said, "It's three o'clock, Gary."

The dive master straightened and looked out to the water with eyes that seemed in a perpetual squint. There were no sails that appeared to be heading to Sapphire.

"Maybe he went over to St. John," he offered. "There's nothing to be worried about. Larry's a good sailor."

Mike nodded. He'd told Gary he was looking for Cavanaugh, nothing more, and the other had no reason to suspect Mike's deep anxiety. Nor did he wish to display it. He wanted to discover his father with little attention before or after. He had no intention of trying to get Charley to return; he understood very well now that could never be. He only wanted to see him, know he was all right, and share what he'd learned about himself with the only person in the world who could really help him—his father.

But as the wait had continued, Mike found his excitement dulling, remembered the flash of premonition in his head three nights earlier in Maine, and as one o'clock had come and gone, he'd begun to feel a dread foreboding.

Now that it was three, he was close to panic and didn't think he would be able to contain his anxiety much longer.

"Tell you what," Gary said, seeming to sense Mike's apprehension. "If he's not back in a half hour, we'll go looking. Okay?"

Mike turned, walked back to the end of the dock, and sat to wait, a growing certainty in him it was probably too late already.

* * *

"There she is," Freddie shouted, pointing ahead to the bobbing mast they could just begin to make out beyond the far point.

The stocky black man veered the power boat sharply to the right, paralleled the small island, and swung quickly left again as they rounded its farthest edge. Ahead, floating peacefully in a small, secluded harbor whose placid surface contrasted the crashing waves at the land's far edge, the Pearson Ensign lay. Its sails were down but loosely tied, as if its occupant intended to return shortly.

244

Freddie cut the motor and the boat drifted up expertly beside the other. Gary jumped into the Ensign and looked briefly into the cabin.

"Nothing," he said as he straightened up. "Just a cooler with some beer and a couple of life jackets. No diving gear at all. He must still be down."

Mike's face paled, and as he clambered back on board, Gary said to him, "Don't worry. Maybe he sailed to St. John's earlier and decided to dive on the way back. He may have gone down only ten minutes ago for all we know." Mike nodded perfunctorily, but he'd detected alarm in the man's voice despite the comforting words.

Without being told, Freddie started up the engine and moved the power boat perhaps fifty yards away. As he cut the motor, Gary was already tossing the anchor. He quickly dove in after it, surfaced again in a moment with thumb and forefinger circled, and climbed agilely into the boat.

The two men moved swiftly. There was no conversation, no wasted motion as within a moment they were fully geared. The speed with which they moved left no doubt in Mike's mind they, like he, feared the worst.

Mike had wanted to go down with them if it came to that, but Gary had flatly refused.

"How many times you been down, Mike?" the man had asked as the power boat had careened out of Sapphire.

"Five or six," Mike lied. He'd only been down three, all of those on this very island when he'd visited with his father nearly five years before.

Gary shook his head firmly, heavy gold chain swinging against his bare chest as the wind whipped their faces in the cockpit of the open boat. "Nope. If we have to go down, you'll only be in the way. You won't be able to help. Freddie and I can handle whatever—" he'd broken it off as he noted the look on Mike's face. "Besides," he'd added, "we need someone on top to watch the boat."

The two men now positioned themselves on the gunwale.

"We'll take the usual tour, Freddie, but as close to the bottom as we can. You take the right, I'll go left."

Freddie nodded affirmation. "If we don't spot him before we get to the passage—"

245

"We'll meet at the entrance. Don't go in alone, okay?"

"Got it," Freddie responded. He positioned his face mask, clamped the mouthpiece in his jaws, and flipped backward into the water. Mike could see the trail of bubbles as the man descended the anchor line.

Gary turned to Mike, seemed about to say something, gave a thumbs up instead, flipped down his mask and was gone.

* * *

Freddie was waiting at the tunnel's entrance when Gary got there, clumps of bubbles bursting from his regulator to rise through the clear waters. He shook his head negatively as did Gary.

Gary moved to the entrance, peered inside, and seemed to consider for a moment. Then he backed out slowly, turned to Freddie, and motioned the other man to the surface.

* * *

Gary was back at the tunnel within moments. This time he didn't wait but moved quickly into the passage as soon as he reached bottom.

Picking his way carefully, he kept as close to the bottom as he could. He'd maneuvered the tunnel more times than he could remember, and professional that he was, did not take it lightly. The walls were narrow, the rocks above so low at points as to give only a few inches clearance even as one hugged the bottom. Gary maintained great care under water at all times but had particular respect for this tunnel.

He moved slowly, not seeing the dim gray light ahead and to his left where he anticipated it. He kept his hand to the wall, felt the bend begin, and pulled himself carefully around.

Ahead, all was black. The light that should have shown from the end of the tunnel where the chimney came was blocked completely.

Despite himself, Gary felt a twinge of panic. No matter what his experience, there was little he could do if danger struck while he was alone in the tunnel, and the blackness ahead made him feel totally cut off. He took a few deep breaths, far deeper than his practiced shallow breathing, felt himself grow calmer, and slowly inched ahead.

He'd almost reached the tunnel's end when something soft brushed his shoulder. He pushed up involuntarily and felt his tank hit hard against the roof of the cave. Thrashing out with his hands at the darkness ahead, he felt something, grabbed and held it. It was a leg, and he knew immediately that what had touched his shoulder was a flipper dangling from the lower part of a torso suspended above his position on the passage floor.

Reacting quickly, he found the other leg, pushed both below him, and worked his way forwards until his hand felt the tank. He crouched on the sand, got as much leverage as he could, and pushed. There was no movement. He grabbed the tank with both hands and tried to move it from side to side, but the result was the same. The tank was solidly wedged.

He knelt on the rocky bottom and took a firm hold on one of the drifting legs. He pulled back as hard as possible with no success. Then he took a leg under each arm and tried to inch his way backwards, but still nothing gave. If he had room he could have easily reached in and cut the harness straps, but the body and tank so completely filled the aperture he couldn't maneuver. There was at most perhaps eighteen inches between the torso and the ocean floor. He decided to try anyway and removed the knife from the sheath strapped about his thigh. Carefully he reached under, extended his arm as far as he could, and could just feel the edge of the knife touch the heavy strap. He moved the knife back and forth with his fingers but realized he couldn't get enough pressure to do any good. He pressed forward again to try to gain the few necessary inches, and as he did so the knife suddenly fell from his hand.

Reaching down to the sand ahead, he tried to find it, but his groping fingers came up empty. The knife must have drifted forward when he'd dropped it, and suddenly Gary felt more alone than ever.

He couldn't go backward through the tunnel, because he'd be unable to keep himself low enough to have his tank clear the rocks above. And the space in which he was now trapped was too narrow for him to struggle out of the harness. If he'd still had his knife—

Now Gary could only wait, wait and hope Freddie would react quickly. Lying in the darkness, he tried to control his breathing but knew he was wasting precious oxygen by taking the rapid gasps that sounded terribly loud to him. He wondered in sudden horror what the last moments of the man ahead must have been like.

* * *

Freddie had followed Gary's instructions precisely but in the end he had to improvise.

He'd retraced the tour as Gary told him and come around the cliff side to the ledge where the chimney rose. Dropping quickly, he'd reached the end of the tunnel to find the body tightly wedged about ten feet inside. The tunnel was still too narrow at that point for him to get enough leverage to pull it free, and he'd given up the effort after a few futile attempts.

Rising to the surface, he swam back to the power boat, propelled swiftly by powerful kicks of his flippered legs.

"Any luck?" Mike asked anxiously as he helped the black clamor aboard.

"He's stuck down there," the man stated as he caught his breath.

As he saw the look on Mike's face, he wondered again what the boy's relationship was to the man below.

"I'll need your help," he went on immediately, not wanting to give Mike a chance to drop into shock or hysteria. Activity would help him get used to the idea, and besides, he really did need the boy.

"You said you dove before," he continued. "Was that true?"

Mike nodded.

"Do you remember enough to go down with me?"

"I think so," Mike managed.

"Good." Freddie quickly helped Mike with his gear and gave him a few brief reminders for which Mike was thankful. "Okay," he ended. "Let's go."

Holding the heavy rope he'd taken from the cabin, Freddie sat on the side and pushed over. Mike followed seconds later, remembering to hold his mask tight to his face as Freddie had instructed.

They swam to the ledge, and Freddie motioned Mike to stay.

The man went down, reappeared in minutes, and signaled.

Mike entered the water and followed Freddie quickly down the chimney. Despite the other thoughts that raced through his mind, he still noted the quiet beauty of the sun-dappled shadows through which the schools of brightly colored fish played against the walls.

When he reached bottom, he stood, feeling the weight of the tank heavy and awkward on his back. He stepped behind Freddie who was positioned at the mouth of an opening and took the rope the man handed him. Freddie nodded and together they leaned back to pull.

* * *

Gary had resisted looking at his pressure gauge but finally surrendered.

Less than fifty pounds.

He wished now he'd attempted to wriggle out of the harness, but it was too late for that. He couldn't have had it both ways and decided the safer way was to rely on Freddie. That it hadn't worked out wouldn't be Freddie's fault, because the man would have already dislodged the body ahead if it were humanly possible. If only Freddie knew he was trapped behind it! Suppose he lost consciousness before—

Gary held the air in his lungs as long as he could, expelled it slowly, and waited again. When he could last no longer, he breathed in shallowly. He'd been controlling the process to an extent he would not have believed possible for half an hour but had somehow managed to keep his panic at bay. It had to be soon, he thought, as he let the air out, waited, and breathed again.

Shallow as the breath was, the pull of air stopped before he'd finished, and the abruptness of the sudden vacuum against which his lungs struggled helplessly was terrifying beyond measure.

* * *

It seemed to Mike the body in the tunnel would never dislodge. They'd been pulling for some moments when Freddie finally stopped, motioned Mike to a kneeling position, knelt himself, and reached into the opening of the tunnel. Mike understood, placed his hands as far forward on the rope as he could, and pulled downward with the other man at the steepest angle they could manage. It didn't seem that would work either, but Freddie gave the rope the barest slack and they pulled again sharply, losing their balance and falling back in slow motion as the rope suddenly came clear.

The body had dislodged, and Freddie, seated on the sandy bottom, reeled the rope quickly out. As the head and shoulders became visible, he stopped, turned to Mike, and signaled the other up. Mike stood and stared at the wetsuit-clad body as if hypnotized. Freddie reached over and grabbed the boy's arm, shook it roughly, and signaled "up" almost angrily when he finally got Mike's attention.

Reluctantly, Mike began the ascent.

When the boy had nearly reached the top, Freddie pulled the body out, grabbed the harness strap, and prepared to go up. As he did so, something caught his eye and he paused for an instant.

Just inside the tunnel an object lay glittering in the edge of the sunlight, and he realized it was a knife. He was not going to stop to retrieve it but was suddenly prompted to do so, and he reached down awkwardly to the sand.

He looked at the knife in his hand for only the briefest instant before releasing his hold on the body and diving into the black hole ahead.

* * *

Mike had just reached the flat ledge above the chimney when he heard the water break behind him.

Looking back, he saw a head bob above the surface and drop again, face down, as the rest of the body began to rise behind. The yellow tank broke the surface first and then, in a slow and profane grace, the lower body rose, legs coming to float prone at the exact moment the outstretched arms came to rest atop the crystal clear pool.

Pushing off the ledge, Mike reached the body in one stroke, grabbed the straps, and made for shore. He hoisted it onto the rocks at the edge of the pool and stood above the prone figure that lay face downward in the trickles of water that spread slowly outward. He's dead, Mike thought as he bent to remove the tank so he could roll the body onto its back.

* * *

Gary's body was dead weight as Freddie pulled it clear of the tunnel. He didn't notice until much later the deep cuts and scratches he'd received on his arms and legs as he struggled backward those long fifteen feet.

When he got to the chimney, he expelled all the air from his lungs, grabbed the other's harness, and with a quick kick of his powerful legs took off as rapidly as he dared for the surface. To ascend those thirty-five feet at top speed with air in his lungs would have meant certain death, since the air would have expanded and burst his lungs. He was running a risk rising so quickly regardless, but he reached the surface in only a few seconds.

Quickly he pulled Gary's inert body to shore, and Mike reached down to help him drag it up. Freddie pulled the mouthpiece from Gary's clenched jaws, reached into his mouth and loosened his tongue. He then stripped the tank, rolled the body onto its back, and without even checking for life signs, bent over the bearded face and began mouth-to-mouth resuscitation.

Mike watched in silence, hypnotized by the drama. He appeared to have forgotten the other body that lay nearby and understood only later he must have been in shock.

He wondered that Freddie didn't give up. He was certain his life-saving attempt was futile as a good ten minutes passed and Gary's chest did not rise and fall of its own accord. So riveted were his eyes on the scene he didn't notice at first the almost imperceptible change of rhythm, only picked it up as Freddie's own breathing began to slacken and the motion of Gary's chest continued to hold.

Freddie finally rose to his knees, his expression grave as he watched the now-breathing man. It wasn't until Gary's eyelids twitched and finally fluttered open that Freddie's own visage broke in a wide grin.

"You okay?" he asked a moment later as Gary lay staring upward.

The pallid face turned to the black man and a squinted eye winked. Freddie said nothing, but Mike saw there were tears in the man's eyes.

Suddenly Freddie looked at Mike and seemed to remember the other task at hand. He rose quickly and walked over to where the other body lay, knelt to look at the blue eyes staring cold and unblinking.

After a moment he rose and faced Mike.

"Do you know him?"

Mike shook his head.

"I do," Freddie said. "He used to teach diving down here four, maybe five years ago."

It was only later after they'd hoisted the body on board the power boat and Freddie was preparing to set sail in the Ensign Mike noticed the leg protruding from behind a ledge of rock on shore.

Swimming back, they discovered the other drowned man, a balding, middle-aged stranger in shorts and a T-shirt. Mike stood over the second body for a long moment, then raised his eyes and looked out to the Caribbean.

* * *

"Two Drown at Dog Rock."

Mike read the headline and remembered the flash that had burned his mind only four nights earlier in Maine. Had those been the words? He was almost certain they had been.

The man who'd washed ashore, the article read, had apparently been unable to swim. There were no clues as to why he'd fallen overboard nor were there any marks on his body.

"Perhaps he got anxious, alone out there, when his companion was overdue. Maybe he tried to swim in," a spokesman quoted in the article suggested.

Mike had a quick picture in his mind of Charley surfacing by the boat, unrecognized in his face mask, and reaching up his hand for the other man to help him on board.

After that...

Mike pushed the thought away and returned to the article.

The other man, the one found in the tunnel, had been an experienced diver, the newspaper said. Authorities were unable to explain how his tank had become so tightly lodged in the tunnel overhang. "I guess he just panicked," Gary was quoted as saying.

Authorities could also not explain what had happened to Larry Cavanaugh, resident of St. Thomas in whose name the sail boat was registered. There was speculation he, too, may have drowned, although an exhaustive search of the area revealed nothing.

There was no mention of Mike himself in the article. Mike had asked the two divers to leave him clear of it, and they'd agreed without comment. Neither he nor they had any idea of what had become of Larry Cavanaugh.

"Maybe he panicked." Mike thought about the statement, knew if it was true for the man in the tunnel it had not applied to his father. He remembered the kidnap-murder, the switch in identities to Charley Frost when his father had been only eighteen. He might never know what else the man had to deal with, but Mike was sure he'd managed with extraordinary aplomb.

His father was gone again now, disappeared, and the timing was such it could not be accidental. That an attempt had been made on his father's life on the very day Mike had found him was too much of a coincidence for Mike to accept.

Mike had been followed, he realized, cursing himself for his carelessness. But how could someone have found Charley that fast? Mike himself had moved quickly and had been fortunate in having his passport with him, avoiding a stop in Boston. He had been lucky in his search on St. Thomas as well—and he had still been too late.

Suddenly he understood. Whoever it was had arrived before him, probably a day earlier. He remembered the phone call he'd made in the early Maine morning, how he'd had to wait until the next day for a flight. In his mind's eye he could see the tap he'd removed from the phone in Weston months ago; he realized now another had been at the place in Maine. And it was likely gone by now, having served its purpose.

Whoever had been after his father had indeed been watching Mike all along as he'd suspected. He'd been wrong to assume they had quit. He wondered how long they would have continued, how long he himself would have, remembering how his quest had seemed dead-ended only days before. If not for the power he wouldn't have known where to look, and obviously no one else would have, either.

The power. Already it had almost cost him more than he'd ever have been willing to pay. His father's life. But could he have changed things? And, if he didn't have the power, would all of this perhaps not have happened anyway?

The questions were impossible for him to cope with and the only man who could help him had disappeared again.

He thought of the irony of his earlier decision to search out Owen Reid for help.

He would search him out now, but with a far different purpose.

CHAPTER 29

Mike drove slowly through the outskirts of Zurich, surprised at the heavy industrialization. Modern factories sprawled in green meadowland; the highways were clogged with traffic. Finally he saw the sign marked "Autobahn" and entered the westbound ramp. The girl at Pan-Am car rental had told him the drive would take little over an hour, especially since he didn't have to stop at the border. There were no customs on entering Liechtenstein from Switzerland, something Mike hadn't known.

Given that fact, he'd decided to buy the gun in Zurich. His plans were still not formulated, but he had nothing to lose by taking the added precaution. His objective was to confront Owen Reid, and he knew he would kill the man if he had to. Or if he wanted to. And, if it came to what he suspected, he would want to.

He hadn't developed any plan for escape if things turned out that way, but the purchase of the gun in a foreign country was at least an intelligent move if he was to be successful. The confrontation had to be in Liechtenstein, because once Reid was back in the states, the security on him would be so heavy Mike could never get close without the senator's consent, which Mike was convinced he'd never get.

He didn't know how he'd get close here, either, but at least the odds were better. And the gun? Well, he'd worry about that when the time came.

He pushed the Porsche to ninety, thought better of it, and dropped back to a more reasonable speed. There was really no reason to speed and risk the police. Fifteen minutes wouldn't make the difference. He had two days. The papers had said Reid was due to leave for Paris on Wednesday.

Not that Mike knew exactly where Reid was. The papers had only mentioned Liechtenstein, but it was a tiny country and Mike had to assume he could find out.

* * *

He arrived in Vaduz at noon and learned where Reid was staying within the hour .

Triesenburg. A short drive south.

There was only one hotel of significance in the small village, a sprawling, gabled edifice that bespoke old world elegance. Mike parked the Porsche in the cobblestone parking lot, pulling up in front of an ornately worked wrought iron railing that must once have been used to tether horses.

He walked into the lobby and went to the desk.

"May I help you, sir?" the distinguished-looking clerk asked him, correctly surmising Mike spoke English. The man stood ramrod straight; his graying moustache was perfectly trimmed.

Mike asked for a room.

"I'm sorry, but we're full. I can't take you until—" the man searched his bulky, leatherbound registry "—Wednesday. You might stay elsewhere in town, however. I'd be happy to call down for you."

Damn, Mike thought. He was certain Reid was here; staying somewhere else would do Mike no good. He wanted to surprise the man, and he could only do that by being in the same hotel and seeing Reid as if by accident. He felt reasonably sure when he identified himself Reid would have to grant him an interview, especially if they met in public. Whatever the man was, he would certainly not order violence done in the open.

A phone call or a message left in his box, however, would give Reid the advantage. He'd know Mike was there and would be able to plan accordingly.

Mike would have no excuse to stay around the hotel all day if he weren't registered there. To attempt it would only draw attention. Still, that seemed the better alternative, so he asked the clerk, "How late does the dining room serve?"

"Until two-thirty," the man answered, glancing at the handsome grandfather clock standing in a corner of the small but well appointed lobby. Mike followed the man's gaze and saw it was well after two. "But sandwiches are served on the terrace until four," the clerk added, "and you can have a drink there at any time."

"Thank you," Mike said, turning away and heading toward the open doors.

The tables on the terrace were only half filled, and Mike was seated at one against the railing. Below him, the mountain dropped sharply, and the view of the valley was spectacular. A large river meandered majestically miles below, and Mike guessed it to be the Rhine. The summer breeze blew fresh and clean, and he might have enjoyed himself immensely on another day.

He ordered a sandwich and a beer, and his eyes searched the lobby as he waited.

* * *

It was four-thirty now, and Mike knew he would have to leave. He could no longer sit over the second beer he'd been nursing for the better part of an hour. The fussy, beet-faced waiter had stopped by several times, making it obvious he'd like to finally clear the table. Several guests had also glanced his way as he'd sat solitary.

He would check into one of the other hotels, he decided, and then come back here for dinner. He figured seven o'clock would be about right with enough time to overlap if Reid dined early or late.

He signaled the waiter, paid his check and rose.

As he entered the lobby through the terrace doors, a burly young man walked toward him. His blond hair was crewcut, which made Mike somehow feel the man was American.

"Mister Frost?" the man asked, less a question than a statement.

Mike nodded dumbly.

"The senator will see you now. If you'll follow me, please."

256

Mike followed woodenly, his mind whirling in confusion. It was only after he entered the elevator he remembered his gun. It was still locked in the glove compartment of his car.

CHAPTER 30

The tall man stood with his back to them as they entered the spacious dome-ceilinged room about which large potted plants were placed on the parquet floors and bunches of freshly cut flowers graced the tables. He was at the open terrace doors, staring out at the view stretching below him, timbered hills tumbling to the river that cut the deep valleys, the same scene Mike had gazed at all afternoon. It seemed to Mike the man was reluctant to turn from it.

When he did, he looked directly at the blonde football type Mike assumed was a bodyguard, and said, "Thanks, Bert. You can leave us alone now." His voice was soft but carried an easy authority, and the other hesitated only briefly before nodding and going to the door. Only after it closed did the senator turn his eyes on Mike. Reid was an even larger man than his photograph indicated, and his ruggedly handsome features set off by the encroaching gray at his temples lent him an unmistakable aura of straightforwardness. Even his clothing—blue-and-white checked shirt above khakis—enhanced that impression.

The gaze was appraising. Whatever Mike had thought his presence might cause the dark eyes to reveal was certainly not in evidence as the man continued to search his face. There was no fear in Reid's eyes, no threat—not even concern. If anything, Mike would have described Reid's expression as one of curiosity and that impression confused him.

Reid must be a hell of an actor, Mike said to himself, trying to retain the sense of purpose that had brought him to this room. But it was hard to feel hatred for the man who looked at him so frankly. So openly.

"Michael Frost," the senator said, enunciating the name with great deliberation, seeming to savor the sound of it.

Mike remained silent. I'm not really up to this, he thought, not with this man. There was a feeling of such self-assurance emanating from Reid Mike felt totally off balance.

Still, he plunged in, opening with the bluff he'd decided on earlier.

"My father's dead," he began, hoping to shock Reid with his abruptness.

The tall man said nothing, although Mike imagined perhaps he nodded in the barest acknowledgment.

"I was there," Mike pushed on. "It happened two days ago. In St.Thomas."

He tried to make the statement challenging but seemed unable to provoke the other man.

"Charley Frost," Reid said after a moment, but his tone carried only a fond, sad remembrance. "We go back a long time."

"I know." Mike felt suddenly comfortable in the senator's presence and tried to fight that. "You knew he was dead, didn't you? I mean really dead this time."

The senator's eyes merely held Mike levelly.

"How?" Mike pushed. "How did you know?"

"How did you know? To be there?" Reid countered quietly, and Mike understood the man had seen through him. Probably knew—

Mike felt a quick impulse to tell Reid all, about his having the power and the rest of it, but controlled the urge. Although the senator must have understood the power well, certainly better than anyone except Charley, he was the last one Mike could trust with that secret. They thought the power lay only with Charley and had died with him, and Mike's only chance would be to perpetuate that belief.

"Like I said, I was there," he fenced.

The senator's look changed to one of gentle admonishment, and Mike knew he'd made a mistake. Whatever he was to learn, wherever this ultimate confrontation would lead, he'd do well to remember not to underestimate the other man's perception.

"What I mean is," he went on, a bit lamely, "I was looking for him. I had been for weeks. At first I just had a hunch, a feeling he was still alive. But after awhile I was certain I was right, and began to think of places he might have gone into hiding."

"And you picked St. Thomas," Reid said. He had moved to the square sculptured dining table that sat beneath the inlaid wooden chandelier and leaned against it, arms crossed over his chest as he regarded Mike.

Did Mike detect a touch of mockery in the statement? He thought so, but realized the senator was more subtle than he'd expected. He wasn't sure of anything about the man. But he felt he was being—toyed with? That wasn't quite it, and Mike couldn't gauge exactly what it was.

Whatever, the other man was definitely in control.

"Yes," Mike responded. "St. Thomas. We'd been there a few years ago, and my father had liked it, so I thought it might be a choice for him. It turned out I was right."

"Your father went to a lot of places he liked. Would you have searched them all?"

Mike tried to hold the other's gaze, but felt his eyes shift as he said, "If I'd had to. Like I said, I knew he was alive. Somehow, I knew it. I got lucky on my first guess." He raised his eyes and looked defiantly at Reid.

"Some lucky. Whoever was looking for him found him through me— and now he's really gone for good. Not dead, like I'm sure you already know, but he might as well be."

His tears came suddenly but he gritted his teeth and bravely held the senator's dark eyes. He had the insane impression the man wanted to come to him and comfort him, and he fought to keep his anger alive.

"You know about that, don't you?" Mike went on, the challenge clear in his voice. "You know all about all of it, don't you? You even knew I was coming," Mike said, the anger dissipating to a sort of wonder as he remembered his shock when Bert had approached him in the lobby.

"I *guessed* you were coming," Reid accentuated softly.

"What's that supposed to mean?" Mike put in harshly. His voice sounded petulant, but suddenly he didn't care. He was so confused, so frustrated, and he had nothing to hang onto now. His hatred for Reid had kept him going these last two days, but no matter how he tried he felt it slipping away. Some part of his mind told him that could be dangerous, perhaps fatal, but it didn't seem to matter.

"Who *are* you?" he asked, surprised at the question as he heard himself utter it. "*What* are you?" he added, and noted without satisfaction the touch of discomfort that crossed the handsome face at that last.

Reid hesitated a long moment and then his features softened. "So many questions, Mike," he said gently.

"You're damn right! And you're the only one who can give me any answers."

"I'll help you all I can," Reid said, and despite himself Mike felt comforted by the senator's tone. "That's why you're here after all," the man added enigmatically. "But first, why don't you tell me what you think you understand so far."

The command was gracefully handled, and Mike welcomed it. Whether he wanted to be or not, he knew he was in the other's hands, and the realization gave him a sudden, sharp relief.

"Okay," he said, taking a deep breath and seating himself in one of the soft leather armchairs that fronted the small brick fireplace set in the near wall beside the open terrace doors. "And then?"

The senator seated himself opposite. "And then," he answered, "I'll tell you the rest of it. All of it. I promise you."

He stretched his legs on to the tiled coffee table that separated them, drew a cigar from his pocket, clipped it neatly, and lit it. "Go on," Reid prompted as he blew the smoke up toward the ceiling.

Mike felt himself oddly at ease as he started. He heard the warning from some other part of his mind but smothered that as he said, "Well, as I told you, I had this feeling after the kidnaping last September my father was still alive. I fought it for awhile, but it wouldn't go away, so I decided to follow up on it. Besides, there were some other things that made me suspicious."

Mike detailed briefly the visit from Barnard, the untraceable FBI man, and the phone tap he'd found still in place eight months later.

"But mostly it was just my hunch," he went on. "I didn't know where to begin, so I thought I'd retrace my father's life and see where it led me. So I went to Saint Mary's," he said.

"The superintendent, Mister Winston, told me how much my father had done for the place," he added, and if he expected a look of apology from Reid for his own lack of involvement with the orphanage of his youth he got none.

"Anyway," Mike went on, "I spent some time with Frank Anderson, the coach, and he told me about when Charley—the real Charley—got beat up after a basketball game one time. That became important later," Reid nodded as he said it, "but then, the most important thing he told me was about the power."

He detected a change in the senator's eyes as he said that but couldn't pinpoint the expression. "He explained about the raffle ticket and the tests at Durham, and he told me what he'd thought that meant."

Mike searched Reid's face as he continued but got nothing more even as he recounted his experience with Dr. Krieger in Durham.

"At that point, I hadn't made any connection with the power and my father. It was just some information I'd picked up, that's all. I did learn, though, you'd been with him when they left—with Richie and Charley. I hadn't known that before. And, of course, that became very important when I began to understand the rest of it."

Mike paused, but as Reid remained silent, he went on again.

"I went to Madison where my father went to school. I met Andy Billingsly, my dad's roommate, and...." Mike then sketched in what he'd learned from the aging college boy—Charley's spectacular success with Mohawk, his abrupt and mysterious departure, his almost brutal abandonment of his sweetheart Alice Winslow. "That part I never understood," he put in. "It seemed so out of character for my father."

He waited, got nothing, and said, "So were some of the other things, too, and that's when I started to get suspicious. I remembered Anderson talking about my father being such a hell-raiser, and I couldn't picture that at all. And then, when I got to California I found out my parents— my real mother—had only been married for four or five months before I was born, and they had probably just met. It just didn't add up.

"That's when I started thinking, and I remembered about the scar Coach Anderson had mentioned. So I called my mother and asked, and when she said there wasn't, everything started to fall together."

Mike rose, walked to the French doors that opened on the terrace, and looked out. The sky was darkening quickly in the late afternoon;

heavy clouds were building on the horizon. The clouds were proud, rich with the promise of downpour, and Mike heard thunder roll in the distance. He took off his sportcoat, tossed it onto the needlepoint side chair by the doors, loosened the tie he'd worn for the occasion, and rolled up the sleeves of his blue shirt.

"The power," he said, turning again to face the senator. Reid's eyes held his firmly, but he did not turn away. This was it, finally, Mike knew. "The power," Mike repeated. "That was it all along. Charley Frost wasn't my father's name. He was really Richie Peters. The real Charley, the 'hell-raiser' with the scar, died in that car wreck in Nevada, and my father switched identities with him. And the only reason for that would be to protect the power, to hide it.

"And you were there." It was the beginning of the accusation. "That's when I knew you were part of it, or at least understood it. You had to. And then I thought about you, how you're going to be president," Mike's voice had a touch of contempt as his original feelings were rekindled, "and I began to put it together. Your record, for example," he went on, and the accusation was unsheathed now, naked in the anger that began to rise in Mike's voice. "Always at the right place at the right time. The farsighted senator from Colorado. You were at the right place at the right time, all right—that wreck in Nevada. That's what made you."

Mike expected a response, got none, and plunged on. "That was your payoff, the price for keeping quiet. My father fed you the information, the things he knew would happen, and you used them to make your way up. Or maybe it wasn't quite that way," he relented slightly. "Maybe it was something you both wanted, a way to better the world or something like that. That would have appealed to my father." The last comment he said to himself more than to Reid.

"Okay," Mike went on. "Let's say it was that way. Not blackmail but a way to achieve a greater good of some kind." His voice flattened out as he felt himself more in control, and he allowed a hard, deliberate edge to replace the anger that had expressed itself before. "Whatever," he ended in that tone, "it doesn't change what happened."

He stopped then, stared down at the senator with a look as hostile as he could manage. He'd played all his cards recklessly and knew the other man now had the total advantage, but he didn't care. He wanted the confrontation and he would have it, on any terms.

"What do you think did happen?" Reid asked finally in a soft voice as Mike stood silent above him.

"I think you got carried away with power," Mike said, his voice as soft and controlled as the other man's. "Your own power. A different power. The power of the presidency." He paused. "I think you used my father to get there, and then felt you didn't need him anymore."

Reid's eyes burned into his, but Mike was over the edge now.

"I think," he went on, very deliberately, "my father represented a threat to you in the end. And I think you tried to have that threat removed."

The look on the senator's face was something Mike had never experienced, and despite his sudden fear, he had a great sense of triumph. Whatever was to come, he'd been right. The man was a monster, he was—

Mike backed up a step as Reid rose slowly. Tall as he was, the senator was more than his equal, and Mike noted the strong condition of the other's body.

He'd never considered the possibility of a physical confrontation, but there was something in Reid's stance that threatened one. Mike balanced himself on the balls of his feet, but he was still unprepared for the slap that crashed against his cheek.

He involuntarily raised his hand toward his face, but his wrist was caught quickly in a vice-like grip.

"What right do you—" Mike began angrily but was cut off by the look in the other's face.

"I have every right," Owen Reid said quietly, though his eyes blazed. "I'm your father."

CHAPTER 31

Mike lay with his hands clasped behind his head, staring mindlessly at the ceiling above his bed. He was dimly aware of the Alpen dawn now spilling soft rose through the billowing drapes of his hotel room. Although he had not slept all night, he knew lack of sleep was the least of his worries.

How could he sleep with the sting of that slap still burning his cheek? With the words, "I'm your father," echoing endlessly in his mind.

"I'm your father," Owen Reid had said those hours ago, and in the vacuum that had suddenly filled the room following that proclamation, Mike had searched the man's eyes and known beyond question he had been told the truth.

"My father," he had finally managed to whisper, but the only confirmation he'd received had been the blazing, unwavering gaze of the man who stood before him.

And that was the only confirmation he was to receive. For, and it was incomprehensible to Mike, the man had refused to discuss things further.

Refused—despite all Mike's entreaties.

"Not now, Mike," Reid had said quietly when Mike was finally under enough control to have posed a faltering question.

"But—"

"Not now!" Reid had cut him off, the gentler tone that had crept into his voice reverting abruptly to sharp anger. "Goddamn it," the man's voice had risen unexpectedly and become oddly shrill, and his arms

265

had seemed to raise of their own volition in a helpless gesture. "Not tonight!"

Reid had broken his gaze away and walked to the window. His stance was resolute as he stood with his back to Mike, arms crossed at his chest as he stared ahead. Mike had the impression the man was almost trembling. He was further confused by that, because after all, the shock was Mike's, wasn't it?

Mike waited for Reid to turn around, but he never did. He did not acknowledge Mike's presence beyond saying tightly, "Come tomorrow at one," and a moment later Mike let himself out of the room.

He didn't remember anything of the drive back to his own hotel; he had only carried the picture in his mind of that broad-shouldered frame silhouetted suddenly against the glare as the first flash of lightning had shattered the somber sky and a drum of thunder rolled.

But once in his room, Mike began attempting to sort out the new pieces of the puzzle, and, oddly, the one he couldn't fit at all was the smallest—Reid's final, dramatic demonstration. Something in that disturbed Mike deeply, something he couldn't quite grasp, some elusive signal he felt was desperately important. For even in his confused state, Mike had sensed Reid's actions in those last moments, after the slap had come, were completely out of character for the man. Mike felt somehow Reid had been badly shaken, but he could not understand how that had come about.

He had been shaken, understandably so.

But Reid?

Even now, after all these sleepless hours, it did not make sense to Mike.

But the rest of it did.

He'd thought about the man's startling revelation and believed he understood now what the total scenario must have been. Many of Mike's unanswered questions made sense now in the context of Owen Reid actually being his father. In that respect, Mike was comforted.

But for the rest—that would take time to settle in, if it ever would. Charley Frost. The man he'd always thought to be his father. How did Mike feel about him now? He tried to focus on the love he'd always felt, the despair that had so totally washed him only days before when he'd seen the dead body on the rocks and thought it to be Charley's. But all he felt was confusion.

And anger.

For despite the arguments he gave himself to the contrary, Mike felt duped, the victim of some complex hoax. And his father's—Charley's, he amended angrily—participation in the deception aroused his fury.

Charley Frost. Paragon of virtue. Supporter of the just, the fair, the equitable. Charley Frost, the man Mike had so hoped to emulate and of whose success he had so long stood in awe, nurturing his own fears of inadequacy as he'd secretly measured himself against that sterling image and inevitably come up short.

Charley Frost.

A fraud.

And Owen Reid? Richie, Mike's real father?

How could he begin to cope with that?

His feelings were so diverse, the questions raised so infinite—he couldn't even attempt to examine them now. He could only open himself to the startling situation as much as he dared and see how things developed.

But for some reason, he realized he didn't feel anger toward Owen Reid. He'd entered the man's room containing a rage that bordered on hatred and had left drained of those feelings. Even the fact the man who was his real father had never seen him—had never even attempted to see him as far as Mike knew—even that fact, which Mike brought again and again to mind, did not raise his ire as he would have expected.

Somehow, although he didn't examine it closely, he knew he could understand that and in fact accept it.

No. The obvious problems with Owen Reid did not really concern him at the moment. What nagged was that final scene, the manner in which Reid had refused to discuss things further. It was as if the man couldn't deal with the situation, and despite Mike's anger and frustration, he could even have understood that.

In anyone else.

But not Owen Reid. For Mike was convinced beyond any doubt this man who was his father would be able to deal with anything—and at any time.

He had to be.

So what had happened? Mike was convinced something had, some-thing of which he was totally unaware. Something Reid had wanted to keep hidden in that moment.

That was it!

But try as he might, Mike could find no answer as to what that might be. No more than he could ascertain, when he thought about it now, whether the man knew he, Mike, also had the power. How should he handle *that* part of it if and when it developed?

He didn't know.

But as he finally rose from bed to prepare himself to meet again with his father, he resolved to move cautiously with the man and to keep his wits about him as best he could.

He sensed now he was in some deep and possibly even dangerous game, and the only man who could teach him the rules was perhaps not only his father but his adversary as well.

CHAPTER 32

The steep trail was rocky, and his horse stumbled from time to time as Richie pushed higher. The trail narrowed so much in places the scrub pines brushed his jeans as he passed.

Then the trail widened again, leveled off, and the trees thinned out. In the distance, he could see the other peaks. Dismounting, he looped the reins over a branch, and walked across the dry red dirt of the forest floor to the precipice.

He stood for a moment and looked out. The long valley stretched below, but the trees began to rise again a few miles away, first in gradual foothills and then sharply into mountains themselves. They peaked at about ten thousand feet, he estimated, just about the height at which he stood.

The vista was all green now, except for occasional outcroppings of red rock, but in a few months fall would come and the aspens would erupt in riots of color.

Stepping back from the edge, he walked to a boulder and climbed agilely to its top. Despite the early hour, the sun was warm, and he shed his lightweight jacket, rolled the sleeves of his shirt to the elbows, and seated himself at the edge of the rock. Dangling his legs, he let his eyes rest on the distance.

Perhaps he could get his thoughts together here, out in the open air. He hoped so. He had only a few hours before he was to meet with Mike again and he had to make absolutely certain of his decision.

After the boy had left, Richie had tried to concentrate on the awe-some implications of what might conceivably be. But he had been hampered in his thoughts, for time and again as he'd let his fancy wander, he was brought back once more to rivet on the sensation he'd experienced when he'd slapped Mike and the stronger one he'd felt as he gripped the boy's wrist.

He hadn't been able to get past that in the long hours he'd sat staring at the darkened windows of his hotel suite. He only vaguely registered the soft pelt of the rain and the rivulets as they traced down the window panes and hypnotically picked up myriad refractions of the dim lights within the room. He paid little attention to the occasional flash of lightning that flooded the room with a quick harsh glare. He hadn't gotten past the sensation then, nor later, as he'd lain wide-eyed in bed and heard the retreating rolls of thunder as the storm passed through.

Finally, when dawn broke, clear, he had risen and gone to the stables and requested a horse. Despite Bert's objections, he had felt an overwhelming need to get out and to have some form of physical activity. He had pushed his horse hard at times as he'd negotiated the narrow mountain trails. He knew the security man waited somewhere just below on his own mount. He could hear the other horse whinny from time to time and was grateful the other man did not infringe on his solitude.

Mike, he thought now, conjuring a picture of the boy in his mind. He seemed like a nice kid, as Charley had said he was. He had open, regular features beneath his reddish hair—strong, cleft chin, bright inquisitive eyes. And Richie had to admire the courage and determination with which the boy had confronted him.

Richie thought about his own father, a man he didn't remember. He had died at twenty-three after falling off a bridge while drunk and drowning in the river below. His death had been ruled accidental, but Richie sometimes wondered about that in later years. And now—

Now his *own* son was here, finally, the son he had so long denied. Mike, with the power, as Charley had suspected.

Mike, whom he had touched—

The feel of the slap, the grasp, returned, capturing his imagination again. But Richie forced all thoughts of the boy from his mind so he could think things through from the beginning. But instead he gave in to another troubling feeling, something that had nagged him on some low level for the past day. He was thinking of his altercation the morning before with Marty Goodman, his campaign manager. Marty was young, brilliant, and totally committed to the person he knew as Owen Reid. Dedicated to him both as a presidential candidate and as a man.

Richie relied on his advice heavily. As heavily as he could anyone's now that Charley was gone.

"Marty," he'd said to the man when the transatlantic call had finally gone through. "Get me all the background on Jason Coleridge you can, will you?"

"Jason Coleridge? You mean that guy in Chicago? The radical? Hell, Owen, he's small potatoes. If you're thinking to tackle the race issue, I've got five guys in mind who—"

"Just get it, Marty!" Richie had suddenly exploded, slamming down the phone and cursing himself a moment later that he'd done so.

He'd called Marty later to apologize.

How could he expect the man to understand how important Coleridge would someday be? How different, how inexplicably different it was when you knew.

Nobody could understand that.

Even Charley had not, not really.

He turned his head south, the way he had come, and could see the outskirts of the village of Triesenberg far below. How much the town reminded him of Estes Park, he thought again.

Estes Park, Colorado. He remembered the town as he'd first seen it nearly twenty-five years ago. It had been fall then and things were quiet. The town had a charm he'd liked, and he'd decided to settle there when he finished law school.

After all, it hadn't really mattered where he started. All he'd had to do was wait.

"Howdy."

Owen tapped the last nail in place and turned to look at the stranger. The burly man stood with hands in the pockets of his jeans as he regarded the shingle. Hectic curls of gray spilled from under the Stetson hat pushed back on his head. The crinkles in the leathery skin surrounding the light blue eyes gave evidence of long hours spent outdoors in the harsh but sunny climate.

"Looks pretty good," the stranger said affably. "'Owen Reid, Attorney at Law', huh?"

"That's me. How about you?"

"Sam Mullins." The man extended a bear paw of a hand that swallowed Owen's own as he shook it. "We'll probably be doin' a lot of business together."

"How so?" Owen asked.

"I'm the sheriff," the man said opening the sheepskin coat to display the badge on the red checkered shirt beneath.

"Good to meet you, sheriff," Owen said. "How about a cup of coffee?"

"Sounds good," Mullins rejoined, following Owen up the stairs and into the house, rubbing his hands together briskly as he did so. "Gettin' cold already."

Owen nodded, removing his leather jacket and hanging it on one of the pegs on the wall of the small foyer. It was only late October but the air already held the bite of winter and even indoors Owen wore a heavy sweater.

"Sit down, sheriff." Owen motioned the big man to one of the leather chairs in the converted living room that was to function as the reception area. A desk for a secretary fronted the near wall, and two chairs were positioned opposite, in front of the fireplace. A coffee table was set between, and a few prints of outdoor scenes lent a coziness to the room.

"Nice set up," Sheriff Mullins said, taking the steaming cup from Owen when he returned. "That going to be your office?" he asked, indicating the sliding door behind the secretary's desk.

"Yes," Owen answered. "The kitchen's beyond and there's a bathroom off the office. And two bedrooms and a bath upstairs."

"Nice," Mullins repeated. "Got a good deal on this place, too—from what I heard."

"Twenty-thousand," Owen said, sure the man opposite already knew the exact figure anyway and not caring that he did. Estes Park was a small town.

"What can I do for you, Sheriff Mullins?" he asked, taking a sip from his cup.

"Nothing really, son. Just stopped by to get acquainted. We don't have too many newcomers moving in, at least not this time of year. And, like I said, you're a lawyer—and I'm the sheriff."

"Besides," he added with a conspiratorial smile, "there's not a hell of a lot I've got to do off season, anyway."

"Stop around any time, sheriff."

"Make it Sam."

"Sam. Come around whenever you like. I don't think I'll have my hands full, either. At least, not for a while."

"Don't figure to," the man agreed. "What made you pick Estes Park anyway?"

Owen shrugged, stood, and walked to the open fireplace where he kicked the smoldering logs into flames.

"Just liked it, I guess. I first came up here seven years ago. It was my first year at the University of Colorado, down in Boulder. It was quiet and I liked the feel of it, and I decided I'd start out here when I finished law school."

Mullins' eyes regarded him quietly over the cup of coffee.

"Not much of a place for a young lawyer to start out, though," he said. "Pretty slow here, and there's already four lawyers in town, pretty well established. You might have some trouble catchin' on."

"I figure to," Owen agreed. "But I'm willing to wait it out."

"Good for you, son," the man's craggy face broke with a smile. "I like to see a young man buckin' the odds to get what he wants. Where you from anyway, Owen? Before college, I mean."

"North Carolina."

"Long ways."

Owen agreed.

"Well, got to be goin'—although I don't know why," Mullins laughed good-naturedly. "But folks like to see my face around town."

Owen watched as Mullins closed the gate and walked to his right toward the center of town. The man gave off a feeling of security, a sense everything was under control. Sheriff Mullins seemed shrewd and competent, for all of his casual air. Owen had detected a steel appraisal from behind the quiet blue eyes he felt could be depended upon when the time came.

He liked Sam Mullins and was glad he did because he knew Mullins would be very important to him one day.

* * *

But that day was not to come for some time, as Owen well knew, and he busied himself doing those other things necessary to ensure he was properly established when it finally did.

A land deal here, a construction project there—all inordinately profitable and all orchestrated under the counsel of the clever young attorney whose timing and foresight proved virtually infallible. His record in court was unblemished, for Owen seemed always to sniff out a winner, including those on occasion other attorneys believed to be lost causes.

It seemed everyone associated with Owen came out a winner, and his reputation spread far beyond the sleepy village.

And he made the right moves politically as well, positioning himself for the moment when it came.

Which it did with a vengeance.

* * *

"That's it, Owen. Keep your head down and bring your left shoulder all the way under when you pivot your body. Now—try it again."

Owen stepped to the ball, positioned his club, and stopped for the barest fraction at the top of his back swing before coming down with a smooth pull and feeling the solid contact as the wood struck. Only after he'd completed his follow through did he look up to see the small white sphere that still rose in a quick trajectory straight out over the center of the fairway.

"You're getting better every day," Rollie said as he clapped Owen on the back. There was genuine enthusiasm in the pro's voice and in his eyes as well, and Owen felt a pride in himself at his accomplishment.

"What say we break now, get a bite, and then we'll play nine. Okay?"

Owen assented, put the driver back into the bag, leaned it against the iron railing, and followed Rollie into the small coffee shop. The dining room was still closed for the season; it wouldn't open again for another month.

There were only two other customers when they entered, two men at the counter over coffee who nodded hello as they took a booth. A pleasant smell of bacon pervaded.

"Grilled cheese, hon," Rollie said when Betsy came over.

"Same," Owen followed. "And coffee."

"Quiet today, huh, sweetheart?" Rollie said, and Betsy nodded. Her green eyes had a worried look, and Rollie took her hand, patted it, said, "Don't worry, hon. It'll work out when the season starts."

"I know," she responded, but Rollie's eyes took on a troubled look as they followed her path to the kitchen.

The man looked back to Owen, shrugged, and raised his eyebrows. His quiet brown eyes carried uncertainty and his youthful face appeared drawn under the early season tan.

"I don't know," Rollie said. "Maybe we made a mistake coming up here."

Owen shook his head. "I don't known either, Rollie. But you knew the risks when you came."

The man nodded. "Sure. Closed all winter and not enough to pay the overhead in spring or fall. Hope for enough action in the summer to make it for the rest of the year."

"You don't know yet it won't work out. You haven't had the season."

"Yeah," Rollie said and heaved a sigh. Through the windows behind him, Owen could see the mountains loom, still draped in heavy snowcover to points well below their peaks. "I haven't found out anything I didn't know already. There's no reason to think the summer won't be good. It's just the waiting that's getting to me, I guess. To both of us."

Owen had met them six months earlier when they'd driven up for their first look at the Mountain View Golf Club. They'd been interested in the purchase and had sought him out to handle the legal matters pertaining to their offer.

"I won't go over seventy-five grand, Owen," Rollie had told him that first night over dinner. "After all, we're only buying the building improvements, not the course itself. I'll be lucky to make out after paying the city for the rental on that."

275

"Well, it's thin, but I think we can work it out. It'd be easier if you had more of a down payment."

"I know, but we had trouble coming up with the twenty thousand down we've got. I couldn't scrape up any more if I had to."

"Well, we'll do our best," Owen said, already knowing he could close but sorry it had to be them.

He liked the eager young couple, wished it could have been someone else. But then, he'd have probably liked the someone else equally well, he told himself as he completed the purchase.

They'd become friends, and he'd been helpful in finding them the small A-frame less than half a mile from the course. He'd settled that for a good price, too. Not that it would matter in the long run.

Now he sat opposite Rollie in the quiet coffee shop, while the man's wife served them lunch.

Owen had never played golf, but realized a decent game would stand him in good stead as he made his way, so he'd approached the golf pro some two months earlier to begin lessons.

As June approached, his game had already become quite respectable.

They played eighteen instead of nine that afternoon because Owen was doing so well. He broke ninety for the first time and Rollie was almost as excited as Owen when they came off the course.

"Keep going like you are and you'll make my reputation," the pro said seriously. "Nothing sells more than the living product."

Rollie turned to face him and ran his hand through his thin brown hair, something he did quite often. The man was squat, no more than five-six, but his arms and shoulders were powerful and he could hit the ball with a force that awed Owen.

"How about stopping over for a drink, Owen? Celebrate that eighty-eight."

"Sure. Thanks."

"Just go on down. Betsy'll be there already. I've got to lock up, but I'll be along in just a minute."

* * *

She opened the door at his knock, brightened when she saw it was he, and released the chain.

"I hate to do that," Betsy said as he entered. "The chain. Especially here," she went on, indicating the mountain vista that was framed like a picture in the massive floor to ceiling window. "But this place is so isolated."

"I don't blame you," he said. "It's a shame, but after last winter—you're wise to take precautions."

"Where's Rollie?" she asked.

"He'll be along in a minute. He invited me over for a drink, to celebrate."

"Well, tell me!"

He paused a beat for the drama. "Eighty-eight," he said.

"That's wonderful, Owen." She came and embraced him briefly.

"Thanks. I'm pretty pleased, myself." Owen pulled away more quickly than he would have liked.

"You should be pleased. Most people never break ninety, and you've only been playing for two months."

"Your husband's a good teacher."

"He is," she said seriously, nodding her blonde head. "I just hope—"

She broke off, turned and walked toward the walnut cabinet in a corner of the large open room that served as living room and dining area. "What are you drinking?"

"Bourbon, if you have some." He watched as she bent to her task, blonde hair soft against her light blue sweater, black skirt tight across her buttocks.

She brought their drinks, placed another for Rollie on the mosaic tiled coffee table, and toasted Owen.

"To your eighty-eight."

He sipped his drink. "It really worries you, doesn't it?"

She nodded. "I try not to show it, for Rollie's sake. But he's worried, too."

"Maybe you should get out, then," he said impulsively. "This would be a good time to sell, right before the season. You could probably get your money back." Don't dabble, his mind cautioned, but something in him rebelled.

She seemed to think about it for a minute, then shook her head reluctantly. "No, Owen. It's been Rollie's dream for so long. We've got to take the chance."

"Maybe you should think about it, though," he persisted. "I know I can get you out reasonably well. And there are other places, probably less risky. Why can't you talk to Rollie?"

"It's tempting, believe me. But his heart's in this and I couldn't discourage him."

"Well, think about it, anyway, okay?" he ended lamely.

"I will, Owen. And I appreciate your concern."

The green eyes were warm and Owen wished he didn't like her so much—wished she weren't Rollie's wife, wished a lot of things.

"Hey, hon," Rollie's voice came from behind as he opened the door. "I guess you heard, huh?"

"I heard it on the five o'clock news before Owen even showed up," she said. "The channel 2 reporters will be here any minute." Rollie came to her laughing and took her in a strong embrace. She was shorter than Rollie, and although he generally preferred tall, slim women, Owen found himself often admiring her full figure.

"Some pupil," Rollie said as he released her.

"Some instructor," she said, handing him his drink. "Here's to the best pro in the Rockies who's going to have a wonderful season."

"I'll drink to that," Rollie said heartily, and Owen joined in the toast.

CHAPTER 33

It turned out to be a wonderful season.

Summer came early. The warm days were inviting, and the tourists made their presence known a good two weeks before Memorial Day. By mid-June, Estes Park was bustling, and as the weather held, the course continued to be crowded.

Rollie's lesson schedule was as full as he could want it.

"Sorry I have to break our date again, Owen," he said one day when he called the office. "I'm just so damned busy I don't have time to play for pleasure anymore."

Rollie's eyes were bright whenever Owen saw him, and the relief Betsy showed was painfully obvious.

"He's so happy, Owen," she told him once. "It's like a dream come true for him."

The three of them had dinner out together one night toward the end of August. Betsy looked particularly vibrant in a yellow dress, and Rollie appeared relaxed and substantial in a well-tailored plaid sportcoat as they sat in a booth in the dim restaurant.

"I'll tell you something, Owen," Rollie confided in a lowered voice, pushing the candle aside and leaning forward with his arms crossed on the table. "We've made our nut for the whole year already, and we've still got a good six weeks to go before things really slow down. This thing can become a gold mine."

He reached over and took his wife's hand.

"Congratulations," Owen offered. His voice was sincere, but there was a reservation in his tone that was meant to capture Rollie's attention.

"What's the matter, Owen? Aren't you excited for us?"

"Sure I am, Rollie. You know that."

"Well, what then? You seem a little worried somehow. Hell, things couldn't be going better."

"That's what I've been thinking about."

He let it hang, and Rollie's face sobered as he regarded his attorney. Betsy placed her drink on the table, looking at Owen with quiet appraisal.

"What are you trying to say, Owen?"

Owen hesitated a moment before plunging. He'd thought it out and decided he needed to at least try. Beyond that, he felt the deeper need to absolve himself. "I think maybe you ought to sell out," he said.

"Sell out!" Rollie sat back with a start, then realized he had raised his voice a bit too loudly and glanced at the other tables. "Sell out!" he repeated, quietly this time as he leaned forward again. "Are you crazy?"

Owen shrugged. "Maybe. But look," he went on, eyes holding Rollie, "you've had a great season. A lot of that has to do with you, Rollie, because you've done a helluva job. You're an outstanding pro, and everybody around here knows it.

"But a lot of it has to do with the weather, too. And you can't control that. You can be the best around, but if the season starts late and ends early, there's nothing you can do about it. And that's a very real possibility up here."

"I know," Rollie responded, dismissing the argument with a motion of his hand. "But hell, we're way ahead of the game already."

"True," Owen came back. "That's what I'm thinking about. Right now, I'll bet I can get you a hundred grand for Mountain View. Maybe more. You came in with twenty-thousand down and you can get out now with more than fifty grand cash after paying off your debt. That's a helluva profit in less than one year, plus the fact you've built yourself a good reputation.

"Look," Owen pushed on, noting the resistance in Rollie's face but also registering the touch of interest in Betsy's, "let me put it this way. You're on top now, but the bottom line is up here you're at the mercy of the weather. One bad season can wreck you, and I've seen bad seasons come. Two years ago you'd have been out of business by August, instead of on top of the world.

"I'm speaking as your friend, Rollie. You two mean a lot to me, you know that, and as much as I'd miss you, I'd like to see you leave. Now, when things are good. And before the winter sets in," he added, "because that's the other thing. It's lonely up here, as you know from last year, especially out where you live. How about it Betsy?" he asked, turning to her. "Do you really want to spend another winter up here? Do you remember what the waiting was like last year?"

He paused for effect, then added deliberately, "And how about the other thing last Christmas? Do you remember how frightened you were, alone out there? The chains on the doors?"

She didn't answer, but he saw something in her eyes that encouraged him. Whatever it was died quickly, however, when she looked to Rollie and saw the expression on his face.

"No, Owen," she said, shaking her head with finality. "We're staying."

Rollie seemed to relax, as if he hadn't been sure of her answer. He smiled broadly, reached across the table to pat Owen's hand. "I really appreciate what you said, Owen. You're a good friend, and I'm glad you care enough about us to worry so much. But, like Betsy said, we're staying."

Owen nodded, trying not to show his desperation. "Maybe you want to think about selling the house, though, and moving out for the winter. After all, there's nothing for you to do for four or five months. You can move down to Boulder, maybe, just come back in the spring . There's nothing to keep you here."

Rollie looked to Betsy, seemed to consider it for a moment before shaking his head. "No. We love the house, and we can't afford a place in Boulder, too. Nope," he concluded heartily, "we're staying. Estes Park is our home—year-round, my friend."

Owen said nothing, and Rollie went on. "Hey. Cheer up. We're celebrating. Here we are on top of the world and you act like doomsday is just around the corner. Come on, drink up," he said, reaching for his glass.

Owen did likewise, avoiding Betsy's eyes.

He had considered telling them all of it, but knew he couldn't. He also knew they'd never believe him even if he tried. And besides, if it wasn't them it would be someone else. Or somewhere else, he told himself, again.

* * *

The season had held well into October, but the snow came fast after that. By Thanksgiving it was already two feet deep on the golf course and Owen doubted they'd see the ground again before March.

* * *

The call came four weeks later. The ring of the telephone was loud as Owen lay waiting in the early Christmas-morning stillness.

"Owen?" He recognized the deep voice before the man identified himself. "Sam Mullins. I'm out at Rollie Harper's and I think you'd better get out here right away."

"What is it, Sam?"

"Trouble. The worst."

He had known what he'd find, but nothing could really have prepared him for the sight that met him as he came through the open door of the A-frame. Nothing could have prepared him for the sight of Rollie sitting on the floor of the spacious, all-purpose room, a bloody ax beside him as he cradled the headless body in his arms.

CHAPTER 34

The trial lasted two weeks and was the biggest thing that ever hit Estes Park.

Newspaper men came from all over the country. Tourists, too, and the motels and rooming houses, which didn't usually even spruce up until May, now found themselves in full swing by mid-March.

Sheriff Mullins was the fourth witness, called by the prosecution after the coroner had testified as to the cause of death and two experts had sworn positive identification of the body through fingerprints and medical records.

Owen rose and walked slowly across the wooden floor of the packed courtroom in the old courthouse building. Dressed in a gray suit with narrow pinstripe and a solid maroon tie, the tall young attorney seemed an imposing figure as he approached the raised docket where Mullins sat and began his cross-examination.

"Sheriff, I'd like you to briefly review for the jury your earlier testimony as to the circumstances under which you discovered the body."

The big man looked uncomfortable in his blue suit as he shifted his body slightly, cleared his throat, and began.

"Well, like I said, I decided to drive out on a few of the more deserted roads, just to see what was going on. Things were real quiet in town, it being Christmas Eve, and normally I wouldn't have made a tour like that for no reason. But after what happened the Christmas before, I was a little uneasy.

"Anyway," he went on, "I'd been driving about an hour, up one road and down another, and I hadn't seen a thing. The snow was falling heavier, too, and I decided to make one more run before calling it a night since it was a little after two already.

"I went out past the golf course, and when I got to the Harpers' I saw all the lights on. So I stopped and got out just to make sure everything was okay. When I got closer to the house I saw the front door was open. I could hear music. Christmas carols on the radio."

Mullins paused a moment, took a deep breath before continuing. "So I went to the door and looked in. And there was Rollie—Mister Harper, the defendant—sitting on the floor with a body in his arms."

"And the condition of the room, sheriff?"

"Like I said before. Blood all over the place. And the bloody ax lying on the floor."

"Blood on Mister Harper?"

"Sure. He was holding the body."

"How was he holding it, sheriff? Was he cradling it, would you—"

"Objection!" Lloyd Jones, the prosecutor rose swiftly from his seat at the long table. Jones was a slight man with a round face that seemed to Owen always on the edge of a smirk.

"Counsel is calling for a conclusion from the witness. The witness has already testified the defendant was holding the body."

"Overruled." Judge Fielding looked to Owen. "You may continue, counselor."

"Thank you, your honor. I'll state my question again. How was the defendant holding the body, Sheriff Mullins?"

"Tenderly as he could, under the circumstances. He didn't seem to notice—"

"Objection!"

"Overruled."

Jones sat again, almost in a huff, and Mullins continued.

"Like I said, he didn't seem to notice the blood running all over him or that the head was missing. He just cradled the body like you would a child."

"What else was he doing, sheriff?"

"He was crying."

A quick sob came from one of the spectators and the judge raised his large, white-maned head but said nothing.

"Did he notice you? Did he say anything?"

"No, sir. He just sat there cradling the body with tears coming down his cheeks."

Owen turned, walked toward the jury, paused a moment, and turned back to face the witness.

"What did you do then?"

"Well, I did a quick search of the premises, but I didn't find anything. Then I called my deputy—and then I called you."

"Because I was the defendant's lawyer."

"Because you were his lawyer," Mullins affirmed.

"Now, sheriff, you testified earlier the front door was open when you reached the house."

"That's correct."

"You just walked in, did you not?"

"Right."

"No locks or chains—nothing?"

"Not in use. Like I said, the door was wide open."

"So anyone, then, could have walked into the house like you did?"

The prosecutor began to rise but seemed to reconsider it and sat back.

"That's right. Anyone could have walked into the house."

"Now, sheriff, how well did you know the Harpers at that time?"

"Pretty well. They'd only been up here a year, but I'd gotten to know them."

"Were they in the habit of locking their doors?"

"Objection!" Jones put in quickly. "Calls for a conclusion on which the witness could have no first-hand knowledge."

"Sustained. "

"I'll rephrase then, your honor. Would you say, sheriff, if a man entered his own home—"

"Objection!"

"Sustained."

Owen changed his tack.

"Sheriff, you stated earlier the door was wide open. Were there locks on the door? Chains?"

"Yes, sir. An inside latch and a heavy safety chain."

"And these were not in use."

"Correct."

"Are there other doors in the house?"

"Yes, sir. A kitchen door and two sliding glass doors to the deck."

"And what was the condition of those doors? Were they locked?"

"Yes, they were." Mullins described the rear door as having been locked and the safety chain set. The sliding doors were both latched, he noted, and the inside bolt between them in place.

"So the house was locked up—except for the front door?"

"That's correct."

"What happened then, sheriff? What happened when your men came?"

"Well, we searched the house real good, but there was nothing more than what was in the living room."

"Just the defendant and the body."

"And the ax."

"No signs of a struggle?"

"None."

"Nothing out of place? Lamps turned over, anything like that?"

"No, sir."

"Now sheriff," Owen continued, turning to face the jury and taking a pace or two towards them, "can you tell us if you found anything outside? Any tracks or footprints—anything like that."

"No, sir. Not really. There were our own tracks, of course, and some indentations that could have been others—but we couldn't really tell."

"Why couldn't you tell, sheriff?"

"Well, like I said before, it was snowing pretty hard that night— dropped about fourteen inches overall."

"And what time did you say you discovered the body?"

"About two in the morning—ten after, to be exact."

Owen nodded.

"Now, you heard the coroner testify the time of death was approximately ten PM?"

"Between ten and eleven—yes."

"So it was a good three hours, maybe four, between the time of death and the time you actually discovered the body."

Mullins concurred.

"And it snowed all that time."

"Yes, sir."

"Sheriff, how many inches would you say it snowed in those—"

"Objection! Witness couldn't possibly know that information."

Judge Fielding pondered for a moment. "Overruled," he said. "The sheriff is not a meteorologist, but after being here for fifty years his opinion is at least informed."

"Thank you, your honor. How many inches would you estimate it snowed in those three or four hours, sheriff?"

"Four inches. Maybe more."

"Enough to obliterate any tracks that might have been there."

"If not obliterate, at least make the signs useless."

"Even tire tracks?"

"Even tire tracks. I was there just over two hours, and when I left I could hardly see the ones I'd made myself."

Owen nodded.

"With that in mind, sheriff, would you say someone could have entered the Harper house earlier that evening, say about ten PM, left shortly thereafter, and not left any track that would have been visible some three or four hours later?"

"Objection."

"Overruled."

"Go on, sheriff. Answer the question."

"Well, I don't know."

"But in your opinion?"

"It could have happened that way."

Owen paused, walked to the defense table, and took a sip of water. He looked at his client. Rollie's eyes seemed glazed and out of focus, as they generally did now.

Owen turned back to Mullins.

"What about fingerprints, sheriff? What did you find?"

Mullins stated that had been done by the Forensic Department not his own.

"But you are familiar with the report."

"Yes, sir, I am."

Owen handed a sheet of paper to the judge who glanced at it, and passed it back. Owen showed the sheet to Jones who nodded, and then gave it to Mullins.

"Is that a copy of the lab report on the fingerprints?"

Mullins looked at it and verified it was.

"Could you tell us what it states?"

"Well, there were numerous prints of both the Harpers, some of mine and my deputy's, Earl Cramer. And the coroner's of course. And a few of friends of the Harpers who'd been there a couple of days before for a party. Including your own."

"You said some of yours, sheriff?"

"That's right."

Owen reminded Mullins he had earlier testified to being in the house for more than two hours and having searched it thoroughly. "Shouldn't you have left more than 'some' fingerprints?" he asked.

The man nodded. "Ordinarily, yes. But remember, it was snowing that night and bitter cold. And the front door was open. I had my gloves on most of the time."

"How about the rest of the men?"

"I'm not really sure, but they must have. I do know Phil Gaines was there, one of my men, and his prints don't show up on the report."

"So the fact that only the defendant's prints were on his own fire wood ax really means nothing, does—"

"Objection!" Jones broke in angrily, his round face red as he shouted the word.

"Sustained," Fielding said, rapping the gavel to quiet the slight murmur of the spectators.

And so it went.

Owen did a creditable job of trying to plant the doubt in the jury's mind. Tracks could and probably would have been covered up had they been there. And gloves would have been worn by anyone.

And wouldn't a man be unlikely to rush into his own home with an ax, decapitate his wife, and not even close the door?

And what about the head, which had never been found?

But there his own argument of the heavy snowfall was turned against him, as the prosecution pointed out Rollie himself could have left, hidden it, and returned. And who but a fool would have locked himself in that house after the fact? Jones pointed out.

On top of it all, Rollie's alibi was weak and unpopular. He related simply in a flat voice he'd returned home at about ten-thirty after having had some drinks with a friend in town. The door had been open, and he'd found Betsy's body just inside on the floor.

He didn't know why he hadn't called the police, only shook his head almost dazedly whenever the question was repeated.

The fact that the 'friend in town' turned out to be a twenty-two-year-old barmaid didn't help his cause, either. Owen himself had been offended when the girl had verified Rollie's story. He wished her hair hadn't been quite so blonde and that she'd worn a dark dress as he'd suggested rather than the snug white sweater.

"And he was with you until what time, Miss Crawford?" Jones asked in his cross-examination.

"Ten o'clock."

"And where were you—you and Mister Harper?"

The girl shifted uncomfortably. "My room," she answered after a brief pause, and the murmur had come from the spectators.

"Was that the first time he'd been to your room?"

"No, sir." The voice was tiny.

"Speak up, Miss Crawford, so the jury can hear you. Was that the first time the defendant had been to your room?"

She raised her head. "No, sir," she said bravely.

"When was the first time?"

She paused again. Her thin figure seemed pathetic in the docket and despite himself Owen felt sorry for her.

"About six months ago," the small voice came again.

"Six months ago." Jones almost idly plucked a piece of lint from the sleeve of his suit coat as he spoke. It was something he did often. "That would make it September if I recount correctly," he went on, eyes leveled on the girl.

"Yes, sir. Just after Labor Day."

"Three months before the murder."

"Yes, sir."

Jones looked to the jury with sorrowful eyes.

"How often did you entertain Mister Harper in your room, Miss Crawford?"

The hesitation was more painful now. "About once or twice a week."

"Sometimes more?"

"Sometimes," she said, but her head came up and her dark eyes met the prosecutor's. "I love him."

Jones let that drop. "Did you know the defendant was married?" he asked.

"Yes, sir."

"From the beginning?"

"Yes, sir."

"And did you know Missus Harper as well?"

"Yes, I did."

"Did you like her?"

Tears seemed to come to the girl's eyes as she answered, "Yes, I did."

"And yet, you carried on with this married man for months while you knew and liked his wife?" Jones' voice was incredulous.

"Yes, sir." The eyes came up again, defiantly now.

"And the defendant was with you the night of the murder?" Jones asked sharply, pointing to Rollie who sat with head down in his hands.

"Until ten o'clock."

"On Christmas Eve," Jones said significantly, shaking his head in disgust and dismissing the witness.

No, Owen felt, his chief defense witness hadn't helped at all. Nor had the fact, which Jones repeated over and over, an identical murder had occurred on Christmas Eve a year earlier, only a month after Rollie had moved to the area. Or the fact the site of that one had been only a half mile down the road from the Harper house, and Rollie was unable to come up with a concrete alibi for his time that previous, bloody Christmas Eve, because his only witness was now dead.

Or the fact the first head hadn't been found, either.

Owen anticipated the outcome with resignation, but felt he'd done a very credible job under the circumstances.

And that, he knew, was the important thing.

So it was with mixed emotions, when it was finally over, he watched the jury filing into the packed courtroom, heard the judge rap his gavel sharply to hush the crowd, and listened as the hollow-cheeked farmer with the patient eyes who was foreman announced the verdict.

"Guilty."

CHAPTER 35

"Sam?" Owen said when he heard the deep "Hello" on the other end of the phone. "This is Owen. Something's come up that..."

It was the day before Christmas, late afternoon, and Owen had not wanted to involve the sheriff until the last possible moment. Although the state of the town was reasonably calm with the "Headhunter," as Rollie had been dubbed by the press, now safely behind bars, it was still Christmas Eve and Owen knew Mullins would be particularly alert. He didn't want to give the sheriff time to prepare; he just wanted to isolate the two of them in this scenario.

They met at six at Bertha's, one of the few bars in town open during the winter season. The place was somewhat crowded when they entered. It was warm, noisy, and smoke filled, but within a half hour most of the pre-Christmas revelers had departed for home, and Owen and Sam found themselves reasonably secluded in the rear booth, drones of conversation and an occasional boisterous laugh breaking over the soft carols that came from the radio.

"What's on your mind, Owen?" Sam said finally.

Owen had spent the past thirty minutes in a brief review of the case, restating his doubts about the verdict, doubts he knew Mullins shared. Now he quickly laid out the rest of it.

"What makes you so sure, Owen?" the sheriff asked when he had done. The steel blue eyes were level, the lids narrowed just the slightest, and Owen was glad he had nothing to hide. Nothing like that, anyway.

291

"I'm not sure, Sam. Like I told you, it's just a hunch I had. But I followed it up, and I noticed no one really drove by there but him. No one without a reason, that is. And he always slowed down when he went by the golf course—not the Harpers' house, or the Stevens'," he added, mentioning the name of the first victim.

"And where do you think they are?"

"I don't know. But somewhere there. I figure we'll wait in the woods and follow him in."

"If he comes," Sam's tone was flat.

"What have we got to lose, except a couple of hours in the cold?"

"Maybe another life," the sheriff said pointedly. "If you're right."

Owen shook his head. "No, Sam. He's too smart for that. Why would he risk exposing himself with Rollie behind bars? He thinks he's free."

"Then why will he go there?"

"Because he has to do something," Owen paused. "It *is* Christmas Eve," he accentuated softly.

Sam thought a moment. "My boys'll be out by now. They're already scheduled. I'll have to get moving so I can round them up."

Owen looked at the man steadily. "Just the two of us, Sam," he said, and there was a grim determination in his voice that made the other nod.

* * *

Owen stood shivering in his sheepskin, legs desperately chilled even under the ski pants and long johns he wore. He'd been out on colder nights but never standing quietly for so long, and he couldn't stop the chatter of his teeth. He wanted to look at his watch but he couldn't bear the discomfort of unlocking his arms to do so.

He figured they'd been there for two hours already. He started to make that comment to Sam when he was silenced by a low "shh" from the other man and felt the strong grasp come down on his forearm.

Following Sam's gaze, he looked out through the trees. He could just make out the shadowy figure skirting the edge of the woods on the far side of the snow-covered fairway.

They stood still for another ten minutes, and Sam finally whispered, "Let's go."

Leaving the shelter of the trees, they moved into the weak moonlight and across the fairway as quickly as they could, picked up the tracks, and followed.

The footprints were sharp in the snow. They had no difficulty following them as they led again into the woods, growing deeper as the slope descended.

"The creek's just ahead," Owen whispered, and Sam nodded, placing a gloved finger to his lips.

They proceeded cautiously, coming in silence to the edge of the trees. Just below, they could see the hunched figure of a man etched against the snow.

Owen waited for the sheriff's cue, turning on his flashlight as the man's elbow nudged his own.

The light was harsh against the snow, but there was no mistaking the hollows of the skulls as they lay side by side on the bank, surrounded by grotesque wisps of blonde hair.

And there was no mistaking, either, the wild and feverish look in the eyes of Lloyd Jones as the prosecutor's round face looked madly into the lights.

* * *

If anything, the second trial was more explosive than the first.

The town was getting used to notoriety, and many regretted the exodus of reporters and spectators when they left Estes Park quiet again in early April.

Everyone agreed justice had finally been served. They hadn't really thought poor Rollie Harper was guilty in the first place, they confessed to each other, and there always had been something strange about that prissy Lloyd Jones.

And everybody agreed, at the very least, Owen Reid would be the next district attorney.

* * *

"Owen Reid?"

The voice on the phone was strong, familiar.

"This is Erwin Darling."

Owen well knew Erwin Darling, the "Darling of Colorado," the aging senator who had controlled state politics for nearly thirty years. Rumor had it he was perhaps planning to retire, finally, and men throughout the state with political ambitions were beginning to mount their forces for next year's election.

"Mister Reid," the senator said, "I think we should have a talk."

* * *

"So there it is," Darling finished.

They were seated in the senator's office, Darling behind the massive wooden desk strewn with papers and files and adorned only by an antique bronze vase in front of which was a framed photograph of some family gathering. On the walls were photographs of the senator shaking hands with a succession of presidents as well as being grouped with a number of well-known public figures.

In the corner, between a window that opened on the highrises of downtown Denver and another that gave a view of the Rockies, stood the flags of the State of Colorado and the United States of America.

Owen sat opposite in a leather wing-backed chair.

His guilt over the Harper affair had diminished over the past months as, with Charley's support, he time and again had reminded himself of his higher purpose. Now that the first major step was finally at hand he felt very relaxed with the senator. Although Darling's heavy-set frame was imposing, the cherub eyes in the round, heavy-jowled face and the disarming smile evoked an image of the grandfather everyone would like to have had. Or so Owen thought.

He nodded soberly now. "Pretty heady stuff, senator," he said. "Especially for a thirty-two-year-old lawyer from Estes Park."

Darling regarded Owen quietly and the friendly eyes narrowed. "Don't take me for a fool, Reid," he said. "You're ambitious, I know that or I wouldn't be here. Save that humble bit for the voters. It might even suit you but don't try to snow me with it." The command was unequivocal and impressed Owen greatly.

Face flushed, he nodded. But he accepted the reprimand and was more sure than ever he'd ended up in the right hands—steady hands that would have to guide him through the difficult shoals of the next few years. Having long foreseen the aging senator would finally abdicate his throne the coming year, the only problem had been to position himself as the man's successor. Not the obvious successor, because that role would have taken far too long for him to establish. Rather, he'd aimed at becoming Darling's personal choice, for with that backing any reasonable republican candidate in Colorado would be unbeatable. And the opportunity had been there, for there was neither a strong public or private choice, the party being badly split from past and unmended attempts to wrest the office from the incumbent.

So Owen had done what he knew to be necessary in his years of practice in Estes Park—joined the Young Republicans, become active in local politics, and above all supported Darling vigorously—and visibly—for reelection five years prior.

And he'd kept his nose very, very clean.

So with the publicity of the "Headhunter" murders and his own dramatic role in the solution of the case, the senator's overture had come on course.

As the senator now detailed his proposal, Owen came to realize Erwin Darling had not achieved his lofty position by chance nor held it by circumstance. The man was tough, there was no doubt of that, and the steel edge could come out quickly as Owen had seen. But there was a warm side, too, a touch of the genuine that showed in his attitude and his questions. And he was a good listener who appeared sincerely interested in what others had to say.

Above all Darling was smart, shrewd, and perceptive in a way that belied his affable countenance. Owen had had a tendency to take the man and his perennial black string tie too lightly, and he suspected now many an opponent still carried the wounds from having made the same miscalculation.

"If you do as I say, follow my advice, you can win."

"With your public support, of course."

"With my strong public support," the man confirmed. "The elections are only a year away, Owen, so you've got a lot of work to do to build your image in this state. Most of the suggestions I have are more gradual, but there is one I'd like you to consider immediately."

"What's that, senator?" Owen asked, knowing the answer before it came and having already prepared for it as best he could.

"I think it would be very wise for you to get married—as soon as possible. And," the man added meaningfully, "to the right girl, of course."

* * *

Without question, Nancy Fielding was an excellent choice. He'd known her for some years rather casually, meeting her occasionally at social or political functions in Boulder where her father was a district judge. She'd always been a pretty girl, and now at twenty-four she had blossomed into a beautiful woman. He found the dark hair and the green eyes exciting, and he doubted there was a better figure in town, even on the full-bosom–strewn University of Colorado campus.

She was intelligent, too, with a good sense of humor and a quick laugh that charmed him.

And she loved him.

He even wondered sometimes if he didn't really feel that way about her. He wished he were less concerned about picking the perfect political mate so he could more clearly experience the girl herself, because he suspected his feelings would run far deeper if he allowed them to.

The problem was, he recognized, in his case free choice had been removed from the process by the very rules he himself had established.

No early marriage, because that increased the possibility of a damaging divorce. That had been one rule.

And no children—ever.

With one notable exception, the rules had been made and the rules had been kept—by Charley as well as himself.

In some ways, Owen often felt, it was a lousy deal. With all their advantages, neither of them would ever really have a life of his own or the freedom to choose. The power was a demanding master. But that was the hand they'd been dealt on that deserted Nevada road so many years ago.

Now that he was committed, though, now that the time was at hand, he comforted himself in his choice and was more pleased than he'd anticipated when Nancy accepted his proposal.

CHAPTER 36

Owen looked up from his paper and saw the slender figure weaving rapidly through the tables in the crowded dining room. As always, the reporter wore a conservative sportcoat that seemed a size too large.

"Sorry I'm late, senator," the man said breathlessly as Owen rose to take his hand. "Got boxed in at the office on a late press release."

"That's okay, Dan. Drink?" he offered when the other sat down.

"No thanks. Just coffee."

Owen raised his hand and an elderly black in tuxedo came quickly to take the order. Owen always chose this room when dining with reporters, for the ambiance of heavy silver, delicate crystal goblets, exquisite linens, and outrageous prices made small but reasonable favors very difficult to refuse.

"How're things at the *Post*, Dan? Keeping busy?"

"More than I'd like."

They chatted for a few moments before Dan blinked his myopic brown eyes and said, "You mentioned you had something to give me, Owen. What's it about?"

"Well, it's no great scoop, Dan, so relax. Just something I'm concerned about I'd like to get a little public airing on. It's about the 'Great Grain Robbery'."

"The 'Great Grain Robbery'? But that was in seventy-two. Old, old news."

"I know," Owen nodded. "But I'm afraid the same thing will happen again unless we change our export policy, tighten controls. I think some clamps really have to be put on Agriculture."

"Why don't you push for legislation then?"

"I am. But, like you said, it's old news, and I'm not likely to get a lot of support for my bill, especially with Kissinger flying so high. He ties our exports to Russia solidly with detente, and my position won't be too popular. And," Owen smiled disarmingly, "I'm still too much of the new kid on the block to really get anything radical through."

"You're as popular as any first-year man I've ever seen, Owen. And in a lot of people's opinions your voting record is one of the best in the senate. Don't underrate yourself."

"I'm not, Dan. But I know a bill won't go, and I'm convinced a repeat of seventy-two is going to happen—maybe soon. I'd hate to see us get caught short on our grain supply, and I at least want to warn the American people of the danger. I thought perhaps a feature in the *Post* would at least make the issue public, maybe arouse enough concern to start turning over some rocks."

The reporter thought a moment, took off his dark-framed glasses and studied them. He shook his head. "I don't think so, Owen. I'd like to help you out, but I don't know I could get that story through even if I wanted to. Not the way you'd want it done, anyway. I just don't think it's big enough news."

Owen felt a familiar rise of frustration, held control as he always did, and, looking directly into the other's eyes, said calmly and softly, "It *will* be big news, Dan. Trust me. It'll be big news sooner than you think." He paused, then added, "Do it for me, Dan."

There was something in Owen's eyes as he spoke that made the man opposite feel almost compelled to acquiesce, and the reporter finally nodded. "Okay, Owen," he said uncertainly. "I'll do my best."

The article ran in the middle of June and as expected drew little attention.

But it *was* big news a month later when, in the final week of July, it suddenly became apparent the Russians had pulled a grain coup that surpassed the 1972 raid.

"Russians Purchase 12.8 Million Tons of North American Grain" screamed the headlines, and this was just the opening salvo of the rape of the American grain stock pile.

George Meany of the AFL-CIO was outraged, and with his approval the International Longshoremen's Association threatened to boycott the loading of Russian bound grain.

But by then it was too late.

Two days later, Owen got a phone call.

"Senator Reid?" the clipped voice said. "This is George Meany. Senator, I just want you to know we won't forget what you tried to do."

* * *

"Senator Reid."

Owen rose, stepped behind his chair, and placed his hand on the polished wood. He was dressed in a dark brown suit that accented the touch of gray just beginning at his temples.

"Mister Vice President. Mister Chairman. Fellow senators." The senate chamber was quiet as the rustling of papers and the scrape of chairs suddenly ceased. Over the past eight years there had been a growing respect for Senator Reid, and rapt attention now was given whenever the imposing figure stood. "For some time now," he began in his deep, resonant voice, "I have been concerned with the safety of our skies. As you may remember, several years ago I called for a tightening of CAB regulations with regards to traffic control. That measure was ultimately adopted, but not before the tragic mid-air collision over California that cost so many hundreds of lives prompted our action."

Someone coughed, but otherwise the chamber remained silent as he continued. "I would hope this new bill receives more serious and immediate attention than that previous legislation.

"Although I realize the implications are costly, far-reaching, and beyond question unpopular, I must implore you to remove the heavy threat from segments of your constituency—as well as partisanship—from your minds when you consider the issue.

"On the one hand, there is no question a cyclical grounding for inspection of an ongoing ten percent of all U.S. commercial airlines will disrupt the economy greatly. The inspections, the controls I urge

299

will be costly to the carriers, not to mention the loss of revenue they will incur. And I fully recognize the impact of delays and other inconveniences to passengers. Optimistic estimates are that air travel will be disrupted for some twelve months, but my own estimate would be closer to eighteen."

There was a murmur and Owen paused, looked about the room, raised his dark eyes briefly to the balcony before continuing. "I realize that some would call me an alarmist—but I am convinced present standards are too low. Disaster is flying our skies at this moment, fellow senators. American lives and others will be lost, tragedies that can be averted by..."

Jase Kolman's attention was interrupted by a nudge at his elbow. Turning his head, the senator from Idaho leaned closer so the man to his right could whisper to him.

"What's he trying to prove, Jase? He knows that bill of his will never get any support. All he's going to do is step on some toes and end up looking like a wild-eyed radical. Owen's too smart for that."

"I don't know, Mason. I guess he just believes in it." Kolman sat back and remembered his surprise at how impatient—angry, actually—Owen had gotten when Kolman had tried to dissuade him from his course.

He ran his fingers through his wiry salt and pepper hair and looked reflectively at Owen as the other continued his appeal.

Owen was summarizing now, doing his best although he knew the bill would never pass. Even he wouldn't have supported it without his special knowledge.

But he had to try, at least on this one. He wasn't sure his conscience could carry this heavy a load if he couldn't tell himself at least he'd done his best.

Owen finished his speech and heard the barest smattering of applause. You poor, short-sighted fools, he thought with a mixture of anger and dread, looking with narrowed eyes around the chamber once more before taking his seat.

* * *

Those same eyes, a study in compassion now, looked out from the various media after the engine broke free of the Boeing 707, causing the plane to crash and take with it three hundred eighty-two lives, the worst single plane air disaster in American history.

Reporters, senators, and political and business leaders throughout the country lauded his courage and foresight while Owen sat quietly watching the TV screen in his Georgetown den, unmindful of the spring breeze that wafted through the open doors from the tiny walled garden in the early evening.

"Coffee, Owen?" Nancy came behind him, put her arms about his neck and pressed her cheek to his. He reached up and absentmindedly stroked her dark brown hair.

"Bourbon, hon."

While she fixed his drink he took out a cigar, bit the end off, and lit it as he watched Harry Reasoner sum up the news.

"Senator Reid seems always to be on the right issue at the right time. His voice has often gone unheeded in the lofty senate halls, but time after time his warnings have been both timely and accurate. He has firmly established himself as a man of uncanny foresight and un-compromising courage.

"With the presidential election still two years away, it would be a bit premature to begin speculation. However," the man went on, eyes direct into the camera, "it is the opinion of this reporter and many others on Capitol Hill Owen Reid is a man to be reckoned with."

He was almost there.

When unemployment soared and things exploded in Lebanon...

The Alpen sun was well risen now and it warmed Richie's face as it shone from above the far hills.

He thought then of Charley, of their meeting two years earlier in this very spot where he'd tried to invest the man with his own growing vision of himself, which extended far beyond the original plan to which they had both adhered so faithfully. He remembered the expected resistance he'd feared, the uncontrollable frustration he'd found rising in himself when Charley did resist, as he'd realized no one else—not even Charley—could ever truly understand.

And he recalled his shame, the deep guilt he'd felt in that encounter with his friend in which he'd attempted to be totally honest. For the truth was, he acknowledged, when Charley had stumbled toward the cliff edge, in the instant before Richie had reached out to save him—in that one mad instant, Richie knew in his heart he'd wished the man would go over, taking Richie's conscience with him.

He looked at his watch now, saw it was already past nine, pushed up to a standing position and stretched. Below him, the valley was still shadowed, but the trees on the far slope to the west were a rich shimmer of green. He took it all in one last moment before climbing down the rocks and walking to where his horse was tethered.

The thoughts of Charley had been painful, and he was troubled again not only by the man's disappearance—for somehow Charley was now beyond his ken—but also by his realization of how sharply his perspective had changed, how isolated he had become even from his only friend, how alone he truly was.

Could anyone ever understand? he wondered again. Even Mike, the son who waited below. The young man who also possessed the power; the boy who might unexpectedly be the key to everything.

At the thought of Mike his excitement rose, but he cautioned himself again, recalling the terrible thing he'd foreseen just the day before Mike's arrival. That must remain uppermost in his mind for now.

I'll have to be very careful if things are going to work out, Richie thought as he pulled up his horse's head, spurred the animal lightly, and began his descent.

CHAPTER 37

"Well?"

Mike had politely refused the senator's offer of coffee and stood leaning his body against the open terrace door, facing the man, arms crossed at his chest, waiting. He's so young, Richie thought, as he appraised the reddish haired, well-built youth neatly dressed in fawn-colored slacks, light blue open-necked shirt and navy blazer. He himself wore an old lightweight gray sweater of which he was particularly fond.

The two stared at each other for a long moment, and finally it was Richie who broke the silence.

"You're not going to make this easy for me, are you?"

"Easier than you've made it for me," Mike said. He wasn't angry with the man. In fact, he was eager and impatient to hear him out, but he had determined to hold back and not be drawn in too quickly. He holds the cards, Mike kept reminding himself, fighting to keep separate the fact this man was his father. There was still so much he was anxious to learn; he couldn't afford to let his emotions get in the way. At least not yet.

"That's fair enough," Richie acknowledged. "It's a long story, Mike—why don't you sit down?" he added, indicating with his head the brown leather armchair opposite his own before the small brick fireplace at that corner of the suite.

"No, thanks. I'm fine here." The day was bright and cloudless, the sun warm against Mike's back as he stood at the doorway.

Richie found himself amused at the boy's so obvious truculence. Was I ever that young, he wondered to himself, that unpolished in dissembling? It was hard to think of the boy as the salvation—and sequentially perhaps the threat—he well might be, and Richie knew he would have to avoid the trap of taking him too lightly.

But for now, he'd do it Mike's way.

"Well," he began, "as I said, it's a long story. And you got most of it right. Most, but not all. I know you've got a lot of questions about—you and me,"he hesitated over the words, but did not break his eyes from Mike's, "but let them lay for a bit, all right? There are other things I want to explain first."

Mike stood silent, frozen in rapt attention as Richie went on. "You were right about Charley Frost. He did die, but not in the crash as you thought. He died before that, just before—trying to kill me. That's right," he repeated as he saw the widening of Mike's eyes, "trying to kill me. He panicked when he believed I wouldn't help him, threatened me, came at me, and—" Richie paused, went back over the years.

"But it was really the power that killed Charley, I guess, when all is said and done," he added, looking at Mike levelly. "None of us had any idea of how to handle it. Not then. We were only beginning to understand what it was. We had never given any thought to the ramifications, the dangers. All we thought about at first, I guess, was the money we could make. Especially Charley, the real Charley," he sighed heavily. "But, we were kids then, and poor ones at that.

"What happened was we'd won the raffle you heard about, and that and some other things started us thinking. The visit to Durham was a setback. It was a while before I figured that out. If I'd understood things then, I'd never have gone for the tests."

Richie paused and Mike nodded to let him know he at least understood that important message. He was pleased he himself had the foresight to decide immediately to trust his secret to no one until he had a chance to fully think things out.

"When I came back," Richie went on, "I was depressed because we'd all begun to bank our futures on the power, and I felt I was responsible because I'd let that happen. We went out for a beer, and I picked up the sports section of the newspaper and happened to notice the racing results. Suddenly there was a flash in my mind, and..." Richie recounted for Mike the rest of it, the money they'd won, the heady excitement as they planned their departure from St. Mary's, their argument. Charley's betrayal.

The scene in Las Vegas. And the fatal struggle on the cliff.

"It was then I realized my only chance was to have anyone who suspected the power—like Barney or Coach Anderson—believe I was the one who had died. Actually, it was originally your father's—the real Owen's—idea," Richie amended. He briefly pictured himself as he'd stood over Charley Frost's broken body on that long-ago night and remembered again that first hard decision. He wondered what was in store for the boy before him. His son. Richie pushed that roughly aside now and continued.

"And he conceived it exactly as you thought. Charley's identity for my own. Simple. But I thought it was too simple.

"We had a long drive north that night and by the time we reached the place where we staged the crash I had a chance to think things out a bit. I began to see what I wanted to do, what I *could* do with the power. I began to realize the more I could cover up my real identity and protect myself the better."

Mike realized the man was now talking about the presidency. He'd decided on it at age eighteen, Mike marveled.

"Simply taking Charley's identity was too risky," the senator went on. "So I set up a decoy in case anyone came looking. Owen Reid. My friend. The man you thought to be your father." The senator let his eyes soften now as he reminded himself how painful this part of the revelation must be for Mike. "He was your father," he said, "and you're lucky to have had him. No one could have given you more—or me more, for that matter," he added. "He was truly the protector of the power, in ways you may never understand."

There was a look on the senator's face Mike couldn't quite place, but he dismissed it as the man continued.

"He was as committed from the beginning as I. In fact, the first sacrifice was his...." Richie went on, telling the boy in no-nonsense terms how they'd stood at the bottom of the slope by the burning car and how, tears in his own eyes, he'd deliberately balled his fist and smashed it into his friend's face. The other had stood stock-still, wait-

305

ing for the blow that left him a broken nose as the real Charley had—another badge to carry along with the dead boy's name.

"So Owen, the real Owen, became Charley Frost. And I—Richie Peters—became Owen Reid. And we hoped the existence of the power would be buried. We separated and were never seen together. We met periodically like spies to discuss our strategy. My goal was to become president because that's where I felt the power could best be used. But the presidency is hardly a low profile position," he smiled, "so I had to go slowly. You understand how I managed—" Mike nodded affirmation, "—but it wasn't as you thought. I fed information to Charley not he to me.

"His job was building the financial end. I'll explain that to you in a bit, because that's the first role you'll have to take over."

Richie paused to let that sink in. He reminded himself again Mike loved Charley deeply. "You'll be amazed at what's accumulated," he went on, "and what's been done. If you were proud of your father, and I know you were, you'll be even more so when you know the truth. The power might be mine, but the spirit, the vision, was something we shared equally. In some ways, he even more than I."

Again that odd expression, but Mike was too caught up in the other's tale to examine it closer.

"In any event," Richie continued, "our plan worked perfectly. Charley made and concealed the assets, and I rose to the presidency—or will soon have, at any rate. Only one mistake was made and that was mine."

Richie paused and looked directly at Mike who already understood.

"Me," he said quietly.

"You," Richie confirmed. "We'd agreed I would not have children. I say 'we' because Charley was very much a part of every decision. I had the power, but I needed someone to talk to, a sounding board, someone to help with the planning. Someone to add some perspective," he added, "and your father filled that role to perfection. He was quite a man—I hope you're as fortunate as I was in finding the proper partner."

He stopped for the moment, but Mike let the implication pass without comment. If the other knew Mike had the power, Mike would find out soon enough. And besides, there was so much to understand and he wanted to hear all of it first.

"Anyway," Richie picked up, "I was speaking of you. I had made a firm decision not to have children, because as president, I would then be vulnerable to the possibility of threat to my offspring, a way to control the power—me—if anyone ever found out. That was the basis for the double switch in identity in the first place. If anyone came looking—as you did, and those who suspected Charley—they'd point to him, and I'd still have the chance to be clear.

"It worked that way, too," he said pointedly. "As I said, all of it worked. Except my one mistake. I was not careful with your mother."

Richie paused and his voice became very deliberate. This part was crucial. He had precious little time to gain the boy's trust, and he had to accomplish that before exploring any of the rest of it. "I want you to understand completely what I am about to tell you. I do not want you to have any illusions as to what happened. I didn't love your mother, but I did like her very much. More than anyone I'd ever known at that point in my life. You were conceived in passion, at least, I can give you that much. And had things been different, I might have married her. But I couldn't. There was too much at stake. Do you understand that?"

"Yes," Mike said truthfully.

"So I called Charley. He was in Wisconsin. He had the ski resort going, and I explained what had happened. And he made the sacrifice. I'd like to believe I would have, had our roles been reversed." Richie looked hard at Mike. "You see, I couldn't let you grow up in an orphanage and that was a very real alternative. Charley couldn't either. That ran deep in both of us.

"She was Catholic, your mother," he put in, "but that wasn't all of it. I believe she'd have felt the same regardless. The point is, you were going to be born. So Charley came out to California, met your mother, and married her. My rejection was hard on her, she thought me ruthless, unfeeling, but the bargain with Charley was still the better way for her and she took it.

"Anyway," he sighed deeply, "they married, and when your mother died in that accident shortly after you were born—"

"That was convenient, wasn't it?" Mike broke in despite himself. He had determined to maintain restraint but some of his conjectures were too painful to contain.

307

Richie met his eyes and held them levelly. "Yes," he acknowledged in a steady voice. "It was 'convenient', if you choose that word. It's a cold word but accurate. Your mother might have posed a threat to me in later years. But it was an accident," he added softly.

"And if it hadn't happened? If she hadn't fallen down those stairs? What would you have done?"

"I really don't know, Mike," Richie said in a tired voice. "And I'm glad I never had to face that decision. I hope you can understand that."

Primed though he was, Mike felt the anger drain from him at the words. He unclenched his jaw, swallowed hard, and nodded.

"After that," Richie went on, "Charley went east with you to begin his end of our operations. He met your mother—Kate—and at least they had sixteen good years together."

Richie paused again, and Mike appreciated the explanation. There'd been no apology, no soft gloves—simply a man-to-man statement of what had happened. He found himself relaxing and coming to trust the man opposite more and more.

"The rest of it you know, pretty well at least," Richie confirmed. "About a year ago Charley came to me and told me he was certain someone was onto him. So we staged the kidnap-murder and hoped anyone who was looking would be satisfied. As it turned out," he went on, "they had been looking, but they weren't satisfied."

"Who are 'they'?" Mike put in.

Richie shrugged, rose, and walked to stand beside Mike at the open terrace doors. On the mountains beyond, the bright sun shimmered the trees in flashes of glossy green as a flock of birds cut the sky.

"American agents—CIA apparently," he said, turning to Mike. "They must have done a check on Charley's background, and someone got suspicious."

"Why the CIA?" Mike asked. "I mean my father—Charley—is one of their own. An American. Why would they want to kill him?"

"I'm not sure they did. My guess is that they wanted to take him alive if possible. To try to control Charley—the power, as they must have believed—if they could. But they didn't really understand what it was. They just knew in the wrong hands the power could be the most dangerous weapon on earth. So the safe way would be to eliminate it if necessary, and that's what Charley inadvertently forced them to attempt.

"But it doesn't matter it was the CIA. It could have been the Russians, the Chinese—anyone. It never really mattered who 'they' were, Mike. It's important you understand that. The end result would have always been the same.

"That was always the problem with the power," Richie added looking into Mike's eyes with regret clearly etched in his own. "In a different world, it could so easily be used to accomplish so much good. The difficulty is one man's good is often another man's evil.

"Charley said that to me once," he added, almost to himself. "If we'd only understood at the beginning, before anyone else suspected." He raised his hands in a helpless gesture.

Mike hesitated before asking the hard question. "But you knew, didn't you? You knew what the future held. You knew he'd be found out. You must have."

Richie waited a long moment before answering. "Yes, I knew," he said finally.

"And you could have stopped it," Mike went on, anger and confusion growing in him again. "Why didn't you?"

Although he'd been expecting the question, Richie hesitated before answering, and chose his words carefully when he finally spoke. "I never try to change the future—not in the way you mean, Mike. Frankly, I'm afraid to try. I did that once, early on..."

Standing braced against the doors, a soft breeze rustling the lace curtains on either side, he trailed off, his expression distant. Finally he took a deep breath and let it out in a sigh of resignation. "Let me tell you about that, Mike, so you'll understand.

"Charley and I were twenty-two then. We were seniors in college, and I met with Charley in..."

Menomonie, Wisconsin. Richie remembered the town well because it was there he—and Charley as well—had occasion to grapple for the first time with the darker side of the power.

As a young Owen Reid, he'd gone out to help Charley select the site for Mohawk, the ski resort his friend had been so anxious to begin. It would be their first actual enterprise.

How excited Charley had been at the thought of finally seeing something tangible. Not just the growing bank accounts and the burgeoning portfolio of stocks that might soon become a problem because of its very size. No—this would be something that, although essentially insignificant in the total scope of things, was at least a creation. Something Charley could touch, work with.

He himself had been excited, too—until that last morning, the day he was supposed to return to Colorado. That was when it finally happened.

"Owen," he had heard Charley call softly from behind. He was sitting at the kitchen table of their small suite in one of the town's better hotels. He sat in his sweatsuit, still in shock, muscles cramped from the tension that filled his body. He slowly raised his eyes to stare at the slender young man in T-shirt and jeans.

"Owen," Charley repeated, concern clear in his voice. "What is it?"

For answer, Owen motioned his hand toward the morning newspaper, which lay on the table before him. The front page carried a picture of President Johnson greeting some foreign dignitary.

"I saw it on the front page, Charley. When I picked up the paper. Exactly like it happened in my dream.

"I picked up the paper," he repeated, as if that was of singular importance, needing Charley to somehow understand, "and before my eyes it changed, the picture changed." He motioned again. "It changed to exactly what I'd seen in my dream."

"What dream, Owen?" Charley probed gently, but his eyes were suddenly frightened. The significance of what he was saying was not lost on his friend, Owen realized. Owen had never had a dream before, not in the "power" sense of things, but somehow Charley seemed to understand he had finally crossed that line.

"The worst dream you can imagine, Charley," Owen had gone on, forcing the words. "It was like I was there. I *was* there," he amended, "exactly like I'm here now." A shudder gripped him. "I was there," he pushed on, "and I saw it all. The bus, the train. The bodies.

"And I heard it all, too. The crash, the sound of metal, like a million pieces of chalk screeching on a blackboard.

"The screams of the kids.

"And the fire. It smelled different than the oil and gasoline. It was almost sweet, sickly sweet, and I knew I was smelling—" Owen broke off, forcing the vision from his mind. He felt a semblance of normalcy settle in.

"I saw it, Charley," he said again. His voice sounded more normal now. "I woke up in a sweat. I thought I'd screamed but I guess I hadn't because you were still asleep. I came out here, fixed some coffee, and tried to calm down.

"Then I picked up the paper." He gestured again to the table. "And the picture—the one of Johnson. It changed. To exactly what I'd seen. And the headline—'Fifteen Die in School Bus Wreck.'

"That's what it said. Just outside of Menomonie."

The silence when he stopped seemed so total, so heavy, Owen almost expected it to forestall the word he knew would spring from Charley's lips. The word he feared. The only word that mattered.

"When, Owen?" the word sprang at him. "When!?"

"Today. This morning. At eight fifty-five." He heard his voice come flat, but he raised his eyes to Charley's and projected the resolve he felt. The astonishment and fury he had anticipated were registered on his friend's face, and he felt an anger begin to rise in himself.

"Eight fifty-five," Charley repeated, eyes widening. "But it's eight twenty now! What have you done about it!" He was almost shouting— in a way that told Owen he already knew the answer.

"Nothing," he said quietly. "Nothing. And I'm not going to."

"Not going to!? But how can you—"

"Goddamn it, Charley," Owen's voice rose sharply as he gave way to the pain and anger that engulfed him. "Goddamn it! Don't you judge me! I've thought about it for hours. Hours! Sitting here at this table with that fucking paper—"

He broke off abruptly, rose, and faced Charley, a determination in his stance and the set of his shoulders that was meant to leave no doubt of his resolve.

"I thought about it for hours," he said again, but his voice was now controlled. "I asked myself all the questions, more than you're asking yourself right now. Because all you're thinking is 'Can I stop it? Is it too late?' That's right, isn't it?"

311

Charley nodded; he seemed fascinated for the moment by Owen's anger.

"That's what I thought, too—at first," Owen went on quickly. It was important to him Charley understand. "Can I stop it? How do I stop it? But then the deeper questions came, Charley. The ones I've been struggling with for hours. The ones you have no right to judge, because the answers—the responsibility—can only be mine." The words, spoken aloud, impacted him more than he would have guessed, but he forced himself to hold the other's eyes steadily. Only when Charley nodded did he continue. "The other questions, Charley. The deeper ones. Not *can* I stop it but *should* I stop it? Do I have the right to stop it?

"Do I want to stop it?"

Charley's eyes widened at that last, but Owen pushed on determinedly. "That's right, Charley—do I want to stop it? Can I risk it? What happens if I bring attention to the power? Is that worth all our other plans?

"And even if I do chance it, then what?" He had said his mind was made up, but he recognized that in posing the questions now, he was again examining his position and seeking reassurance. But hadn't he said the responsibility was his own?

"Then what?" he pursued, confused by his sudden anger. "What happens if I *can* stop it? *Can* change the future? What then? Where does it end? I change this, and something else comes along. Then what do I do? Change that, too? And the next thing—

"Maybe something worse will happen." He felt the dread fear of that rise and pushed it down again as he had those long hours. "I don't know," he managed to say.

"I *don't* know," he accentuated, his voice imploring the need for understanding—his own or anyone's—naked in him. "And where does it end, anyway, once I start?"

He made his statement final, forced his resolution uppermost. But some part of his mind tortured him with the thought—Jesus, fifteen kids!—and an unwelcome image of the St. Mary school bus of his childhood raked his mind. Despite what he'd said, he knew it now rested with Charley, and he was almost relieved when the other suddenly broke his gaze and looked at his watch.

"It's eight-thirty, Owen. Where? Goddamn it, where!?" he shouted angrily, taking Owen's shoulders roughly. "I heard what you said, and I understood it—and maybe you're right. But now—now I know, too! *I know!*" A perverse pleasure, a feeling almost of revenge that surprised him, touched Owen as he heard the words, "I know, too, and I can't sit on it. Now tell me—where!"

Charley had mindlessly begun to shake Owen but stopped as he awaited a reply.

"Where?" he whispered again.

"Route 140. At the railroad crossing about five miles north of town. A Washington County school bus heading west. Number one-oh-eight."

Charley started to respond, nodded instead, and moved quickly to the phone. Owen marveled at the relief he felt as his friend took charge.

It was eight thirty-five by the time Charley dialed the bus company to which the operator at Menomonie High School had referred him, and he paced in agitation about the small kitchen for what seemed like moments before he finally spoke.

"Your bus—number one-oh-eight," Owen heard him say. "Is there any way you can reach the driver? This is an emergency."

Charley held the phone a moment before hanging up.

"They can't reach the driver," he said in a flat voice, turning to Owen. "Not until his next stop. At nine o'clock."

It was all back on Owen and he was terrified. Without a word, he grabbed his car keys from the counter. He caught Charley's eyes but couldn't fathom their message. There was something there, certainly, but he didn't want to think about it. He couldn't think about it now as he broke the gaze and slammed out of the apartment with Charley on his heels.

Eight-forty, he noted as he pulled away from the curb.

They had fifteen minutes.

It would be on Route 140 about five miles north of town. Luckily, he knew how to get to the road. They'd taken it east only yesterday.

Five miles. They could make it. They could make it easily, he thought with mounting impatience, if not for the rush hour traffic. Owen cursed the slow-moving vehicles ahead of him, honked when one hesitated at a light and ran a light himself, the last one, as he reached the edge of town and headed north.

313

Eight forty-eight.

Maybe three miles now, he estimated. On the open road, he could make it.

He pushed the car to seventy, gripped the steering wheel with white-knuckled hands, and prayed as Charley sat silent beside him.

It was eight fifty-one when he came around a curve and saw the bus dead ahead.

Owen released a breath he hadn't realized he'd been holding, turned, and caught Charley's grin of relief. He moved out to his left, overtook the bus, and pulled in front. Slowing down, he put his arm out of the window and flagged the bus to a stop.

As he pulled over to the shoulder of the road and noted in his mirror the bus did likewise, a touch of wonder overcame him.

I stopped it, he said to himself.

"I stopped it," he whispered aloud, and he heard Charley say, "Thank God you did."

Owen got out of the car and heart pounding, walked to the driver's side of the bus where the man leaned out the open window.

"What's the trouble?" the driver asked, a hint of reserve in his voice. Beyond the man, in the confines of the bus, Owen could see a crowd of kids craning their necks to get a glimpse of what was going on.

"What's the trouble?" the man repeated impatiently when Owen did not respond immediately. His only thought had been to stop the bus, but now—what did he say?

"Why'd ya flag us down?" the driver insisted. The man was middle-aged, forty-eight, Owen was to learn later, with a drinking problem he struggled to overcome and that manifested itself in his agitated motions and in the lackluster of his watery blue eyes and the surliness of his narrow mouth.

The cap on the man's head looked comically out of place. Owen later remembered thinking that at exactly the moment when he opened his mouth to speak.

The same moment when the man suddenly put the idling bus in gear and pulled out, almost brushing Owen as he did so.

"Hey!" Owen screamed. "Hey!"

He ran after the bus, waving his arms, but the vehicle picked up speed. Quickly, he jumped in the car, didn't respond to the, "Oh Christ!"

Charley muttered through clenched lips, and took off in pursuit, cursing himself for not having thought things through.

He'd been intent only on stopping the bus and in that he'd succeeded. It had never occurred to him what to say once that had been accomplished, and now—too late—he understood the consequence of that oversight.

He had frightened the man with his hesitation, a stranger wildly flagging down a bus load of kids on a lonely road.

Oh my God, he thought as he picked up speed and closed on the yellow vehicle ahead. Oh God—let me stop it again!

Eight fifty-three now. Still time, he thought, thankful for Charley's silence, getting himself under control as he came up close behind the bus. Through its rear window, he could see a bunch of young faces pressed to the glass, six, eight, ten kids perhaps, all staring at him wide-eyed as he pulled left to pass the bus again.

And grinning at him as the bus, too, pulled left, into the center of the road, blocking the other lane.

Jesus, he thought, cutting quickly back before trying to maneuver out again.

But the bus moved out, too, keeping him blocked, and he heard Charley cry, "That dumb bastard!" as he leaned out his own window to wave warning.

Eight fifty-four, he saw on his watch, and panic hit. He swerved the car from side to side, but the bus held the middle of the road firmly.

"Oh my God," Owen screamed, honking his horn frantically, waving his arm from the window to the delight of the young faces that pressed to the window bare yards ahead of him.

They were waving, too, blurs of white arms that moved beyond grinning faces as they mocked the crazy man in the pursuing car.

As beside him Charley intoned, "Oh no, oh no! Oh my God no!"

Owen leaned on the horn, pressing down as if his strength might make a difference. It was only when he took his hand off for an instant, thinking to press down harder still, he was able to hear the train whistle. It sounded clear and not far away, almost wistful like he'd heard it drifting down on some long ago night in Carolina. It touched something in him that made him slam on the brakes and skid to a stop as the bus plunged on.

315

The whistle was loud as he watched from the car, louder than anything he had ever heard, louder even than his dream, but not nearly as loud as the crash that came, the grinding crash as the locomotive roared from the periphery of his vision and slammed dead center into the bus ahead.

And the screech that followed—the never-ending *screeeeccchhh* that tore at every nerve of his body as the train fought the steel of the tracks—finally bringing the battered shape it pushed ahead to an agonizing stop. That *had* sounded exactly like a million chalks being drawn across some colossal blackboard.

Exactly as Owen had remembered.

And the fire smell—the sickening sweet odor that overrode even the rank scent of oil and gasoline. That was there, too.

But worst of all, worse even than the bodies he could see, the broken things that lay sprawled like discarded rubbish—worst of all were the screams he could hear, the wails that rose from within the burning thing that had been a bus and floated heavenward with the thick, gray smoke.

Somehow, he had forgotten that part of the dream.

Tears streaming down his face, he ran from the car to the scene of carnage where help, too late, was already gathering.

Was I to blame? he wondered as he frantically helped Charley pull a blood-spattered girl from the wreckage and realized from the awkward sprawl of her head she was already dead.

———

"Could I have stopped it?" Richie still pondered years later, facing a sober-eyed Mike in the sunlit hotel room. "Changed the outcome, if I'd thought things out better? They were in my hands, those kids—once I stopped the bus!

"Was it my fault it got away?"

He stopped momentarily, then posed the harder question, exposed the deeper fear that had always lurked. "And worse, Mike—would they not have heard the train whistle, except for my horn? Wouldn't the driver have heard and stopped, if he hadn't been panicked? Did I *make* it happen?"

A silence stretched between them as each deeply searched himself for that for which neither had an answer.

"God," Mike finally intoned, breaking the spell.

Richie nodded heavily. "God is right, Mike. It's a dangerous game to play." The man seemed about to say something more but instead pushed away from the open terrace doors, walked to the wet bar set against the far wall, and fixed two drinks. Coming back past the sculptured dining table, he handed one of the cut crystal glasses to Mike, then proceeded to one of the arm chairs placed before the small brick fireplace in the corner and seated himself without comment.

Mike stood framed in the doorway, mountains green in the distance behind him as he regarded the imposing figure now hunched in his chair. He felt very close to the man at that moment, recognized they alone shared not only the most unique of gifts but its awesome burdens as well.

Taking a welcome sip of his drink, Mike crossed the room and took the chair opposite Richie. The man met his eyes, and Mike detected the gradual shift from torment to some weary resignation.

"It *is* a curse in a way, Mike. But I can't change that. I can't change what I am."

And what I am, Mike thought with a shudder.

"But then there's the good side—the court where Charley played. Let me tell you about that."

Richie's face cleared as he spoke the words, and he hunched forward with forearms resting on his thighs as he spoke to the boy who now sat opposite, face sober but all traces of wariness gone.

"Charley first came here, to Liechtenstein, in nineteen-sixty-eight, the year before you were born. He was only twenty-three then, but..." and as he detailed the Eur America operation Mike remembered the thought that had nagged, the connection he couldn't quite make when he'd read of the senator's visit to the tiny country. Andy Billingsly had mentioned Liechtenstein as one of Charley's ski haunts, and Mike smiled to himself as he pictured that long ago young man embarking on such a heady enterprise.

"...Klaus Von Horst," Richie was saying. "He's expecting someone, Charley's replacement, and now that you're here..."

317

There was something more in the statement Mike felt he should pick up, but couldn't isolate it. "In any event," he followed Richie's voice again, "the first step was to amass the fortune we'd need..." and he recounted the quiet rise of Eur America, its dramatic entrance into the American market place with the cash purchase of United Motors, the concept of the safer, more practical Aquarius, which was now the third best-selling car in the country.

"And then came Quality Housing," he went on, and Mike followed in fascination as Richie explained the vast inner-city projects, the improved living conditions for so many Eur America had supported.

The grants, too, were staggering. "We've given over one billion dollars in environmental research grants so far," Richie said. "No one except the IRS has any idea of the scope of our funding. We've kept a very low profile, but we give more annually than any other single foundation in the United States."

He said the last with a great pride, adding, "And there's a lot more to be done. Much more. That'll be your job, Mike. At least for now."

Mike nodded, surprised at how quickly he was beginning to feel a part of it. His mind was still awhirl with unanswered questions, but he sensed a strong feeling of the rightness of things already.

"How will I go about it?"

"We've had papers prepared for a long time—in case anything happened to Charley. They were transferring ownership to me originally.

"But since you've come in the picture, I've inserted your name instead." *That* should certainly gain the boy's trust, Richie thought, noting with satisfaction the wide-eyed young face. "Here," Richie said, rising and walking to a briefcase that lay on the antique parson's against the wall opposite the terrace. He spun the combination, clicked back the lock, and reached inside for a folder, which he brought back to where Mike sat waiting.

Opening the folder, he spread several documents on the tiled coffee table between them.

"Read these," he said.

Mike scanned the papers quickly. The documents were quite simple. They assigned all the assets of Eur America from Charley Frost to his son Michael for the consideration of one shilling.

Billions in assets, Mike thought in wonder, "for the consideration of one shilling."

Just below, Charley Frost's signature was scrawled on the page.

There were three copies, and Mike noted Charley's signature was on each.

Mike looked at his father for a moment, then took the pen from the man's hand and signed his name.

"And here," Richie added, handing Mike another piece of paper, feeling a shiver pass through him.

It was a simple statement that in the event of Mike's death, all assets of Eur America were to be transferred to Owen Reid.

Mike signed that, too.

"You knew I was coming, didn't you?"

"Yes," Richie replied, and Mike imagined again an odd expression crossed the man's face but if it had it was quickly gone.

They sat in a silence broken only by the rustle of the white lace curtains as a delicate breeze came through the terrace doors. Finally, Richie said, "So now you know all of it, Mike. Everything."

The boy nodded, his thoughts still spinning from what he'd heard. "And?"

Mike looked up. His father seemed to be waiting for something.

"There's something else, Mike, isn't there? Something *you* haven't told *me*." Richie let that sink in before asking gently, "Don't you think you should?"

Mike met his father's dark eyes patiently appraising him.

He knows, Mike thought. He knows.

"The power," he said finally. "I have it, too."

"Why didn't you tell me that part, Mike? Didn't you think it was important—perhaps the most important thing of all? That business about St. Thomas, all your other 'hunches'—were you going to let it go at that in this conversation?"

"No," Mike responded quickly, shaking his head. "I would have told you. It's just that so much else…"

Why *hadn't* he told him, Mike wondered. He should have realized the man would know, and, as much as anything else, he wanted to understand that part of himself. Now he felt he'd made a miscalculation, had in some way given himself a subtle but important disadvantage.

319

"You knew about me?" he asked. "About the power, I mean?"

"I wasn't sure until you told me about St. Thomas. I only suspected from things Charley had said. There were things he had begun to see. He'd been through this before, remember—with me. So we planned for the eventuality," he said, indicating the documents that still lay on the table.

"And if I hadn't come?"

"Then you'd have been contacted on your twenty-first birthday. By Von Horst. There's a sealed letter in his possession that explains all of what I've told you. Except for the fact it states Charley had the power."

Richie paused. "But you did come," he went on, "and I'm glad of it. We've finally met. That's very important to me."

Mike began to feel for the first time the sacrifices this man who was his father must had to have made. With all his obvious advantages, it could not have been easy.

"What's it like?" he asked. "The power. How does it work for you?"

Richie shrugged. "The same as for you, I suppose. At first I didn't recognize it at all. I got what I thought of as hunches. Then I began to feel they were more than just hunches, but I didn't know what exactly.

"Finally," he said, "I came to isolate it in the form of flashes in my mind, almost like headlines, if you will. Things to come, events that were to happen." Mike nodded as Richie paused a moment. "The first time I understood it clearly was with that racing thing with Barney. How differently things might have turned out if I'd *really* understood early on," he mused. "Charley, the real Charley, dead. He *was* a hell-raiser, too." He shook his gray-templed head. "You'd have liked him. And your father—gone now, too, if in a different way. All because of the need to protect the power."

"But that's over now for you." Mike's statement was half question.

"It's over," Richie said reflectively, but in such a way Mike again thought there was something he was missing. "The important thing," Richie went on, "is that you keep your power secret. You've seen how deadly even a suspicion of its existence can be. Just keep a low profile as you do what you have to do. And as for the rest of it—" he ended it there.

"But how about you?" Mike asked. "You said keep a low profile, and yet you'll soon be president."

Richie said nothing for a moment. Then he turned his eyes from the window where they'd drifted and settled them on Mike.

"How do you feel about that?"

"About what—your being president?"

Richie nodded.

Mike paused an instant before answering. "Good, I guess," he said. "I mean, I never really thought about it before, not personally if you know what I mean." He looked into Richie's eyes and grinned suddenly. "But, yeah—I feel good about it—great, in fact. Hell, my father's going to be president of the United States!" he exclaimed as that connection finally hit. "Even if nobody else knows you're my father," he added with good-natured rancor.

"Do you think it's right?" Richie eyed Mike intently.

"Right? Sure it's right." Mike stood abruptly as he said the words, prompted to activity as his thoughts raced. "I mean," he went on, pacing back and forth as he did so, turning at times to Richie, "I mean," he said, "why not? Look at all the good you've done—all the things you can do now. Sure, you should be president."

"Charley wasn't sure." The statement was so quiet it sobered Mike immediately.

"Wasn't sure?" he repeated, incredulous. "But I thought—"

"Oh," Richie said, reaching into his pocket and taking out another cigar, "that was the plan, and we followed it. Faithfully." His eyes were on Mike as he struck a match. "But Charley had his doubts sometimes."

"That you could make it?" Mike asked in disbelief.

Richie blew out a slow puff of smoke as he shook his head. "No, Mike. Not that I could make it. That I *should* make it."

"But why?"

"Because," Richie answered, rising himself now and walking to the window where he stood with his back toward Mike. Careful, he thought. Probe the boy carefully. If what you suspect is true, you will need his absolute commitment on this—assuming you somehow get through the next three days, he reminded himself. "Because," he continued, "Charley feared that power—any power but especially mine—could corrupt."

"And has it?" Mike stood very still as he asked the question. "Has it corrupted you?"

321

Richie hesitated a long moment before answering, and when he did so he turned and looked at his son directly. "I don't think so. It's hard to tell sometimes, Mike. But—no, I don't think that it has."

"What's bothering you then? You've done a lot, and now you can do even more. What's wrong with that?"

"Nothing, Mike. At least, not as I see it. But you see," he added in a tone that alerted his son, "I'm beginning to think I should do more than that."

"More than that?" Mike's words were a whisper.

"Yes," his father answered, coming to stand directly before him, eyes bright as his voice came slow but challenging. "Yes, Mike—more than that. All of it."

Mike stood frozen as the beginning of understanding came. He tried to sort out the confusion rushing his mind as his father spoke again.

"Yes, Mike," Richie repeated, searching the boy's face carefully. "You said it yourself before—why not?"

He walked toward the terrace and turned to face Mike after a few paces.

"Why not, Mike," he posed again as he stood framed against the open doors, the afternoon sun now strong at his back. "I can do it, if I manage things carefully. And I believe I should do it."

"Well, yeah, I guess you can," Mike began tentatively as the thought took hold, his face beginning to flush as he saw it.

"Think about it, Mike," Richie went on, heartened by his son's reaction. "As president, I can use my knowledge to manipulate things far beyond the borders of the United States. War. Starvation. Economic depression. Most—if not all of that—gone, Mike. A better world."

"Yes," Mike exclaimed, eyes suddenly as bright as Richie's own as the idea took further hold. "I can see it that way, too! And I'd like to help—that would make it easier for you."

Mike looked to his father and was warmed by the satisfaction evident on the man's face. "Come here," Richie said.

Mike approached the man and to his complete surprise, Richie embraced him. Mike stiffened inadvertently but something inside—something that had a desperate need to crumble—gave, and he found himself returning the embrace, stirred almost to tears as he pressed his cheek to his father's.

"That's true, Mike," Richie said lightly, stepping back but still keeping his hands on Mike's shoulders, eyes brighter than they should have been, a fact Mike overlooked in his own swell of emotions. "You *can* help me. In so many ways. And you don't know how much it means to me to be working with—my son." He'd paused deliberately at the last words, and Mike was touched as he heard them spoken.

This amazing man is my father, he thought, and for the first time the realization totally registered. He was in his father's hands, those strong hands that gripped his shoulders, and as he looked into Richie's dark eyes he felt a seductive comfort growing.

Richie held his gaze as a soft smile slowly break his face, and he squeezed Mike's shoulder a last time before letting go his hold. "It *is* good to have you here," he said, reseating himself and looking up at the boy. "There's so much to catch up on, so much I've missed. Eighteen years is a long time."

Mike nodded but felt no bitterness at the loss of those years. He understood why it had to be, regretted only that it was so. He sat again, facing his father, and grinned with excitement. "Well, we're together now," he said.

"We are indeed. Tell me something about yourself, Mike. The sort of things you think I should know. I'd like to know all I can."

Mike hesitated, wanting to share it all with the imposing figure opposite him but not knowing where to begin. "I guess—" he started, "—I guess I'm pretty average. At least I was, until the past year. I got pretty good grades in school, kept out of trouble mostly—a lot of the usual kid stuff, you know, but nothing ever serious. My father—Charley—did a good job with me. I can see that better than ever now."

He paused a moment as a sense of loss welled inside, continuing when Richie nodded understanding. "I'm a good athlete," Mike went on, warming to his task, sitting forward a bit as he noted his father's interest. "Tennis and basketball, especially. I think I'm good enough to play in college.

"I played football for a while, too, running back..." Mike spent some moments detailing those things about himself he believed would be of interest to his father and felt rewarded as Richie listened attentively.

And Richie was attentive, enjoying not only the sketch of himself Mike was giving but gratified in his appraisal of the boy. Mike showed wit and intelligence along with the courage and determination he'd already displayed, and Richie's excitement grew as he gauged the enormous possibility Mike might represent. Finally, he could contain his need to know no longer.

"I'm glad you told me all that, Mike," he said. "And there's a lot more I want to know. As much as I can. But we'll have plenty of time together to catch up. Now, though," he said, a mischievous gleam suddenly bright in his eyes, "—now, let's have a little fun together. I've got a surprise for you."

The abrupt change of pace jarred Mike. His father was regarding him in a challenging way the boy couldn't fathom. Richie turned away and walked to the rosewood cabinet at the far wall, and removed something from a drawer. When he turned, Mike saw with surprise he held a pack of playing cards in his hand.

"Not gin rummy, Mike," Richie said in response to Mike's expression. "A headier, more exciting game. We're going to test your power. You'd like that, wouldn't you?" The tease was gone from his voice now, although his eyes still glittered.

Mike's gaze riveted on the deck of cards in Richie's hand while the other seated himself on one of the ornately carved chairs about the dining table. He beckoned Mike to join him.

"Here we go," Richie said after Mike had slowly come over and seated himself. Richie shuffled the cards several times, thoroughly, as he explained what they would do.

And why.

"We're doing more than test your power, Mike. I'm going to be teaching you something I didn't understand for years." Richie had thought about this ploy long into the night; he had alternately embraced and rejected it as a viable approach but now committed himself to it without hesitation. He would be accelerating the boy's development, teaching him things that might have taken years for him to learn on his own. He knew it could be a risk if he did not win Mike over.

If he handled it delicately, however, he might gain the boy's trust on a level no other way afforded, and at the moment that was uppermost if there was even to be a future. And toward that end, he himself had something to learn, something absolutely vital, and he felt he could accomplish it in this way.

And time was running out.

"Remember the tests I took in Durham?" Richie continued, idly shuffling the cards as he spoke. "Well, that's a perfect example of how the power was for me in the beginning. Random. Undirected. As I would imagine it is for you."

Mike nodded, eyes fastened on Richie as he waited for these secrets to unfold, unconsciously pushing the rolled sleeves of his blue shirt higher on his arms. So intent was he on searching the other's face he was quite unaware his father was similarly occupied.

"The Durham tests. I saw those cards three weeks in the future, and I didn't even know it. Even the horse races. I could predict them, but I was at the mercy of chance, limited and directed by those things that came to me.

"It didn't occur to me for some time I could train myself to ferret out those predictions I wanted. But I could and did, and now I'm going to begin to teach you to do the same."

Richie shuffled the cards a final time before passing them to Mike. The boy was mesmerized by the red-patterned deck as he forced himself to make the cut. He hardly felt himself breathing, and his fingers registered almost no sensation as he touched the deck. He might have been someone else, some other, phantom Mike who watched and listened as his father explained the test.

"It's simple, Mike," Richie's tone was easy, reassuring, "but I've found it to be an excellent exercise, even today. Keeps your skills sharp, even after you've mastered what you have. And—like anything else— you do have to practice, even with the power, to keep yourself where you should be.

"All we'll do," he said, speaking carefully, "is place the cards here." He put them in the center of the table. "Then turn them one by one. Before we turn each, we'll both concentrate and see if we know what the next card will be. Okay?"

The instructions were simple enough, but Mike hesitated before he finally answered.

"Okay," he said, exhaling the deep breath he'd been holding.

It was one thing to know he had the power.

It was quite another to test it.

But he would now for the first time, and suddenly he was excited.

"Okay," he repeated, lips tight, anxious for it to begin.

"The first card, Mike," Richie prompted.

Mike stared at the top card, shut his eyes tightly and concentrated. After a moment he opened them and looked to his father. Richie smiled reassurance, reached his hand out, and placed it lightly on his son's forearm. "That's what I did, too, at first. And it didn't work for me, either. Now—touch the card while you think about it and see what happens then."

Mike hesitated before placing his hand on the top card. He closed his eyes, concentrated again, and suddenly a flash seemed to burn in his mind.

"Seven of hearts," he said, opening his eyes and turning the card over.

"The seven it is," Richie confirmed. His eyes were bright as he met his son's, and Mike reached without hesitation to touch the next card.

"Nine of diamonds."

"Right," Richie said, even before Mike turned up the correct card. There was emotion in Richie's voice, and Mike grinned as he met his father's eyes.

"Jack of spades," Mike announced, touching the top card but not bothering to close his eyes now, knowing he didn't have to.

"Right," Richie responded, keeping his eyes locked with the boy's, his hand resting on Mike's arm.

Both only perfunctorily glanced at the jack before Mike touched the next card and said, "Queen of clubs."

Mike turned the queen.

Jesus! Mike thought to himself, excitement mounting as the correct cards continued to fall.

At the twentieth card, Richie said, "Now do it without touching them, Mike. Just concentrate and see what happens."

Mike took his fingers from the deck and stared at the top card. Throughout the process, he'd had not only a growing confidence as card after card had turned right, but he'd felt, too, actually *felt* the power sharpening.

With his hand off the deck, however, he suddenly felt different, strange—isolated in some way. As long as he'd touched the cards there had been some sort of communication, some connection with the secret contained on the underside.

But now, his hand removed, all tactile sensation was gone with only his mind challenging the next card. He was totally alone.

And not frightened by that sense, for in that moment Mike had his first understanding of how it felt to be all-powerful.

"Six of clubs," he said, and Richie nodded.

He turned the six.

"Ace of hearts."

And the ace turned.

Mike was breathing easily, a shaft of sunlight highlighting his reddish hair, grinning at his father as card after card came up correctly. Over the boy's shoulder, Richie noticed a sparrow had lighted on the stone railing of the balcony.

They were nearly through the deck now, and Richie, hand on Mike's forearm, felt the power full in him as he had throughout.

Try it now, he told himself, feeling the force swell.

"Eight of diamonds," Mike said.

"No, Mike," he said, holding the boy's eyes and masking from him only by the greatest effort of will any indication of the sharp anticipation that was welling within him. If what he believed was true, he would have to be able to carry off this and more without arousing suspicion until he had the time not only to test things fully, but also to truly convert the boy. To completely gain his trust and confidence without limitation.

"No, Mike," Richie repeated softly, strengthening ever so slightly the grip he'd held throughout on the boy's forearm. "Not the eight of diamonds," he said, envisioning the red eight that waited.

The boy looked at him almost with disdain, disbelief clearly etched on the young face.

How quickly we come to take *any*thing for granted, Richie reflected, saying again, "The king of spades, Mike."

Mike held his father's eyes and reached for the card with slow and calculated deliberation, an almost-smile on his face. As he turned it,

327

Richie's heart leapt and he had to fight not to reveal the exhilaration he felt when the black king came up.

Holding his emotions in check, he cautioned himself again to be very careful now. He knew he must tread very delicately, because the boy could not yet be allowed to learn the true nature of what Richie himself had discovered and the next moments would be crucial to that end.

Mike sat holding the king of spades, the look of dismay so naked on his face Richie could not help but smile. Good, he thought as he did so. Smile. You are, after all, the mentor here, the kindly, patient father helping his son chart waters no one else ever had.

Establish yourself now beyond any question as the authority figure and things will develop more easily, he told himself

"Try another now, Mike," he said, removing his hand from the boy's forearm. His voice was quiet but firm, and like an automaton, Mike stared at the deck.

"Three of diamonds," he said, finally, but his voice held no conviction.

He turned the club ace Richie had known to be waiting.

"Mike," Richie said softly, although his heart was pounding at this second, all-important setback of his son. "Mike, that will happen to you from time to time. A wrong guess, a flash that seems just as strong as any of the others but that turns out to be off. And then another. Perhaps many and for a long period of time. That used to happen to me often when I was your age, but it hasn't now, not for years. Part of that was practice, as I told you. Sharpening your skills.

"But part of it—the biggest part, I think—was simply growing. The power grows, Mike. It did in me, as I'm sure it will in you. It's been a long time since I was wrong—more years than I care to remember," he put in lightly, and felt the boy relax when he did. "But when I was your age, I was wrong from time to time. As you will be. It took years before I could totally trust the power.

"But look what you did, Mike," his tone brightened, as he pointed to the pile of upturned cards on the table. "Nearly a full deck without a miss. You can't really be disappointed in that now, can you?"

Mike looked at the pile and back to his father's face. He shook his head and grinned.

"I guess not," he said. "And I guess I took myself a little too seriously. It's just that it came so easily—and I was so sure..."

"Like I said—that happens. And it *will* happen. Understand that and accept what you have—which is quite remarkable. You'll get the rest in time. And besides," he added, reaching over and tousling the boy's hair, "in our league, there really isn't any competition is there?"

CHAPTER 38

The late afternoon sun was strong, but it was cool in the shadows of the deep forest as they walked alongside the stream. Mike heard a splash behind him and turned to see a large spotted trout shimmer briefly in the air before it hit the water again to skitter quickly to the shadow of a rock.

They were above the village, following the same trail Richie had taken with Charley during his previous visit to Liechtenstein two years before. Mike, who was still bubbling with excitement over what had happened with the cards, was glad his father had suggested the hike. It felt good to be out of the hotel room and into the open air.

Looking up at the small white clouds that decorated the clear sky, he breathed deeply. The scent of pine mixed with the smell of earth was strong, and Mike, although still torn by conflicting emotions, nonetheless felt a surprising contentment. Most of yesterday's doubts had now been soothed.

The experience in St. Thomas still hurt, and he knew it always would. The man he'd known and loved as his father was gone, and his anger when he'd learned of the life-long deception, his initial disappointment in the man at that revelation, had faded now and a deep sense of loss had settled in. But he'd met another man, his real father, and the warmth, the security he was coming to feel in that discovery somehow dulled the other ache.

He *had* felt alone for so long, he thought to himself as they side by side walked in silence, the ever-present Bert trudging somewhere behind. Since Charley's disappearance Mike had been out of things, and the cross-country odyssey had only added to his feeling of confusion and isolation. And with the discovery he had the power—

Had it not been for these past two days, he didn't know how he'd have handled things.

But Richie had made him whole again, more whole perhaps than he'd ever been. Now he had an image of himself that, although different from anything he would ever have suspected, was nonetheless highly defined. And so to Mike, on that perfect day, the future held an exquisite excitement.

Glancing to his side as they proceeded up the rocky path, Mike noted how elegant and authoritative *his father* seemed even in khakis and sweatshirt. *His father.* Mike was awed by the total presence of the man.

Mike wondered again how he really felt about his father's power and remembered the look in his eyes when Mike had thought to include himself in his father's grander plans.

"About yesterday," he said, finally breaking the silence. "When we first talked. I'm sorry for what I said. About what I thought you'd done."

Richie looked over at his son. "Don't worry about it, Mike. You couldn't have known."

The stream came in again just to their right. Richie stopped, bent to pick up a flat stone, and skimmed it with authority across the calm water.

"Seven," he said, counting the skips before the stone was finally swallowed.

Mike picked up a similar stone, threw it side arm, and managed five.

"There was a creek at Saint Mary's," Richie began, eyes soft in a way Mike had not seen before. "Sometimes on hot summer days, Charley and Owen and I—"

He broke it off, put his arm around Mike briefly, and removed it as they continued up the path.

Shortly, they reached a small, almost hidden break in the trail, and Richie turned to his left and led them through the woods. They'd only gone perhaps twenty yards when the trees ended abruptly at a clearing that bordered a precipice. Large boulders lay about the sparse grass cover and wildflowers sprouted at random.

Bert waited at the edge of the trees while Richie and Mike went forward.

"I was here with Charley two years ago," Richie said, looking out to the view ahead.

"This would have been his kind of place," Mike commented, following his father's gaze.

Richie nodded. "We had a fight that day," he said.

"A fight?"

"Not a fight, really. An argument, though. About what I mentioned to you earlier."

Mike thought a moment. "The world part of it, you mean?"

"Yes."

"But why was he so against that?"

"Because he felt the power had to end somewhere. That it couldn't be limitless." Richie eyed Mike closely as he spoke.

"Well, I can see that," Mike began slowly. "I mean, I had the same kind of thought myself when I first understood I had the power, too," he said, raising his eyes to his father. "Anything—even the power—had to be limited somehow, I thought. But I didn't mean it *should* be limited beyond where it could go."

His father said nothing, but Mike detected a look in his eyes that encouraged him further.

"I mean," he added, "I really think the power should go as far as it can, if it's used right."

Richie's face glowed, and the light that had sparked his eyes grew brighter as he took them from his son and gazed out again at the expanse before him.

When his voice came after a moment, it was soft and touched with emotion. "It's good to have someone, finally, who can understand that. You said yesterday you've felt alone, but you don't yet know how truly alone you can become. Because the truth is no one else can possibly see what you see.

"The world, Mike," he said, but speaking of it in a different way than Mike would yet understand. "That's what I see."

"And me?" Mike's words came soft. "Where do you see me in it?"

Richie turned to stare at his son, an intense look settling on his face as he came back from his vision. "You'll be part of it Mike—a big part of everything," he said putting his hand on the boy's shoulder. "You'll be running Eur America as of now. And I've also decided—" he let it trail off significantly.

"What?" Mike pursued eagerly.

"I want you to join my team, Mike. Work with me during the campaign. Be at my side."

"I'd like that!" Mike exclaimed, thinking of what Richie could teach him, what he'd already learned about himself through the man.

He was silent for a moment. "Does it change things for you—my having the power?" he asked then on impulse.

"Change things?" Richie's voice sounded odd to Mike, almost clipped in a way, although he smiled easily. "Why should it change things?"

"I don't know," Mike shrugged. "I just thought maybe it would. I mean, now you're not the only one in the world with the power." He looked into his father's eyes directly and saw them narrow just the slightest.

"What are you trying to say, Mike?" his father asked softly after a moment.

"Just that I want to be part of it, too."

"But you will be. A big part. I've told you that."

Mike hesitated. It was all so new; there was so much to think about. For already Richie's vision had become his own, and Mike found his imagination running rampant as he explored with his own growing wonder how it really could be.

Perhaps he should stay silent now, he thought, think about it more. After all it *was* so new.

But something in him pushed.

"I know you've said I'll be part of it, and I'm sure you mean that," Mike began, carefully. "But I don't want it to be just tag-along." He paused and caught Richie's eyes directly. "I want to be part of all of it. I have to be," he stated.

"And what does *that* mean?" Richie's own gaze deepened.

"Damn it," Mike said angrily, shrugging his father's hand from his shoulder. At the side of the woods he saw Bert stiffen slightly and he held his voice lower as he went on. "You know exactly what that means. I have the power, too—the good and the bad of it. And I've got to live with it, too. Just like you," he added, holding his father's eyes fiercely. "Because that's what I am," he continued, "just like you."

"And where's the problem there?" Richie asked lightly, but the narrowing of his eyes belied his tone.

"Suppose," Mike said slowly, "just suppose I didn't agree with your ideas about taking the power further, manipulating things all over."

"But you did," Richie came back softly, thinking to himself, it's coming. Sooner than I thought. The power takes hold quickly.

"But maybe I was wrong," Mike went on. "Maybe I'll change my mind. After all, the stakes—maybe there are things you'll want to do I won't."

"Or vice-versa?" The challenge was quiet, but Mike was so caught up in his own rising vision that he missed the ominous note.

"Yes," he exclaimed, frustrated by the new confusions in his mind and desperately needing to sort them out. "Maybe vice-versa. Suppose I do see it differently. What then?"

"Mike." Richie's voice was calming. "Mike," he said, "don't get yourself worked up. I'll help you, I promise. We'll work together."

"I'm your father, remember—not your enemy."

"My father!" Mike exploded angrily, tears suddenly in his eyes, understanding in that instant at least one of the conflicting emotions coursing through him. "Where the hell were you all those years?"

"Mike—I explained that." Richie held out his hand but Mike brushed it angrily away. Out of the corner of his eye, he was aware Bert had edged closer, but he pushed on anyway.

"The power. That's all you ever cared about—the power. Rule the world. You always wanted that, didn't you? That's it, isn't it?" he challenged, voice rising. He knew he was losing control and didn't realize his outburst was in fact triggered by the conflicts about himself his burgeoning plans had engendered. "Rule the world. That was always it, deep down in your mind. Use anybody, anything. Maybe my father— maybe Charley was right. Maybe—"

Mike broke off suddenly, took a deep breath, and got himself under control.

"I'm sorry," he mumbled, raising his eyes to his father, whose face held a look of perfect understanding.

"That's all right, Mike," Richie said quietly. "As I told you, it's hard. And you're very alone."

Mike nodded, beginning to understand that now.

"You said we'd work together. Now," he went on after a moment, when he was fully calm again.

"Yes. I'm going to Paris tomorrow for a late morning conference. I'd like you to come with me."

Mike looked at him questioningly. "I'd like that very much," he said. "But how? Won't there be a lot of questions asked? I mean, how will you explain me?"

Richie shrugged, cautioned himself again to tread carefully with Mike. The boy had already flashed a touch of independence and belligerence that boded difficult negotiation.

"It won't create comment," he said. "After all, as far as anyone will know you're the son of an old friend, someone who was once very close to me. It wouldn't be unnatural that we met, and that I offered you a position suitable to your age. Polling young voters, perhaps, or maybe even directing that area of my campaign. The young vote."

"I understand that," Mike said, "but that's not what I meant. I mean, it seems to me there is a risk in me, Mike Frost—Charley Frost's son— being connected with you. After all the lengths you went to keep any link between you hidden. I mean, wouldn't those men, those CIA people, the ones who were after my father—Charley—wouldn't they maybe…"

The boy was right, of course, and Richie had the urge to tell him everything then but instead held back. He could not risk unduly upsetting the boy before he'd had a chance not only to gain his confidence further, but also to test as much as possible in these next two days the feasibility of the desperate plan he had conceived.

"Don't worry about all those people, Mike," Richie said easily. "I know things will work out or I wouldn't have suggested your joining me."

Mike held his eyes a moment and nodded, acknowledging the other's special authority.

"You'll come to Paris with me," Richie went on, "and then we'll come back tomorrow night and spend another day or so. I'll let you meet with Von Horst and begin things there. It will give us a little more time to get to know each other better. I can think of nothing more important. Nothing in the world," he added emphatically, placing his arm about Mike's shoulders and looking out at the roll of valleys that seemed to stretch forever toward the lowering sun.

Suddenly he saw the sky darken and Richie stood in moonlight alone at the edge of the precipice. The vision was gone almost as quickly as it had come, but as he stood with his arm about the boy he was pervaded by an inexplicable sense of foreboding.

CHAPTER 39

Still in sweatshirt and khakis, Richie stared at the small stack of cards that remained unturned on the table. Since coming back from their hike, he'd gone through the deck twice and had selected each card correctly as a matter of course, almost automatically pursuing the exercise as he opened himself to recapture the awesome force that had momentarily been his when in physical contact with Mike.

But he hadn't felt it coming, and he knew he was only wasting time by putting things off and prolonging the uncertainty. Now, he said to himself, summoning up whatever force he could as he reached for the next card.

Now, he willed. *The ten of clubs.*

He touched the card and conjured an image of the black ten in his mind, willing it there until finally it seemed to obliterate the red four that lay waiting.

Ten of clubs he forced again, seeing the picture clearer now, feeling a heartening, suspecting that it was only his imagination, but hoping against hope as he touched the card and turned it. The four of hearts lay exposed.

Richie stared at the card. After a moment he slowly took it in both hands and almost idly tore it down the middle.

Rising from the table, he walked to the bar on the far wall of the living room and fixed a drink. He took a small sip and turned back to the room. As he passed in front of the terrace doors, he barely noticed that the late afternoon sun, lowering in a crystal sky, was casting the far trees in long, cool shadows.

Richie finally acknowledged he was tired, more tired than he would have expected even after the long day. He felt drained in some way. Shrugging off the feeling as best he could, he seated himself in an armchair by the brick fireplace and stretched out his legs onto the coffee table. As if by rote, he took a cigar from his pocket, bit off the end, and lit it.

Inhaling deeply, he held the strong smoke in his lungs before expelling it steadily toward the ceiling. Only then did he allow himself to begin assessing the situation, and he cautioned himself to be exact in his conclusions. No ego here, no complacency, nothing taken for granted. Those were luxuries he could ill afford.

He would only deal in the cold facts and whatever logic they subsequently dictated.

What he had suspected the day before, during his first meeting with Mike, had in fact proven true. There was a force created when he touched the boy that gave him the power to change things—not conceptually as he'd done in the past, or even more specifically as he'd recently envisioned, but to directly alter things that undeniably were to be. Somehow, his power was sparked by that of the boy and made greater. As was Mike's, for at this stage the boy would never have gotten the cards right without Richie's hand on his arm. With that power in hand, under his control, what couldn't he accomplish!

Except it wasn't his to command without restriction. He needed Mike for that. He needed the boy's touch and ultimately his concurrence, for he could not keep the secret from the boy for long. No matter what his choice might otherwise have been, he had only two days now at best before revealing all to Mike if the terrible vision he'd foreseen was to be thwarted. They would have to be in total accord, similarly and unquestionably committed, and two days gave him very little time. Mike was beginning to trust him already, but there was a reserve in the boy that, under the circumstances, was only natural. There had to be resentment there, feelings that hadn't as yet really surfaced.

Eighteen long years without contact, for one thing.

And Charley's abandonment and disappearance for another, which Mike would ultimately have to lay at Richie's feet. That Charley was a victim of the power was unquestionable, despite how it had come about.

He would have to move cautiously with the boy and use his wits, because when he drew on the force their touch created—as he now felt an overwhelming desire to do again—the power generated could well be at Mike's command rather than at his own, if the boy recognized and captured it. And if that occurred prematurely, before Mike was won over—

But the prize! The ability to change things, to create! The anticipation to begin was irresistible. He needed only the boy's total understanding and agreement.

And to get them both safely past the next two days, he reminded himself.

Richie looked at the glass in his hand, long forgotten as he'd immersed himself in thought. The cubes had melted down to mere opaque pebbles that barely tinkled as they brushed the sides of the glass when he swirled it lightly before taking a sip of the watered-down bourbon.

He returned to the bar and fixed a fresh drink. He had been vaguely aware of the late afternoon dwindling at some point into twilight and looked out now at the velvet of the Alpen mountains, dark in silhouette against the deepening blue sky. A star—only one—was discernible, reigning solitary in the gentle evening.

Richie gazed at the star. As he did, another began to come clear at the extremity of his vision, a tiny star that seemed to struggle to take hold, shining and fading in a delicate balance until it asserted itself. As he watched, it became clear, fixed in the heavens with an intrinsic promise of brighter light to come.

An accord with Mike, Richie thought, appraising the difficulties from yet another viewpoint. From his own experience, Richie recognized that if not for the unique opportunity Mike afforded, he would never have considered allowing anyone, even his son, to be involved in his plans. That had once been true with Charley, in the early days and even for some long time after, but it had been years since he had felt a need for an outside opinion. The perspective, the decisions, had come to be totally his own, and he'd settled into the isolation the power had fostered.

Those same feelings would come to Mike. They were already stirring, as he'd seen on the mountain.

He looked again to the window. The two stars beyond were of equal intensity, and he smiled to himself.

Equals, as are we, he thought, except Mike did not as yet understand the game. But when he did, Richie reflected, when Mike did understand the quantum force and realized it could be his to harness as well—what then?

CHAPTER 40

"The nine of hearts," Mike thought to himself.

Reaching out, he turned the nine face up onto the small desk where he sat by the light of a delicate brass lamp.

There were only two cards left in the deck now, and he suddenly decided to up the stakes for himself.

Two at once.

Why not?

He concentrated and at first only a confused image filled his mind. But he persisted, refraining from touching the cards, keeping his eyes open, too, as he had for these past hours, concentrating harder, focusing, and suddenly they sprang clear for him.

The ace of diamonds and the four of spades.

Mike turned over the cards and looked at them triumphantly.

At just that moment, when he'd barely savored this latest victory, the mournful sounds of the ancient clock in the watchtower on the hill beyond slowly drifted through the open window of his hotel room.

Three o'clock, he thought to himself, registering the stiffness in his back and shoulders from the prolonged position in the straight-backed chair. He had ignored the growing discomfort for some time but gave in to it finally as he rose and stretched.

He didn't have anything more to prove to himself now, anyway.

He knew beyond question what he had and how to work with it.

When he'd first returned to his room after his solitary dinner in the hotel restaurant below, he'd tried to relax, but the events of the day had kept crowding. He'd gone out, taken a brief walk in the deserted cobblestone square below, had sojourned briefly through the pines up the narrow, stone-stepped trail to the very watchtower from which the clock had just struck, and had returned to his room to pace there.

Finally, he'd gone to the desk drawer and removed the deck of playing cards he'd purchased late that afternoon when he and Richie had come down from the mountain.

Opening the pack, he'd shuffled the cards several times, and placed them before him on the table.

He looked at the first a long while and thought it to be the jack of spades. But he was uncertain and had not been surprised when a five had turned.

The next card he imagined as a nine and a seven showed.

He'd tried five more unsuccessfully before pushing away from the desk. Walking to the window, he'd drawn back the lace curtains and opened the creaking French windows to the night air.

In the sky above, some part of him registered two bright stars, but he was too preoccupied to notice them.

What happened, he wondered.

When he'd turned the cards with his father, he'd been so confident, so sure. He had actually felt the power growing in him, surging as his successful string had continued.

Until those last two attempts.

On the first miss, he'd felt confused, almost angry, because he'd been certain it was the eight. Instead, it had been the king of spades, as his father had predicted.

But on the second miss, even before turning the wrong card, he'd felt defeated, as he felt now. Why had he been so successful, so powerful earlier and so impotent now?

He took a deep breath, turned from the window, and walked resolutely back to the table. He reached out his hand this time, concentrated on the top card, and turned a six.

He'd conjured a queen.

Not conjured but forced, he admitted, because no image had been forthcoming.

He tried again and a deuce turned instead of the ten.

Still he didn't give up; he kept trying, and finally on the third time through the deck, something happened. It wasn't that he was concentrating harder, but rather that somehow his concentration seemed to shift. It was almost as if two blocks that had been slightly out of position suddenly moved together in perfect sync, and his concentration had a different quality, a focus that seemed to zero down to the final, brilliant intensity of the last pinprick ray made by a magnifying glass.

Three of diamonds, he thought, knowing it would be the three this time, absolutely certain even before the card turned.

The three of diamonds lay exposed.

He touched the next card, pictured the five of clubs.

The five turned.

The ace of spades was next, and it came up.

After several more cards, he took his hand from the deck. He felt the same isolation, the coldness, he had experienced when he'd done the same in his father's room, but he knew the focus was just as acute.

Nine of clubs he thought, reaching out to turn the nine.

That had been a good three hours and Lord knows how many decks ago, Mike thought now as he stood at the window.

And in all that time, he'd never touched the cards again as he'd focused in.

Nor had he once been wrong.

He'd even conjured two at a time as his finale, pushing the focus just a little harder and feeling the blocks coalesce tighter still. As he stood now looking out, rolling his shoulders to ease his cramped muscles, he knew beyond question those blocks were in place and would not be dislodged.

He had the power and he could direct it.

And, most important, he could trust it. Of that, he was absolutely certain.

CHAPTER 41

Jonathan Barnard, although that was not his real name, sat before the television set in his den, nursing a second brandy. The collar of his white shirt was open, his tie long discarded and hanging over the arm of one of the chairs that surrounded the bridge table by the bookcases.

The children had been put to bed two hours earlier, for which he was grateful, and Sandy, who sat crocheting on the couch beside him, would turn in in a few moments, as soon as the eleven o'clock news was over.

For that he would be even more thankful.

She was getting on his nerves more and more of late, boring him to distraction with her mindless chatter and endless anecdotes. The incessant clack of her knitting needles was becoming an increasing irritant.

The kids, the towheads too, were getting on his nerves these days, especially Jackie who, at age six, seemed to whine at bedtime almost as a matter of course. And his five-year-old sister Marge was beginning to show signs of fast following his example.

Barnard was impatient now for the news to end, the flying needles to cease, and silence to follow. And when, a moment later, his wife rose and turned off the set, he kissed the cheek she offered with a gratefulness she mistook for affection.

"Will you be long?" she asked.

"A bit. I've got some tax papers I want to go over. Don't wait up."

"Not too late," she cautioned. She thought him an accountant—which in fact he had been once—and worried at the hours he put in at times.

"Not too late," he agreed, and she blew him a light kiss before leaving the room.

He listened to her footsteps as she mounted the stairs and heard their bedroom door close. He rose and freshened his brandy from the decanter on the silver tray in the bookshelves.

Coming back to the armchair, he sat and took out a cigarette. He seldom smoked in her presence—never in the children's—but heavily when alone, especially when he had some deep thinking to do.

And tonight was certainly such a night.

If what he had begun to suspect was true, it would be the biggest coup ever.

And it was all his. He was the only one who knew the pieces, the only one who could possibly make the connection.

Owen Reid.

Was it possible? Had it been he all the time?

Barnard was beginning to think so, and he was more glad now than ever he'd decided to go it alone at the end.

When Mike Frost had returned to Boston following his cross-country search, apparently having found nothing new, Barnard had finally acceded to the pressures and called off the chase. They had the Eur America connection made and had a frightened Von Horst firmly in place to alert them when Frost's successor finally surfaced. And that had been their objective.

The Richie Peters thing had only been a spinoff at first, the result of Barnard's hunch to follow up a coincidental reference to the man garnered during his quiet check of the anonymous tip linking the investor Frost to Eur America. It had been the first break in the long search to uncover ownership of the powerful corporation. After his trip to Durham, the tie-in of Frost to some sort of "power" had opened exciting possibilities, but only he had held the nagging doubt Frost was still alive following the explosion of his plane. They'd let him play out that fragile string for longer than he could reasonably have hoped.

So when Mike returned home Barnard had called it off, written an official *finis* to the operation, marked the Charley Frost/Richie Peters file closed.

And then he'd asked for a week's leave, told Sandy he was off on business, and headed to Maine. There he bugged the phones, set up shop in his van nearby, and hoped he wasn't just wasting his time.

He'd hit it lucky after only two days.

The kid, Mike, had come up, and in the early morning had called and made reservations for St. Thomas.

That could only mean one thing, Barnard had surmised, and acting on his own, he'd immediately made contact with the men in Florida, who had gone down.

Larry Cavanaugh, as Frost's name had turned out to be, had somehow gotten away and eliminated both his assailants, leaving no possible connection to the supposedly deceased Boston businessman.

And Barnard's associates in the network would hardly be alerted. The disappearance and possible drowning in St. Thomas of a local citizen would be of absolutely no concern to them. It would never even come to their attention. And besides, they were already convinced Frost had died in the airplane.

The chapter was closed for everyone but himself, and Barnard had been anticipating with pleasure the impact his announcement would have when he revealed in the end he'd been right as he detailed the final episode in the saga of Charley Frost.

How good *that* would look in his file. He'd planned to spring the surprise tomorrow, but now—now he had more to think about. Bigger things, he reflected, as he lit another cigarette.

Now he had Owen Reid.

Maybe.

But if he was right, he wouldn't have to worry about his file. He'd be at the top of the heap in one jump.

And all because of his persistence. That bulldog trait about which he had so often been teased as a kid. That need to see the final dot in place, which had taken him into accounting, led to investigation of tax fraud, and ultimately brought him to the middle echelons of the CIA.

It had been that need, that obsession to be certain everything was buttoned up, that had led him to follow up on Mike even after Frost got

346

away again. The boy hadn't come home from St. Thomas. Barnard, using some pretext, had called Mike's home and been informed Mike was "away."

Something in the way that had been said by his sister told Barnard the family didn't know where Mike was. On a hunch he'd tried a contact at the Miami Airport, and he'd hit pay dirt again.

The boy had booked himself a flight to Zurich, where he had to use his passport and therefore his right name. Barnard had been surprised at the move but had immediately understood.

Liechtenstein. The boy was Frost's successor at Eur America.

Had Mike made contact with Frost in St. Thomas? Barnard doubted it—he wouldn't have had time. If not, then he must have had the information all along, all during the months they'd tapped the phones and the weeks they'd trailed him in his cross-country search for Frost.

But why had he waited so long to make his move?

That had troubled Barnard, and was what had kept him from submitting his final report.

Barnard had puzzled over it for two days now, keeping the facts to himself, safe in the knowledge the pressure on Von Horst would keep the man under control. The trap was set, and when Mike surfaced Barnard would be there as well. Perhaps they would even snag the elusive Charley Frost in the net.

Earlier tonight, he had decided to present his report tomorrow regardless, to bring the others into it again before leaving for Liechtenstein. Just in case. They'd certain listen to him about Frost now. They would have to, he had thought, picturing the impact his revelations would have, feeling the anticipation rise.

But that had been before he'd read the evening paper.

It was just an insignificant article, almost buried on page four of the *Times*, but it had leaped out at Barnard. "Reid in Liechtenstein," the headline announced, and suddenly the pieces began falling into place.

Owen Reid.

He'd been a friend of Frost's at the orphanage, Barnard had known that, but the connection had seemed to end there twenty-five years ago. To Barnard's knowledge—according to the files—the men had no contact in all those years. But Reid had left Carolina with Frost. And with *Richie Peters*. Barnard remembered that now.

And that accident?

Sandy had called him for dinner then, and it was only now, hours later, he could hone in on the rest of it.

That accident.

Yes.

Why shouldn't he assume Reid had been there, too?

That made sense. It was in fact a probability now that he thought it through.

And if that were true—

He took his mind from that trail and concentrated now on the man himself, for that suddenly clicked in place.

Owen Reid.

The next President of the United States.

The man who had achieved that position by always being at the right place, on the right issue—at the right time.

Uncanny perception. He remembered that phrase being used in one article to describe the man.

Uncanny perception.

Of course!

The connection, the modus operandi of the two men was now obvious.

And Reid could as easily be Richie Peters as Frost might have been!

It was a fascinating idea, but yes—it played the same way. And if it were so—

Barnard lit another cigarette.

He wouldn't turn his report in yet, he determined. He'd sit on it a bit, leave tomorrow, do his own tracking, and maybe wrap the package up all by himself. In fact, the thought took hold, he might not turn his report in at all—except to Owen Reid, the next president of the United States, the man who would soon be at the very center of power.

The more he thought about it, the more he liked that idea.

CHAPTER 42

The tuxedoed bartender stood waiting, watery blue eyes patient as they peered through wrinkled lids set in a gaunt face distinguished only by a perfectly clipped salt and pepper moustache.

"Bourbon," Richie said.

The man nodded and looked at Mike who ordered Coke.

The man turned away and was back in a moment, placing the glasses on soft coasters that would protect the deep, rich polish of the handsome mahogany bar at which they stood.

Richie's foot rested on the brass rail below, and as he raised his glass to Mike's, he saw Bert pretending not to notice them while he nursed his own drink at the far end of the crowded bar. He caught the man's eye and winked; Bert grimaced despite himself.

Bert was never comfortable when the senator was in any crowded atmosphere, especially when Bert had to act as sole security. But that was Bert's problem, Richie told himself, turning away from the man, anxious for the afternoon to begin.

Going to the races had been Mike's idea, but Richie had jumped on it eagerly. His conference had been dull, the long morning hours increasingly tedious. So when Mike had made the suggestion over lunch, Richie had agreed, seeing it as an excellent opportunity to test things further.

Longchamps was an exciting place, charged with the electric atmosphere of any racetrack but with the added elements of tradition and elegance—especially here, in the exclusive Men's Bar that, to Richie, gave the Paris course a unique dimension. The exceedingly well-dressed patrons, who crowded the high-ceilinged room with its broad expanse of windows, talked animatedly among themselves in a variety of languages, looking first to their papers, back to the tote board, then to their papers again as their arm-waving discussions continued.

"Lord, I'd never figure this out," Mike commented, next to him. "Even if it was in English." The boy was looking at the voluminous racing form over which he'd pondered for some time before finally giving up. Richie felt proud as he regarded his son and thought how handsome the boy looked in the well-tailored blue cord suit he'd purchased on the Champs Elysées that morning. He knew that, in his own navy blue which flattered his graying temples so well, they made an outstanding pair.

He smiled at Mike, reached over, and touched his arm. Despite the vision that lurked, Richie was feeling very expansive today, even more so now as, in physical contact with Mike, he felt the power surge again. He was nostalgic, too, a mood to which he was not often prone, but somehow he felt as he had in the early days, those days with Charley, when they'd haunted the tracks of the Southwest, two kids building their opening stake. Perhaps looking at his son's young face brought that back, he thought.

"You don't need that, Mike," he reminded the boy, indicating the thick newspaper the boy had discarded. "All you need is this," he said, touching the official program that lay on the bar before them, the form that merely listed the horses and their jockeys.

"Yeah, I guess," Mike agreed, but Richie noted just a trace of disappointment in his tone.

Just like Charley, he thought, remembering that stubborn characteristic of his friend. Charley had a compulsive need from time to time to risk something, to be unsure of some outcome.

To not know.

The need to not know had never been a problem for Richie. He'd found *knowing* heady enough.

And so will Mike, he thought, reminding himself to be careful and to keep things in perspective. He's already given you cause for concern, remember, just yesterday on the mountain. That belligerent streak he showed. Don't take him for granted. And more important, there's the other thing to deal with first.

"Who do you pick in the first race?" Richie asked, moving over slightly so his arm rested on the bar against the boy's.

Mike ran his finger down the column of horses, then stopped at the name Pierot.

"That's it," Richie confirmed. "Why don't you make the bet?"

"How much?"

"Oh—not a lot. Never a lot. Just—something reasonable."

The boy nodded, looked at the form again to check Pierot's number, and walked to the door to mingle with the growing rush of other men who would be descending the stairs to wait in the long lines already forming before the parimutuel windows below.

So much I can teach him, Richie thought, remembering himself at Mike's age as his reddish-haired son merged with the crowd.

Sighing, he turned from the bar, brushed Bert's studiously unconcerned face with his eyes, and walked to the window where he secured a place from which to watch the race. The horses were already on the track, galloping in spurts before they would make their final turn and head back toward the starting gate.

He spotted Pierot, number four, a gray gelding whose jockey wore black and red. The horse pranced restlessly in the strong check held by his rider.

Eight to one, Richie noted, looking at the tote board in the center of the track's enclosure.

Briefly, he wondered what it *would* be like not to know. *Was* there some mystique there, some meaningful dimension of life he was missing? He hadn't always known, and he tried to recall how he'd felt in those youthful days before the power, but he could only conjure up the orphan's fear of the future that had run deep in him.

No. It was better to know, especially if you were the only one who did. He felt the familiar arrogance rise in him as he looked at the crowd of people who milled below him, jockeying for position at the rail, so as to see the race now about to begin.

Mike came up next to him, and he moved over to give the boy room at the window, careful not to make contact with him. He'd done so at the bar but that had been to allow the boy to pick the winner correctly.

Other than what was necessary to his immediate purpose, Richie did not want to risk on this last day Mike's premature discovery of the power's greater dimension.

Mike held up his hand, showing Richie the tickets. "Fifty dollars," he said with a grin. "At eight to one."

Richie quickly calculated the tickets he held would total closer to one hundred, and he suddenly suspected the boy held more in his pockets.

"They're off!" the announcer's voice barked through the loudspeaker. Mike and Richie watched as the horses broke from right to left, racing the course clockwise in European tradition.

"He's on top already," Mike said excitedly and Richie nodded, watching as the gray horse settled into the early lead. He ran steadily, adding to his advantage just before the far turn, and easily withstood a late challenge from the favorite who attempted to close amidst the rising clamor of the crowd.

Richie turned to Mike and saw the boy's eyes were still on the track. He noted Mike clutched the pink tickets tightly in his fist.

"Why don't you go to the cashier's line now?" he suggested. "Beat the crowd."

"Good idea," Mike said, turning from the window. As he walked to the door, Richie saw him touch the pocket of his jacket.

Richie shook his head and wondered if he'd been that shortsighted at Mike's age. He didn't remember it that way.

He walked to the bar, ordered another bourbon, and nursed it until Mike joined him.

"Nearly five hundred dollars," the boy chortled, showing Richie the wad of bills in his hand.

Richie forced a smile.

"What's the next race?" the boy asked eagerly.

"Quarter mile," Richie said, looking at the program. As he'd explained earlier to Mike, unlike the American the French racing program contained a variety of different races on the same afternoon. There was the standard mile or thereabouts, as they'd just witnessed, interspersed with quarter-mile sprints and also a steeple chase or two that was run over the obstacle course whose hazards were permanently established on the infield of the track beyond the large tote board.

"Who do we have?" Mike asked.

"You pick," Richie said, moving next to the boy, resting his arm lightly against the other's. Let him believe he can do it on his own, Richie told himself.

"Jacques d'Or," Mike pronounced, pointing to number three.

"Right," said Richie, casually moving his arm away.

"Want to place the bet this time?"

"No. You do it. Besides, it would make Bert more nervous than he is if I went into that crowd."

As Mike walked away, Richie caught the bodyguard's eye. Bert *was* nervous. When they'd first entered the men's bar after having been ushered through the gate by the attendant who carefully screened all patrons for pedigree, several people had turned to look with recognition at the senator, and more and more had done so as the afternoon progressed.

A few had even nodded when they'd caught his eye, and he'd inclined his head perfunctorily in return. Now, though, he saw one nudge another as Mike walked up, and he wondered at that.

They watched together as Jacques d'Or, at three to one, broke quickly and led all the way to win the sprint.

And they watched as Charley Oh, who Mike also picked, came from behind in the mile and paid five to one for first place.

"We're already two thousand ahead," Mike said excitedly as he came back from the cashier's window after that third race.

Richie started to respond but froze when he noted a cluster of men standing beyond Mike's shoulder. The men were staring at them, whispering and gesturing. It wasn't his imagination. And they were speaking of Mike, not himself.

"Mike," Richie said, holding his emotion in check. "Mike—how much have you really won?"

The boy looked startled for a moment, then seemed to reach some decision and grinned widely. "Twenty-five thousand," he admitted.

"Goddamn it," Richie said in a low voice, grabbing the boy's elbow roughly and squeezing so hard Mike winced. "I told you to keep it low key, not to draw attention to yourself. For God's sake, it's only money— you don't need it. But now look what you did! There must be a dozen men at the bar all staring at you!"

353

Richie lightened his grip and Mike turned to the bar. The group of men quieted immediately but kept their eyes on Mike; there was open admiration on their faces. Despite himself, Mike smiled, and the men seemed to relax, nodding in his direction. One even gave a thumbs up sign.

"Well—what the hell," Mike said as he turned back to face Richie. "So I made a mistake. So what? They'll think I'm just some lucky rich kid, that's all."

"For God's sake, Mike. You can't afford any mistakes. Look what happened to me, to Charley. Look how we had to live, the precautions we had to take."

"That's right—look at how you had to live." There was anger in Mike's eyes as he faced Richie. "What's so hot about that, anyway? What makes you think you've got all the answers?"

"Mike," Richie began in a calming voice, reaching out towards the boy but stopping himself. "Mike—remember the stakes, the rules."

"Your rules," Mike broke in sharply. "Your rules, remember. Maybe they don't have to be mine. It's my life."

"What are you thinking?" It was all Richie could do to keep his voice a whisper. "Nobody can know about the power or even suspect it. Nobody!"

"Why not?" The words hung like some insolent banner as Mike met Richie's eyes. "Why not?" the boy repeated. "I've been thinking a lot these past two days. And I'm not so sure your way is right, at least not for me. It's taken you so long—twenty-five years!—to get to where you can even start making things happen. I'm not going to sit on the sidelines and—"

"Mike!" Richie's tone was harsh, desperate. "You don't understand yet. There's so much—"

"That's where you're wrong." The words were touched with anger and arrogance. "I *do* understand. I've got the power and I can control it—as well as you can. I've proven it to myself."

"You have," Richie said, letting the sarcasm come.

"Yes, I have."

Richie held the boy's eyes, but Mike didn't waver. Although the anger receded from the young face, the determination remained. Richie nodded, acknowledging the boy's position, and Mike seemed to relax.

"We'll talk later," Richie said. "But no more heavy betting today until we do talk, agreed?"

"Okay," Mike said, seeming to accept the compromise in good spirits.

What had brought that on? And what had Mike meant when he said he was so certain of his power? Richie wondered as he turned again to the window and stared down at the track. He was badly shaken and could not fathom the confidence—the insolence—with which the boy had challenged him. He had a long way to go—further than he would ever have suspected—in totally winning Mike over, if in fact that was even a possibility. For now, though, he determined to put all thought of that aside and concentrate on the more immediate concerns at hand. The problem now was to control Mike, to make him feel dependent, to knock some of the cockiness out of the boy so he could begin to deal with him on the crucial matters he must.

The next race was a steeplechase over the obstacle course, and Richie decided what he would do. Turning to the boy, he said, "I'm sorry, Mike. I guess I did take too much for granted. But remember, it's new for me, too—having you here. I promise I'll hear you out, and then we'll talk things through together. Meanwhile—let's back off and enjoy ourselves."

Mike, his tension obviously gone, held the program questioningly to Richie who shook his head.

"You pick, Mike," he said, moving next to the boy, because it was of paramount importance Mike be certain of this choice.

"Ardourette," Mike said without hesitation, pointing to number one, looking to Richie for confirmation.

Richie shook his head. "You're on your own now, like you said," he stated, annoyed at Mike's cocky grin.

Richie moved aside slightly, glancing down at the program again as he did so.

He forced his eyes past Ardourette and settled on number eight.

Chanson de Guerre. Song of War.

He thought the name particularly apt.

When Mike returned with his tickets, they walked together to the window and watched as the horses promenaded on the track below.

Ardourette was a sleek chestnut and the sun glistened on her flanks as she pranced and snorted.

Mike was watching her eagerly, but Richie's eyes turned to the black horse, slightly smaller in stature but very powerful in the chest.

Chanson de Guerre, he repeated to himself, burning the name in his mind.

The horses were led into the infield and moved up behind the rope that served as the starting line for the steeple chase.

Then they were off, and as they lunged forward, Richie casually put his arm around Mike's shoulders. The boy was intent on watching the race and did not appear to notice.

There were ten horses in the field, and after the third hurdle, two horses had already fallen and Ardourette was running second, moving easily. Seconds later, Chanson de Guerre also cleared the hurdle, landed clumsily but righted himself, and regained his gallop to maintain the fourth position.

Come *on*, Guerre, Richie willed, and the horse did indeed appear to increase his stride.

Now, Guerre, now, he willed, and the horse moved up to third. Just ahead of him, Ardourette gracefully cleared the water hazard and moved past the leader as the crowd cheered. And just behind, Chanson de Guerre was continuing his move.

Come on Guerre, Richie intoned, instinctively squeezing Mike's shoulder, and the black gelding in turn eased past the faltering early leader and moved up to challenge Ardourette.

The two were on the straightaway now, only one hurdle left, which stood shortly before the finish line, and they battled neck and neck as they pounded across the infield turf.

Come on Guerre, Richie willed again, focusing as hard as he could, and the horse indeed seemed to be gaining the advantage.

But suddenly Ardourette increased her stride, drawing from some additional reservoir of power that had not seemed apparent, and the chestnut filly moved ahead, gaining ground over its rival at every stride.

As beside him, Richie heard Mike yelling, "Go, Ardourette. Go! Go!"

Urging his horse on.

Willing him on! Harnessing the quantum force without even realizing he was doing so!

"Go, Ardourette. Go!" Mike's chant grew louder, more intense, and Richie continued with his own silent incantation.

Come on Guerre, he willed, focusing now as if it were a matter of life and death. Come *on*, he forced harder, but as the two horses approached the final hurdle, the cords of their graceful necks straining as their powerful legs pistoned again and again, Ardourette maintained her lead and seemed now the apparent winner.

Come on, Richie willed once more, but beside him Mike screamed, "Yes, Ardourette. Go. Go!"

Not this way. I won't win this way, Richie realized.

And I *must* win.

The horses were only strides from the hurdle now, and as Ardourette rose from the ground in her final leap, the answer came to Richie.

"Look, Mike!" he called, pulling the boy closer yet. He embraced Mike as tightly as he dared, focusing on Ardourette and watching as her foreleg, which looked as if it would easily clear the hurdle, dropped suddenly to catch the hedge. He heard the sudden gasp of the crowd as the filly tumbled and sprawled on the far side.

He watched as the dislodged jockey rolled under the shelter of the hedge to avoid the flashing hooves of the black horse behind, Chanson de Guerre, who settled easily after clearing the hurdle and galloped on to the finish line.

Then he took his arm from Mike's shoulders.

Mike turned to his father, confusion on his face.

"Remember yesterday, Mike?" Richie said. "With the cards? As I told you then, it happens. Whether you think so or not, you've still got a lot to learn." Richie spoke matter-of-factly, careful to keep from his voice the pleasure he felt as he noted the young face marked in such confusion. But it did feel good to see this cocky son of his get his comeuppance, regardless of the weightier considerations that loomed.

"I'm getting a beer," Mike said after a moment. "Want anything?"

"No. I'll wait for you here."

As the boy walked away, Richie turned back to the window. It had worked! Not only had he changed the course of the race, but he'd also managed to mislead Mike into doubting his own power. That would leave the boy more open to counsel, more willing to accept his father's lead once they got beyond the critical days ahead.

That would be important, for Richie had learned something else during the race, something that disturbed him greatly despite his success in altering the outcome. But the fact was that if not for Richie's cunning, the boy would have prevailed. Had Richie not distracted him in that brief instant as he focused in and willed Ardourette to stumble—if not for that, Mike would have won the battle in which he'd unknowingly been engaged. Somehow, the boy's power was potentially the stronger, although he didn't realize it yet.

It was too dangerous a game, Richie told himself, and he would have to go with what he had at hand. He would have to trust that the boy's inexperience and misinformation would be sufficient to allow him to be handled until they were finished with what awaited in Liechtenstein.

Richie felt suddenly weary as he looked over at the bar and saw Mike nursing his beer, his young face lined with thought.

And Mike was in thought, deep thought, as he tried again to reconstruct what had happened while at the same time attempting to come to terms with his feelings.

He regretted his earlier outburst. He was sorry he had so openly and prematurely challenged his father, but he had been unable to contain his resentment of the man's easy assumption Mike would follow directions without question. He had the power, too, didn't he? And it *was* his life, as he had said. He owed Richie a lot, he acknowledged. He knew he could learn much from the man, but he was tired of being treated like a kid.

He hadn't intended to challenge Richie so blatantly, though. That had been a mistake, for it was certainly an overstep. He really hadn't thought through his position clearly. He did not know if he in fact was at variance with the other's views but just had faint stirrings of that. He had simply felt the need to assert his independence, his individuality, so Richie would start thinking of him as an equal.

And now he was doubly embarrassed. After what he now saw as a childish confrontation, his power had somehow failed him, and he sensed his father had taken delight from that. Maybe he deserved it after his bigshot statements, Mike thought, but he still didn't like the idea the man was mentally putting him down.

But the fact was his power *had* failed him, and he wondered again at that.

He'd known Ardourette would win; he had known it as surely as he had his other picks.

And it wasn't like yesterday with the cards, as his father had suggested. He'd gone far beyond that during those long hours in his hotel, when he'd gone countless times through the deck without error, which for some reason he had not shared with Richie.

He had come to trust what he had without question, as he still trusted it.

What, then, had happened?

Mike pictured the race again in his mind; he could feel his heart pounding as his horse, an apparent winner, had risen to take the last jump. He could see the forelegs reaching up. He could hear his father call, "Look, Mike!" then saw the foreleg drop suddenly and—

He stopped his train of thought abruptly and ran it back like a reel of film to play again in his mind.

He heard his father call, "Look, Mike!"

Then he saw the foreleg drop.

Then.

After his father had called out.

And squeezed him hard, because he could feel that now, too, the squeeze and the odd force that seemed to surge in him as it had on the two previous occasions when he'd been conscious of the man doing that.

He'd first noticed it on the mountain in Liechtenstein yesterday, when they'd turned to go and his father had put his arm about him. That had seemed natural enough, but when the man had squeezed his shoulder the feeling in Mike had been so strong it had startled him.

Then for some reason, the picture of the black king came to his mind. The king of spades had turned when he'd *known* it would be an eight. He could see that scene clearly in his mind, the card held stiffly in his fingers.

And Richie's hand placed firmly on his forearm.

And he could feel, too, the sense of loss he had a moment later, the feeling that his power had drained away as it had proven to when the next card had come wrong. He remembered the look on his father's face when he'd turned to him in disappointment.

The man had been sitting with a smile of reassurance on his face.

And his hands clasped before him.

Mike stayed at the bar a few moments longer, finished his beer in one long gulp, put the glass back on its coaster, and returned to the window where his father waited.

"Well," he said with a deliberate air of indecision, "who do we like in this race?"

Richie was tired and would have preferred to leave, but it would help for the boy to lose again, he thought. And Mike had little chance of randomly picking the next race, which would be won by the long shot Redoux. "You pick, Mike. Don't be down just because of one miss."

Mike seemed to hesitate, then nodded and said, "Okay," and picked up the program. His eyes stopped at Redoux, but he looked down further and selected the fifth horse.

"Argentine," he said, looking to Richie.

"Like I said, Mike—you're on your own."

The boy didn't seem to mind. He seemed almost to saunter as he turned away to purchase his tickets.

So cocksure, Richie thought, amazed at the boy's resurgent arrogance, anxious more than ever for Mike to have yet another comeuppance.

"Got 'em," Mike said moments later when he returned, holding up the tickets for Richie to see before placing them in his pocket. "Number five. Only bet a hundred, too, so don't worry." There was something in his voice Richie couldn't place, but it somehow bothered him.

Mike took his place next to Richie, and neither spoke as the horses neared the starting gate. Argentine, Mike's selection, was as black as the winner Guerre had been.

And Redoux, the long shot, was a bay with a white forelock.

The horses broke and Redoux moved quickly to the front. Richie knew from the form the horse broke quickly and was a frontrunner with little stamina who almost invariably faded well short of a mile.

But not today, Richie knew. Today he was destined to win; he was already in front by four lengths and was widening that lead.

Argentine, Mike's choice, was in sixth place, moving at what appeared to be a lackluster pace.

"Come on, Argentine!" Richie heard Mike yell beside him, and suddenly he felt the boy's hand hard on his forearm. "Come on," Mike urged, eyes intent on the field, appearing not to notice that his grip was increasing on his father's arm, lost in his mounting excitement as his horse began to move, coming wide on the outside and suddenly overtaking the horses bunched ahead of him.

"Come on, Argentine!" the boy yelled as the black horse closed further on Redoux. Richie tried to move his arm away, but the boy held fast. "Come on," he urged again, seeming lost in the race.

Suddenly Mike turned his eyes from the window and looked directly into Richie's. He held the gaze for just a moment then turned again to the field. "Go Argentine, go!" he urged, and the horse moved to within a length of the leader as they entered the home stretch.

"Go," the boy shouted, and Richie turned his own gaze to the track. He zeroed in on the bay, which still held a slight lead. He focused as totally as he could and silently intoned, "Go, Redoux. Go. Go!"

The horse seemed almost to get a second wind, increased his pace, but Argentine still crept up further.

"Go, Redoux. Go!" Richie screamed in his mind as beside him, his son urged on Argentine.

The horses were neck and neck now, the finish line scant yards away, and the crowd was cheering them on.

"Go, Redoux. Go!" Richie didn't realize he'd shouted the words aloud until he yelled again and Mike turned to him, an almost-smile on his face.

The boy turned quickly again to the field and yelled once more, "Go Argentine. Win it!" He squeezed harder yet on his father's arm as the black horse gave a final surge.

Only then did Mike take his hand away.

He did so almost casually.

"How about that?" he said, turning to face Richie with wide, innocent eyes. "I won."

CHAPTER 43

The flight from Paris to Zurich took nearly two hours, the drive to Triesenberg an hour more, and throughout Mike and Richie did not exchange a word. As they passed through the rolling countryside, Richie stared ahead seeming deep in thought, eyes closing from time to time. Mike, seething anger emanating from his tense body, arms crossed at his chest and as far away from his father as the rear seat of the limousine allowed, watched fixedly through the window as twilight deepened over the far mountain peaks. It was only after Bert had settled them into Richie's suite, satisfied himself the rooms were secure, and left at Richie's request, the two even met each other's eyes.

"Well," said Richie in a tired voice, taking a deep breath and expelling it. He removed his jacket and hung it over one of the high-backed velvet chairs set about the dining table. "Drink?" he raised his eyebrows at Mike, who nodded tightly.

While Richie walked to the bar, Mike removed his own jacket, the blue cord he'd bought only that morning in Paris, and folded it onto the chair next to the terrace doors. He pushed open the doors to the evening breeze and saw that pinpricks of stars were already visible beyond the aura of the bright full moon, which cast the valley below in ghostly shadow.

Richie came next to him and handed him a glass. He raised his own in a halfhearted gesture of toast and, when Mike merely swirled his drink so the cubes tinkled the cut crystal, raised the bourbon to his lips.

He stood beside the boy in the doorway and looked beyond the terrace to the deep silhouettes of the far hills.

"We have to talk," he said finally.

"You're good at that."

"Yes, I am. But that doesn't change the fact that whatever you must be thinking won't be resolved by silence."

"Okay—talk." Mike turned from the doorway, went to the farthest of the armchairs fronting the brick fireplace, seated himself, and looked up at his father, who had followed him into the room.

Richie stood at the opposite end of the tiled coffee table, shirtsleeves rolled and drink in hand. In the light cast by the wooden chandelier that hung from the domed ceiling above the dining table, the man appeared tired. His shoulders drooped and crow's feet accentuated the hollows of the deep-set, piercing eyes.

Mike experienced a perverse satisfaction that this omnipotent man could evidence such an air of resignation.

"You know," Richie began in a quiet voice, "if circumstances were otherwise I'd probably haul you out of that chair and slap the shit out of you. And if you don't get that insolent look off your face, I may do it, anyway."

Mike's eyes widened at the unexpected thrust and his body tensed. Despite his calculations, his father obviously still saw himself as unquestionably in control, and Mike fought to keep his anger bright and not to fall on the defensive.

"Your feelings are hurt, right? You feel I tried to manipulate you. I tricked you—treated you like a kid, in other words. Isn't that so? And guess what," he went on quickly before Mike could respond, "that's exactly how you're acting—like a spoiled kid."

He placed his drink down on the table in ill-restrained anger and rose to full height. As he loomed above Mike he looked powerful indeed. "What do you think we're playing at here, anyway? Kids games? You think the power—all of that—" he gestured to the open terrace doors, the world beyond "—you think it's a game, an ego trip, a test of one-upmanship?

"Sure I misled you. And I'd do it again. Do you honestly believe when I touched you and came to understand that together we could actually, *physically* change things—do you think I took that lightly?

We're beyond the power now, on some new dimension I can only guess at, and I had to give myself time to feel that out. Do you think I would have jeopardized the implication of that so as not to hurt the feelings of a poor troubled son who's never seen his father in all his eighteen years? You've got the power, too, Mike—and you'd better start understanding what that means. I've had twenty-five years to do that."

Richie ended the tirade abruptly, and when he did the anger seemed to drain from his body. His shoulders stooped almost imperceptibly, and his blazing eyes seemed tired again.

"Look, Mike," he continued in a reasonable tone, "I understand how you feel—at least I think I do. Here you are, the man who raised you, whom you love, disappeared to Lord knows where. And another man reveals to you *he's* your natural father. On top of that, learning you have the power and desperately seeking answers and having the one person in the world who could help you hold out on you—trick you, as you would see it.

"That's a lot for anybody to handle, and I don't blame you for being upset. But what I said is true, Mike. That's a luxury you can't afford. Protecting the power is paramount—that's something I learned the hard way, and something you have to accept immediately and without reservation.

"Can you even imagine the excitement I felt that first time I touched you and suspected what might be?" The blaze in Richie's eyes was such that Mike, even through his anger, realized the man spoke the truth. "Can you envision the thrill that gripped me when I considered the incredible implications? I've been living with this for twenty-five years, Mike. All that time I've been thinking all sorts of things beyond your wildest imagination—awesome and wondrous things that suddenly might be realized in a far different way than I had ever conceived.

"To change the world, Mike—not by manipulation but by direct action! To create! Even though you were the most vital part of it, how could I share that secret with you? You didn't even trust me. I had to keep it to myself until I at least knew what I suspected was true and began to understand the potential, the limits it has. If any."

"And?" Mike prodded. During the latter part of Richie's discourse he had uncrossed his arms from about his chest and placed them on the arms of his chair as he looked up at his father with eyes which, while reserved, still showed absolute attention and interest. "What *do* you understand?"

Richie sighed heavily, reached down, and retrieved his drink from the coffee table and took a long sip. Although the temperature in the room was pleasantly cool because of the summer night breeze flowing through the open terrace doors, Mike noticed sweat stains ringed the underarms of his father's blue shirt.

"I don't understand much more than you do, Mike. I haven't had time to test things beyond what little we've done so far. All I know is when we touch, the power takes on a quantum dimension. It allows either of us not only to foresee the future but to change it as well. Together we'll have to learn what that can mean."

He held Mike's eyes, and the boy felt himself surrendering. "I don't trust you," he said. "I want to and maybe I will some day, but right now I don't. Too much has happened too fast. Whatever we do together we'll have to go slowly to give me the time I need. And you've got to promise never to lie to me again. One more time and I'm gone—I mean it."

"I won't lie to you again, Mike. I promise. But I've got to learn to trust you, too. This afternoon at the track, for instance—when you drew so much attention to yourself by betting so heavily. That was dangerous. I've got to believe you understand how vital it is to protect the power."

Mike nodded his head, embarrassed by what he now recognized to have been a foolish display.

"But with regards to the other, Mike—the going slow for a time. I'm afraid we don't have the luxury of that."

Richie sat in the chair opposite Mike, hunched forward, and told him about Barnard.

"And he's got Von Horst in it, too?" Mike asked, eyes wide in his young face when Richie had finished.

"He must have. I'd foreseen his coming and confronting me, and I'd decided to temporize with him, to give him what he wants in exchange for his silence. But I couldn't have allowed the situation to remain for long, not with that knowledge in his hands. Now, though—now that together we can directly change the course of things—I don't think we have a choice but to move immediately. The risks of waiting are too great—for both of us."

"There's more, isn't there?" Mike asked, cocking his head as he eyed Richie. "Something you still haven't told me."

Richie met the boy's eyes and Mike was startled to see something far beyond sorrow in his father's gaze when he answered, "Yes, Mike, there is."

Richie rose and stepped a pace away toward the open doors. He stood with his back to Mike as he stared ahead and took a slow sip from the drink in his hand. Without facing his son, he said, "You told me before you don't trust me. But I'm afraid you'll have to, Mike."

He turned to face the young man, staring down at him with tortured eyes. "I'll tell you the rest in a few minutes, I promise, but first I have to determine something. Will you help me?"

Mike, hypnotized by his father's face, nodded dumbly.

"Come here," Richie said, and Mike rose and went to his father. "I'm going to teach you how to focus on yourself now, Mike, so you can see exactly what you'll be doing at some given point in the future."

"You can do that?" Mike whispered in awe.

"Yes. It took a lot of understanding and experience, but I can. Not beyond certain limitations, of course, but I can focus on either myself or on any place I choose and see exactly what will take place at a specific time in advance. And I want to do that with you now."

Without awaiting a reply, Richie placed his hands firmly on Mike's shoulders, and the boy closed his eyes and listened to his father's voice.

Mike's first several attempts brought nothing. He tried to concentrate harder and more selectively as Richie directed although he would not have thought that possible for his eyelids were already straining from his effort and his jaw was becoming stiff from the fierce clench of his teeth. But suddenly the darkness cleared and there he was, milling with the stream of colorfully clad tourists inspecting the windows of the shops lining the cobblestone square in Vaduz. It was three in the afternoon, he knew, for the deep bell from the watchtower on the hill was resounding the hour.

"I've got it," he exclaimed. "I see myself—three o'clock tomorrow, walking the square in town."

"Wearing khakis and a white shirt. You're just in front of the watchmaker's window."

"That's it!" Mike's excitement rose when he realized his father had honed in on the vision.

Together they watched as Mike strolled the street, paused in front of an antique shop, and entered.

He made for the counter and they listened as he negotiated the purchase of a small music box from a middle-aged woman with fleshy arms; they followed as he left the shop, package under his arm, to proceed leisurely around the square.

Richie released his hold, and the two were back in the darkened hotel suite, Mike facing his father with wide eyes. But before he could even comment on the extraordinary experience, Richie's hands were hard on his shoulders again.

"Hold on now, Mike. I want to try something. Let's go back to that antique shop."

Mike closed his eyes and watched as he entered the shop again. He moved to the counter, spoke to the fleshy-armed woman, but when she placed the small box before him he felt his father's fingers hard on his skin. He heard Richie say, "Shake your head, Mike. Not that box. Choose another."

They watched the abrupt change in tempo of the scene, saw the shake of Mike's head, watched him point to another box in the display counter, saw the woman remove it, then wrap it up after Mike's inspection.

"Now open the package," Richie directed, and Mike saw himself on the street once more, tearing open the wrappings and looking at the box.

"Now just put the box down by that hedge and walk away," and Mike watched as he did that.

"We learned something there," Richie exclaimed, as excited as Mike when the boy opened his eyes.

"What—" Mike began, but Richie's "shh" quieted him quickly. "One more time, Mike—let's go back to the shop."

He relaxed his grip on the boy's shoulders, merely held them lightly, and Mike concentrated again, saw himself back in the shop and watched the transaction for the box he pointed to in the display case.

Observed as he opened the box and walked down the street after discarding it by the hedge.

367

He opened his eyes and looked at his father.

"It happened the way we made it," he whispered.

"Yes, Mike, it did." Richie removed his hands from Mike, his eyes brighter than ever in an otherwise weary countenance.

An inkling of what the man still withheld began to take hold in Mike's mind, and he said, "Tell me the rest of it now. All of it."

Richie looked deep into his son's eyes. "Your meeting with Von Horst. Tomorrow night at eight. Let's go there. And, Mike—brace yourself."

Heart pounding, almost unable to breathe, Mike closed his eyes and honed in as Richie had taught him, and the spacious office of the president of the Alpen Bank came clear. Mike was seated before a massive glass desk behind which was a barrel-chested man with curly black hair. The lighting was subdued, accentuated here and there by the spots that shone on the massive abstracts gracing the paneled walls.

They listened to the exchange of information between the banker and the youth, watched the signing of papers relating to the Eur America Corporation, and heard Mike's further instructions to the man. Suddenly they saw the massive office door open and Barnard come in.

They noted the look of hatred on Mike's face and the infuriatingly placid expression of the other man as they faced each other. They listened to the uneven exchange, one voice angry and the other irritatingly calm, heard the names "Owen Reid and Richie Peters" come from Barnard's lips. They froze tighter yet as they saw Mike suddenly go for the man and Barnard's quick side-step and the fluid grasp of Mike's arm that turned the boy and threw him violently toward the glass-topped desk where his head struck with a sickening thud.

Watched the sudden fear on Barnard's face and the horror on Von Horst's as they stood above the body that lay face up, glassy-eyed, blood spreading from behind the reddish hair to stain the thick off-white carpeting.

Mike was trembling. He forced open his eyes and saw his father's face was as white as Von Horst's had been as he looked down on the body at his feet. Richie's eyelids came open and his eyes met Mike's.

The vision hadn't changed from what he'd seen not only days before but again only yesterday evening when, after returning with Mike from hiking the mountain opposite the hotel, he'd called up the scene in Von Horst's office once more.

"Now you know," Richie said. "I didn't tell you before, Mike, because I didn't know how. And I didn't know what to do about it, what I could do about it."

They stood looking at each other in silence. Through the open terrace doors, the soft call of a cicada drifted in on the evening breeze.

"What happens if I don't go?" Mike asked finally in a hushed voice.

"I don't know. I can only foresee what *is* to happen, and I've never tried to change that, not since the bus."

Mike thought about that, considered his father's fears, his own.

"But if I don't go, it'll all be up with the power, anyway, right? No matter what else happens."

Richie nodded his head slowly. "Barnard knows it all."

"But you do have a plan," Mike stated, eyes full on his father's face.

"Yes, Mike," Richie said, reaching his hand out to the boy. "I do have a plan."

CHAPTER 44

Zurich lay below in a late afternoon sun that glinted on the river meandering beneath ancient wooden bridges. The gabled roofs and watchtowers lining the narrow streets of the medieval city center stood in marked contrast to the sprawl of modern factories that invaded at the city's edges.

Barnard looked down in casual interest as the plane banked left and made its final approach.

He used his regular passport going through customs, sacrificing the additional time in exchange for the relative anonymity. His special papers would have seen him through immediately, but they might be remembered later, calling unwanted attention to him, and perhaps that might be important. He was uncertain of the outcome, but he knew it could play out several ways. He believed he held all the key cards and was anxious for the final game to begin.

Walking briskly to the Hertz counter, he rented a car and got directions to Vaduz from the attractive brunette at the counter. An hour's drive, she said. He glanced at his watch, saw he had plenty of time to catch dinner before the meeting, picked up his valise, and made for the glass doors beyond which was the lot where he would pick up his car.

As he left the counter he noticed another man come up. He recognized the bearded face with the piercing blue eyes as having been a fellow passenger on his flight from London and dismissed him from his mind as he hastened toward the doors.

CHAPTER 45

It was seven o'clock. The drive to Vaduz was twenty miles, and Mike needed to leave if he was to arrive early as he intended.

Unexpectedly, Richie pulled Mike to him and embraced the boy.

When Mike stepped away, he turned and left the suite with a wave of his hand that was almost flippant, looking fresh and handsome in a lightweight tweed jacket with leather patches at the elbows.

I wish I was so confident, Richie thought as the door closed behind the boy. For the first time in many years he was uncertain of some outcome, and the feeling lent him a sense of impotence. It frightened him almost as much as did his immediate concerns for Mike. Without thinking he walked to the terrace doors and pulled them shut.

* * *

In the shadows of the trees that lined the far end of the parking lot, the bearded man sat in his car as he had for the past half hour, watching the entrance of the hotel, uncertain how to proceed. If his suspicions were correct, it might be fatal to announce his arrival. He would be safer taking the senator by surprise, but that would be difficult to manage.

He was about to leave the car when he saw a figure emerge from the lobby and stand at the entrance. The amber light cast by the lamps set in the stone walls shone on the reddish hair, and the bearded man froze.

He watched as a black Porsche came up to the entrance, saw the boy come down the steps, tip the attendant, and drive off in the car.

Quickly the man turned on his ignition, pulled out, and followed.

* * *

It was just past seven-thirty when Mike pulled to the curb on Englestrasse about half a block past the Alpen Bank. He locked the car and walked back beneath the linden trees that lined the empty sidewalk toward the lighted entrance at which a security guard stood, taking no notice of the gray Mercedes that passed slowly up the street and parked just beyond his Porsche.

The security guard had been alerted and ushered Mike into the deserted bank when he gave the prearranged identification. The elderly, ruddy-faced man waited until Mike entered the elevator and watched as the doors closed after Mike had pushed three.

The third floor was an open, richly carpeted area with an aisle of secretarial desks that led toward a set of massive oak doors, which stood ajar. Light came from within, and Mike heard the murmur of a voice. Von Horst must be speaking to the guard, he thought, for he and Richie had foreseen that the banker would arrive early for the meeting and alone.

Mike had almost reached the door when it opened further and Klaus Von Horst stood framed in the aperture. Mike felt an odd sensation as he recognized the figure from his vision, barrel-chest, thick neck, with a shock of black curls that ringed a strongly featured, well-tanned face. The man was dressed exactly as Mike had foreseen, a fawn-colored suede sportjacket of obvious quality, blue shirt open at the neck with a scarlet cravat beneath, and dark brown slacks that touched lustrous Cordovan loafers.

Mike himself had worn a different outfit, exchanging the blue cord suit in which he'd envisioned himself lying on the floor of the man's office for a lightweight tweed jacket, white shirt, and tie.

"Mister Adler?" Mike asked, activating the code the man had established with Charley so many years ago.

Von Horst nodded, eyes fixed on Mike in fascination. He's amazed I'm so young, Mike thought, wondering what sort of man the other might have expected to show up and take control of the powerful Eur America Corporation—what his expression might have been if the man who was recognized as Owen Reid had come instead.

"Mister Cooper?" Von Horst queried, completing his end of the code, and Mike came forward to take Von Horst's hand. He liked the man instinctively and prayed things went as he and Richie had envisioned. He immediately brushed the surfacing doubts aside.

"My name is really Michael Frost, Mister Von Horst. I'm Charley's son."

* * *

Barnard turned onto Englestrasse. Looking at his watch, he saw it was seven forty-five. The bank was only three blocks down, in range of the receiver tuned to the small transmitter taped behind the large abstract on the wall to the right of Von Horst's desk.

Reaching over, Barnard opened his briefcase and snapped the switch, in case whoever was coming had gotten there early.

* * *

Von Horst sat behind his massive glass desk explaining the United Motors corporate structure to Mike. The man seemed nervous and preoccupied, although he did his best not to show it. Von Horst was under tremendous pressure Mike knew, accentuated by the fact Mike had arrived unexpectedly early.

Mike had a difficult time masking his own rising anxiety and forcibly restrained himself from glancing again at his watch as Von Horst reached for another cigarette.

It was then they heard the crash, the screech of wheels followed by the grinding clash of metals that shattered the quiet of the street below. Racing to the window, Von Horst drew the drapes, raised the frame, and leaned out, Mike at his side.

Just below, to their left where the cross street came in, two figures were scrambling from a mangled automobile. Quickly they dashed away, farther down to a safer distance, casting long shadows beneath the linden trees in the fire light that came from the overturned car burning in front of their own.

* * *

Mike emerged from the bank on the run, reached his car in seconds, and pulled away squealing from the curb.

The crash and the burgeoning fire had captured the bearded man's attention, and the boy was past the tree where he waited before he even realized it. He ran to his car, wrenched open the door, swung out, and gunned the engine to gain ground on the rapidly receding taillights.

* * *

It had all gone exactly as they'd directed and foreseen when they'd joined hands the night before and projected a new ending to the meeting in Von Horst's office. When he saw Mike drive away from the bank, Richie released his breath, opened his eyes, and let the vision go. Summoning it had been unexpectedly difficult and holding it more so. Richie understood now that what was happening to him was as he'd feared, but he had made the choice and was determined not to dwell on second thoughts.

He rose, walked to the bar, and freshened his bourbon, taking the drink through the open doors out onto the terrace. Far below in the shadowed valleys, he saw patches of the Rhine flash like scraps of silver ribbon in the moonlight.

He was calmer now that Mike was out of danger, but he was still deeply troubled. Their harnessing of the quantum power generated between them had indeed enabled them to change the outcome of the night's events, saving Mike's life and putting an end to Barnard and his knowledge of their secrets as well.

But what other changes were in store? Richie wondered. Unexpected changes precipitated by those they had already initiated? And beyond that, perhaps most important of all, Richie realized as he anxiously awaited Mike's return, that for the first time in twenty-five years he was uncertain of the limits and reliability of his power.

* * *

Mike's heart was still pounding as he pulled into the cobblestone parking lot of the hotel in Triesenberg. The crash had occurred a half

374

hour ago, but the grind of metal and the pillar of fire still hammered his mind as they had the night before when he and Richie had held hands and envisioned them.

The experiences were exactly the same, but somehow the actual event had been far more shattering than the vision had been. Mike wondered how he would assess his future ventures with that side of the power after he had a chance to think things through. At the moment, he wanted nothing to do with it ever again but realized on some deeper level that feeling would alter.

They had, after all, cheated fate. He was alive, Barnard was dead and his knowledge with him. Von Horst was free to carry on as before. And the power was safe. There was certainly value in all of that, he thought.

He parked his car, sat a moment to get his breathing under control, and had just stepped out when he heard the voice call softly, "Mike."

Looking around, he saw a stranger approaching through the shadows, a tall bearded man who stood only yards away. "Mike," the man called again in a reassuring voice, but Mike was already running, cursing their miscalculation that Barnard had come without backup, concerned now only to lead his pursuer away from his father and protect the power as he had pledged.

Racing through the parking lot, he crossed the road, and entered the woods on the moonlit trail he'd hiked with his father. Through the night air he heard the sound of the bearded man scrambling up the path behind him.

CHAPTER 46

Richie paced back and forth between the open terrace doors and the bar at the far end of the suite. He held a drink in his hand, his third. He was breathing in a heavy, measured cadence and was conscious of the perspiration on his face and neck as it was cooled by the fresh evening breeze.

He hadn't felt this way in a long, long time. He hadn't experienced this level of anxiety and fear since that spring day with Charley twenty years ago when they'd raced down that country road after the school bus filled with arm-waving kids. He'd been torn by his foreknowledge then, afraid to change what he'd known was to come but unable to resist trying. He had never been sure since that his attempt at intervention had not actually caused the tragedy.

He felt the same way now, despite the weighty evidence to the contrary. He had *averted* tragedy this time, hadn't he, in saving Mike's life? In addition to protecting the power as they had in fact done by destroying the heavy threat of Barnard, wasn't his son's survival alone worth the risk of altering what he had envisioned?

Still, the action threatened him, for no matter how high the purpose, he feared in some way a line had been crossed. Try as he might he could not quell his anxiety as he paced the floor and awaited Mike's return.

But that wasn't all that troubled him, he acknowledged. It was his final secret, the one he'd still withheld from his son, uncertain as to when—if ever—to share it with the boy. But the loss of his power to

Mike, the subtle shift of strength from himself to his son whenever they harnessed the quantum force, that sway of balance of which he'd become aware during the last horse race in Paris hung heavy. It was accentuated now by his unquestioned difficulty in conjuring and subsequently holding the vision of Mike in Von Horst's office and of Barnard's vehicle as the other car struck.

Only days ago that would have required no effort on his part, but tonight he'd hardly had the strength to keep the vision through Mike's hasty retreat. Their preparations the night before had taken more from him than he'd realized, and although he hadn't hesitated over that decision, the thought he could no longer rely without question on his power was almost crippling.

The half hour struck. Eight-thirty, he noted, glancing at the grandfather clock that stood against the far wall next to the parsons table. Where was Mike? Why had he let the vision go when the boy sped from the bank instead of following until Mike arrived, despite the intense effort that would have taken? Now the boy wasn't here as expected, and Richie would have difficulty honing in on him to ascertain all was well and his rising fears were groundless.

He paused in his pacing and tried to relax so he could concentrate. He sensed the boy's presence nearby. Forcing himself further, he honed in on the hotel corridors in a search for the boy, swept through the lobby and out into the parking lot, then froze as he saw the black Porsche Mike had rented sitting empty in the shadows of the trees. Where was the boy? he wondered, casting frantically about the parking lot but unable to pick him up.

He took a deep breath to calm himself and felt his eyes drawn to the road. Beyond it lay the mountain he and Mike had hiked just days ago, and some instinct moved him to the trail they'd taken. Honing swiftly, skimming above the tree line, he followed the outline of the path as it meandered through the moonlit forest, past the spot where the stream curved in. He suddenly registered the sounds of motion in the underbrush. Focusing, he saw Mike running up the path, jacket discarded, panting and stumbling as he negotiated the rocky trail perhaps fifty yards ahead of the bearded man who pursued him.

At just that moment Mike stopped. He seemed to be looking for something and made to his left for a path that was almost hidden in the night shadows. Richie's heart leaped when he recognized it as the trail to the precipice. Something clicked in his mind and suddenly he recalled vividly the quick vision he'd had of himself standing alone in that clearing, the vision that had filled him with a dread foreboding when he'd stood there with his arm about Mike's shoulders, feeling the surge of the quantum force.

There was something else that tugged at his memory, and he mustered what strength he could, settling his eyes on the man behind Mike whose breath came in ragged gasps as he pushed onward. There was something sharply familiar about the figure, even in the deep shadows of the narrow path.

But at just that instant the vision faded and, heart pounding with terrible premonition, Richie opened his eyes, made for the door, took the steps two at a time, and rushed through the lobby out into the night.

CHAPTER 47

Mike stumbled through the edge of the trees and out into the clearing. Gasping for breath, he looked around. The full moon bathed the landscape in an eerie glow, but the deep shadows cast by the occasional boulders that lay about seemed to offer inadequate cover. The trees stretched behind, the precipice lurked ahead, there was no hiding place where he stood, and the sound of his pursuer came closer.

Mike had hoped to elude the man by taking the almost hidden side trail Richie had showed him. He crept stealthily through the woods after turning off, but somehow the man behind had known, and Mike had felt a sharp twinge of fear when he'd heard the sound of crashing underbrush as the other pressed behind in open and abandoned pursuit.

The man was almost on him now, and Mike turned to face the woods where he would soon appear. He stepped forward a few paces to move further from the brink of the sharp drop behind him, tensed his body in a slight crouch, and prepared to take the man's charge. Whatever was to come, he would fight as best he could to protect not only himself but the power as well, for he had come that night to respect on a totally new level the unique treasure that was his.

The sounds stopped, and Mike stiffened. He had expected his pursuer to come crashing out of the woods as he himself had done and to make for Mike when he saw him trapped in the clearing. Instead, the man had stopped and was watching silently from the shelter of the trees, and the sudden shroud of night quiet was far more terrifying than the sounds of thrashing underbrush had been.

Mike held his breath, strained to listen, and heard a twig snap. He turned in that direction and caught the rustle of a footfall. He backed up involuntarily and dropped to a full crouch, feeling naked, exposed, and totally vulnerable out in the open. Keeping his eyes riveted on the woods, he reached out his hand and felt about the ground beside him. His fingers touched a loose rock and he clutched it tightly.

Suddenly a shadow separated from the woods and moved toward him. A figure materialized, moving slowly, cautiously, and Mike squeezed the rock he held until his fingers cramped. Sweat oozed from his palms as the man, tall with a beard that glowed dark as he stepped into the moonlight, came closer.

Mike could wait no longer and was about to spring from his crouch and fling himself headlong at the man, when the other stopped and raised his arms above his head. To Mike's surprise the open palms held no weapon as he had anticipated.

"Mike," the voice came in a rasp, for the man was panting heavily from his run. "Mike—it's me—Charley. Your father."

Mike stood slowly, recognizing the voice but as yet unable to put it together with the long-haired man who stood waiting.

"Dad," he managed, loosing his fingers from about the rock, hearing it hit the ground with a soft thud beside his planted foot.

Then he was running, sprinting the few yards to the arms that dropped about him.

"Dad," he whispered, pressing his cheek to the other's in the strong embrace, tears streaming down his face and mingling with those of the bearded man.

After a moment, Charley stepped back, held his hands to the side of Mike's face and looked at it searchingly. They stood at eye level, and Charley said, "You've grown."

It was Mike who laughed first, a chuckle coming from deep in his throat that gave way to a series sobs as he felt most of the tension, not only from the events of the night but of the last year as well, drain from his body. He stood in the moonlit mountain clearing with the precipice at his back and held the man he only moments before had feared might kill him. The man he'd thought never to see again. The man whose first words had been a comment on his height. Mike heard the rumble of laughter from his father, a laugh as rich and deep and uncontrollable as

380

his own. It was a sound he'd never heard before and in unison they threw their heads back as if to howl at the moon.

Shaking his head and wiping his eyes, Mike looked at Charley, made a fist and brought it lightly to the man's beard. "Blue eyes, huh," he commented, for despite his deep relief in at last finding Charley, he felt somehow violated by the man's altered appearance although he well understood the reasons. But this was not the face he'd carried in his mind through the interminable months of the past year. "You look good," he said. "Younger than I remember. St. Thomas must have agreed with you." Mike wanted to recall the words, but the pain and anger he'd endured because of his father's disappearance surfaced, more active than ever in the man's presence since he now knew the act to have been voluntary. "You didn't change your appearance for those other passports," he went on, suddenly breaking into tears.

Charley pulled the boy toward him and after the briefest resistance Mike surrendered to the embrace. With Charley's arms tight around him, he sobbed openly into the man's shoulder.

"You've found out a lot, haven't you, Mike? Even what's in the safe." Charley stepped back and appraised the boy. Not only had he grown, he'd filled out as well. His son now had the body of a man, but as he stood in the clearing in his ripped shirt, sleeves rolled above the elbows, red hair matted with sweat, and tears rolling from brown eyes down flushed cheeks, he looked very young indeed.

"I know all that and more," Mike said, taking a handkerchief from his pocket and wiping away a combination of tears, sweat, and dirt from his face. He took a deep breath and felt calmer, his anger dissipated. "I was in St. Thomas the day you got away. I even dove with Gary and Freddie to find you. And then we found the other body instead and the one on the beach."

Charley nodded slowly, but his eyes showed a sharp curiosity. "How did you come to be there, Mike? And how did you get here?" he asked. "To Owen."

"To Richie, you mean." Mike almost spat the name, for despite all the high purpose, the fact remained the man in front of him would never have had to run had he not been connected with the senator.

"Tell me all of it, Mike," Charley said in a calming voice, taking Mike's arm and leading him to a large flat rock that sat toward the far edge of the clearing. "Tell me everything and then I'll explain why I came."

Mike seated himself on the rock and looked up at Charley, who placed his foot beside Mike and rested his arm across his raised knee. He, too, was in shirt sleeves, and the hair of his forearms glistened dully in the moonglow.

"Well," Mike began, "after the plane exploded and they said you were dead, for some reason I didn't buy it. Then some other things happened," he went on, detailing Barnard's visit to the house and the taps on the phones. "So I decided to search for you," he said, and took Charley through his trip to St. Mary's, his meeting with Anderson, and his subsequent discovery in Durham.

"That's when I began to understand about Richie, about the power," Mike continued, and filled Charley in on his cross-country odyssey, the scene with Andy Billingsly in Wisconsin where he learned about the ski resort, his confusion at the dates on the certificates he'd found in California, his return home, and the shattering realization that he, too, had the power.

"So that's how I got to St. Thomas," he said.

Charley felt a great relief as Mike described the events that had taken him to the island, for he had believed it to be Richie, the only one who'd know his whereabouts, who had sent the men down. That was why he had come, to make peace with the man, for he couldn't run forever. At least his friend had not betrayed him, Charley thought, feeling a sharp pang of guilt at his own secret defection.

"And you were gone again," Mike said, winding up the events that had taken place in St. Thomas. "The only door left was Owen Reid—so I came here."

"And found Richie instead."

"Yes," Mike went on, explaining how that had happened. He told Charley of the slap in that storm-darkened room. He detailed Richie's disclosures, becoming excited now as he approached the final revelations, the discovery of the quantum force and what he and Richie had done with it. Those things would stagger the imagination of anyone, and Mike suddenly realized how anxious he was to share with the only other man he could the knowledge of who and what he really was. And of what he might become.

Mike delighted as Charley's eyes widened when he told him of his victory in the horse race and how that had come about. But Mike sobered as he described the vision of himself dead in Von Horst's office. Charley's face was expressionless then, his eyes flat as Mike filled in the final pieces—the joining of hands with Richie and the projecting of the vision that had changed the course of events, eliminating Barnard and allowing Mike to cheat fate.

Charley was silent when Mike was finished. In the moonlit clearing there was no sound at all except for the occasional call of some night bird from the dark forest beyond.

"And what will you do now, Mike?" Charley asked finally in a soft voice. "How do you and Richie plan to use this new power of yours?"

Mike shrugged. He'd struggled with that same thought an hour earlier during the drive back from the bank. "Right now I'm afraid of it. And I don't really trust Richie yet," he added, telling Charley of the scene they'd had in this very clearing as they'd stood by the precipice. Charley's eyes were riveted on Mike's face and the boy was engrossed as he recounted Richie's talk of a world managed by the power and Mike's own mixed emotions about it.

Neither was aware that behind them a large figure crept stealthily through the shadows of the trees. Richie moved cautiously, his breath still coming heavy from his run. He was careful to mask that and any other sound as he slipped from tree to tree toward the edge of the clearing where the two figures talked in a drone of low voices.

Mike sat on a rock facing him, and Richie could see the earnest expression on the boy's face as he responded to the questions from the man who stood above him, arms resting across his knee as he leaned into the rock. The man's back was to Richie, but he was certain the man held Mike at gunpoint. He tried to focus but found the effort too great. He felt an unfamiliar panic rise as for the first time in years he was not in total control of some situation.

"Anyway," Mike concluded, "the whole thing scares hell out of me." He paused. "Richie said he talked once about that to you, too, and you were against it."

It was now Charley's turn to fill Mike in, and he hesitated so as to get his thoughts together. Mike's tale had gripped him from the start, taking him on what seemed like a flashing roller coaster ride through the peaks and valleys of his life. But the final revelations had filled him not only with awe but with dread, for it was because of the very conversation with Richie to which Mike alluded, two years ago in this same clearing, when the man had revealed his secret temptation to take the power to further limits—it was because of that Charley had done what he had.

"We did talk about it, Mike," Charley began finally. "Richie told me what he'd like to do, in much the same way as he said it to you. And I was against it, as he told you. If it scares hell out of you, it terrified me. And now, with this new force of yours—" Charley broke it off. "Anyway, I opposed it."

"And what was his reaction?" Mike's question came in a way that let Charley know the answer was all important to the boy.

"He was angry," he said. "We had an argument, close to a shoving match. I almost stumbled over that precipice there," he gestured toward the space that yawned beyond Mike, "but Richie caught my arm and pulled me back."

"And it was after that you disappeared in the phony kidnaping." Mike stood and faced Charley, taking a step backward to better search the man's face. "It was then somebody came looking for you, after all those years, made you run. Richie Peters!" Mike shouted the name.

Charley straightened and faced the boy. Painful as it would be, he would have to tell Mike the truth. That the implications of Richie's further ambitions had pushed him beyond the brink of handling the double life that had already become too much for him, that he'd grown weary of being a thrall to the power, that he'd believed Richie would never let him and his knowledge and his opposition to Richie's plans go if he thought Charley's defection was voluntary. That it was he, Charley, who had alerted the CIA to his connection with Eur America, triggering the crisis from which he'd been forced to flee, abandoning his family as well for what he'd seen as his only chance to finally be free.

Richie had been watching the quiet conversation, moving closer and positioning himself at the edge of the nearest tree where he readied to make his assault on the man who held Mike hostage. Suddenly he saw Mike rise abruptly, step backward, and heard him shout "Richie Peters!" Barnard's man had gotten what he'd come for, Richie thought, the final secret, and the figure stood to face a boy who was now expendable!

"Mike," Charley began in a placating voice that was cut off abruptly as the sound of Richie's rush came. Charley had no time to even turn before he felt a body slam into his back, thrusting him forward. His arms were pinioned in a vicelike grip as he was hoisted off the ground, spun about, and released suddenly to stumble of his own momentum over the precipice before him. The last thing he heard as he dropped into the black void was the "Noooo..." Mike wailed, a sound that mingled with his own scream and the rush of air that tore at his face.

"Noooo!" Mike stood screaming at the edge of the precipice, looking down, beating his fists against his thighs.

"No!" he yelled again and again as Richie moved up to calm him, although he himself was badly shaken not only by what had transpired, but also by some nagging memory that had flashed in his mind as the man's body had pinwheeled toward the edge.

"Mike," he said, touching the boy's shoulder softly.

Mike spun about and faced the other, eyes blazing.

"You're safe now," Richie said, raising his hands as if to calm the boy. "It's over."

"Over!" Mike screamed. "How can it ever be over? You took him away from us, made him run—and now you killed him! And you say it's over!?"

Richie's face was frozen, bloodless in the moonlight as Mike's words sunk in.

"Charley?" he croaked.

"You know damn well it was Charley!" Mike exploded, stepping closer. "You wanted to get rid of him because he knew everything and wouldn't go along anymore, and you did it. You bastard!"

Charley, Richie whispered to himself.

He faced the rage in Mike's eyes, shook his head in disbelief, muttered, "Charley—Mike, I didn't know."

"Didn't know! You—with the power!—you didn't know?!"

Charley—Jesus, Richie whispered to himself as he saw Mike's arm rise, heard the torrent of rage spew from the boy's lips.

Charley gone! His power diminished! And all because of Mike, he thought, raising his own arm in reflex toward the fist that came at him.

I wish you'd never been born! he thought in the instant he grasped Mike's flesh with his own and felt the awesome force surge within him.

He heard a soft whoosh like the suck of a vacuum and felt a wind pull through his clenched fingers.

He opened his hand to nothingness.

I wish you'd never been *born*! his numbed mind echoed as he stood alone and looked about the clearing. The trees surrounded him like a silent Greek chorus, and a soft night breeze played across the empty moonlit clearing in which the occasional boulders cast deep shadows.

It was on just such a night he'd envisioned himself standing here alone.

He turned his eyes heavenward, resting them on the moon and the sprinkle of stars that surrounded it, and finally brought his gaze down to stare at the edge of the precipice and the blackness that yawned below.

EPILOGUE

Penny was reading in the den, light spilling from the table lamp at her side and casting the far corner of the room where her father's desk sat in deep shadow.

The October night was chilly, and she had a sudden wish for a fire in the grate. If her father or Mike—

Her thought was cut off by the ringing of the phone.

"Hello?" she said.

She listened a moment, felt chillier yet as she said slowly and carefully, "I'm sorry—he's not here. Who's calling, please?"

Penny heard the unfamiliar name stated, then replied, "I wish I could help you. But we haven't heard from Mike for three months. And we don't know where he is. We're terribly worried," she said. "Can I take your number? I'll have him call you when we hear from him. And please," she put in "do the same if he calls you."

She jotted down the number and replaced the phone. Looking at the area code number on the pad, she wondered where it was.

In North Carolina, Susan Mallory slowly replaced her own receiver.

She should have called sooner. Now her options were truly narrowed.

She was nearly four months pregnant, she thought, feeling very alone.

What would she do now? Her parents couldn't help, and the idea of involving Mike's family, especially under these conditions, seemed beyond her capabilities.

A thought of St. Mary's, the orphanage near Asheville, suddenly crossed her mind.

After what Mike had told her of the place, it was a possibility.

GIVE THE GIFT OF

A Long Way From the Creek
TO YOUR FRIENDS AND COLLEAGUES

CHECK YOUR LEADING BOOKSTORE OR ORDER HERE

❑ **YES**, I want _____copies of *A Long Way From the Creek* at $24.00 each, plus $3 shipping per book (Iowa residents please add $1.20 sales tax per book). Canadian orders must be accompanied by a postal money order in U.S. funds. Allow 15 days for delivery.

My check or money order for $_____ is enclosed.
Please charge my   ❑ Visa   ❑ MasterCard

Name _____

Organization _____

Address _____

City/State/Zip _____

Phone _____

Credit Card Number _____

Exp. date_____ Signature _____

Please make your check payable and return to:
Ad-Lib Publications
P.O. Box 1102
Fairfield, IA 52556

Call credit card orders to: **(800) 669-0773**
or Fax: (515) 472-3186

389